Copyright © 2011
La Leyenda de La Princesa Dorada: La perdición de Bandah

Copyright © 2013
The Legend of the Golden Princess,
The bane of Bandah

Yesenia Cardona-Müller

All rights reserved.

All character and events in this book are fictitious. Any resemblance to persons
living or dead is strictly coincidental.

The scanning, uploading and distribution of this book via the Internet or via any
other means without the permission of the publisher or author is illegal, and
punishable by law. Please purchase only authorized electronic editions, and do not
participate or encourage the electronic piracy of copyrighted materials. Your
support of the author's rights is appreciated.

Todos los derechos reservados.

Todos los personajes en este libro son ficticios, cualquier semejanza a una persona
viva o muerta, es una coincidencia.

Cualquier reproducción parcial o total de este libro e uso no autorizado por la casa
editorial, publicitaria, o sin permiso del autor, está prohibido. Por favor compre
obras de mercantes legítimos, no apoye la piratería. Su apoyo a los derechos del
autor le es apreciado.

Unedited Version/Version Inédita

LeyendaPrincesaDorada.info@gmail.com
Primera Edición 2012, Segunda Edición 2013
First Paperback Edition 2012, Second Edition 2013

Hecho en U.S.A
Printed in the U.S.A.

The Legend of the Golden Princess
Book I: The bane of Bandah
By Yesenia Cardona-Muller

Unedited Version 'aka' Poor Writer's Edition

Translated by Yesenia Cardona-Muller from the Spanish Edition: La Leyenda de La Princesa Dorada Primer Tomo: La Perdición de Bandah also by Yesenia Cardona-Muller

.... In loving memory of my malevolent prince...

Dedicated to those who gave me breath
when mine failed me,
to those who loved me... in spite of the tempest.
To all those who always believed
that I was destined to write...

The Legend of the Golden Princess

Millenniums past, longer than we even had a concept of many years ago, a council of magical creatures came together with the mission to safeguard the future of their world and its inhabitants. Amongst such an illustrious counsel were ancient magical races such as that of elves, dragons, trolls, ogres, dwarves, fairies, humans and benevolent spirits. They all had in common the desire to bestow upon the world the certainty of peace and harmony as best as they could, through magic. An eternal spell was forged and cast, which when necessary would befall on a newborn girl (preferably of noble kind), if there were signs that an evil force threatened, or was about to be unleashed upon the world. The spell would find a girl predisposed in character to be courageous, strong, and wise; and above everything else loving. The girl would be bestowed with immense magical power, control over magical creatures and the rightful possession of the Golden Sword. The child would be blessed with gracefulness and the ability to see into the heart of others to guide her. She would come be known in the land as the Golden Princess, true monarch of all kingdoms...

Index

10

Chapter 1: An invitation to court

The story about to unfold before your eyes is nothing but a fairytale, very much like others, full of fantasy, adventure, magic, and not much novelty. It is worth mentioning that the true mission of this tale is to open our hearts to all the possibilities in life, good and bad. How we weight those at the crucial moment when a decision can chart the course of our entire existence. For it is us who can ultimately cherish the true value of courage, loyalty and love in the face of misfortune. Lets place our story in a world far away, were two beautiful kingdoms lay next to each other, so close that even their fates get tangled. Bandah is the minor kingdom, separated from its neighbor by a willful chain of the rockiest mountains you could ever imagine. It is only in the northern and southernmost part of this indomitable terrain that two main ways are open to allow ground trade between the kingdoms. Towards the northeastern part of the mountains, tucked in past a magical forest, the beautiful kingdom of Astra the major is found. Although this kingdom is quite important, for the moment it will not play an interesting part in our immediate story. Our tale truly takes form in the kingdom of Bandah...

What the happy citizens of this world call the Kingdom of Bandah is a large landmass, full of geographical and climatological diversity. It is divided into several ruling domains that are led by the capital of the kingdom, aptly named Bandah. It is here on the outskirts of this city that one could spy a magnificent bridge made entirely of solid white marble. Bridge, which happens to end right at the majestic gates of the Royal Castle of Bandah. This castle, made by the muse of fairies, is the home of Queen Violet and her king, the just and beloved monarchs of the land. Like any other court, along with the royal couple, a cadre of councils and legislators, ensure that the kingdom operates efficiently. All these important people lead fruitful and happy lives within the walls of the castle, creating their own micro cosmos and needs. Thus making the royal household one of the largest employers in the vicinity. It is fair to mention that the thousands of souls that come daily to serve at the castle do so gladly and with the intent to make life comfortable for the sovereigns.

Amongst these affable servants was the Royal Cook, a woman with a job of utmost importance; keeping the taste buds of the queen and king extremely satisfied. Mistress Flora was a handsome and portly woman of pleasant manners and unmatched culinary skill. She resided with her family in a little house tucked inside the forest by the castle grounds, away and close from everything. She was a woman of loving smiles and friendly character that still pined for her husband with adoration, whom she was happy to share a life with. They only had a daughter, who was the love of their lives, and who filled their days with laughter and joy. However, their daughter's looks were cause for speculation amongst some of the inhabitants of the castle. The rumor mill had spun its nasty tales against Mistress Flora, suggesting that in spite of her nice semblance, she led a double life. It was rumored in the palace that once the moons were full, Mistress Flora would escape to the city of Bandah for illicit promiscuous encounters, and the having of too much of a good time. Not only that, but she was also accused of consorting with drunken elves to steal secrets of eternal youth and magical spices. It should be noted hereby that it is always wrong to speak ill of people, even though we can't always ignore an amount of truth in rumors... In this case they were all false, the suspicions that Flora's daughter aroused in others about her fathering were all positively wrong.

Mistress Flora gave birth on a warm summer solstice night, when the three Bandian moons splashed their glow over the kingdom. Howling wolves shattered the silence, followed by the powerful cries of a newborn child, a girl emphatically announced her arrival in the world. It is said that all those present at the birth remained quiet when they saw the tiny figure, which resembled more an elf kind than a human. The little one had the rosy glow of a marine pearl on her white skin; her hair seemed a platinum mantle of moon glow, and her eyes a brilliant turquoise (they always kept that sparkle that shone in the moment of her birth). Her father, Master Lorean, took the little girl in his arms and lovingly accepted his daughter, in spite of the imprudent glances of those present. They named her Koren, and raised her amongst the other servant's children in the castle grounds, regardless of her physical distinctions. No one ever knew for sure if Koren, had elf blood, but that belief certainly intensified later on, due to certain magical aptitudes she possessed. It was not a secret; however, that there was no one fairer in the castle than Koren. Every time her steps were heard it was not uncommon for people to stop their labor just to steal a glance at the beauty. She secretly smiled; enjoying the effect she had on others, aware that she had something that made her stand out. Soon new rumors began to spread; it was certain that someday Koren would be invited to the queen's court. It was common knowledge that only noble ladies or extremely magical creatures were at the queen's service, since working for the queen was one of the highest honors possible, yet there had been exceptions that allowed for women of extreme beauty to enter the court...

The call finally arrived an afternoon in the springtime, when Koren was about twelve years of age. An envoy from the queen arrived at their little home; all dressed up in royal garb of exquisite black velvet and silver, the official colors of Bandah. Koren had been sitting in the kitchen unraveling some woolen yarn, trying not to annoy her mother as she sharpened her knives, when they heard the knock.

"Go get the door!" Mistress Flora ordered peeking over the contents of a boiling cauldron and grabbing another knife to file. Koren obeyed her mother dropping her incomplete project on the table with a dull thud, glad to be doing something else. The girl opened the door only to be instantly paralyzed by the sight of the handsome young man standing there. Who without wasting any time with pleasantries parted his lips to carry on his messenger duties. The young man's voice was richly melodic as he spoke, yet his body incredibly stiff.

"I have come in the name of the Royal Family of Bandah, in the name of the sovereign majesty, her Royal Highness Queen Violet of Bandah. It is the queen's wishes that the girl, Koren of Lorean and Flora, come along with her mother, Mistress Flora of Umber and Dian, to the Royal Palace at tea time, to sit with the queen." The young page finished his recital in one breath, barely able to speak anymore and deeply blushing. Mistress Flora, upon overhearing these words, dropped everything she was doing and ran to the door to accept the invitation.

"Young man, please let her majesty know, that we are honored to visit... we will be there.'" The lad bowed his head and clicked his heels as an affirmative salute, while turning with great pomp to return to the castle. After his departure Koren couldn't help but notice how her mother's disposition immediately changed to utter happiness. Mistress Flora began to smile widely and spin in little circles as she hummed a song to herself, returning to her labors with less care.

"Why are you like that, mother?"

"Oh, I have a feeling that the queen is going to ask you to work for her..."

"Why is that so good? I'm going to end up working for her anyway, don't we all? Besides, I wouldn't want to work for her, I've seen her ladies, and all they do is nothing." There was a slight tone of disapproval in Koren's voice, bordering on disdain.

"Child, they will give you an excellent education, you can have the most exquisite dresses, you will travel the kingdoms and go to wonderful balls with the queen. You will be the envy of every girl in this castle."

"But I am already the envy of every girl in this castle. I'm the most beautiful girl in the kingdom of Bandah, besides what is wrong with the local school?"

"Koren, don't say those things! There is no one more beautiful than the queen, it is very few that see her, yet we all know that her beauty is insurmountable." Flora spoke tenderly.

"We shall see about that... What if I don't want to work for the queen?"

"It would be an insult to the Royal Court, but no one is going to force you into it. We all chose our destinies, only as much as we accept the opportunities life presents us, though. What could be better than working in the palace? You will be treated like royalty." Mistress Flora tried to reason with her daughter, whom only responded with doubtfulness in her eyes.

Flora took her daughter by the hand and led her to her room, a modest sized dormitory full of coziness, where she immediately took out all the trunks hidden under the bed to sift through their contents. She found a lovely pink lace dress that flowed beautifully upon her daughter, accentuating the loveliness of her skin. Koren's silky hair, she braided in delicate tendrils that fell on her shoulders like silvery vines. Flora's chest expanded with pride as she beheld the loveliness her daughter was, only to be reminded that she should also be presentable. Flora ran to her room, tearing through every corner like a little tempest, angry and frustrated by not having decent clothes, but mostly for realizing she no longer fit in her youthful attires. She had the misfortune of having to wear a brown silk tunic she had worn to a town party a few years back, which was not up to par with the queen's tea garden. Flora left her room after applying some colorful powders to refresh her look, and then sat in the living room to wait. She nervously began to knit, then read, move things around, check the soup every second, all to the annoyance of her daughter who remained unaffected. Koren could hear all the movement from her room, were she had remained thinking about the situation at hand. As she sat on her desk, little thought regarding the prospect of working for the queen ran through her mind, uncertain about the expectations. In the end, she told herself she should decline the queen's offer to join the court. At least she would be able to see for herself if what her mother had said about the queen's beauty was true.

After an hour of being lost in thought, her mother finally came to get her to walk to the palace, which lay in the heart of the castle grounds. Koren could see how her mother radiated excitement, little beads of perspiration glistened upon her forehead, as she pulled on her daughter to walk faster.

"Just imagine if we are lucky enough to bump into the king..." Flora said almost out of breath.

"I thought the king knew you. Haven't you been cooking for him too for years?" Koren laughed at her mother.

"Don't be so mean, of course I've seen him, but it is always an honor."

"Mother, wouldn't you like to be a queen?"

"What? Not every one wants to be a queen or a king. I would never want to be either; I'm a cook because I like to cook. I would not want to be the king even if he offered; he has to take care of a lot of things, belong to everybody, and lives with the fear that somebody wants the throne. There are always the rumors...It is not easy to have so much power, when you are older you'll come to realize that there are things that take away more than they give. Regardless of how good they seem..."

Flora and Koren approached the inner part of the castle, making way through one of the many royal gardens to the palace, surrounded by lively colors of the varied vegetation. A little ways past that wonderful sight, they found the large plaza that preceded the entrance to the Royal Palace. Koren looked around full of curiosity and admiration, since those grounds had been off limits to her in the past. Her mother was not affected, having worked so many years in the castle allowed Flora to navigate the grounds easily. For any visitor this would seem a never-ending maze impossible to penetrate, thus needing a royal escort to the grounds.

Anyone coming from Bandah, would have to cross the bridge to reach the castle's gates, at which point they would then have to declare the reason of their visit at the main military office. The office was inside the castle's fort, which was a complex of many offices, barracks and a well supplied infantry. The kingdom of Bandah counted proudly with a small but very efficient militia (was mostly for show since peace had reigned in the kingdom for many years). From there, one kept going to the plaza, right behind the fort, a preceding ground to the palace out in the open, where no one could escape the military force's sight, or reach. The plaza was not meager in proportions and it contained several ornate gardens that were a pleasure to stroll at any time of the year.

The Royal Palace was indeed a beautiful edifice that enthralled the eyes, made with the most precious materials on earth, and adorned with exquisite platinum windows and doors. The architecture of the palace had been based on the muse of mermaids and fairies, the structure being the part of the castle composed of celestial towers, great halls and lovely quarters. From all the palaces in the castle the Royal Palace stood out by its beauty, since its only function was to house the queen and king and their immediate court. Mostly hidden behind the Royal Palace, was the Royal Government Center of Bandah, were the king met day after day with the chancellors to legislate under the queen's orders. It was an austere edifice of such insufferable blandness that the castle's designers had the good sense of tucking it away from sight. On one side of the Royal Palace one would find the Royal Academy of Bandah, were the outstanding scholars and talents of the kingdom would be found studying advanced matters of the physical, non-physical and magical worlds. On the other side was the Embassy Palace, a round and stout building where delegates from the vice kingdoms of Bandah would come to address matters of state. The embassy was divided in different sections, and each quarter reflected unique characteristics of the vice kingdoms that it served. There was an official section for the Bandian delegates, which was always the busiest one. Another belonged to Stella Maris, a northern coastal kingdom. One section was for Nubis, from the northeastern land. Also Cyrus, which was far to the south, and Polaris below the desert areas. The latter was famous for its treacherous weather and for being a well-regarded point of trade by the kingdoms of Bandah and Astra.

Koren had ran about some of the castle grounds throughout the years, yet had never seen inside the Royal Palace, and she couldn't help but feel a little anxious about the prospect of setting foot inside. As they came closer to the palace the number of guards present dramatically increased, all in their stunning black and silver uniforms, carrying their fire spears. Fire Spears were the most powerful and feared weapons the royal army possessed, they were almost indestructible, yet simple and easy to use. The weapon was merely an innocent looking staff, which had a short white magical flame of about a palm's length. However, this magical fire disintegrated everything it touched, making it an extremely deadly weapon. Soldiers were not allowed to carry the spears unless they had been rigorously trained for years at the military academy. Koren began to feel a little intimidated as she walked past the tall and muscular men, who seem quite willing to defend at any moment, the royal castle. Flora didn't even wince at the soldiers, she had seen them so many times, just that day she had been there in the morning at the Royal Kitchen to give orders for the day. She just smiled as she walked past their curious glances.

"Greetings, I'm Flora of Umber and Dian, I have come by royal invitation to share the tea with the queen, the sovereign majesty, Her Royal Highness Queen Violet. This is my daughter, Koren of Lorean and Flora, also a guest." Flora announced in the most formal voice she could muster, having always accessed the palace through the servant's entry, she wanted to keep the formalities. Momentarily, she had the horrendous doubt that perhaps she was expected to use the service entry as usual, however the soldiers smiled as if expecting them. The gate guards also unashamedly looked at Koren with curious interest.

"Her Royal Highness Queen Violet, welcomes you to the Palace, her home. Please proceed to the Hall of Fountains." A guard spoke in a friendly manner, and only when he noticed the look of confusion on their faces, did he realize that they probably had no clue where this place was located.

"Go on into thorough this main hall, stay to your right, it will lead you to an opening through a grandiose bronze gate, where you will see a beautiful garden of blue roses, once there you will hear the soothing murmurs of the fountains. Past that, there will be yet another courtyard, in there you will see a beautiful glass dome with bronze frames, you will find the queen there…" The guard spoke as if threading a fairytale, as if the mere thought of such a place already made his life extraordinary. He sent them off with a smile and straightened his large frame by the entry to keep guard one more time. Flora and Koren cordially bid farewell, trying to follow the directions as closely as they remembered, they went through a hallway that indeed took them to a hall whose splendor left them agape.

The hall's standout feature was its floor, made of smooth glass that gave the appearance that one was stepping on ice, which bounced off the light from large platinum chandeliers in the ceiling, similar to the light reflections the sun flicks off the crest of a wave. Awe was bringing Koren to a standstill, her mother had to tug at her arm just to get her to move along, yet there were so many details to spy upon, that you could barely see anything with one glance. Flora started to fear that they would be late to their appointment with the queen; she had not calculated properly the magnitude of the palace. She breathed a sigh of relief when finally she spotted the garden with the blue roses that the guard had spoken of. Once they set foot in the garden they were engulfed by the subtle smell of the roses, but it was their color that surprised them most, the rose petals were so blue that they thought they must be made of sapphires. Koren reached to touch one of the petals, just to make sure they were plant and not precious stones, her skin felt the tenderness of the petals, the softness…

"Mother, how is it possible? The roses…"

" They must be from another kingdom, probably Nubis, they have fantastic vegetation there, and the witches and the fairies love color." Flora walked faster noticing that the garden was just as big as the hall they had just left, impatience making her feel even more nervous. After what seemed to be an interminable amount of time, they finally heard what appeared to be the murmur of running water. They saw large fountains, each with a different theme. One had a mermaid sitting on a giant shell, the statue looked up to the sky trying to reach for it with her hands, from which colorful water spouted. Another fountain was like a waterfall, which had a shallow pond where colorful fish swam about merrily. Koren had to resist the urge to touch anything, or sit by a fountain to take it all in, there were magnificent fountains all around. One could not see them all at once, but they led a fabulous aquatic concert in unison, that let their presence be known.

The glass dome came to sight, much to Flora's relief, the queen's committee immediately visible as well. A group of beautiful maidens dressed in silver played a lovely and relaxing melody, their delicate fingers breezing through the chords of harp like instruments. One of them, which had a lovely lavender hint to her skin, sang a barely audible song, letting her voice go on about, much like a harmonious breeze. Koren couldn't help but stare at the lovely maidens, their elegant and delicate bodies, all different in color and shape. She had never seen lavender skin, or dark, or teal, or green. A dwarf maiden caught her eye, not having seen a dwarf in her life; she had thought that they were not real, only part of fairytales. One thing that didn't escape her was the fact that every one of those women present had one thing in common; they were all owners of extraordinary beauty. This alarming thought made her look at them in detail, to ascertain that no other was more beautiful than she; finding no match made her smile to herself. As Koren and Flora got closer they could see that there was a group of about thirty people in the place, amongst them a smaller group that seemed to stand out. This group was in close proximity to the queen, the women were visibly relaxed and wore more elaborate garments than the others.

The visitors saw as some of the women played games, painted, chatted animatedly, and knitted. Overall, every one of the women seemed to be having a good time in whichever activity it was pursuing at the moment. Koren thought that this was no work at all, they were just wasting their day away in silliness, merely to keep company to the queen. She wondered about what had brought any of these women to the royal court... nobility, character, skill, or beauty. What would the other women of the kingdom think of not having such a life of luxury simply because they were just too common? Suddenly she was quite proud of her beauty, feeling that perhaps her mother was right and she should accept the queen's offer of employment. She had been indeed blessed with something that made her stand out above the others; even so, a tinge of fear took her by surprise. What if the queen didn't think she was beautiful enough to enter the court? If the queen didn't extend an invitation the whole world would know that she had not been worthy of becoming a Lady Maid of Honor. She would be the laughing stock of the kingdom; her mother would continue to be berated by the gossip in the castle. The girl stood up straight and tried to walk elegantly, raising her forehead in what she thought was a dignified manner, showing confidence. Knowing that she was there already to meet the queen, it was now up to her to distinguish herself from the others. Inevitably, her heart began to pound, the weight of what was about to happen finally bearing down on her delicate shoulders.

The ladies stopped their activities, once they realized that visitors had joined them. Smiling warmly, specially at Koren, the women barely hid their curiosity. At that precise moment a subtle scent of jasmine and roses overpowered the breeze, followed by a pleasant feeling of well-being. The newcomers finally found themselves in the queen's presence where they lost their breath, taken aback by the sheer power of her presence. Queen Violet was a tall and elegant woman, full of grace and beauty. Her tan skin radiated the heat of the desert where she had come from, her straight black hair laid on her shoulders like a curtain of darkness, while her silvery grey eyes seemed bright stars stolen from the winter's sky. Koren felt she could not take her eyes away from her, even though she knew that it was impolite to stare, she was powerless. The queen observed her visitors, greeting them with a smile and signaling for them to be seated. Koren and Flora barely moved to the seats provided, unable to take their peasant eyes from the mighty queen of Bandah.

"Welcome, I hope it has not been too long of a walk to get to the garden. I think is such a lovely place to take the tea..." The queen's melodic words rang exquisitely while a maiden started to serve fragrant tea right on cue.

"No your majesty... your highness, the way here was very pleasant and as always your palace is so beautiful, I could walk around here all day long. I have only seen other parts of the palace, this is more than I imagined... I have never seen anything so beautiful in my life." Flora spoke animated by her euphoria, making the queen smile broadly, while Koren felt a surge of embarrassment in light of her mother being a simpleton. Inexplicably, Koren felt a deep unease as she realized that the queen indeed had beauty exceeding hers. A feeling of anger raged through her heart, while disdain shook her body. Shame filled her as she faced these emotions, more so when she noticed that the queen was staring intently at her, almost as if she could read her thoughts. Violet smiled again, this time in a manner that soothed Koren, almost as if sending the girl some magical warmth to embrace her body.

"I will be honest with you, you are here because it has been brought to my attention that the maiden Koren of Lorean and Flora, is the beholder of extraordinary beauty. I can see her now, and she is truly beautiful."

"Thank you, your Highness." Koren tried to hide her intense blushing by humbly lowering her gaze. Meanwhile, her mother could barely hold back the tears of pride swelling in her eyes, as she too lowered her head.

"It is custom of the Royal Palace to invite maidens of such beauty to serve in the queen's court, as an opportunity to serve their kingdom. It has been said in the past that this is a highly discriminatory tradition, yet every extraordinary subject of the kingdom has always been welcome at the castle, so I do not agree with that assertion. I firmly believe that extraordinary beauty should be celebrated and cherished, since it is one of the most authentic forms in which Mother Nature manifests its excellence." The queen paused momentarily to sip from her cup, never taking her eyes off of Koren.

"I would be very pleased if Koren would join my court. I would offer her a post as Lady Maid of Honor, not just simple lady in waiting."

Upon hearing these words Flora felt her soul leave her body momentarily, soaring about with the powerful wings of maternal pride. Koren felt intense relief, as if an imaginary load of boulders had been lifted from her back. She would have never admitted it, but it would have been impossible to recover from such a phenomenal rejection had the queen not provided the invite.

"Your majesty, your highness, what honor you have bestowed upon us! I would be honored to have my daughter join your service."

"Thank you, yet I believe the decision ultimately belongs to Koren. You may ask any questions..." The queen turned to face Koren.

"Your majesty, what exactly do I have to do for you?" Koren spoke timidly.

"The ladies and maidens at my service must, on top of everything else, be loyal to me and the kingdom of Bandah. Every one of them has an important role in the operation of the castle and the court. Also, you would receive a necklace of onyx and platinum with my crest, that would give you access throughout the kingdom as my envoy in special royal affairs... You would be expected to join the Royal Academy and educate yourself properly in your chosen subject of interest. Of course, life will be very pleasant, but you will see that there is much to do in a castle. We do convene here oftentimes, not just for tea, but also to settle matters of court. And as you can see these women are more than companions to me, they are my family."

"Will I be able to see my mother?" Koren inquired, quite preoccupied with the prospect of having to leave her family.

"Of course, you are welcome to live at the palace or remain at home with your family. You will come to find that the palace is a lovely place, and once you have a routine worked out you will have plenty of time to enjoy it."

Koren was silent, thinking hard about the incredible decision before her. How could it be that she had to decide on this while being so young and inexperienced? All eyes were on her, surprised that she was actually thinking things through, as if they had never expected that a decision needed to be made. Flora began to perspire profusely.

"Your majesty, it would be a great honor to serve you and the kingdom of Bandah." The reply was full of certainty, enough to bring plenty of smiles about. Flora jumped from her seat, unable to contain her joy as she squeezed her daughter tightly in her ample bosom, while her eyes welled with tears of pride. The queen and her ladies watched merrily, accepting the emotional outburst.

"Well then, return in the morning, you will be greeted by my personal assistant, Lady Althea. She will guide you to my office chambers, were we immediately will tend to the particulars of your education and office in the palace." The queen spoke as Althea smiled warmly, welcoming her to the court.

"Althea, is not only my personal assistant, she is my main counselor and great friend. Whenever I'm not available feel free to approach her for any assistance you may need, this is also yours now." Violet extended her delicate hand, holding a little silvery silk pouch, which she gave to Koren. The pouch seemed surprisingly light to Koren, making it seem impossible that there would be anything in its interior. To her astonishment she actually pulled out an exquisite necklace of onyx and platinum, just as the queen had said. The necklace had a round pendant, where the relief of a rose had been carved within the onyx; Koren and Flora had never beheld anything so precious with eyes or hands.

"I can help you put it on." Althea offered, as she was the closest one to her.

"Thank you, I have never had anything so beautiful." Koren genuinely thanked the queen; who smiled pleased by the girl's response.

"You will have many more things, but above all an education. For today, enjoy the music and the garden, tomorrow your life will become very interesting, I promise you." Violet smiled broadly. The afternoon melted away rather quietly and fast, Flora and Koren very much enjoyed the stay at the garden while getting to know the other ladies of the court. For the first time in her life, Koren felt an extreme uncontrollable happiness, although she wanted the day to end so she could come back to the palace and resume her new identity. Once they were dismissed, Koren and Flora skipped happily all the way back home.

"Ah, the queen is so beautiful... I think she must have elf or nymph blood." Mistress Flora mused out loud.

"I really didn't think I could stop looking at her, I felt so insignificant, yet knew that she was welcoming me somehow. How strange to be next to someone and not know what to do."

"Don't worry, once you see her everyday, you'll get used to it. You are so fortunate. People only get to see the monarchs once in a while at official events, and never too close..." Flora laughed at the thought, already feeling the looks of envy, as word got around that she had had tea with the queen. She enjoyed the thought of knowing that her daughter, would in fact, be part of the queen's ladies. Her heart welled up with joy and she permitted herself some vanity, after all Koren was her daughter and resembled her a bit. Koren's thoughts were less complicated, she was aware that her friends would feel a little bit more envy of her, perhaps intimidated by her new position. No one would really care though, she was used to being alienated by the other youngsters in the castle for standing out so much physically, and her beauty had been a bit disquieting to the others. She was actually glad to find a place were she would not feel like an oddity, a place where perhaps she would fit in once and for all. Seeing that there were two girls about the same age as her, made her welcome the possibility of making new friends as well...

Inside the little house in the forest, Master Lorean anxiously awaited the arrival of his women by, pretending to read quietly in their small living room. He was a tall and lean man, with long white tresses that tapped his lower back. His long years of life had wrinkled his skin mercilessly; he was almost on the verge of his three hundred years of age. What people didn't know about him, was that in spite of his simple human appearance, he was born from the illicit union of a fair elven lady and a dragon, it was from his side of the family that Koren had gotten her elfish looks and more... No one suspected that he had any connection to those races, not that he would be advertising it much, humans tended to mistrust the offspring of those of unions. People feared the results of those mixes, for they borne extremely magical creatures, which seemed too human for any one's taste. Specially, given that for a common human, the knowledge and practice of magic required rigorous training that oftentimes lasted years. Master Lorean had never given any indication that he was adept at anything other than the care and training of magical beasts. The only thing that could possibly raise brows was the issue of his longevity; he had already lain to rest two of his human wives, their children and grandchildren as well. It wasn't until he had his two hundred and seventy years that he considered again the idea of taking another wife.

Lorean met the woman who would become his third wife one sunny afternoon in the spring. As he walked around in the forest the scent of food captured his senses and left him disoriented. Following the exquisite aroma he found himself right before a young maiden cooking a hare on a small pit by a brook. She raised her skirt a bit and invited him to more than her delicious meal, and from that moment on they had never been apart from each other. Flora had always liked the idea of marrying an elf, without any regards to all the problems that it might entail.

"Papa, I'm going to be a Lady! Look at my necklace!" Koren exclaimed launching herself at her father, ignoring his inquiring eyes. He resigned to wait for an explanation as to their whereabouts, while kissing her face and holding her lovingly.

"Of course, I told you. You are the most beautiful girl I've ever seen, and this poor old elf has seen lots of things..."

"The queen is beautiful, and she has skin like the sand, maybe a little darker. And her eyes, oh her eyes, they are like stolen silver stars sparkling on her face. Mama thinks she could be a demi-goddess... Now, look at this necklace!" Koren almost shoved the pendant in his mouth.

"That is quite perfect, I'm sure it's the collaboration of elf and fairy handiwork. The details and its lightness are quite unique; the stone is too perfect and dark for it not to be magical. I'm so glad that you are happy about this opportunity." Her father held her tightly, again softly kissing her head. Flora couldn't stand there watching them any longer; she joined their tender embrace, feeling her chest well up with happiness.

"Enough of that lets have some supper. You, my love, must be rested and cleaned up for tomorrow." Flora declared as Lorean kissed his daughter's cheek one more time. The girl ran off to bathe before eating, preparing the bath and summoning her father whom with a touch of his finger left the water the perfect hot temperature. Flora found herself hugging her husband at every corner of the little home, both enraptured by loving parental pride.

"I wished you had seen the inside of the palace, the queen, the gardens..." Flora told her husband.

"I have seen plenty of palaces, I'm just happy for the two of you. I can tell Koren is excited, I always knew her beauty would bring her good fortune."

"Don't think she only looks like you! I had some doing in that affair..." Mistress Flora reminded him with a suggestive smile.

Not feeling hungry at all, Koren retreated to her room in order to prepare herself for the big day ahead, still hearing the muffled voices of her parents in the contiguous room. She smiled to herself feeling their excitement, her own increasing. Plagued with a little bit of anxiety, knowing that in a few hours she would belong to the royal court. Her mind was flooded with memories of the day that had past, her thoughts immediately falling upon the queen. An image that had been seared into her reminiscence, to the last detail. She could clearly see again the redness of the dress the queen had worn, almost like a flow of lava bearing into itself amber and ruby notes. The sleeves of the dress had been velvety lace swirls that seemed to gently caress the skin it covered. The thought of having clothes of such marvelous confection, made her almost euphoric, she fell asleep dreaming of life in the palace, along with teatime and fancy garbs.

Chapter 2: Beauty amok in the palace

Morning greeted Koren with the busy chirping of the forest birds and the sun's inopportune rays. Her eyes suddenly opened, like those of one who realizes that sleep had lasted longer than intended. Running to her mother's room, she hurried to arouse her, not having heard the usual morning noises that filled the home. Only her mother's snoring could be heard throughout the house, surely her father laid next to her immune to the thundering sound. Koren watched their sleep lovingly for a few seconds, before jumping on them to scare them out of their wits.

"Wake up! You have to walk me to the palace." Her giggles bubbled in her throat as her father tickled her, barely seeing her through blurry sleepy eyes.

"Its true! We must not let Lady Althea waiting..." Mistress Flora jumped out of bed on a mission, pulling the bed covers with a swift tug so that her husband would have to get up too. Master Lorean huffed and puffed showing disapproval, he was not so happy to have parted with his sleep at that point, and so abruptly. Koren returned to her chamber to dress, allowing for her parents to do the same, very pleased after catching her reflection in the mirror. Had it not been for the queen, she was certain she would have been the most beautiful creature in the land. Her parents swallowed the sight of her greedily, full of pride, they served her a light breakfast and kissed her head often.

"Mama, now that I will have so many opportunities and riches, you won't have to work at the palace anymore, you can have your own cook. The first thing I'll do is find you one..."

"Don't you dare! One of the things I love the most is cooking. You see, the pots and the pans, they are my beauty." Her voice let Koren know that she was touched by the offer, even if she had declined.

"But you are always saying it's a lot of work, that you are tired."

"Yes, my love, but that doesn't mean that I don't want to do it."

"Papa, what about you? What would you like to do now?"

"Thank you for your good intentions, but I've have done enough... I'm quite content with what I do right now. My life is simple, yet very happy, and that is how I enjoy it most." Her father smiled. Koren remained silent, trying to understand why her parents would not take advantage of her new position to find different opportunities in life. Hurriedly, they parted to the palace shortly after breakfast aware that it was a bit of a walk to get there.

The morning was pleasant, and it was always entertaining to see how different parts of the castle came alive as you walked by. It could be seen how scholars, young and old, would run about with multiple books cradled in their arms. Carriages pulled by enormous Pegasus arrived by air and land, while servants scurried in between them to their particular palaces. The servant's different garment colors were a blur in the swarm of people, creating a swirl of hues; but it was by color that one would know which palace they worked at. Soldiers arrived all ready and in formation; there would be one or two yawning audaciously, yet every one trying to be alert for their rounds. Even the smells of the castle seemed to be waking up, the gardens would release their perfume prodded by the gentle kisses of dew, the ovens would break their nocturnal hibernation to welcome the risen loafs of bread.

Hundreds of footsteps muffled the echo of the little unnoticed family's steps atop the stone bricks that led to the palace.

Master Lorean kept pace with his beloved women, spying the castle's daily routine and enjoying the smiles he received from the matutine revelers. It was rare that he would witness the well planned daily choreography of the castle, since he preferred to be at home taking his time to breakfast, hike in the forest or stop to chat with the little creatures there. After a morning of leisure at home he would then head out at his convenience to the Royal Stables. Of all the creatures in his care, he loved the Pegasus the most, for their intelligence, strength and corpulence. The knowledge that only a select few could really be at ease with a Pegasus, given their demands, rarity and dangerous dispositions, made him very proud of himself. Although at that moment the pride that swelled in him came from his family. He glanced over at his wife and smiled, she walked as if in a dream, enjoying her daughter's newfound importance. Still, he could tell her mind was already starting to plan the day at the Royal Kitchens; surely she was thinking about all the orders that she had delegated to her underlies the day before.

As they reached the palace entrance all their thoughts were replaced by the image of Lady Althea waiting at the door, ready to welcome Koren to her new life. The whole kingdom knew that Lady Althea was the most powerful witch ever to work for a monarchy, she was well respected, and it was also rumored that she might even be the most powerful witch that ever existed. Her presence stood out anywhere she went, and in that moment she seemed every inch a mythical creature. Mistress Flora took advantage of her proximity to observe the Lady with greater detail; she was tall and slender, with hair as deep red as the most delicate wine, and eyes greener than the prairies beyond the mountains. Her skin was fair and creamy, it made Flora think of sweet cream, there was no hint in it of the two hundred years she had lived. Delicate tattoos adorned her body and face, declaring the history of her tribal affiliations to ancestral witching families in Nubis. Lady Althea wore the loveliest lace gown Flora had ever seen; it was made of caramel colored lace, with emeralds sown in, easily declaring the high status she had in the palace.

"Good morning, and welcome." Althea's smile was warm and welcoming as she moved to greet them, allowing them to smell the scent of sage mixed with the sweetness of her skin, a most aromatic perfume.

"Good morning, Lady Althea, we hope we have not made you wait long for us." Mistress Flora excused her family.

"Do not worry, I came out here quite early, just to see the comings and goings of the castle. I try to chat with the guards, they see everything, and you have no idea all the things I find out…" Althea winked and regaled them with a conspirational grin.

"Lady Althea, I assume you must have met my husband, Lorean of Kai and Dhur." Flora introduced her husband, without noticing that he paled a bit.

"Dhur… that's curious. I had no idea that was your ancestry; it is a very old family name, Master Lorean. I sort of suspected Koren was not an average human girl, now I know for sure…" Althea spoke with emphasis on her last words, Lorean looked away, certain that the witch knew a lot more than she would admit to.

"I would love to stay and chat, but I'm afraid I'll have to tear your daughter away from you. There is a lot to learn and do, we are meeting at the queen's offices really soon to get our commands for the day. We think she'll get along just fine with the rest of us."

"Certainly, we only wanted to walk Koren here, it being her first day at the palace and all..." Mistress Flora and her husband hugged her daughter one more time. Koren started to feel unease after seeing how her parents were so affected by the whole situation, making her double guess if she had made the right decision. Unexpectedly, she felt a strong attachment to her parents and hesitated before taking the first step towards Althea on her own.

"Have lovely day, if you can escape, find me in the kitchen. Behave, ok." Her mother caressed her hair almost on the verge of tears. Master Lorean had to pull Flora away by the arm recognizing that she didn't want to let go of their daughter.

"Good bye, mama. I'll see you in the afternoon." Koren's voice seemed very small; she felt a pang of anguish as her parents walked away, disappearing in the crowd.

"Oh, don't feel like that... It's okay to be a little nervous the first time you do anything, but you'll get used to the palace and find it quite mundane after a while. You'll see." Koren nodded in silence and followed Althea into the palace, not sure of what her presence in the court would entail. Judging by her parent's reactions, she began to think that the severity of the situation was perhaps too abstract for her. Both women entered once again through the fabulous front hall that Koren had already seen, this time turning the opposite way of the garden, directly into a hallway that led into another greater hall.

This great hall was decorated in its entirety by depictions of the different races in the land; the walls were covered in exquisite murals, alongside statues of marble. Koren couldn't see all the figures or details, but she could make out glorious mermaids, fairies, centaurs, and unicorns amongst others. She couldn't help but notice that there were also some maleficent looking creatures depicted. She would have just loved to stop and study every inch of the place, quite the impossibility, specially when she had to follow the fast pace Lady Althea carried. At the end of the hall they came upon a grandiose pink marble stairway that Koren assumed would take one directly to the sky, given its seeming endlessness.

"This stairs will lead you to the waiting room in the first floor of the queen's tower. From there we go to her majesty's offices, where we meet early every morning to receive our orders for the day and report back our duties to her. You must try not to be late for the meetings; it really throws the day off. Try to be cautious in the palace these first few weeks, it would be terrible if you got lost in here, if you do, just place your hand in any wall and call for the queen, she'll hear you."

"How would she hear me?" Koren asked astonished at the notion.

"You have entered a world full of magic, the palace is more so than anywhere else in the castle, it carries the queen's blood, it's an extension of her. You'll get very used to all the magical oddities, don't worry." Althea was only able to confuse the girl even more

"I don't understand, what do you mean that the palace has her blood?"

"You will study the history of the queens of Bandah, but I'll give you a brief summary. Part of being queen is giving yourself in your totality to the kingdom. Every time there is a new and legitimate queen, she must go to the heart of the castle and give her blood to the kingdom of Bandah. This act of sacrifice seals a magical pact that ensures the well being of the kingdom." Althea paused briefly, thinking of what to say next.

"You are aware by now that lineage follows the infallible mother line, thus ancestral magic is purer when it comes from the mother, the queen is sort of Bandah's mother. Violet, being the legitimate queen, was given immense magical power that she can share with the people."

"How does she share them, though?" Koren tried to unravel the tangle of new information in her mind.

"In the heart of the castle there is a small fountain, which is the starting point of a river, that feeds into the main waterways of the kingdom. The queen puts her blood in this fountain once, letting her magic flow through the land to give it life. This simple act ensures better crops, greener forests, pure water, and good rain. Overall, it just smoothes along the cycle of life in accordance with nature."

"I thought all that was part of nature, isn't Mother Nature in charge?" Koren expressed her skepticism.

"Yes, its all part of nature, so is magic. They work together to become one, to work in harmony. We have known of kingdoms that have not taken into consideration Mother Nature, only to be obliterated by her later, guess you can learn all those particulars later, as you study." Koren remained silent, wondering what place did magic really had in the world. The thought that the queen's blood was in the drinking water of Bandah seemed gross and barbaric.

"And how much blood is in the water?" Koren finally asked indignated.

"One or two drops." Althea confessed, laughing heartily as she realized that the magical concept had not fared well with the girl.

At the end of the stairs and right before their eyes another great hall appeared, however, this one had been turned into a perfect forest. Koren couldn't believe that inside a palace there could be a thriving environment of such magnitude. The forest had a brook, tress as tall as the eye could see and the floor had just turned into moist fresh earth. The sun's rays mysteriously infiltrated from the outside, glistening wildly where it touched the leaves, or falling upon some unsuspecting forest creature. The air was fresh, fragrant and embedded with the green scent of happy foliage. Koren had no doubt that in any moment she would bump right into a unicorn in this magical forest.

"Beautiful, isn't it?" Althea inquired noticing how Koren admired the forest.

"I can't believe I'm seeing this, the last thing I imagined is that we would walk right into a forest. How is it possible? No, don't tell me... magic, right?"

"Yes and no. It did start out magically, and then nature took over. Magic brought the trees and the water, the rest came on its own."

"Why not just do all of it with magic?" Koren demanded.

"If we resolved everything with magic we would never experience the process, we would never have seen the plants and trees grow, the birds make their little nests, perhaps the end result would have never been so wonderful. Even if we tried we could never imagine the perfections that nature can." Althea explained, she then whistled and a little bird came to rest upon her hand. Koren watched fascinated almost thinking the whole creation was absurd.

"Magic can help us sometimes, my dear, but it takes away too much. Once you become adept in magic you'll come to realize that things only matter to us, if we have lived them. No matter how small, or how hard they might be." With these words Althea raised her other hand and squashed the blue bird hard, turning it into a cloud of yellow dust.

"I would use magic for everything, everyday..." Koren confessed with enthusiasm, in spite of having shuddered when Althea dismissed the bird so easily.

"You will certainly have the opportunity, but I hope not. The real danger of magic lies in that it takes you away from reality. Only you are real..." Althea said cryptically, before continuing the tour.

"To our left there is a music conservatory, we always have concerts, try to make one or two. The queen loves music... Also, back there is a lovely terrace where you can get some fresh air and enjoy a wide variety of orchids, all real, no magic. That terrace has access to the queen's main office; on its other side there are baths. There is this little pond of warm botanical water, than is quite soothing. There is also a sauna, with plenty of marine infusions right from Stella Maris, and if you feel like a nap after all the luxury there is a nice place for you to sleep it off as well. Try not to sleep the whole day; it is tempting once you are so relaxed. Just go the third floor in the tower; all the entertainment is there... Theater, atelier, gymnasium, athletic courts, anything you can imagine. I recommend a massage daily, it's my favorite treat."

"I'll remember that." Koren replied almost in a trancelike state, unable to keep track of all the things that Althea was throwing her way.

"On the fourth, fifth and sixth floors of the tower you'll find all the apartments designated for Violet's ladies. There are seven apartments per floor, each with six chambers, waiting room, vanity room, bath hall, kitchen, garden and service. You will be assigned your own apartment, so that you can live in the palace if you so desire, even your family is welcome to move here with you. My sister lives with me in mine; she has even found work as a gardener. She is very pleased to have found work, she is ancient, been around for almost five hundred years and has lost most of her faculties. Had to retire from magic, she kept forgetting her spells and causing too much trouble. Once she tried to fly somewhere and was only able to send her clothes... without her." Koren could not help but laugh at the thought.

"What's in the other floors?" She asked Althea enjoying the fact that the witch seemed to like chatting openly about the palace.

"The seventh floor is solely for the queen. She has a private garden, bath, waiting rooms, study hall, atelier, jewelry hall, orchestra chamber and a nursery, ready for the arrival of the princes of Bandah. The very uppermost floor is just an observatory, you may visit the cosmos from there in the company of the queen's

Pegasus'. Just be careful, they are very ill behaved and full of mischief. One of the ladies was pushed off the tower by them, had it not been for her flying abilities, well..." Althea warned sternly.

"I'll for sure remember that." Koren was terrorized by what she had just heard, seemed like life in the palace was more dangerous than outside.

"Here we are, the royal offices, come here directly next time. I gave you the longer route so that we could talk, but skip all that, never be late."

Althea led Koren into a great office where a giant desk made of onyx laid at the end, commanding attention thanks to its color and the many delicate silver engravings that contrasted in it. The queen sat behind the desk in her silver throne, her back to multiple large glass windows that let the light in unrestrained, creating a halo of morning glory around her figure. In front of the queen's desk were rows of more modest silver chairs were the other ladies of the court already sat patiently and comfortably. There where shelves covering almost every wall, each fruitfully packed with colorful books, while every so often a break in a wall would reveal a majestic portrait. Each painting depicted one beautiful woman after the other; Koren assumed they had all been queens of Bandah, since each wore the crown of Bandah upon her brow. The women in the office noticed Althea and Koren's arrival, thus ending the lively chatter that had filled the room moments before. The queen stood out as a heavenly vision, more so with the dress she wore, a sky blue garment trimmed with delicate pearls.

"Good morning, Koren. Welcome, we are just about to start our session and we wanted to wait for your arrival. Today it will be a little less formal so that we can welcome you to our group." Violet spoke in the melodious voice that Koren already had come to love. Then she motioned to an empty seat in the second row, given that there were only five seats per row and they were already taken. Koren nodded, walking over to her place feeling sweat in the palms of her hand, nervous about being there. Sitting as elegantly as she could, while trying to smile and wave her hand to greet the friendly faces that turned to face her, she joined them. For a moment she thought Althea would sit next to her, but the witch walked past the chairs and stood up by the desk, close to the windows.

"We are not quite formal here, we are more like sisters, and such is my preference. The only thing that must be clear is that all of you work for me, and by addition, for the kingdom of Bandah. It is our duty to keep this palace in shape; it is a complicated daily operation, impossible to carry on without the work of many. I would go insane." The queen confided the last words smiling broadly.

"I'll begin with introducing to you the other ladies in my personal court, with some brief information about them, hopefully you will get to know each one of them properly." One of the ladies sitting in the front row stood up and turned to face Koren.

"This is Lady Marussa, she comes to us from Albah, close to the central mountains. She is in charge of all the artistic endeavors of the castle. Art, architecture, decoration, restoration and the preservation of art fall under her jurisdiction. Obviously, all the final decisions come from me, but I'm always pleased with her work." Koren observed Marussa briefly, her first impression being awe of her youthful appearance. Her skin was dark as night, allowing for her lavender eyes to stand out amongst her perfect features. Her smile was warm and embracing, making her think suddenly in the perfect symmetry of flowers.

"Beware, she is a nymph and if you look too long at her you'll be lost." The queen warned, this time seriously. Marussa sat, allowing Koren to return to her senses, asking herself how she would be able to withstand the nymph in the future. Immediately after, a beautiful young woman with long silvery hair similar to hers rose from her seat. Koren was certain that this maiden must be an elf, her piercing blue eyes and the way she carried herself were uncommon to humans. Her skin had the warm iridescence of a white pearl; her hair was similar to a whisper carried in the breeze. Her lean and languid body seemed to delicately flow through time and space. The sharpness of her features was unlike those of humans; specially the pointiness of her ears and chin. Koren was admiring the fullness of the elf woman's lips when the queen interrupted her appreciative stare.

"Palea is from the elves of Cyrus, she is in charge of the culinary division of the castle, including the pantry, stock, utilities, sales of food, and events... It was her that saw you first when you came to the Royal Kitchen with your mother." The queen informed Koren surprising her, since she had convinced herself that her beauty's reputation had preceded her. This new piece of information, even though a small detail, made her feel ashamed of her simple origins. No one had spoken openly of her beauty in the castle, she had merely been found in a kitchen. Her thoughts turned to immediate gratefulness towards the elf woman.

"The following lady is Talma, who is in charge of the incredible task of keeping this castle clean and orderly. Keeping this place impeccable is nearly impossible, only a dragon could perform such a task handsomely." Talma smiled broadly showing her very sharp teeth for the first time. Koren was alarmed as she had formed a completely different idea of a dragon would look like in her mind. For some reason she hadn't expected them to have a human form... Talma was an impressive woman, with a mop of silky black hair from which little cinders spewed out every so often. It was her eyes that more clearly indicated her true race, they seemed as if they had been made out of fire, and very similar in form to a reptile's. This sight only lasted a few seconds, for the dragon changed her intimidating eye color to a darker one, probably not to incommodate the newcomer. Her skin appeared to have a warm golden tone, however if one looked very closely, diminutive scales could be made out. The biggest impact Talma had imparted on the girl had not been her eyes or her skin. There was no escaping the thought of those lethal teeth once having seen them. Even as the dragon sat with great poise, it was difficult to believe that she possessed such dragon like features at all.

Next, a diminutive woman who seemed to barely reach Koren's knee greeted her.

"She is Pumzi, obviously a dwarf. She is in charge of all the gardens and please do not be scared if you see a moving plant, it is just probably her rearranging. Although if Talma has not made away with her at this point, I think all is well."

"Don't listen to them, I'm three hundred years old and no one has dared step over me!" The little woman announced proudly with her sharp voice. Koren couldn't believe someone so tiny was real; she reminded her more of one of her wooden puppets than a living thing.

"Now meet Lenna, a fairy, comes to us from Nubis. She is in charge of music and literature in the castle; however from now own you will take over the literature part. She is quite happy about this; reading is not her favorite past time. You will get instruction about your duties from her." Lenna seemed very young. She had lovely lavender hair reminiscent of amethyst, while her skin was more of a carnation pink color; one must have to see her to know that these colors actually worked together in a person. The fairy wore a little crown of flowers upon her brow to compliment the sky blue of her tunic. Koren took notice of the delicate and almost transparent blue wings that peeked out from behind the young woman's back

"Anari is in charge of the many clothing ateliers in the castle, she is our main designer. Anari is truly skilled in all the aspects of fashion, design, fabrics and style. As soon as you can, go to her so that you can both work together on proper palace attire for you. She's got in common with you and I our human ancestry, although that doesn't hinder her duties at all, she has mastered her magical skills as well as all the others. Only in very few years…" The queen spoke candidly of the young girl, whom Koren observed, taken aback by her striking beauty, specially her skin and hair. These were gold, as the color of honey; even her eyes were golden reminiscent of the undulating fields of barley. Koren smiled at her invitingly, hoping to strike a friendship with her more than the others, lured by the knowledge that they had the ancestry of the human race in common.

"You already know Althea, and to put an end to the introductions, meet Lady Kloe. She is the official Royal Liaison, or spokeswoman of the castle. Parts of her duties are to organize all the government details of the queen's offices before attending the legislative council, as well as orchestrating embassy matters. On top of that, she is responsible for our military training, as you can see she is an Amazon." Kloe nodded courteously, clearly indicating she was the most reserved of the ladies. The woman was extremely tall and had an amazing physique, her muscles visibly outlined under her simple silk tunic. The stunning black dress she wore complimented her green eyes and intense green locks.

Koren looked around appraising the different attributes of such a spectacular group of women, all unique in their own way and from different races that she had not even imagined existed until minutes before. The knowledge that she was there merely by her beauty left her feeling humiliated and lucky to find herself among them. She quickly resolved to stand out in any duty that would be relayed to her; she would prove that she could distinguish herself not only by her beauty, but also by her intellect. Silence had fallen in the office as the introductions had ended, leaving all of them waiting for the queen to proceed. However, it was Althea that addressed them.

"In a few days we will depart to Cyrus on a diplomatic mission, we have to resolve a dispute between the heirs of the Viceroy. The younger son has been chosen by the people and the father to rule the kingdom; the viceroy wants to retire now. The eldest son is not happy about this twist of fate and has build up a sizable allied army. Some of these alliances are with questionable creatures, and his intent to stop the younger prince from inheriting the throne is clear. The queen will meet the two brothers and will try to ask the eldest son to desist his attempts to take the throne by force. Bandah's royalty is upholding the subjects of Cyrus' decision and will support the younger son as heir to the throne. We have to keep the formalities and give them both an audience, but we know the outcome of the matter is already resolved in favor of the young prince. The King's entourage will depart in the morning, we will follow in the afternoon the day of departure."

"Even for this reason I'm excited to go back to Cyrus, I would love to visit with my family." Palea announced, straying from the seriousness of the matter.

"I'm sure that will be fine, once we are settled in the castle in Cyrus you may have a few days leave to visit your loved ones." The queen spoke casually.

"I will make sure security is tight and the travel plans are already in order. Do we know what sort of creatures we are speaking of when we refer to "allies" of the prince?" Kloe addressed the group from her chair, returning the conversation to its original point.

"We have intelligence that tells us that Prince Orion has brought to his service some southern trolls and Lagartunes." Althea responded.

"Anari, make sure all our garments are made of lavender silver thread from Nubis, its scent repels the Lagartunes, we might need chainmail with moonlit filament in case the trolls do attack us." Kloe spoke to Anari, making much more than a suggestion, but rather an explicit order. Anari nodded, as she understood what was requested of her.

"Koren, you must find any new information about the trolls and the Lagartunes to make sure we have the most recent intelligence about both. There is no room for surprises in these matters…" Althea's voice made Koren shudder in her seat, realizing that she was being given her first task in the palace.

"Koren, Lenna will take you to the Royal Library, and then we will reconvene here at tea time to make sure that all is as expected. Make sure to be on the lookout for recent articles regarding those races." The queen remarked again, while the others rose from their seats and chatted animatedly. Koren could barely make out what they were talking about, only able to tell they were excited about the upcoming trick regardless of the reason they were undertaking it. The bonds of friendship were immediately visible amongst the ladies, all the while Althea and the queen spoke softly in front of the windows looking at the horizon. Talma and Kloe seemed to speak emphatically, making energetic hand movements at times during their conversation. Marussa stood nearby interjecting every so often with an unwelcome suggestion. Lenna and Anari were so deeply enthralled in their conversation that neither noticed that Pumzi and Koren had been completely left out of the group. One had no idea what to say and the other too small to be able to be heard without the others having to bend over. Finally, both thought best to seat next to each other and watch the rest of the group go about their business.

"Don't think it is always this exciting, most of the time the meetings are very boring. It's been about two years since we've made a special trip anywhere, so this is an important event. Our last trip was to Astra, to the majesties' wedding, it was quite an impressive affair, even the queen was taken aback by it." Pumzi commented.

"I have never been out of the castle grounds, to me this is an important trip as any. Not only am I getting out of Bandah for the first time, but also I'm going on a Royal diplomatic mission, that is just incredible. How will we travel?" Koren contemplated the possibilities in her head.

"The queen prefers to travel by Pegasus. We all have our own, except Althea and Talma, one flies as a dragon and the other likes to show off the archaic art of flying a broom. Althea concedes that it's an obsolete symbol of the past, yet she likes to show off her lineage. Witches…" Pumzi shrugged and smiled.

"If not by Pegasus, how else would we get there?"

"Oh, we could fly a dragon, or teleport, or by horse or carriage…" Pumzi rolled her eyes indicating that the possibilities were endless.

"I noticed that every one stiffened when Althea spoke of Lagartunes, do you know what they are?" Koren took advantage of the moment to ask the question that was burning in her mind.

"Those nasty creatures… Lagartunes come from the swamps, sort of humanoid reptiles. They have a complex language of shrills and are quite intelligent, however they are mostly mercenaries. Lagartunes love wars and conflict, they see them as perfect opportunities to get something they have an insatiable appetite for, human flesh. If you ever come across one, always be careful, they sneak up on you and have a very long tongue, similar to a whip, which they adeptly use to strangle their unsuspecting victims." Pumzi spoke sternly.

"Do you think we'll be in danger?" Nerves started to get the better of Koren.

"We always are." The dwarf replied enigmatically, leaving Koren feeling uncomfortable. Lenna approached them with a smile on her face, not a friendly smile though, rather a blank one.

"You must come with me. I guess I should hand over the library duties to you as soon as possible." The fairy informed Koren. Both departed from the office in a hurry; Lenna moving with incredible speed. Koren realized that the fairy's feet were barely touching the ground; it was her wings that helped her glide along effortlessly.

"It will seem to you that the library is not very big, but the larger part of it lies underground, it is said that its chambers are twice the size of the castle itself. Luckily all the information has been organized in such a way that you can have immediate access to whatever you are looking for. We only keep some of the most valuable physical books deep inside the library, so in reality what you get is an astral copy of any given book. Don't worry; it is just like having a real book in your hands… We receive hundreds of thousands of books and manuscripts from all over Bandah every week, sometimes from other kingdoms. We do have a panel of readers, mostly scholars, which have to make detailed summaries of each new acquisition so that they can be catalogued properly. If they are important, they will reach the Royal Librarian… you. As director of the library, you must read all the summaries that the readers bring to you. If you see anything that stands out you must pass it on to the queen, keeping her up to date with news and tidings within the land." Lenna spoke fast, not letting Koren absorb all the information that she was throwing at her.

"I'm going to spend my whole life reading! And how am I supposed to know what to give the queen?" Koren was already starting to feel frustration, and she hadn't even started her new duties.

"Just focus on scientific, magical and military advances, although she really has a particular interest in philosophy. She always demands to read it, make sure to pass on the lectures from the notorious scholars, better not forget that. The queen once told me that we have to respect the thoughts of those dedicated to it. I guess more often than not the people's thoughts hide behind the mouths of philosophers... Oh yeah, and if there is anything about legislature make sure she gets that too."

"The queen reads a lot!" Koren declared incredulous.

"Yes, that's why we try to help with everything else, even the king has to read as much. A lot rests on his shoulders, he has to rule above the chancellors, and decide if a new law passes to legislation. He is always worried about being fair and just, the more he educates himself, he says, the wiser he will be. Of course, the queen must approve everything, but she trusts him wholeheartedly."

"It must have worked for him, he is a great king."

"Greatness, justice and truth lay not in books, but in the heart... The queen said that." Lenna smiled wryly.

Following a grand hallway passage, which led them to a magnificent wooden gate, they came upon a large staircase that seemed to descend endlessly. Fortunately, the white luminescent fire of powerful magical torches lit their path. At the end of the steps was a hall, where the shields of Bandah adorned the walls. Where vases full of colorful blooming roses perfumed the air, perhaps trying to conceal the smell of dampness and earth that assaulted the senses. The hall had a comfortable lounge, vivid tapestries decorating the walls along with the shields, and inviting chaises abounded.

"This is the reading hall, normally it is busy, people must be away trying to prepare for the trip to Cyrus. From here you go to the Reader's Chambers, there is about twenty readers in the group. They are fascinated with reading it's quite unnerving. Past that, you'll find the archives, the real library system." Koren remained silent assenting with her head, she could tell that the library was not Lenna's favorite place; she seemed to be uneasy there. They finally reached the archives, careful to be as silent as possible, lest they interrupt the readers that had their noses buried in thick books. Both visitors spied them as they read, wrote and worked on what they assumed were the summaries for the queen.

"Here we are, the archive." Lenna gestured nonchalantly with her hand, showing Koren a room of formidable size. Where the walls were lined with shelves full of thin document files, except for one wall where there was a window. The window seemed out of place, Koren thought that perhaps it was a frame that someone had forgotten to fill with a portrait. The gilded wooden frame seemed to be decorative enough to bear the semblance of a royal.

"All these documents you see around here are summaries, to your right are the new ones that you should read. To the left are the ones that the queen and king have read, and are ready to archive. They are sorted by date, so make sure to write the date on them when you give them to their majesties, and when you return them here. This window is the librarian, it will give you what you want, literally." Lenna led Koren to the window.

"I come in the name of her majesty and highness Queen Violet, this is my key." Lenna spoke to the dark interior of the window's frame, as she raised the pendant in her necklace, as if some sort of invisible entity would see it. A light appeared pulsating inside the window, giving the impression that it had come alive. Koren was too shocked by what she was witnessing to be able to utter a word at the moment.

"I need information about the Southern Trolls and the Lagartunes." Lenna spoke at the light loudly, almost uncertain of her words, perhaps a little afraid.

"There are two thousand, six hundred and twenty seven items including information pertaining to the matter." A deep voice announced from the window, Koren couldn't help but try to peek inside to see who owned such a voice.

"I need something more recent, not so many items, maybe a hundred years back only. Something that describes them, their customs, attributes..."

"There are three hundred and fifty one titles available, should we present them all." The mysterious voice continued ignoring Lenna's exasperated sighs.

"This is not possible, isn't there something from the last ten years?"

"There are one hundred and eighty items available..." The astral voice replied calmly while Lenna rolled her eyes and kicked the ground frustrated.

"This is exasperating..."Lenna commented full of indignation.

"I thought you said it was an easy to use library system, let me try now." Koren offered as she faced the window.

"I come in the name of her majesty and highness Queen Violet, this is my key. I need the most recent and comprehensive summaries regarding the Southern Trolls and Lagartunes, no more than two titles per subject matter." There was a silence in the room; the voice did not respond. Koren was uncertain if she had been heard at all, until four dim lights appeared floating out of the window's frame. Lenna grabbed them all at once and she placed them on the nearest desk. Each of the lights transformed into a book, with beautiful covers of their own, and ready to be read.

"This was just not for me, I'm glad you have taken over." Lenna smiled at Koren.

"Unbelievable! This is amazing!" Was the only thing Koren could say as she touched the thick pages, making certain that they were indeed real. Inside the book cover she found what would be a book summary, it had the dates when it was last read, seemingly recent.

"Once you are done reading just throw them through the window, that's it." Lenna informed her as she stood to leave.

"Are you leaving? You are leaving me here by myself?" Koren was a little uneasy about the prospect; it didn't feel right to her somehow to be there unaccompanied.

"You don't need to be concerned about anything here, just make sure to be on time to the meeting. Haven't you noticed how well you did on your first visit? Besides you are never alone here, the castle is with you." Her voice was hurried, she was anxious to leave the place and made no effort to hide the fact.

"The castle?"

"Yes, the voice you heard belongs to one of the spirits who works here. I'm quite sure all those stupid readers will die in their seats and float right on to the archives some day. The spirits are in charge of all the magic in here; there are even some royals who decided to reside here forever... This castle, like the kingdom, thanks to the queen's blood is alive and magical. It will even talk to you or serve you, you just got to pay attention." Lenna left at once, not even trying to wait for further comments from Koren.

Koren looked around nervously, not being able figure out exactly why. Maybe it was the knowledge that she was buried deep in the heart of the castle. Moss was noticeably imbibing with a greenish hue the whiteness of the walls. Every so often the laconic drip of some invisible water leaked audibly as well. The light in the window seemed to continue its pulsing, indicating that it was still ready to serve. The furniture seemed to mysteriously want to swallow her, while some unseen eyes spying the room could be felt. Koren walked over to a golden chaise, which seemed extremely comfortable, and it was so. Surprisingly a little footrest scooted over on its own, offering itself and lifting her legs comfortably. She couldn't believe what had just happened, thinking that magic was going to take a lot of getting used to, when a nearby table approached her carrying some tea. Looking around the room, certain that she was being watched, she found herself alone. She decided not to question these events anymore acceptance was just simpler.

"I'd like some pastries too, with the tea..." Koren smiled sheepishly at her brazenness, yet she enjoyed the mysterious attentions. Immediately, a little silver tray full of delicate confections was right next to her cup of tea, making her believe that they were there all along and she had foolishly overlooked them. Taking one and putting it to her lips she savored the delicate flavor of honey and almonds, her mother had probably made this confection, yet how it got there was purely a matter of magic. She reprimanded herself for wasting so much time in these small luxuries, no matter how stupendous they seemed, reading was supposed to be the focus at the moment.

"Um, I'd like to be alerted when tea time is getting close, to be on time at the queen's offices." She spoke to the empty room once again, trusting that somehow her request would be satisfied. Without further ado she grabbed the first book, dedicating herself completely to the duty of reading. Her main concern was to deliver a great report for the queen, under no circumstance she wanted to botch her first mission. Time seemed to have disintegrated when the austere voice scared her out her wits with the onerous announcement that time was up.

"A quarter of an hour to tea time..." Once again Koren couldn't locate the owner of the voice, yet she gratefully murmured thanks and rose from the comfortable seat to depart. Following Lenna's advice she flung the books into the window, where they returned to their luminescent shape and disappeared from sight.

"Thank you, that is all for now." Koren spoke out loud as she left, noticing the window returning to its lifeless state. Trying to avoid a late arrival to the queen's office she ran most of the way, yet in spite of her race the other ladies were already there. The group chatted amicably and sipped hot tea, the queen sat behind her desk lost in the reading of important papers at hand. Koren found a spot next to Pumzi trying not to attract any attention to her.

"Am I too late?"

"No, we are all early, the queen hasn't left the office at all, she's been tending to new reports from the queen of Cyrus." The dwarf spoke softly. Althea left the group to approach the queen, speaking something into her ear, and prompting her to incorporate right away to start the meeting.

"Thank you all for being here a little early, the queen of Cyrus has written and demands the matter be attended to soon. We depart for the lesser kingdom of Cyrus tomorrow morning. The queen fears the elder son will attack any minute, perhaps even kill the king before any compromise is made."

"Why would he do that?" Koren couldn't help herself from exclaiming out loud.

"If the viceroy dies, the kingdom goes automatically to the eldest daughter, in the absence of one, to the eldest son. However, the viceroy upon announcing to retire before his term is due has allowed his people to decide which of his heirs should rule. I believe we already explained this… The official ceremony of succession has been set for the summer solstice. The queen fears that Orion, the eldest, will take advantage and strike before then, needless to say he would never admit having part in any tragedy that befalls his father. I'm ordering the succession ceremony to be done at once, we are taking a sizable military force to support the chosen heir until he is officially crowned viceroy." The queen spoke to all, but threw a curt glance at Koren, apparently not liking to repeat herself.

"If the young brother is crowned, who will stop an attack against him?" Koren braved to ask.

"We have considered that as well, I'm afraid that once Prince Atle becomes viceroy the eldest son will be exiled. We will strip him of his royal title and riches, he will not be able to support an army and cause any more trouble." The queen answered with aplomb settling the matter once and for all, by announcing her intentions to the others as well.

"You majesty, all our garments have been readied for the trip, following all of Kloe's specifications." Anari announced becoming the center of attention.

"Well done. Koren, have you gathered any new information for us?" Koren blushed ferociously after becoming the focus of too many inquisitive eyes.

"Yes… The Southern Trolls, are very aggressive, they love conflict and wars solely for the purpose of dying or killing. Their main weapon is the mace, followed by the bow and arrow, which they use with great skill. The trolls are fond of fire missiles, to protect themselves in battle they wear a magical blue coral armor sealed in dragon's blood." Koren paused briefly wondering how would Talma feel after her references about dragons.

"Trolls have thick skin, oozing an acidic sweat that corrodes metal and the flesh of almost any creature that comes in contact with them for too long. Best to not touch them at all if they sweat. Trolls will spit at each other to show affection and because their saliva protects them from each others acidic sweat, so if you get sweat on you, somehow try to get Troll spit on it. They don't seem to be highly intelligent creatures, unless it's about military affairs, although their loyalty can be earned by feeding them and the promise of battle. Usually, trolls return to their territories after battle to mate, or die in their tribes. Due to the inhospitable areas were they reside the Southern Trolls are amongst the biggest and sturdiest of their kind."

"Perfect, what about the Lagartunes?" The queen questioned after listening intently.

"Those are quite intelligent, we already know they live in swamps and are very aggressive. Their instinct focuses solely on the consumption of flesh, especially human, since they consider it a delicacy. They have that in common with Trolls as a matter of fact. Lagartunes are reptilian that stand tall, much like a human but a couple heads taller, they go into battle with the purpose of defeating its enemy to feast on it. Their skin is scaly but almost impenetrable, their neck is their weakest spot, usually its covered with some sort of magical metal neck brace. Possibly titanium, seems like it doesn't irritate their necks like other metals can. Whenever they smell the grey lavender of Nubis, they become disoriented; in large quantities they could temporarily lose their sight. Just like Trolls, they are loyal to whoever promises them human flesh, even though they battle just for the joy of it. As far as I could tell, they never show affection to each other, but they consider it very disrespectful if their tails get stepped on." Koren inhaled profoundly after letting go of all the pertinent information that she could think of.

"Fortunately, there are no novelties, it is good to know our adversaries are not unpredictable. Great job Koren. Talma? Kloe? Anything else we should know?"

"We should be armed with fire spears whenever possible, they are the best defense against both." Kloe spoke as Talma assented to her suggestion.

"Should battle break out, I'll lead the front with the soldiers, at least to face the Trolls, its very hard to break their armor if it has dragon's blood, but one dragon can fight another, I should be able to cause quite some damage." Talma spoke sternly.

"I will keep that in mind, remember the king also will be there with his knights and entourage, you are there to protect me and we will not compromise ourselves at any point if they can fight. I doubt the mischievous prince will dare attack a royal committee, its doubtful an attack can be feasible, and they don't expect our arrival yet." Violet declared confidently, allowing herself the reassurance that there would not be any setbacks.

"Oh, lets forget about all this dreary talk, lets just go to the atelier and try our new clothing. The grey lavender infused dresses are all ready to, thank you Lady Pumzi for gathering so much of that unique lavender for us in such short notice." Violet smiled gracefully at the dwarf as she stood up, leading them all into the third floor where the atelier for their clothing was located. Koren took part of the procession following quickly, surrounded by the flourishing lashing of the ladies' heavy skirts.

Koren had only briefly glanced at the atelier when Althea showed it to her. Once in there she couldn't take in all of its grandeur, although everything she did get to see seemed extraordinary. She could barely wait for the day to be over so that she could relay to her mother all the events and sights of her first day at the palace. Keeping her pace as best she could, and trying to see as much as possible, was a full time distraction all on its own. The fear of getting lost at such a crucial time was not at all impertinent. The group went through a spacious vanity hall with multiple mirrors and gilded chairs, all the way to another room that was full in its entirety by rows upon rows of beautiful dresses. Anari led the group into the room, where with an elegant swirl of her hand she made the dresses come alive. The dresses all lined up in perfect formation, as if invisible soldiers had possessed them. Koren could barely hold back a laugh at the ridiculous sight.

The dresses floated about elegantly, all of them exposing similar colors and designs, except for one that stood out by its silvery fabric and lilac lace detail. Koren thought that it would be the most beautiful dress she would ever see, it was obvious that it would belong to the queen. A deep sentiment of envy unlike any she had ever felt engulfed her voraciously. It was not fair that the queen had to have always the best of everything... Why not make all the other dresses fabulous too? Koren's eyes fell on the silky silvery fabric, delicately resplendent like a dim star's sigh, wishing with all her might that the dress would disappear. She told herself that if the beautiful dress couldn't be hers then it couldn't be anybody else's. Unexpectedly, something magical and sudden happened that left the group in terror. Powerful blue flames emerged from out thin air and swallowed the dress whole, burning it instantly, leaving behind merely a fistful of ashes. Every one in the room ran to surround the queen ready to protect her, frenzied eyes searching around for the culprit of such a sinister act. Koren stood frozen and unable to react, not knowing what to do. Never thinking she would have been capable of doing such a thing, even asking if it was possible at all that she did it.

"Do not move." Althea spoke authoritatively, leaving the group surrounding the queen to search around the room, placing her hands in the walls and studying every corner. Althea closed her eyes every so often, deeply inhaling, as if the truth would come to her through thin air.

"Nothing. There are no clues that something has caused this to happen. It was one of us." The women let out a cry of alarm almost simultaneously, looking at each other confused, even though it was obvious that the only one that was standing still and not reacting was the newcomer. The queen moved away from the parameter the ladies had established and walked to where the ashes were piled up, a tense silence befell the room. Koren's heart raced, she was scared, knowing that soon enough the truth would be known... she did indeed burn the queen's dress. Sweat started to dampen her skin, the fear of the consequences already hammering at her brain; it could be the first and last day in court for her... Would they throw her out of the palace? Her legs began to tremble, the queen's proximity was too much to bear, and her face felt like it was burning. Tears of guilt began to flow freely.

"It was me your majesty, it was me!" Koren declared shamefully as she wept. The queen turned to look at her sharply, without saying a word.

"Impossible!" Althea bellowed, not so much incredulously, but in amazement. The queen approached Koren smiling, and hugged her, surprising her tremendously.

"Don't cry like that, if it was you I'm glad that you have been honest. I don't know why you did it, yet I know that you are a young girl and it is hard to sometimes control some of our emotions." Violet wiped her tears away with her delicate hand.

"Anari can replace the dress, but tell me, what did you feel?"

"I was jealous because your dress was the most beautiful... I wanted it to be mine." Koren confessed to the queen.

"I understand. You, however, must understand this now once and for all, I am the queen. You and the others are my servants. The best is always for me; this is what sets me apart from the rest, as it should be. Being the queen is the biggest honor to befall on any woman, not because you are the sovereign, but because it is through the woman's line, my own, that magic will be sure to flow through Bandah. My garments have to be made by certain traditional specifications, ripe of magic, that won't be of any use to any of you..." The queen's voice was stern yet reassuring, Koren felt calm as she listened in silence.

"I'm really sorry, your majesty." She finally found the courage to speak almost inaudibly.

"We shall not dwell on the past, lets see the other dresses. Anari, order another dress be made immediately for me." The queen faced the others and smiled, encouraging them to accept the situation without further comment. It was obvious she didn't want to make Koren feel out of place, even though every so often the ladies found themselves throwing furtive glances at the girl. It took a few hours for the burning dress to be forgotten much to Koren's dismay, they were finally able to relax as they tried on all their new garments and commented gaily about the colors and fashion. Koren enjoyed the occasion quite enthused, regarding her image in the mirror with great admiration.

"It is time to retire for the day, soon it will darken and the moons are full of magic." Althea announced. The women left the dresses at the workshop, certain that the servants would pack them in their trunks at one point. They each hugged and kissed chatting amicably, knowing that they would see each other the next day. Violet was the first one to retire to her tower, although before she left she spoke briefly with Althea, it was a quiet conversation that the others could not hear. Koren was ready to go home, she felt exhausted and her senses needed a rest from the overexcitement of the first day at court. She daydreamed of sitting on the little couch in the living room, her mother bringing her some piping hot tea, while her father read quietly... her bed beckoned her alluringly too. As she entertained these thoughts she began to walk away only to have Althea step right in front of her, bringing her to a sudden halt.

"Not so fast, we need to talk, follow me." Althea walked ahead of Koren in her hurried pace, the girl dared not follow the order. After what seemed an endless walk, Koren realized that they were in the sixth floor of the tower, probably in Althea's apartments.

"This is my home, welcome. My sister Lula is here, she usually sits by the fire to keep warm, and she'll show up any minute. We can talk at ease; even if she were here she couldn't hear much of what we said. We can sit in the living room it is more comfortable there... Don't look so sullen, I just want to speak with you briefly, you'll make it home in time for supper." Althea offered her a seat and Koren obliged settling on a large black leather chair, which was quite comfortable. The witch found a seat across from the girl so that she could look at her while they spoke.

"I'll be honest, the reason I wanted to talk to you is to know more information about you. Have you ever had anything similar events to what happened at the Atelier before?"

"No." Koren responded faintly.

"I just want to help you. You performed some seriously powerful magic today, which means it is imperative that you learn how to control it. The palace is a place ripe with magic, it will make yours stronger, and we cannot have an untrained force running amok. That is dangerous, given that magic can be good or bad, ultimately the person has to learn to control it and use it for their intended purpose."

"But it wasn't unrestrained, what happened was exactly what I wished, I wanted the dress to vanish." Koren confessed trying to explain that she had felt in some sort of control of the situation, implying that her magic wouldn't cause any harm unless she wanted it to.

"That's even worse, it means you are ignorantly squandering your magic with your poor control. You could have just disappeared the dress without having to burn it, just by closing your eyes and not using so much... black magic." Althea tried to explain, but Koren felt she was hiding something from her.

"What do you mean black magic? That kind of magic is evil..." Koren spoke sort of scandalized by what Althea was insinuating.

"Look, there are a lot of people who would categorize what you did as black magic, although I believe all magic is the same. Black magic, white magic; there are only intentions behind them, which constitute their true nature. If you use magic for good, then it's white, if you intend to hurt, destroy or cause damage, its black. Quite simple. For example, there is a spell that can be use to grow hair on fire victims, this is white magic because it helps. If you use the same spell to make hair grow on someone excessively to traumatize them or make them a laughing stock, then it takes a whole other turn. Do you understand what I'm trying to tell you?"

"I do. The problem was not the magic, it's that I used it to destroy something. I should've never wished it happened..."

"Don't be so hard on yourself, you are young and need to learn, just be aware that our intentions are reflected in our actions."

"Where did the magic come from, really?" Koren demanded confused.

"You've always had it in you, it hadn't bloomed yet. Just like I said, the palace will bring out magic by the tenfold. Some people study and practice magic for many years, while others just feel an urgent desire to change reality and without knowing, they do. You are in the latter group, and I think you should also have a conversation with your father..." Althea advised.

"What happens to me now?"

"After seeing what you are capable of doing, it is obvious you have a strong magical line in you, we will train you so that you can take advantage of such a wonderful gift life has given you. Once we return from Cyrus, I will help you train, although most of the best lessons will come from yourself. There is an excellent dragon, Erasmus, who teaches at the Royal Academy, his instruction is unparalleled. We can only point you in the right direction; however, you are in charge of the rest. If I were you, I'd take advantage of the library access and start reading about hereditary magical skills... And you must be aware of your negative desires from now on, try to only do things, which you can live with after they are done. You have just begun to live and hopefully you'll live as long and fruitful a life as mine. Believe me, you will enjoy it much better if its good and content." Althea smiled warmly.

"I promise I'll be more careful, I didn't know I could do things like that."

"Unfortunately, that is a very common statement... no one fully knows what they are capable of, sometimes until its too late. You will find information in the library about all kinds of magic, white, black, pink, blue, it doesn't matter, ultimately the choice is yours." Althea reiterated.

"But how exactly is it that books work for magic?"

"First, they'll give you a lot of information, and secondly, they'll help you train your mind to use the power confined there. And of course there are always spells, which are only a simple formula to achieve an end result with as little magic as possible, sort of a cheat sheet. Powerful entities need no such things; they are able to carry on magic from beginning to end solely with the power of their minds. Always keep in mind that you must respect nature, even if you don't think so it will always have the upper hand."

"I guess I won't be using so much magic after all this is all to complicated, too delicate."

"Oh please, I'm not trying to put you off on magic or anything of the sort, perhaps I'm not expressing everything I wanted to tell you correctly. It's been a while since I've had to talk to an impressionable young woman, but trust me, magic has been sort of like a sister to me..." Almost as if on cue, Althea's sister arrived unannounced. The ancient woman's eyes where completely an off white color, her irises visibly worn down by time, the same way her hair resembled threads made out of silvery cobwebs. A simple frock made of wool, whose sole embellishments were dirt stains and grit, covered the woman's skeletal frame. Koren was taken aback by the old witches' appearance, unable to grasp the fact that a woman of such stature as Althea kept her sister in such a state.

"Yes, I'm the old hag, the sister. Blind, deaf, mute... but here I am you majesty. Althea did not announce your visit; otherwise I'd worn a shawl. Today I fell from the fourth floor balcony and landed on the stables. The Pegasus' were very upset, yet a kind dragon-man helped me to the palace again, he said his daughter works for you your majesty..." The old woman's sweet voice surprised everyone in the room, probably her more than the other two present; surely they had all heard it.

"That man you speak of is my father, and you are very confused, I'm not the queen..." Koren explained kindly.

"She can't hear you, you have to let her touch you so that you can communicate with each other. I hadn't heard her voice for decades; I doubt it'll happen again. You can always open your mind to let her read it. Let me formally introduce you to Lula, age has been a little merciless on her, sometimes I fear for her safety, being so confused and all. Look at all the foolishness she has spoken right now." Althea commented shaking her lustrous locks.

"She is the queen! She will rule, mark my words, Althea!" The old witches' screams thundered in their minds making them jump.

"Lula, calm down! Violet is the queen, you know her. This is Lady Koren..."

"Stupid witch! Half wit, brute, evil… that is her, the queen… she will hold the scepter!" Lula yelled agitated as she kicked the floor, signaling at Koren with her mangled fingers. Althea rose from her chair and held the woman by the shoulders tenderly, trying to calm her down; the old witch seemed very sleepy all of a sudden.

"I think its time our visitor returns home and we have supper…" Althea led her sister away, pacing forward slowly, in a trance. She stopped by the door to the main chambers and turned to bid farewell to Koren.

"Good night, dear Koren, thank you for stopping by."

"Good night." They disappeared from sight walking slowly into the dim-lit room, holding each other affectionately by the arm. As much as Koren felt sad for the old woman's decay, she felt greater admiration for Althea's devotion. Feeling left behind, she immediately departed with the idea of hugging her mother, and able to let out all the days troubles on her loving arms. The way from the queen's tower to the forest took about a half hour racing to complete, anxiety to get home did not allow for any stops along the way. Koren's heart pumped relief throughout her body as she saw her little home come into view at the end of the dirt road in the forest. It was such a small yet welcoming place, with warm golden lights, which led the way in the darkness. From far away Mistress Flora's figure could be seen sitting expectantly in the great armchair by the window, reading casually as if pretending that she had no cares in the world. Koren ran faster to seek refuge in her mother's lap as she had done so many times in her short life, knowing that soothing warmth and kisses would engulf her. The door opened right as she arrived, her mother had heard her steps as she got closer, and indeed she opened her arms to receive her. It had been a stressful day for both, neither knowing what would transpire that day, were each one would be truly on their own for the first time.

"Mother…" Koren held her tightly, like she had never before.

"Don't squeeze so hard! I can only imagine what sort of day you've had! I've missed you tremendously today, but come in; we have not eaten yet waiting for you. Come, my love, I've made you a mushroom stew that will have you happy in no time, come, come…" Mistress Flora ushered her daughter directly into the small dining room by the kitchen, where her father already sat holding a steaming mug of tea.

"So we finally have our daughter back, what time is this to be returning from the palace? If you will be leaving so late then we must be there to walk you back, I was getting worried." Her father returned her hug before she sat next to him at the table.

"Oh Papa, you shouldn't worry, you know the castle is safe. Other than that, it has been an impossible, incredible, phenomenal day!"

"Tell us then, I'll serve supper while you settle in…" Her mother went about preparing dishes and ladling stew into earthenware.

"I don't even know where to start, mother. The queen's tower is hallucinating; and the other ladies are extraordinary… One is a dragon!" Exclaimed Koren making her mother jump from excitement.

"A dragon, go figure!" Mistress Flora murmured shaking her head.

"There is also an elf, a dwarf, a nymph, a fairy, an Amazon… Oh and the queen is marvelous… She is just incredible! And… I have magic, mother! Magic!" The young woman nearly exploded as she announced the news, making her mother cover her mouth to suppress a cry of surprise. Master Lorean smiled seemingly pleased.

"Magic, huh? I was wondering if you got some of that..." He remarked casually.

"Yes, Papa, I have lots of it, Althea said that she will train me herself when we return from Cyrus." The proud announcement was given at last.

"Cyrus? What trip to Cyrus?" Flora inquired visibly upset.

"They've been trying to keep it hushed, the queen and her ladies will depart tomorrow morning to Cyrus on a diplomatic mission. I get to go too! On a Pegasus no less!" Koren exclaimed almost losing her breath.

"Wait a minute, the king is gone and the queen was not supposed to go unless there was any trouble. Why is she leaving so soon?" Her eyes squinted full of suspicion.

"Because of the evil prince! There is a prince that wants to fight for the throne, which has already been promised to another prince, one that the viceroy and the people have chosen." Koren seized the opportunity for drama, moving her hands about animatedly.

"Holy goddesses! This sounds quite dangerous, they better not think about taking you with them, you are only a child."

"Flora, don't be so dramatic. Koren is not a girl, she is a young woman and I doubt there will be any dangerous situations over there. The majesties have an impressive military service; the queen has her ladies, and the king has the knights. I sincerely doubt that the prince would dare take on the majesties of Bandah, it would be suicidal." Lorean admonished his wife, he knew that the military forces of Bandah were to be trusted at all times in the rare likelihood of an attack.

"Also, if they are traveling in Pegasus' that means that they don't think danger is likely, otherwise they'd go on dragons, or just appear over there." Lorean added. Mistress Flora remained silent as she sat to eat, serving Koren a second serving of stew, which she received happily.

"Oh, I forgot to tell you that I'm now the castle's librarian." Koren swelled with pride as she surprised he parents again.

"Darling, you have no idea how important that position is. Every written book is there, it is even rumored there are books written by deities themselves, which may carry within the secrets of life." Master Lorean spoke in a low voice.

"Don't tell her those things, you are filling up her head with falsehoods, or truths, that is best she doesn't know." Flora rebuked her husband quite upset.

"It was just a comment!"

"Why would it be bad for me to know those things, Mama?" Koren demanded with sudden interest in the conversation.

"Its not that it would be bad, truth is never bad, dear. It's just that the secret of life and things of the sort are hidden inside us, trying to find them elsewhere is just asking for trouble. Trouble that we might not know how to handle."

"But you just said truth is not bad..." Koren confronted her smiling.

"Yes, but that doesn't mean that it always has to be overexposed." Mistress Flora replied grumpily. Supper went on undisturbed from that point on, each happy to retire after such an eventful day. Koren laid her head on her pillow, enjoying the darkness of her room, with the intention of playing the day all over again in her head, however sleep stupefied her into submission rather quickly.

Chapter 3: A defining moment

Koren arrived early at the palace only to find a terrifying silence. Wondering where everyone had gone, the ordinary sounds of the place were loudly absent, and the halls empty. The servant's steps were sorely missing as much as their gossipy giggles. Koren ran as fast as she could to the queen's tower, her heart full of fear, thinking that perhaps the queen had left without her. As she got close to the office she heard voices, which made her sigh with utter relief.

"Good morning Koren, ready for the trip?" Talma asked welcoming her in.

"Yes, I'm a little anxious, it's the first time I leave the castle, and my mother's nervousness must have rubbed off on me. My dad suggested I visit the Pegasus' stable before we leave, but I don't think I'll have enough time to do that."

"Well if you do, be on your guard, they really have a mean spirit." Pumzi informed.

"I still clear from them, it always makes me hungry." Talma laughed out loud, leaving the others open mouthed, by the implications of her words.

"Ah well, you would scare anybody, doesn't your race eat every magical creature it can?" Pumzi reminded her, to which Talma shrugged and muttered "I'm a vegetarian". Just in that moment they heard a multitude of steps approaching the office.

"The king!" Pumzi exclaimed her eyes wide open with excitement, as she made sure her hair was perfectly in place. Koren turned to face the entrance to the office; expectantly awaiting to see the man she had only heard great things about.

The elegantly royal figure of the king of Bandah appeared through the threshold with an air of dignity and power. The queen rose from her desk to bestow her husband a dashing smile, full of the complicity of very intimate moments. Koren held her breath, dumbfounded at the sight. King Papo was tall and impressive, with skin made of pure gold. His hair was lustrous and wavy, the color of chestnuts and fell on his broad shoulders. His royal uniform was impeccable, the dark cape he wore flung about the ground like a shadow trailing his leather boots. The silver symbols of Bandah stood out over the pitch darkness of his whole ensemble. The thought that she would never see such beautiful a man, crossed Koren's mind as she admired him. The king returned his wife's smile, focusing his intense brown eyes on hers, while he walked. Once if front of her he fell to his knee to salute the queen, grabbing her hand ever so tenderly when she offered it to his waiting lips.

"Your majesty, I have allowed myself to return to Bandah. It is my desire to lead the travel committee along with my men, in order to be at your service. As soon as you give the order we shall depart to Cyrus." As he spoke Koren realized that he had come with a group of men to the queen's office, she had been so absorbed in his appreciation that she hadn't noticed the others. There were at least ten men in the entourage; they also were on one knee, except that they all solemnly looked to the ground.

"My beloved husband, rise. Give the order to prepare for departure right at midday." She smiled at him blushing. He kissed her delicate hand again and rose to his feet, their eyes met electrifying the room with the passion that radiated from their hearts. The king's men remained stoically quiet, however one of the ladies present allowed herself to let go of a heartfelt sigh. The king turned to leave, yet was detained by the queen, who embraced him feverishly tossing aside all the pleasantries of court. She whispered something in his ear that made him lose his composure, allowing himself to kiss her passionately, and forgetting that they were not alone. Koren blushed and turned to look at the other ladies to spy their reactions, most were blushing or smiling, or both, by the affectionate display. Althea, who was standing close to the queen, had a broad smile on her face, appreciating the temporary lack of decorum the monarchs of Bandah allowed themselves. It was clear that over everything else they happened to be, they were two people madly in love.

After letting go, the king turned to face the ladies and with a handsome smile bowed his head in a gallant salute. The men on the floor finally rose one by one once the king had gone right through them and headed to the door. The king led his men away, who walked behind him in perfect formation, to the astonishment of Koren.

"Oh believe me, if I had known he was like that from the very beginning, I would not have resisted becoming queen for so long..." The queen commented merrily, once the men were out of sight, causing all the women to laugh as well, as if they were familiar with that story.

"You have heard the order, we leave soon. The trip is long, I chose the Pegasus' to enjoy this beautiful weather we are having, and because I want to spend the night at Albah. We will stay at the nymph's temple, Arkana, the Demi-goddess will have a feast in our honor." Applause of pleasure erupted in the room, letting Koren know that the other women had been there before, and that they had probably enjoyed their stay. The happiest of them seemed to be Marussa, her joy made her glow; surely she was excited to be back to the place she was born.

"Koren, since you are new to the palace I ordered Althea to prepare your belongings for the trip. I'm certain you'll find what she has prepared for you enjoyable." Violet informed the girl.

"Thank you, your majesty. Althea." Koren lowered her head with humble gratitude to both.

The women stayed in the office for another hour, until the queen gave them permission to leave and make any arrangements they saw fit before leaving the palace. Koren ran to the Royal Kitchen, knowing her mother was there, so she could bid farewell one more time. The kitchens were known territory; Koren was familiar with all five of them having visited often. There were so many since sustaining a large palace demanded a lot of food to be prepared. They were loud, full of vapors and intense smells. The kitchen cooks and their helpers ran about like mice, coordinating the operation of food preparation like the manning of a large ship. Mistress Flora was the Head Royal Cook, in charge of organizing and delegating duties to others, and personally preparing or ordering the preparation of their majesties food. Koren ran happily inside the long corridors, in between cooks and delicacies, as she had done for so many years of her life. She raced past the bakery, and would artfully grab a delicate pastry without the pastry cook noticing. He would've yelled obscenities at her had he noticed, which made Koren laugh harder than anything else could in the past. Then she would go past the cavernous ovens, lined by huge simmering pots that finally led to the main kitchen, her mother's den. Place which also served as a culinary academy where the best cooks of Bandah came to hone in their skills and perhaps secure work at the palace. Koren couldn't help but be proud of her mother; after all she was the most envied and revered cook in the whole kingdom. The queen had personally chosen her for the office!

Flora was behind a beautiful copper pot, from which a delicate aroma of cooked sweet milk came up in threads. Her face was flush from the stove's heat, her hair tucked away behind her silver bonnet and her frock had many insignias created by the process of food creation.

"Mother I'm here!" The shout made the woman jump, almost tossing up in the air the ladle she had in her hand.

"Koren! I've told you so many times not to do that! You are going to make me spill scalding soup on me. And I see you've been stealing pastries again, you know well Master Obreu gets very upset." Her mother reprimanded sternly.

"Oh but they are so-oh good, Mama..." Flora grunted disapprovingly, then gave her daughter a kiss on the head, returning to her soup.

"What are you making? It smells fabulous..."

"It's the king's favorite soup, you can have some in a minute. He sometimes gets a little anxious before traveling with the flying horses, this soup is calming, he requested it."

"I saw him for the first time! He is so handsome!"

"Yes, he is. I remember the first time I saw him, myself very young when I started working here. Don't have a clue how the poor boy ended up in the kitchens, possibly hiding from everything. I had him sit on that corner while I fixed him something to make him feel better, and I did, this very same soup. From that day on he asked the queen to make me the head cook. Wish you'd seen the senior cook's reaction, but regardless the king's will had to be obeyed."

"What's in it?"

"When you come back I'll teach you how to make it, it's very simple. Only healing milk from the Kanibian cows, butter, cinnamon, sugar, scented salt from the mermaid kingdom, a little bit of flour from Polaris and a few petals of the Treste flower..." Mistress Flora recited the ingredients, as if they were the sonnets of a love poem. Pouring a good amount of creamy liquid into a porcelain bowl, she smiled offering it to her daughter. Koren carefully put the steaming bowl to her lips, immediately aware of the delicious milky smell. It smelled scalded, sweet, soothing... reminiscent of fresh air, green pastures and a kiss of sun. Koren felt transported back to her own little home, to her favorite spot by the fire on a cold winter night. The thick liquid entered her body like a reviving breath that made her close her eyes briefly and smile.

"Ahh, that is so good. Why don't you always make this for me?" She reprimanded with a smile on her face.

"It just didn't occur to me, you always seem so happy."

"I have to go…only stopped by briefly to say bye. We leave in a couple of hours."

"I know, the king asked if I wanted to come along with his company, but I declined. I'm too old for that and I've never liked to travel, really. Besides all those diplomacy matters always make me nervous…"

"Mama you should've come, we would've been able to see each other the whole time."

"No, his entourage is just as big as the queen's, we would have been in different places all the time. Your father hasn't been feeling well, I don't want to leave him by himself."

"What's wrong with him?" Koren was preoccupied.

"I'm not sure, maybe time is catching up with him. He has been having strange nightmares; he never wants to speak about them, or the bad signs that I know he can perceive… Oh well, don't fear, he has magic blood and he'll outlive me, you bet."

"Stop taking like that." Koren threw herself at her mother, getting lost in the comfort of her arms, as if the thought of her parents not being there was an absolute abomination.

"You better go, I have to get this soup to his majesty and if you keep making me so sentimental, I'll change my mind and you'll have to stay here." Flora warned Koren, hugging her hard. The girl set the bowl down, kissed her mother again and ran back to the queen's office the same way she had come. She found a spot to sit by Marussa and Lenna, who sat reading quietly.

"Where is everybody else?" Koren looked around curiously for the rest of the ladies.

"They are still getting ready, even the queen is running late. Why haven't you changed?" Marussa answered her question with a welcoming smile.

"Why should I change?" Alarm was palpable in her voice.

"Your official travel garments, they should have been in your chambers…" Lenna informed her rather uninterested.

"Nobody told me…" Koren felt faint.

"Well you better get going, hurry up and change, the queen is not going to be pleased if we have to wait around for you." Marussa advised. Not to be delayed further, Koren ran out of the office as quickly as she had arrived. She was upset about the situation, why didn't anyone have the kindness to tell her about all this minutiae. The distance to her apartment seemed suffocatingly far, her legs ached as she pushed on, knowing that it would also mean a race back to the office. Her heart pounded her chest, if only she could fly to the apartment… At that moment and to her surprise, her body elevated above the ground with a shove, almost flying her straight into the ceiling. Trying not to be thrown off by the new discovery, she focused on getting to her apartment by taking advantage of the sudden burst of magic. Almost in a blink the threshold to her quarters were incredibly and pleasantly visible. Pride swelled in her knowing that she had been capable of using her magical skills to her favor. Running inside her sumptuous accommodations, which she hadn't even had the opportunity to explore, she found a vanity hall where a closet room full of gowns awaited her. Without any time to decide, she grabbed the first dress to catch her eye, a lovely orange gown that upon closer inspection showed delicate red details. There were also perfectly matching slippers encrusted with rubies to compliment her jewelry and tiara. Undressing in a hurry, she put on the fancy gown impressed by how perfectly it fit her, allowing herself a few seconds to admire her image in the mirror. She was quite satisfied with what she saw.

Standing out by the exit door she closed her eyes firmly, trying to repeat the same magical feat that had brought her there so quickly. Her thoughts turned to anything inviting of the act of flying... to the queen, and to the office. She visualized arrows, floating, and yet nothing was happening. Her anxious heart beat faster, and then she darted forward unexpectedly, falling in some sort of precipice where she could barely discern the world about her. Walls went by in a blur, the hallway and stairs melted away to give her a direct view to the queen's offices. Seeing how close she was to the entry she reduced her speed, when suddenly a blinding light hit her. Screaming in terror she crashed hard against the walls.

"Koren!" Althea's voice of alarm cried out as she ran to her aid. The girl tried to stand, too dazed to be able to, and with several limbs experiencing intense pain.

"What happened?" Koren asked disoriented, trying to hold on to the witch for support.

"It was me...I'm so sorry. You appeared out of nowhere bolting about like a ball of fire, I thought someone had infiltrated the castle to attack us. It never occurred to me that it was you; only skilled magicians can fly like that! And they usually do so employing questionable magic..." Koren kept trying to incorporate ignoring what Althea had just said, yet when she tried to do so she screamed in pain. They both looked down to realize that one of Koren's ankles seemed grotesquely out of place.

"Oh Goddess! What am I going to do?" Koren cried horrified.

"What do you mean? If you can fly like that, you can heal yourself. Do it!"

"I don't even know how I got myself to fly!" Koren yelled at her barely able to withstand the pain.

The commotion drew the rest of the group to the hallway, Queen Violet making her way through the ladies to get there first.

"What has happened? What is going on?" The queen demanded to know after seeing the girl squirming in pain against Althea, her leg visibly hurt.

"Your majesty, I attacked her by mistake, it's my fault. She was flying over, flying! I thought it was someone attacking, it's a miracle she has survived!" Althea explained guiltily, shrugging her shoulders, knowing that she had done what protocol suggested.

"What are you waiting for? You should've tended to her leg immediately!" The queen was fuming while she sat on the ground next to Koren to check for other injuries.

"But... I was trying to make her heal herself, she is powerful..." Althea hesitated to act.

"Have you lost your wits? I don't care what you are trying to teach her, you are only torturing her." Violet reprimanded Althea while furiously pushing her aside. The queen's proximity made Koren feel immediately calm, warmth flooding through her body, making her feel that pain did not exist; as if it was merely a figment of her imagination. Gently, the queen exposed Koren's leg entirely to visually inspect the injuries, and then she placed her hand on it. An indescribable sense of freezing cold traveled from the queen's hand to Koren's skin, making her believe that her leg would freeze and break in shards. The girl couldn't stop screaming in pain, sending shivers to the others whom watched in silence. In spite of the intensity, the pain only lasted briefly; Koren inspected her limb through teary eyes to discover that it was perfectly healed. She rose tentatively and put some weight on it, there was no discomfort or pain, and it was back to normal.

Violet gave her a hug and a comforting smile; she also kissed her forehead after trying to fix her messy hair a bit.

"It is always best to teach with compassion, not with pain..." Violet glanced at Althea when she said the words, turning to head back to her office and ending the matter there. The other ladies followed, while Koren and Althea stayed back for a minute staring at each other silently.

"She is right. I'm very sorry, that was horrible of me..."

"I'm okay now." Koren accepted her apology with a little bit of resentment wedged in her heart. Finally at the office, Koren was having a hard time paying attention to all the travel details. Her mind kept wandering back to the recent episode and the queen's magic; she kept spying her with renewed interest. How much magic did the queen truly possess? What else was she capable of? Where did she learn? Where? The questions flooded her brain, bringing with them promising implications. The queen supposedly was human, but her magic was exceptional. How long did it take her to become so skilled? Was it the palace's magic? Something else? Did she get more magic when she became queen? This question was fascinating, since she pondered what would happen if a powerful person became queen and got more... The bells of a nearby tower shattered her reverie and announced to every one that it was time to depart. Violet rose from her throne, allowing a view of her beautiful red dress with orange details, reflecting the window's light with an incandescent glow. The queen led the procession out of the office, immediately followed by Talma and Althea, Kloe and Marussa, Anari and Lenna... leaving Koren and Pumzi their obvious place in the formation. They walked in a quick pace and upon reaching the grand hall; they were met with a formidable battalion of Amazon guards.

The women's Amazon origins were obvious thanks to their height, their musculature and their mostly green hair. Koren observed how the heavily armed soldiers stood perfectly still carrying fire spears, crossbows and multiple close combat weapons. It was truly an intimidating sight. Especially the menacingly large arrows that could be seen hanging from their special bag on their belts, and the cold sharp dagger strategically placed on the outer part of their tall leather boots. The Amazons wore simple clothing, white linen tunics, and chain mail covering their chests, their hair tied up with supple jungle vines. It was a sight to behold, the women looked like the kind of threat you would never want to battle against. Their formation was so precise that when they kneeled to greet the queen, it was as if one had done it, and her reflection spread through the hall. One of the Amazons, which Koren thought to be the leader, thanks to the queen's symbol on a small crown she wore, approached the queen. The Amazon woman held in her hand a dark scepter, she kneeled looking at the ground and gave the queen the ebony staff. Queen Violet lightly tapped the long scepter on the ground, causing a terrible boom that made the whole room tremble. The Amazon captain returned to her place amongst the others, whom rose at once and marched in unison to lead the procession.

The group made its way to the Royal Stables were the king and his men, were ready waiting for the women to arrive. The king's group seemed to be twice the size of the queen's, yet they all fell to the ground on one knee at the sigh of the queen and her entourage. Koren was so impressed with all the well-rehearsed formalities that she didn't even remember that she hadn't chosen a Pegasus for her trip. Young pages led the Pegasus' out of the stables one by one, setting them all in line seven in total. Koren noticed that Althea wore a long red robe, her hair tied up in a tight bun, as she held a beautiful broom. To the side she could see Talma wander far away from the group, where she extended her arms and began to be engulfed by intense blue flames. The flames seemed to be coming from her feet, shining intensely as their size increased, swallowing Talma. Koren was scared when she saw what had happened yet remained still, no one seemed to be affected by the scene. The fire kept growing and growing in height almost to double in size to the enormous edifice in which the stables were situated. As the fire waned, the terrifying figure of an enormous black dragon was left in its place. Koren swallowed dry in sheer terror of the creature, unable to believe that it was her friend Talma. Wings similar to those of a giant bat extended from Talma's back, lifting the dragon above with a subtle thrust. The people nearby tried to hold their ground in spite of the strong current of air that the lift off had caused, even though a few of those present inevitably fell. Talma circled above a couple of times before being joined by a smiling Althea. The witch took off like an arrow, her robe flapping wildly in the wind.

Gigantic carriages started to arrive pulled by even bigger birds of blue plumage, and similar to swans. The king's men proceeded to embark the large transports until they were full. With a signal from the captain in charge the birds whipped their magnificent wings and lifted the carriages gently into the air, heading south. After the soldiers left, the king and his men followed in Pegasus', except for two of the knights who also changed into their dragon form. Koren was not as impressed with their transformation, they seemed to be smaller in size compared to Talma. Perhaps, just like in some species the female was the larger and sturdier specimen. After the first part of the royal committee departed, the queen came close to a Pegasus and mounted effortlessly. The other ladies did the same trying to mimic her gracefulness. Koren tried to copy the others, yet when she approached the Pegasus that was to be her mount fear gripped her. The Pegasus was thrice the size of a sizable farm horse; its corpulent white body's glare almost blinding. The creature's wings seemed endless.

"Don't be afraid." A deep voice spoke to her. Koren looked around to see who had spoken, petrified with fear.

"My name is Zaur. I will be your Pegasus, you father has chosen me for you." The Pegasus looked at her intently nodding his head, she remained silent and surprised.

"Go on, we must depart, grab my hair and use the leather steps to get on my back, the seat will hold you securely." The girl did as instructed without hesitation. She knew that the other ladies were traveling this way; there was no other option. From the seat she could see the vastness of the queen's entourage, whom upon making sure everyone was ready for travel lifted the scepter indicating departure. The Amazons filled up two other carriages like the ones the soldiers traveled in, and once those were out of sight the queen's Pegasus joined Talma and Althea in the air. Koren shut her eyes tight the moment Zaur stretched out his wings, feeling how his body contracted and with a smooth impulse began to fly effortlessly. Even though, Koren was still holding on for dear life, grabbing his mane tightly as she felt the earth fade away.

"Open your eyes, it's a wonderful view from up here, the wind is not blowing too hard today, it's perfect." Zaur spoke kindly, while she wondered how was it possible for him to communicate with her. Wasn't he a horse after all?

"A horse? Do not offend me; I'm as much a horse as you are… Our magical race is ancient and intelligent." The Pegasus joked.

She finally opened her eyes after what seemed an eternity, Zaur prodded her to do so once they where settled in flight. All the while she had been leaning her head on him, enjoying the cold wind on her face and its delicious smell of moisture. Althea came to sight, waving her hand at her, obviously enjoying the travel. Koren saw they were in the middle of the group, she could see the ladies, the flying carriages, and the dragons… However, it was upon gazing at the firmament that's she was stunned, the blue vastness was like a round mantle that spread endlessly before them. With barely enough courage, she dared look down at the passing earth, only to shiver with fear at its distant and diminutive blur. The hills and mountains were obviously visible, the fields and towns, less so. The rivers looked like silvery serpents, the roads crooked threads, and the lakes similar to stunning mirrors. Koren placed her face closer to Zaur, just to feel a little safer and enjoy the warmth radiating from his body. The rocking motion of Zaur's powerful wings served as a soporific that left the girl profoundly asleep.

"Wake up, young lady. Its about time…" Koren awoke gripping Zaur's mane instinctively, having lost track of time but not of the circumstances. Sunset was already coloring the sky in several ethereal hues of red and orange, which indicated to Koren that she had slept quite a while.

"There is about a quarter of an hour to get to Arkana's temple." The Pegasus informed.

"Oh no! I was looking forward to see the city of Albah…" Koren was disappointed.

"On the way back then…"

"I slept for hours, I can't believe it. How long do you think?" She let out a yawn.

"Three hours or less."

"At least it made for a short trip, no offense, but this flying mode is not for me."

"Didn't seem to bother you, you were snoring soundly. Now, if you look down you can see some of the villages and temples where the nymphs reside. They are very colorful and round, sort of like little nests, it is one of my favorite landscapes. Soon, you'll also see the Demi-goddesses temple, right there in the middle of the forest…" Koren searched the scenery as best as she could, taking it all in gladly, until her eyes found the rectangular edifice surrounded by gigantic trees. It was a large structure where a large glass dome had been placed in the middle to allow the free passage of light. Amazingly, the temple itself was of a deep red color, and all its gold windows, doors and gates stood out fiercely.

"Its beautiful!" Koren held her breath admiring the vision. Noticing that part of the king's entourage was already on the ground below, organized and prepared for the queen's arrival. Talma was the first to land, followed by Althea and the queen, Koren almost ripped Zaur's mane as she held on tight for landing. Much to her surprise the creature circled the air a few times descending slowly and touching down in a swift gallop. Zaur headed to where the other ladies had formed their line and joined them, glad that his passenger's fear had not resulted in a scalping.

The golden gates of the temple opened slowly, allowing a group of women with long tresses to come out, playing melodic harmonies with whimsical musical instruments as a welcome. Amongst them was a woman of impossible beauty, whose skin glowed as if she were a moving candle, and spreading as much warmth. The woman's hair was chestnut, full of red highlights, and her eyes of the same color, lined by an abundance of lashes. Red lips that carried an alluring smile, a lithe figure that seemed to float and delicate hands holding a lovely bouquet of fresh flowers. Thus she welcomed the group, while a fresh scent of earth and sandalwood laced itself with the breeze, elevating all the spirits of those whom had just arrived. Arkana wore a light blue dress, almost transparent against the admiring light, which flowed about every time her naked feet caressed the ground. Earth welcomed her every step by giving away the seeds it carried inside, allowing for magical blooms to sprout beautifully all around her. The Demi-goddess made her way to Queen Violet, to whom she handed the flowers she held.

"Welcome to my home." The queen kneeled in front of the Demi-goddess, thankful for the inviting words.

"We thank you for allowing us entry into your temple." Violet smiled. Arkana extended her hand to help the queen incorporate, as they both headed towards the king's entourage. King Papo saluted both women with the necessary formalities, all the while keeping a serious semblance, which softened as he took his wife's hand. The trio led the way to the large temple, followed by those who knew would be allowed to enter. Uncertainty grabbed a hold of Koren as she looked about for the others to shadow their behavior. The ladies walked behind the queen, followed immediately by the king's knights. The rest of the travelers had been led to a nearby building; it was not as fancy as the temple, but bigger in size.

The first thing to welcome the newcomers was an intense smell of fresh dirt, followed by the sweaty scent of the vibrant vegetation lining the walls. An imposing fountain pelted the air with its sonorous chant, as well as the freshness of its clear water. Smiling nymphs, of every conceivable shape and form came upon them to cover their path with fragrant petals. Some of them also anointed the visitor's hands with wonderfully smelling oils. Koren watched everything fascinated, trying to spy every detail to no avail, the place was truly an assault on the senses. The group arrived at a majestic white marble terrace, whereupon was placed a long wooden table displaying an array of delectable foods. Trays were overflowing with fruit, vegetables and other appealing dishes. Surprisingly the hall was devoid of chairs; guests were expected to use the many colorful cushions that surrounded the low table. Towards the end of the terrace there was a small, elevated stage, several nymphs sang to the music of their silver mandolin like instruments. Arkana sat on a huge indigo cushion indicating that the others follow suit. Appreciating the lack of formalities, the king and queen sat next to each other and let the others seat as they pleased. Koren took advantage of the situation by placing herself as far as possible from the guests of honor, that way she could oversee the crowd, especially the king's knights. She had taken notice of them and was captivated by their appearance, having never seen such an impressive collection of elegant and handsome men before.

The nymphs began to serve the feast, starting with a delicious soup of spiced artichokes. Thereon dish after dish came by the laborious hands of the smiling women whom joyfully jumped about not caring to disguise their excitement. The smell of food was overwhelming; every bite seemed more delightful than the last. Koren smiled as the thought that perhaps her mother had a little bit of a nymph in her crossed her mind. She was after all the best cook in the kingdom... As she thought this a blue skinned nymph with intense purple lips arrived to serve her perfumed vegetables from a golden tray. Koren was delighted with the dish's complex simplicity; to think that not one of the dishes served had any meat on them was an eye opener for her. As she enjoyed the food, she kept numerous mental notes to pass on to her mother once they returned to Bandah.

"My dear Violet, you must visit us more often, look how happy my nymphs are. The last time you were here was to leave the Golden Sword in my care." Arkana commented with a wide smile.

"You are absolutely right, I do not get out of the castle that often. Life in there is not quite as pleasant as here, that's for sure..." Violet laughed heartily enjoying the wine.

"My poor neglected queen..." The king faked a whine.

"I remember that last time very well, we had such a delightful time here with the majesties of Astra." Arkana added.

"I agree. I hope we get to see them soon." Papo sipped from his wine.

"You will. You know I cannot divulge the future, but I dare say that next time you see them it will be a joyous occasion." Arkana spoke with a soft voice, the king and queen smiled at each other, accomplices of an unspoken secret.

"Lets then celebrate now to that." The king raised his cup and solicited a toast from the crowd. The retinue toasted with the king and after a sip from their cups, applauded to celebrate their majesties. Koren joined the cheer, although she resented the shameless adulation bestowed on the monarchs. Destiny had placed a throne at their feet, what had they done to deserve the honor? Nothing. They had been born lucky. She didn't know the particulars about the life of a monarch, yet the whole affair seemed rather ridiculous. Arkana's eyes fell on her, as she realized that it was quite possible that the Demi-goddess could know her thoughts. Instinctively she cleared her mind, such as it is when sleep takes over consciousness.

"Beware…" Arkana's voice made its way through Koren's darkness. Their eyes met briefly, Koren's upset with the Demi-goddess' intrusion in her mind, and the woman's triumphant. Arkana gazed away smiling at all the other guests that surrounded her, letting the girl be. Even though the brief connection had been severed Koren felt surprised that it had happened at all. Koren was not ashamed of what she had thought, certain that others might have felt the same way at one point or another. Animated chatter rose and fell sporadically around the table. Koren found a solicitous nymph willing to share culinary secrets and who explained that meat was forbidden in the temple out of respect for living creatures. Night came serene and tepid, one by one the exhausted nymphs fell asleep in every corner, some cuddled in the bigger cushions. Koren let out a loud yawn that attracted an elderly nymph's attention.

"Oh, dear girl you are so tired, allow me to take you to the guest chambers." The melodious voice summoned. Koren followed her out of the terrace until they reached a spacious room where an oversized round bed could be found. Pumzi and Lenna already lay between the silky sheets soundly asleep. Koren slid in and sank into the soft bed, feeling the warmth of some mysterious invisible fire. Even before she tried to think, sleep had overcome her.

The refreshing wetness of rain rose Koren from her sleep early in the morning. Looking out the window she found that the sun was out, perhaps the rain she had felt was nothing but an illusion. Lifting her head she realized she had slept partially on top of Marussa, who was still sleeping. Trying not to make a sound she escaped the bed littered with dormant beauties, leaving the great chamber without any particular destination. Deciding to explore the temple, she moved about aimlessly, knowing that at one point or another a nymph would pop out of nowhere to offer her breakfast. Her feet led her outside, where she found a beautiful lake of crystalline water, surrounded by beautiful gardens. She couldn't help the tempting allure of the cold water, dipping her feet in it while inhaling the wonderful aroma of jasmines at the same time. Koren kept her eyes closed as she savored the moment, abruptly interrupted by the sound of giggles.

"You can come in if you like." Arkana was in between some gigantic aquatic plants nearby, in the company of a small group of nymphs, that Koren had failed to see.

"No thanks, I just wanted to get my feet wet." The girl replied somewhat uncomfortably.

"This small lake belongs to the aquatic nymphs, they truly enjoy bathing those who come to visit." Arkana added.

"No, I'd rather not." Koren reaffirmed feeling a little bit more uncomfortable as she noticed that all the women were naked in the water. A natural curiosity attracted her towards the naked bodies, which made her feel self conscious, so she lowered her gaze.

"You don't need to feel ashamed. The naked body is part of nature, Mother Nature is sacred, thus good." Arkana smiled, making Koren smile and raise her head, free of shame.

"Your temple is beautiful. I have seen the gardens and they are truly a paradise fit for a goddess." Koren spoke watching as the nymphs rubbed oils and plants all over Arkana's body, which was halfway exposed.

"Thanks. It is a paradise, not only for me, but also for the other creatures that live here. I'm very happy..." Arkana looked amorously at her surroundings.

"I'm really sorry about what happened last night..." The girl ventured a declaration of guilt.

"No, you are not. Its fine though, I'm glad that you are aware of everything that affects you and that you show no fear of talking about it. I only advised that you be careful, that is all. Actions are borne out of thought... Thoughts are comprised and compromised by our feelings, however it is not those that betray us, it is our thoughts." The Demi-goddess spoke softly undisturbed by a nymph grooming her hair.

"It's normal to feel good and bad things, besides, I'm only a girl."

"You are not a little girl anymore, you are on the verge of womanhood, don't even pretend to use that excuse. It doesn't matter which stage of your life you find yourself at you are always you... What makes you think feeling good and bad is natural?" Arkana questioned, curious to hear the reply.

"You said so yourself, nature is always good, yet good and bad are parts of nature. For example death, isn't it a natural event?"

"You are very shrewd, yet you fail to assume that death is bad." Arkana laughed making Koren lower her gaze again full of resentment for being mocked.

"Koren, you must see beyond that which is visible. You are young and have a lot of power at you reach; yet I fear that you won't see enough before destiny calls upon you. I cannot tell you much, but I hope love will trump all your doubts. Always remember that for love to be pure, it must remain the good kind..." Arkana submerged herself after releasing the enigmatic words to the air. The water greeted her body with a spectacular array of splashes and squirts, which made the plants shiver with delight and bloom. Koren returned to the temple pondering the words that the Demi-goddess had pronounced. Which doubts had she referred to? Had she possibly hinted at a future event that was about to come? Love? As she got close to the building she spotted Marussa waving at her.

"Have you seen my mother at the lake?"

"Arkana is your mother?" Koren exclaimed surprised at the news.

"Yes, I thought you knew that." Marussa shrugged.

"How would I know? I barely met both of you. She's out there bathing at the lake, I just spoke to her briefly."

"Really? She is not one to speak casually to mortals... Anyhow, she is taking too long and breakfast is ready." The nymph showed some exasperation.

"I think she was almost done." Koren replied as she continued on to the terrace where they had dined the previous night. The table reminded her of a farmer's stand full of fresh fruit and cheeses. The king and queen of Bandah led the group in animated chatter. Anari was talking too close to one of the king's knights, deliberately giggling at his words, while Talma spoke to a young dragon. Pumzi sat between Lenna and a nymph laughing hysterically at some joke, further apart Kloe and Althea spoke privately to some knights. Marussa sat by her sisters inquiring about the happenings of the temple in her absence. Koren observed everything with an uneasy feeling of not belonging; a deep desire to return to Bandah swept her. She wanted to go home, to her mother, to her old life. As she found a place to sit a lovely silvery nymph brought her a small tray full of little dumplings and fruit. At that moment the commotion of Arkana's return brought the place to a standstill. She presented herself wrapped in her luminous glory, radiating energy all around her. With great ceremony she sat at the table with her guests and urged them to carry on with breakfast.

"Please forgive my tardiness, I had important business to attend to. I was trying to change the future..." Arkana smiled broadly after her declaration, inciting laughter amongst the guests. They all knew, ironically, that she was forbidden to do so. Koren was the only one that remained serious, wondering why Arkana had made such a statement, given that it was probable that it had to do with her. The Demi-goddesses' enigmas fell heavy on her, as she thought that perhaps those beings were useless and obsolete. Once again she felt Arkana's eyes on her, instead of being surprised this time, Koren smiled and raised her glass. The woman echoed her movement, yet her face remained blank, she sipped the wine and nodded her head. Cheers, Arkana...Koren laughed in her mind, enjoying the liberty of her insolence. The secret interaction had gone unperceived by the people at the table, giving Koren another reason to smile...

"When are we departing?" Koren turned her attention to a nearby nymph.

"Arkana has told us that you are all leaving soon after breakfast."

The parting ceremonies began shortly after the guests had been fed and properly prepared for travel. Koren though all the details were just a boring waste of time, how many times must the ancient traditions be carried out before someone realized their uselessness. She was just glad to leave that chimerical place where she had felt somewhat uncomfortable and out of sorts. Zaur was happy to see her, relating his wonderful time in the magical pastures by the temple, where he had been in the great company of wild unicorns. Koren barely paid attention to his ranting; a particular subject that had been in her mind for too long troubled her.

"Why is the Golden Sword so special?" She blurted

"Why do you ask?" There was caution in his voice.

"Just out of curiosity, Arkana mentioned that it is at the temple."

"Hmmm. It is never spoken of, unless..."

"Unless what? Why don't you just say it already!" Koren was growing impatient with the Pegasus as they readied for departure.

"It's a long story... A long time ago, longer than you can imagine, a powerful enchantment was cast. The Golden Sword is a magical artifact that is part of that enchantment; the person who wields it would come to have great power. Usually it is kept for a hundred years in a different kingdom for safekeeping, that way no one can claim that they truly possess it."

"Yes, yes... everyone is familiar with the legend, but what does Arkana have to do with it? She is supposed to be a non-meddling demi-goddess."

"I'm not sure. Its is true that deities of any kind are not to meddle in worldly events, the sword should not be in the temple... there is something else... perhaps she mentioned it as a warning." Zaur explained as they became airborne.

"Perhaps, being that she is just a Demi-goddess traditional rules don't apply to her. She did mention something about trying to change the future..." Koren suggested as she leaned her head once again on Zaur's powerful back, enjoying the rocking motion created by his wings. All the while observing the beauty of the landscape that was swiftly disappearing under their flight. In about little over an hour, a giant wall of trees came to view. Trees so tall that their tops seemed to be swallowed by the thick white clouds that surrounded them.

"We are almost there, that which you see is Cyrus."

"What do you mean? Where is it? How do you get in? It seems that if we keep our current course we will slam into those trees!"

"As we get closer you'll see it's not a solid wall, on the contrary, one of the beauties of Cyrus is that it is an ever changing live kingdom." Koren saw those leading the group disappear through the thick foliage. Zaur had been right, the enormity of the trees allowed for the whole entourage to move about freely in between their branches. Elaborate tree houses began to be noticeable throughout the scenery, of all shapes and sizes, but with enough roundness to seem to blend in right into the branch in which they sat. Crowds of curious people came out of their abodes to watch the spectacle of the arrival of the Queen of Bandah and her retinue. They cheered and waved merrily as the flock of Pegasus went by. Koren waved back at them and smiled, enjoying the smiles that welcomed them, and trying to grab a few of the fragrant petals that started to rain on her.

"We are flying through Upper Cyrus, the cities here are obviously perched on the higher part of the trees. Underneath, Lower Cyrus is earthbound, the other half of the kingdom, which is mostly an agricultural society. The land there is quite fertile, and its northern part has the swamps and a few underground cavern systems."

"This place is amazing! It seems to be bigger than the whole of Bandah." Koren exclaimed impressed.

"Yes, it is bigger than Bandah, and much older. Just not as ambitious. The inhabitants are very peaceful; solely preoccupied with the fat of the land and the positive energy they get from the trees. Close your eyes and take a deep breath, there is nothing like the air in Cyrus." Koren obeyed the Pegasus, shutting her eyes and taking in the fresh smell of humidity from the leaves. Enjoying the sweet scent of wood and the coolness of the air. She could imagine being a squirrel in that forest, hugging tight the trunk of one of the Cyro trees and being happy. A loud humming sound caught her attention; she opened her eyes abruptly to see a flock of gigantic birds fly by, navigating through the trees effortlessly. They were the same kind of birds that she had seen pulling the carriages that brought the soldiers from Bandah, except that this time she saw riders on their backs.

"They use those birds for transport too! Looks like fun." Koren spoke excitedly.

"Fun... The birds are original from here, they are part of this forest, they are mild mannered and stupid, if you ask me." Zaur spoke disdainfully.

"You are just jealous!" She joked, although he didn't find it funny at all and remained silent. They began their descent as they approached the biggest tree ever imaginable, in which an impressive castle had been carved into its trunk. The tree was in the heart of Cyrus and it was of such a large diameter that it was not possible to see its whole circumference in a half-day's flight. The people of Bandah were lining up at a spacious beautiful garden that preceded the main entry to the castle. The gates were wide open; a large battalion of guards welcomed everybody with great pomp. Zaur lined up next to the other ladies, in perfect synchronicity. At that moment trumpets began to play announcing the apparition of a smaller group of soldiers dressed in light blue uniforms. The men carried seemingly heavy shields with the feather emblem of the Vice-queen of Cyrus. They stepped aside to flank the sovereigns of Cyrus, who also wore beautiful celestial garments. Koren could tell that in spite of all the cheerfulness and welcomes, the Vice-queen seemed somewhat tense. The Viceroy smiled kindly, yet he seemed tired, going through the well rehearsed welcoming ceremonies like an automaton. Koren noticed that the monarchs didn't seem that old, she wondered why they wanted to retire.

Queen Violet elegantly dismounted her Pegasus and walked towards the royal couple, which fell to their knees holding hands and lowering their gaze. Violet raised her royal scepter so that it was clearly seen by everyone, and then gently lowered it to tap the ground. Koren braced herself for the impact, knowing that the little tap would cause a magnificent boom. Sure enough, the scepter let out a loud explosion when it touched the wood, causing a magical gale that almost ripped the crowns of off the kneeling monarchs. Koren smiled and enjoyed watching that swift ceremonious assertion of power, which seemed to serve no other purpose other than the humiliation of those standing nearby.

"Viceroys of Cyrus, in the name Bandah, I now enter you land as sovereign." The trumpets blared on cue a triumphant march, as the viceroys stood up. King Papo walked to where they were, also kneeling briefly before Violet and then standing by her side. The Viceroy of Cyrus took Queen Violet's hand, as Papo took the Vice-queen's and together marched slowly towards the castle. The queen's ladies were the first to follow, then the knights, and finally the rest of the visitors.

Koren hated the procession, she was eager to enter the wooden castle and see what its interior was like. Her dreams were fulfilled as she gaped at the detailed carvings that adorned the generous tree. The wooden floor was polished so impeccably that it seemed like a placid chestnut lake. The walls had intricate wooden carvings of incredible detail, while gigantic wooden chandeliers hung from the cavernous ceilings to impregnate the place with their luminosity. Statues of ebony, oak and rosewood in the shape of majestic birds graced the hall. Ivy plants would cover parts of the walls here and there, especially to accompany the lovely fountains, or the wooden statues of maidens.

The group was led to a large assembly hall, decorated with delicate white blooms, where a generous feast awaited. Servants led the guests to their places at the table, immediately pouring in their glasses a refreshingly sweet rose wine. Hurried maidens brought warm cloths to the travelers to wash their hands, while another group of servers began to present the steaming hot food. To the back of the hall a handsome young man overlooked the event, visibly pleased with what he saw. Once everyone was ready to eat, the Viceroy rose from his chair to invite the young man to join the feast, and both men seemed a little nervous.

"Your majesties, allow me to formally introduce to you my youngest son, Prince Atle. As you can see he has turned into a fine young man." The young prince came close to the table and literally threw himself on his knees in front of Queen Violet. Who immediately signaled him to stand, allowing him to kiss her hand before doing so. Prince Atle proceeded to gallantly salute King Papo with a deep reverence, and then sat by the empty chair next to his father. Koren tried to surreptitiously glance his way, trying to conceal her curiosity, given that she had never seen a real prince so closely. Atle had lovely brown hair, and intense green eyes; his skin was rather pale although it somehow complimented his masculinity. The prince seemed too austere for his age, in spite of all his elegance and poise, the roundness of his face betrayed his youth.

Barely a half an hour had passed, when a commotion arose in the hallway, and the hall's wooden doors were slammed open with a sudden thud. At the threshold stood the figure of a young man, similar to Prince Atle, but haughtier. He had a tanned complexion and fire in his eyes, which he spread in a lordlike manner all over the room.

"I'm offended that my presence is not necessary to entertain our guests, you have begun the feast without me." The young man admonished arrogantly as he approached the table. The Viceroys of Cyrus stood up quickly from their seats, seemingly tense, though remaining silent. The newcomer headed directly to Queen Violet and kneeled by her in an overtly reverent gesture.

"Your majesty, highness, goddess… allow me to introduce myself. I am Prince Orion, the firstborn child of this castle and true heir to the throne of Cyrus."

"You may rise. Although, I'm certain you would do so even if I had not allowed it, don't you think? Besides, it is true that you would inherit the throne, but only if your father had died and left you the crown. He has decided to abdicate and thus different rules apply, which I'm sure you are well aware of." Queen Violet spoke arrogantly and firmly, fixing her eyes in his with a blank expression on her face. The prince stood up at once, walked over to where his brother sat and pulling him by the shoulders besieged his seat. Young Prince Atle blushed furiously, however apparently deciding to avoid a confrontation in front of the guests, by moving on to another seat nearby. His actions did not appease the rising tension at the feasting table, which was now under the spell of a threatening dark cloud.

"Well then, now that we are all here, lets proceed with the festivities…" Viceroy Plutarco cleared his throat uncomfortably as he made his proclamation. His voice sounded affected, as he tried to avoid the glaring looks his eldest son bestowed upon him, creating great discomfort. The guests tried to carry on unhampered by the display of insolence by Prince Orion, as if by doing so they devoided him of the pleasure of ruining their fete. Koren observed the prince astonished by his beauty, there was truly no other word that could describe him or do justice to his semblance. His stunning face was masculine, strong and imposing. She could feel herself blush intensely, feeling her heart race desperately, as she tried to admire him at every opportunity. Orion's hair was a dark chestnut, highlighted with reddish streaks that fell on silky waves over his shoulders. His eyes were as green as the emerald leaves of the Cyrus, with the intensity of a preying beast. A strong jaw line, fleshy lips and chiseled cheekbones, along with the glow of masculine youth, were unto themselves a feast for the eyes. Koren was lost in her daydream, spying the moment his lips parted to speak, or as he flashed his cynical smirk at Queen Violet. Suddenly the prince looked her way and smiled, drowning her in utter embarrassment after being so flagrantly caught in the act of adoration.

"In honor of the majesties of Bandah, the Royal Academy of Arts will present a piece for your entertainment." Prince Atle announced as a large group of performers gathered at a stage on the further part of the hall accompanied by musicians. The perfect musical score of flutes and large drums gave magical life to the limbs and bodies of the muscular dancers. Koren was making a supreme effort to focus on the fluidity of movements in the choreography, yet always stealing glances at Prince Orion, who seemed to be enjoying the spectacle. Her glances brought to her attention that the viceroys and Prince Atle were not enjoying themselves so much. The group shared uncomfortable glances, avoiding altogether any visual contact with Prince Orion. The crowd's applause indicated that the function had ended, the Viceroy rose from his seat to address the guests once again.

"I hope the performance has been to your liking, we give you a warm welcome to our beautiful kingdom. We wish you a restful night's sleep." The servants scurried about retiring the plates and offering warm cordials. With a dramatic gesture, Prince Orion swallowed the contents of his glass in one gulp, slammed it on the table and stood up without any regard to royal formalities.

"My dear highnesses of Bandah, sweet dreams." Orion made a curt bow and left.

"Your majesty, please excuse our son. He is so young, so arrogant, and he has been taken by surprise by your arrival…" Vice-Queen Juli implored forgiveness. Violet smiled kindly.

"My dear Juli, no need to excuse the boy, each person is responsible for its actions, he is not an exception." The chatter around the table died down eventually, after which, the Vice-Queen gave the order to the servants to show the guests to their accommodations. Koren was exhausted, wanting to lay in bed badly, the travel and the pleasantries of court having drained her energy. She had made no effort whatsoever to join the ladies in their conversation as they walked to their rooms.

The women talked about the feast and inevitably the topic of conversation turned to the reviled, yet admired Prince Orion.

"I would say he is the most beautiful man I've seen, too bad he is so arrogant." Anari confessed as she let out a sigh.

"I'd give anything to kiss him!" Lenna giggled coquettishly.

"Me too!" Palea added blushing.

"You are all so silly, being led on by just a pretty face..." Kloe mocked the ladies.

"You can't deny that the boy is to die for." Althea added perhaps a little bit too seriously. Koren remained silent, unable to speak about Orion, the greatest implausibility of her life. The question of it being possible to fall madly in love with a person after only seeing them once crossed her mind.

"Yes, he is very handsome." Queen Violet's voice spooked the ladies, as they thought themselves unheard.

"You scared us! Where did you come from, your majesty?" Anari asked surprised by her appearance.

"I went to say good night to MY prince. Papo agrees that it is best to sleep in separate quarters, it is harder to carry out two attacks ... He is a little worried after he has seen how open Orion is with his ill demeanor. It is best to be on guard, who knows what he is capable of."

"The boy has presented himself quite assertive." Talma added as the others nodded in agreement.

"He is so young, what a pity..." Marussa sighed shaking her head.

"Oh please, we are being negative here, perhaps the boy knows what's good for him. After seeing Bandah's support for his brother he might just adjust his attitude and cut it out." Pumzi shared her thoughts.

"That is my hope." The queen declared sternly.

They reached a grandiose dormitory comprised of several chambers, the larger one prepared for the queen. Koren waited until the other's had picked their places and then went to hers without delay. The bed seemed comfortable and looked exquisite; it had lovely silk drapes hanging from the tall canopy. An older maid helped her undress as she looked around the room, where she spotted a remarkable painting of a hunter at a magnificent prairie. She was delighted to see that the hunter was none other than Prince Orion, surrounded by his hunting dogs, with his bow extended as if a mortal arrow had already departed. The maid quietly bathed her and prepped her for bed, letting her know that she would be at her service should the need arise. Koren thanked her and tucked herself in bed, thinking about Orion one more time before sleep wrested her into submission.

The chirping of some birds floating about her room aroused Koren, as the sunrise's rays of light and the morning's coolness filtered in through a window. Walking out of her room she noticed that everyone else still slept, it was probably quite early in the morning, as the sun had just started to peek out. Deciding to venture out to a little outdoor terrace she had spied the night before, she walked quietly hoping to find a servant that could offer her some breakfast. Right outside the grand chamber she saw a few ladies in waiting comfortably slumped on large lounging chairs, they had fallen asleep by the warmth of the waiting area's fire. Her steps made the women jump up straight, brutally aroused from their slumber, yet ready to serve.

"Good morning Lady Koren. May we offer you anything? Breakfast perhaps?" They curtsied.

"Yes, thank you. I would like to have breakfast in the terrace, if I may. If anyone else wakes up please let them know where I've gone to."

"Yes milady. Please allow me to suggest you wear a proper cape, it will be very cold out there." One of the women offered.

"Oh, I don't have one with me, I'm afraid if I go back I'll wake them up. Can you make one available to me?" One of the women nodded and briefly disappeared, only to come back holding an exquisite royal blue cape.

"Milady, the cape. Mali will make a nice fire for you in the terrace, I will bring your food." After saying this, the maid curtsied and left, while Mali led Koren to the terrace. The maid immediately created a glorious pink fire in the outdoor furnace before retiring. Koren draped the cape around herself observing how light and warm it was in spite of its generous size. A nearby bench provided the perfect spot to take in the beauty of the intense foliage and the tangled tree branches. One would be pressed to believe that this world had been placed in a tree trunk, especially since a garden of lovely lavender blooms extended like a carpet as far as the eye could see. Garden fountains and all... A multitude of birds flew about and chirped joyfully announcing the start of another day, their constant chatter delighting Koren. She was so enthralled in the marvelous affairs of the tree creatures that she had not noticed that she was no longer alone in the terrace.

"Good morning." A deep masculine voice startled her, and to her surprise she turned around to find Prince Orion. He had a small tray full of bread, jam and butter, which he placed in a nearby small table.

"I have taken the liberty to bring you a small breakfast myself." He explained smiling broadly.

"Thank you, your highness." It was all Koren could say, making every effort not to faint in his presence. Her legs trembled, not from cold, she was thankful for the cape that would also cover her nervousness.

"I hope I'm not imposing. This is one of my favorite spots, even though it's a bit far from my tower. I love the delicate blooms and the tranquility." He spoke casually taking a small cup of tea to his lips as he sat next to her on the bench. Her mind was racing trying to think of what she could possibly say to him that didn't come out sounding childish. Surely the prince saw her merely as an adolescent girl, but she felt an intense urge to be seen as a woman.

"You are not imposing your highness, on the contrary, I find your presence to my liking." She said trying to sound demure.

"I couldn't help but notice that you were constantly watching me last night." He looked at her in the eyes as if trying to read her; all the while she lost her composure over the unexpected confrontation.

"Please accept my apologies your highness, it was not my intention to incommodate. I had never seen a prince…" She tried to explain feeling awful, her head down.

"Hey! Don't feel bad, please. I was not offended. I'm used to all kinds of stares, I only wish all of them were like yours…" He replied tersely. Koren could not believe the moment was real, feeling as if she would explode with emotion. Here was the prince of her dreams in the flesh, sitting next to her, and talking to her.

"I suppose your highness knows why we are here…" Koren ventured, although she regretted the words as quickly as she had spoken them.

"Yes, I know. I appreciate your openness; no one talks to me like that anymore. I have become the shame of the kingdom as I have declared my disdain to the injustice fallen upon me." Orion took another sip of his tea and found her eyes again.

"Injustice?" Koren asked, allowing him to take the lead in the conversation, uncertain if he wanted to talk about his distress.

"Hmm, my father favors my younger brother, they are similar in character. It's probably why he thinks Atle deserves the throne. They like to read about government, legislature, things that are nothing but ideas about ruling… instead of having actual practical experience." He said airily.

"But the people of Cyrus have chosen…" Her voice was shy although not hampered by his presence.

"Ah, the people! The people are only a group of ignorant farmers that are stuck in tradition and don't know what is good for them. While my father was ill recently, I took charge of the kingdom and by my doing we were able to dam part of the northern river. This way we were able to provide better irrigation to a large part of the southern Lower Cyrus. Obviously, a few peasants lost some land, but it was all for the greater good."

"What happened when the Viceroy got better?" Koren inquired curiously.

"He sought my mother's consent to undo everything I had done. The lands were returned to the peasants and it was declared that South Lower Cyrus must promote the use of its resources, not depend on the ones of the north." Orion mocked the idea.

"Perhaps he is right…" Koren offered.

"No, my father is just a conservative, he is of the opinion that Cyrus has operated well during millennia, so there is no necessity for innovation." He explained.

"Oh." It was all she could reply, as she had nothing else to offer. The workings of the kingdom of Cyrus were unknown territory to her. The whole matter seemed complicated and complex, yet she couldn't help sympathizing with the alienation that Orion must have been feeling.

"I really didn't come here to bother you or discuss my frail fate, that was not my intention… perhaps you are too young to understand." The prince apologized causing indignation in her.

"Don't pretend you are much older than I. You are barely five years my senior, I may seem young to you, but I'm very wise. I can think just as much as anyone, and the queen has chosen me for her court." She replied airily.

"Please forgive me, milady. You are right, you must be an outstanding person to serve in the queen's court, beauty aside." He admitted, more to himself than to her.

"I'm very powerful." Koren declared staring intently into his eyes. She was aware that the statement was almost true, since she had only experimented with her magic recently, but her desire to impress him was greater than her reason. He flashed her a dashing grin.

"I don't doubt it." He declared. Silence settled amongst the two as they let their eyes wander through the landscape.

"Don't go to the audience hall today. Pretend you have fallen ill." Orion suddenly blurted, the words sounding more like an order than anything else.

"Why?" She replied feeling nervous. At that moment the older maid approached the terrace, but turned away drastically after seeing them sitting next to each other.

"Soon they will come for you." Orion observed the obvious.

"I know."

"Casualty has not brought me here." The prince confessed avoiding her eyes, allowing her to observe his chiseled profile.

"No? Why have you come then?"

"Yesterday, when I saw you, I felt your eyes burning through me. It bothers me that your are still so young... I don't know what is wrong with me; I spent the night wide-awake... Your beauty... someday you will be a woman, and someday..." Orion turned to face her, leaving her breathless.

"Someday, if you'll have me, I will make you my queen... I swear." His chest compressed by emotion rendered him vulnerable, like those who wantonly abandon themselves to fate because they know it's useless to fight against it. Orion's emerald eyes burned with the intensity of a passion that Koren did not understand yet. She felt that his words were seared into her soul; a promise of love carved in the stillness of time, a time that perhaps would never come. Both knew their lives would never be the same from that moment on. Orion stood up and kneeled in front of her, asking for her hand, she trembled as she placed it in his. Closing his eyes to hold back a tear of farewell, he softly kissed the terse hand. He knew she was not ready for him yet, and he had nothing to offer...

The touch of Orion's warm lips on her skin electrified her whole body. She wanted to embrace him, to avoid the sour taste of farewell, and to protect him from whatever fate awaited him. Questions besieged her mind uninvited. What would happen to Orion if he fought for the throne? Would he really wait for her? Did he really want her? Nothing mattered, not reality, much less the doubts; from that moment on she had absolutely surrendered her heart. Orion would be the only man in her life and somehow she knew this to be true. Koren watched him walk away, his steps agile and firm, tears threatening to emerge. He turned around to face her one more time, smiling and giving a small wave of the hand. His eyes glowing with the brilliance that only love could bestow. At that moment Koren understood that it was indeed possible to love someone just because. Reasons, words, and time were not necessary. There only existed a mysterious bond that united and choked, eased only by the closeness of those whom we love. She remained seated at the bench, waiting to wake from her cruel dream at any moment. The kiss he deposited in her hand burned savagely, the conversation that had transpired replayed in her mind over and over. She would be his queen... this unsettling thought filled her with excitement and fear. She heard voices approaching; she turned to see the queen and the ladies who were walking over hurriedly.

"The maid has told us you were here and we saw Orion leave. Is everything alright?" The queen demanded to know right away.

"Yes, your majesty, everything is fine. He only found me here, apparently he likes to visit this particular garden often, or so he said." Koren shrugged.

"He hasn't said anything else?" The queen seemed somewhat surprised.

"No, not really." She lied serenely.

"We must be careful... I wouldn't be surprised if he tried to find allies amongst my people." The queen warned all the women.

"How so?" Koren asked feeling sort of anxious.

"It is quite obvious, Orion knows his charms... Anyone of you could be a direct link to me. If he were able to put me in danger somehow, he'd have an advantage. I'm not saying you could betray me, its him I don't trust." Violet added. Her words falling like sharp daggers on Koren's mind, bleeding increasing doubt about her beloved's intentions. Doubt disappeared as soon as it had reared its halo, she could inexplicably feel in her heart that Orion had been sincere. The other ladies regarded her with curiosity, perhaps envying the fact that she had been close to the enigmatic young man.

"It is best we get ready for our day ahead. We must attend audience with the viceroys addressing officially the dispute of succession. It is very important that you remain awake and alert, even if these proceedings are long and tedious. We don't know what could happen." Violet informed as she led them back to the guest chambers to change into their official garments. All the while, Koren followed fretting nervously about the warning that Orion had given her; she knew her duty was to inform the queen what he had said. Her lips trembled as she hid the words, unable to betray the first proof of faith that her prince had bestowed on her.

"You are so lucky! Being so close to Orion, tell us everything." Lenna demanded in a whisper, although Anari heard and squeezed herself close to Koren intent on listening.

"He really didn't say that much... But I got to look at him! His eyes are hard to describe, green like the heart of the forest, his voice is deep... he could easily put you in a trance. He had a cape run down his back that made him look so regal, and he smelled wonderful, like the fresh and sweet aroma of moss. It's like someone put together the best scents and visuals of the forest and compressed them into a person. I almost passed out; my legs were shaking terribly, since he had caught me by surprise. At the beginning I was sort of intimidated by him, but then I realized there was nothing to fear." Koren shared in a soft voice, happy to be able to tell the others about Orion. Once at the rooms, maids helped them get into their lovely dresses, which were warm velvety tunics fitted at the bodice with silver details. A small breastplate covered their chests and abdomens, complimented by a thin cape of delicate chain mail. Thin bejeweled tiaras were on their heads, with the symbols of Bandah visible. The queen led them to the waiting chamber close to the royal audience hall, were the king and his men awaited her arrival. The king also wore his royal outfit, looking every bit the part of a glorious monarch, alongside his distinguished knights. The large assembly made its way to the Royal Audience Hall, where the Viceroys of Cyrus and their chancellors also awaited in all their royal regalia.

The large hall was similar to an amphitheater; towards the side of the hall there was an elevated wooden platform were the Viceroys sat on elegant thrones. As they saw the queen and king of Bandah, they stood up to allow them to sit where they had been, symbolically relinquishing their kingdom to them. The viceroys occupied simple thrones to the right of the majesties from where they could see and take part in the proceedings. The ladies and knights of the royal courts sat on the left side, while several rows full of chancellors and dignitaries filled the rest of the hall. In the middle of it all, two beautiful but remarkably empty chairs faced the majesties of Bandah. Everyone in their place, the trumpets flared away the announcement of the arrival of the Princes of Cyrus. Prince Atle walked into the hall austere and solemn, sweat giving away his state of distress. The trumpets filled the hall once again; Orion stepped in with his singularly elegant and firm steps, looking majestic. Koren's heart began to hop as if it were a little hare fleeing, she watched as he made his way to one of the empty chairs facing them. Cautiously looking at him, and searching for the loving sparkle in his eyes, she only found the coldness of a blank stare. She didn't know where to place her gaze, seeing him there faced against the whole royal retinue was too much to bear. Both princes, however, seemed to be carrying on their predicament with dignity and composure. The booming voice of a man dressed in the official blue colors of Cyrus announced the beginning of the audience. An official welcome was given to the Queen of Bandah; the never ending introductions and every other formality was carried out as the crowd obliginly applauded.

"We are gathered here to settle the matter of succession to the throne of the mighty kingdom of Cyrus. Viceroy Plutarco, rightful heir to the throne by wishes of Vice Queen Juli of Cyrus, wishes to abdicate the throne to his younger son Prince Atle of Cyrus, favored by the people according to their delegates. The Vice-Queen Juli does not wish to chose between her sons, and has decided that the matter be settled by the majesties of Bandah." The crowd let out an "Aye" acknowledging the session's topic.

"An objection has been raised by the formal heir to the throne Prince Orion of Cyrus, firstborn of the royal line of Cyrus. Citing tradition and formality of succession he requests the majesties of Bandah rule in his favor." The man added.

"Has there ever been a similar instance in Cyrus? What has been the precedent?" King Papo spoke, given that he was the queen's official spokesman.

"This particular situation has not occurred before in our history, your majesty, thus we have requested your help. Traditional laws of succession stand the same as in Bandah, upon the death of the reigning couple the firstborn daughter inherits the throne, if no girl, then the male heir. However if the rightful heir to the throne abdicates, it may choose a successor that it deems fit. Until now, no prince or princess has refused his or her fate after someone else has been named heir." The man answered the king directing a heavy glance at Prince Orion.

"Prince Orion, what do you have to say about the allegations?" King Papo asked, while Orion rose from his seat to speak.

"Your majesty, since an early age, by my status of firstborn I have been preparing myself to the throne. My training has included government, military and legislative theories and practices. My father's abdication has been a surprise and disappointment to me, more so when he has chosen my younger brother to rule, given his lack of experience and character." Orion spoke unshaken.

"When you speak of experience, can you elaborate more? It seems to us that you are quite similar in age and you have both been raised in the castle with the same instruction."

"Your majesty, my brother Prince Atle buries himself all day long in government books, while I have taken part in the relevant governing councils and proceedings, having had contact with all these delegates here at one point or another. I have performed my duties as ambassador to the viceroys satisfactorily. Also, I am familiar with every corner of Cyrus, given that I get out and visit my kingdom to ensure its well being."

"May the delegate's representative approach." King Papo requested. An obese man wearing a long blue robe came forward, he bowed as best as his large frame allowed and remained standing to speak.

"Please address Prince Orion's allegations." Papo requested.

"Your majesty, in the name of all the delegates of Cyrus here present, allow me to speak. Its is true that Prince Orion has been present in many government proceedings, but when he has, he has been nothing but a hindrance with his unnecessary ideas of innovation and governance. He is of the belief that just because an idea floats about in his head we must abide by it and implement it, without regard to the consequences of its execution. One example, has been the damming of the northern river when the Viceroy was indisposed to rule. Prince Orion decided to construct a dam and a system of channels in some of the agricultural land of Lower Cyrus. Act, which destroyed the frail ecosystem of several species and landscapes, took away the land and livelihood of many subjects of Cyrus and brought great wealth to some of his friends. The system in place prior to that allowed many to use freely the water resources in order to farm the land properly, while the new system fell in the hand of a chosen few who immediately took advantage of the situation. Incredible fees for the use of the irrigation channels were placed upon the backs of peasants. Not only that, but the delegates from those regions have pleaded with Prince Orion to ask the Viceroy for a review of the situation and he refuses. As to his knowledge of all our regions, this is also true, for it is more than a rumor that he has made alliances with questionable races." The man exclaimed with indignity in his voice causing a stir in the hall of such magnitude that the king had to restore order with a thunderous clap.

"We shall focus on facts, not rumors. Prince Orion, do you have anything to say?" The king commanded the hall.

"Your majesty, there might be undesirable races in our kingdom, but that does not mean that they are not subjects of Cyrus. As to the problem with the channels, yes it is true that water use was limited and a few people were financially benefitting from the enterprise, but the benefit was to recover their investment in infrastructure. The delegate fails to inform that by the canalization of the river we were able to triple the total of our agricultural area, creating more opportunities for farmers."

"Your majesty, Prince Orion fails to see that even though the farming area increased there was no need for it, he ruined precious land that had been thriving for thousands of year. The current agricultural area meets and exceeds the requests of our food supply and production. There were no new opportunities for the farmers, the fees imposed by the owners of the water system left them in poverty, a state they had never known before." The large man explained airily.

"Your words have been duly noted. Prince Atle is there anything you would like to say?" King Papo addressed Atle, who seemed ready to pass out.

"No, your majesty. The people have spoken on my behalf." The prince mustered the courage to speak firmly, avoiding his brother's eyes.

"In this instance, we must not focus on what has or has not been done, but in the real issue at hand. In this whole discourse there has not been presented any piece of information that contradicts the Viceroy's desires of succession. The subject's desires trump tradition, as we have heard from the Senior Delegate that the people stand with Prince Atle. Prince Orion has failed to bring forth any evidence that would deem him any worthier to rule other than his birth order. Thus, a vote is in order. All those in favor of Prince Atle as successor to the throne please stand." Queen Violet addressed the members of the audience. The majority of those in the hall stood at once.

"Prince Orion of Cyrus, in light of the overwhelming support of the delegates in favor of Prince Atle, I see no reason to carry on these proceedings any further. Your father and his subjects have deemed Prince Atle worthy of ruling; therefore your claim to the throne is hereby rejected. If you further your dispute you will be stripped of your titles and riches, sent into exile or imprisoned for treason. The final decision rests on the Queen of Bandah." King Papo announced, Orion received the news in silence, but color seemed to drain from his face.

"The kingdom of Bandah, represented by me, concludes that we will continue to trust the judgment of Viceroy Plutarco and its subjects, and thus allow him to choose his successor, Prince Atle. He will be recognized officially in ceremony as the future Viceroy of Cyrus by the ruling kingdom of Bandah." The queen proclaimed with authority. Cheers of joy and celebration erupted in the hall as many chanted:" Long live the Queen of Bandah!"

Orion left his seat, expressionless against the tumult, without heeding to the required formalities. A numbing silence fell upon the congregation as they gaped at the prince's lack of decorum. Seconds later, thunderous steps were heard storming in from the outside, people turned to watch in confusion to see what the commotion was about. Prince Orion had returned, this time sword in hand in the company of a hideous battalion of trolls and Lagartunes. The attack took all by surprise; having felt secure in the castle grounds, terrifying screams began to surface, followed by some of pain and death. The delegates found themselves unarmed and easy prey to the invaders, trumped mercilessly in a matter of seconds. Soldiers tried unsuccessfully to halt the flow of assailants whom clogged the doors, not letting anyone in our out. The audience hall had become a death trap. A river of deadly creatures seemed to overflow into the amphitheater bearing with it the swift scythe of death. King Papo jumped from his throne sword in hand followed by his men, while the ladies surrounded the queen creating a human shield. Viceroy Plutarco joined the fray after sending off his wife with the queen and the ladies.

"Stay together!" Queen Violet yelled at the ladies, although she knew that the battle was getting close to them and they would have to possibly fight. It was clear that the attackers outnumbered the soldiers and the casualties were beginning to mount considerably.

"Your majesty, I request permission to join the battle." Kloe fell to one knee before the queen.

"Granted. May fate guard your future." Queen Violet gently caressed the Amazon's forehead. Kloe turned away and ran almost desperately to fend off a pack of trolls nearby. She was like a jungle beast, fighting with everything under her command, sword, hands, feet, and dagger, causing great damage to anyone in her path.

"Your majesty, I request permission to join the battle." Talma kneeled too.

"Granted. May fate guard your future." Violet touched her forehead and saw her disappear into the mass of violence unfolding in the hall. Koren wondered if Talma would transform into a dragon, but noticed how she remained in human form, although completely unarmed. A large troll jumped at her, who was received with a forceful fist that smashed the creature's chest. Fire spouted from her mouth and nostrils, while her hands shredded her opponent, sometimes through dismemberment or beheading. However, as many of the enemy fell twice as many seemed to be arriving, turning the amphitheater into grotesquely violent scenario.

"Your majesty, we request permission to join battle." Marussa and Palea fell to their knees holding fire spears in their hands, their faces stern.

"Granted. May fate guard your future." Both women entered battle and with great dexterity overtook several assailants.

"Why are you letting them go?" Vice-Queen Juli asked the queen in a panic.

"They have requested to join the battle, protocol allows for the ladies to join military service if needed and I cannot restrain them." Violet replied a little dazed by all that was happening.

"Why doesn't Talma just turn onto a dragon and finish them off?" Koren demanded to know.

"She can't, her size would destroy the castle, and kill us all. In moments like these it is hard to tell friend from enemy so it's best to stay able to discern. The situation is out of hand at the moment, not need to complicate things…"

"Your majesty, I request permission to join the battle." Pumzi's little voice came through in spite of the noise. The queen remained silent as if pondering the request heavily, until finally she tenderly touched the small forehead and allowed the request.

"Granted. May fate guard your future." Pumzi ran away while suffering a horrible transformation, no longer was she an adorable little dwarf. Sharp claws sprouted from her hands, her golden locks turned to lethal spikes and her face darkened in a demon like manner. Her mouth was the most grotesque sight, forming an elongated moonlike shape where rows of sharp thin teeth appeared. Pumzi jumped ferociously at a large lizard she spotted, climbing his stature as easily as if she were a squirrel in the forest. The creature was taken by surprise, unable to see what was attacking it, only feeling as claws stripped its flesh open. Once the dwarf neared the creature's neck she began to bite so ferociously that she decapitated him almost effortlessly.

"Your majesty, I request permission to go into battle. This attack is moving too quickly for my liking, we are surrounded and I see no escape, fight is inevitable. There is too much dark magic in the place and to teleport would be a mistake, furthermore I'd advice that you do not use magic, it would announce your precise location." Althea conferred as a guard, not as a friend.

"I would never leave Papo alone..." The queen desperately searched the melee for her husband.

"Your majesty..." Althea implored. Queen Violet nodded as her face darkened, giving her friend permission to fight since it seemed the attack was not letting up and the front was approaching swiftly. Koren observed the horrific scene through acrid tears, holding tight the ladies that remained behind with the queen, as she tried to shut out the atrocious sights assaulting her eyes. It was the first time that Koren had seen blood shed, heard the chilling screams of pain and death, or the sharp shrill of swords. She also saw how Althea dispatched magical balls of blue fire, which incinerated her opponents on the spot. Koren searched desperately for Orion between the tangled mass of fighters, but it was impossible to see past the action right in front of them. Suddenly her thoughts were distracted when the queen doubled up and began to vomit.

"Oh! What is going on?" Screamed the Vice-queen petrified at the sight.

"She has been poisoned!" Lenna screamed as they all witnessed the queen's helpless retching, while collapsing to her knees.

"Impossible! We must do something! Your majesty..." Anari yelled above the loudness in the hall. The queen was unable to utter a word; unable to regain her composure she lost consciousness. The ladies screamed in terror, not knowing what to do, and unable to call for help. Althea, who usually would know what to do, had disappeared from sight much to their despair. Koren looked around hopelessly for an exit, but they had been cornered against a wall.

"Your majesty, what is there behind this wall?" Koren asked the Vice-queen with a sudden flash of inspiration.

"Well, behind that one and that one is the main hallway, and that one is by the waiting area..." Juli pointed at each explaining what lay on the other side not sure what the girl was planning to do. Koren got close to the nearest wall, thinking that it didn't really matter where it led to, the only way they would be able to escape was if she was able to take the wall down. Her heart raced in a panic, wishing she had had magic instruction prior to this event, as she faced the wooden wall. Althea's words entered her mind, reminding her that in magic she needed to wish for something badly for it to happen. Yet wishing that the wall would explode didn't bring any results.

"The queen!" Anari screamed as Violet was regaining consciousness. Violet looked around confused, making an effort to get up and then passing out once again. Koren saw her slump and a fury grabbed hold of her, turning to the wall she uttered the words: "Get out of my way!" A section of the wall exploded sending wooden shards all around, and a small opening had successfully been created. Lenna and

Anari grabbed the queen with great haste and without hesitation, pulling her out from the audience hall as the Vice-Queen Juli followed. The queen barely woke up enough to try and walk, the ladies ended up dragging her away as she was still too weak.

"Your majesty, where can we take her?" Koren asked the Vice-Queen.

"Lets take her to my tower, from there we will send word that reinforcements are needed at the audience hall... this area is quite isolated from the rest of the castle."

"We can't take that long! If we go to the tower and then come back to ask for help, the enemy would have annihilated everyone by now, if they already haven't. We must sound the alarm right away!" Koren was anguished as she spoke, nearly losing her breath.

"Do not question me child, I'm in control!" Juli said curtly.

"No! This is wrong, I will not take the queen there!" Koren came to a halt, motioning for Anari and Lenna to do the same, as they helped the queen stand.

"You rotten peasant! And to think my son has noticed you...we haven't planned this for so long to have you ruin everything!" Juli glared at Koren full of hatred.

"You poisoned the queen!" Koren accused full of fury.

"No! Who knows what's wrong with her! But it was I who gave my beloved son's army entry into the castle, so that he could get rid of his useless father, and capture the queen while at it. All would have been well if it had not been for you taking Violet out of the hall." Juli spat furiously as she spoke. Violet tried in vain to incorporate, Lenna and Anari continued to hold her.

"You have betrayed us..." Violet spoke faintly.

"No, you have betrayed my firstborn, he is the true heir to the throne. You were supposed to follow tradition, none of this would've happened if you had!" Juli accused the queen.

"What have you done to me?" Violet demanded to know.

"I don't know what you are talking about, we haven't done anything to you, we need you alive. Although, I hope you do die for denying my son the throne." The woman spoke full of hatred, then suddenly kicked the queen hard in her leg making her fall forward in excruciating pain. Anari and Lenna didn't even have time to get the queen out of harm's way, losing their balance and falling to the ground with her.

"Atle is also your son!" Anari yelled full of indignity.

"I'm so fed up with you!" The Vice-queen said coldly as she pulled out a hidden dagger from her belt, with the obvious intent of stabbing Violet. Lenna and Anari tried to cover the queen with their bodies, which incensed Juli, who began to stab at them in a frenzied state. Every exposed limb was under merciless attack, their backs and shoulders bearing the brunt of the strikes, as they struggled against the woman trying to withstand the pain. Blood flowed bright red through their delicate gowns, as their chest plates and capes protected their torsos. Koren leaped on the Vice-queen's back, causing her to retreat momentarily from the others. Juli was able to break free from the girl by throwing her to the ground, and then kicking her violently on the face before turning to the others again. Koren was dazed, her broken nose gushed morbid streams of warm blood. She saw how Juli grabbed Anari's hair and pulled her out of the way, stabbing her hands as she tried to protect herself. Lenna held on to the queen who was again prey to convulsive vomiting. Koren decided to attack again, knowing that the others couldn't use their magic for fear that it would put the queen in danger, or because they couldn't focus enough. She jumped at Juli's back grabbing at her hair and pulling with all her might, making her retrocede by several steps. Once away from the others she grabbed the woman's body tightly and thought about fire. She thought about the huge bonfire at the fall ceremonies, she thought of the powerful fires that swallowed a hut once… Blue flames appeared unexpectedly to engulf the Vice-queen's body who began to scream as the fire intensified and she fell to the ground as Koren let her go.

"What do we do now?" Anari asked weakly.

"Lenna, take the queen to the chambers and hide her in the armoire. Don't alert anyone yet; we don't know who is friend of foe. Anari try to fly to the guards and tell them what has happened, I will search for Althea, and she will know how to help her highness." Koren said assertively.

"Koren, you saved my life…" The queen was breathless.

Koren didn't stay one second longer, time was racing against her, not only did she want to find Althea she wanted to see Orion. The thought that he might not be alive pounded at her heart ferociously. She didn't care if he was behind all that had happened, she only knew that she loved him and that she wanted him to be alive. Running swiftly, her heart heavy, she entered the hall the same way she had exited. The battle scene that greeted her was the most horrible and violent anyone could have ever conceived possible. A thick bloody mist permeated the air sinisterly floating above the dead, the tired and the fighting. Reinforcements had not arrived yet, after all that much time had not transpired, regardless of the attack seeming like an eternity. There still was a ferocious struggle carrying on inside the hall, like an infernal vortex intent on swallowing life and limb. The combatants trampled on the dead and some Lagartunes had stopped fighting to feast on the bodies of humans. The trolls attacked anything on their path, even their own kind, just for the love of violence. Koren searched for Althea and Orion through the moving bodies, having to get close to the battleground. She made her way slowly, hiding behind some of the upturned furniture, trying not to slip on the pooling blood. A familiar delicate hand stood out from a pile of dead bodies, dread filled her chest as she crawled over to try to confirm what she terribly feared. Tears flowed freely, almost blinding her, as she pushed with her legs the inert bodies to uncover Palea's lifeless one. Screaming in pain Koren threw her body at her friend's, not able to grasp the reality of her death. Somehow the thought that any of the ladies would die fighting hadn't crossed her mind. A deep gash nearly separated Palea's head from her body, from where intensely purple blood no longer flowed. She tried desperately to pull the body away from the rest, when suddenly giant hands grabbed her by the back and flung her into the air, the force of the landing knocking the air out of her. A terrifying troll was heading towards her, his massive sword intent on destroying her. Paralyzed by fear by the creature's rage, and unable to control her magic, she was utterly defenseless.

"No!" Orion yelled, stopping the troll dead on its tracks, and giving Koren the opportunity to fire an unexpected fireball at it. The fire engulfed the troll, who let out thunderous roars of pain as his sulfuric skin scorched. Orion ran towards her sword in hand intent on coming to her defense, but was suddenly halted by a blinding blue flash. Althea had seen him run at Koren and propelled a lethal fireball at once, thinking he was on the attack.

"Orion!" Koren let out a gripping scream after witnessing his collapse, and the blue flames starting to burn him alive. She wished with all her might that time would stand still so that the fire would not kill him. The powerful thought created a gigantic sphere of brilliant light which burst from her chest, and pulsed overtaking the audience hall entirely, leaving everyone unconscious. Running to Orion, she kneeled next to his body, placing her hands on his chest. His heart still beat, she could feel it, then she ordered the fire to leave his body and burn her instead. Her intent was to trade her life for his, but it was not necessary, the blue fire crept onto her arms burning her skin but dissipating. She wanted to caress his face, yet the blistering burns in her arms impeded it.

"Please tell me you are alive..." Koren begged in tears.

"Koren... you are okay. I didn't want any harm to come to you... I told you not to come. My mother was supposed to protect you if you did..." Orion spoke troubled by pain, the fire was no longer burning him but a deep wound in his chest left evidence of the attack.

"I have to get you out of here, you'll bleed to death... I don't know how much longer the rest will remain knocked out..." She tried to pull his body away.

"You won't be able to carry me. Go. I do not want to live in disgrace, it is best that I die here, things didn't turn out as I planned..."

"Never... you promised you would be my king." Koren closed her eyes clamoring for her Pegasus. A familiar voice responded with alarm: "Where are you? Reinforcements are on their way. I'll come too."- "Zaur, come for me in the amphitheater, find my thoughts. There is an entry on the wall towards the left flank end of the hallway... please hurry."

Zaur arrived in seconds, peeking through the hole in the wall that Koren had described. The Pegasus was stunned when he saw that every soul in the place was on the ground, seemingly dead or asleep. The guards were minutes away from being able to come through the doors, having to make their way through a horde of trolls guarding the hall.

"They are all not dead, some are unconscious, perhaps not for long." She explained trembling. Zaur came to her and kneeled allowing her to mount.

"I'm not coming with you, I want you to take this man to safety. He needs help."

"What are you doing? That is Prince Orion! You cannot help him escape; he has attacked the kingdom of Bandah. You will be charged with high treason if you help him, so will I." Zaur warned airily.

"Then its an order! You are at my service and I'm an envoy from the royal court. Please... he will die if you don't help. Do it for me, please... take him to Bandah, to my father..." She implored going down on her knees.

"He will not survive the trip." Zaur responded drily.

"We have no time for arguing, take him somewhere and then I'll decide what to do. If I'm found out I will not speak your name..."

"This is madness... I'll take him to the stables with me. Come as soon as you can. His wound needs attention, but doesn't seem urgent, he will be fine for a couple of hours..." Koren helped hoist Orion on the Pegasus. Bodies of the living were beginning to stir, Zaur made a daring dash to the stables wondering what kind of fool he was. Koren followed them out to the hall making sure that guards had not stormed the area yet, her heart tight as she hoped that they would make it out unnoticed. After that, she raced to the guest's chambers to inquire on the queen's condition, noticing that the maids and soldiers were already in attendance.

"Your majesty, how are you?" Koren spoke softly as she got close to her bedside.

"Where is Althea?" Violet responded.

"Still in battle, your highness, reinforcements had just made their way through." Fresh tears began to descend as Koren informed the queen of the news.

"What else has happened?" The queen asked full of alarm, sensing that Koren was the bearer of bad news. The girl remained silent unable to speak, scared to upset the queen's condition further.

"I order you to speak." The queen demanded sharply.

"Your majesty, Palea is dead. I don't know about the others..." Koren replied tearfully. The queen began to cry, letting out a sad wail; Lenna and Anari joined her grief upon hearing the dreadful words. The ladies held each other for support. A maid approached and tapped Koren gently on her shoulder, asking if she would like to be cleaned and healed now. The girl nodded and gladly allowed to be led out of the room, walking in a trancelike state and wondering how much more she could take. The woman stripped her of the bloodied clothes, guiding her to a hot bath, where she poured fragrant oils. The water felt incredibly soothing, although she could not place her arms in the water yet. Another maid appeared with salves and potions she smeared on her injuries, making them more bearable.

"Milady, these will soothe your wounds until you see the healers."

"Thank you... I must ask you where is the Vice-Queen, is she alive?" Koren was terrified of the answer, knowing that without Juli's help, Orion was finished.

"The majesty is in her tower, near death. She suffered a magical attack, which might as well have killed her. We know she plotted against the queen of Bandah with her son. It is a sad day indeed..."

"Take me to her..." Koren ordered grabbing the maid's arm with force.

"Milady, I cannot do that, the place is guarded and entry is restricted. Vice-Queen Juli is a traitor..." The woman explained trying to break free.

"You have clearance with the court, you are serving here... Give me your clothes. It is and order, and if you say a word or leave this place I will find you and set you on fire." Koren threatened with a chilling stare. The woman undressed quickly, weeping at her predicament, grabbing a robe to cover her trembling body. Koren moved swiftly through the halls, finding her way by asking passing soldiers, whom didn't suspect her because of her clothing. With great care she made it to the Vice-Queen's chambers miraculously undetected.

"I have come to care for the Vice-Queen." Koren said whatever came to mind first, trying to bury her face in her hair, pretending to be shy.

"The healer has left just recently, she didn't mention anyone else coming." One of the soldiers mentioned.

"I'm just a lady in waiting, I was sent here from another tower to make sure no extra help was needed, I'll just go back and tell them you denied me entry." She shrugged innocently pretending to leave, all the while hiding her broken nose as best as she could. The men looked at each other and stepped aside, noting that she seemed to be a shy palace servant and too young to cause trouble. A disturbing tranquility in the chamber was intermittently disturbed by the Vice-queen's moans of pain. The healers sat on a corner nearby as if in a trance, aware that they would not trump death's card. Koren approached and went to Juli's bedside aware that the others took notice of her presence and would soon demand to know what she was doing there. The woman lay covered in wet dressings, which tried to calm in vain the sting of her deadly burns.

"Who goes there?" Juli asked weakly after feeling her proximity, her face covered in bandages.

"It is I the Royal Chambermaid... I have a message. Orion needs help..." Koren said the last words almost inaudibly so that the others couldn't hear.

"My son...my son..." The woman moaned.

"Shhh! Be quiet... he has been wounded, he is hiding on the stables, I don't know how to heal him."

"You! What are you doing here? You serpent! I know your voice, damn you!" Juli spat her hatred through clenched teeth.

"I'm only here for Orion... I hope you die soon." Koren replied with a hiss.

"I will send someone to heal him, I have allies... He must runaway, they'll send him to the dungeons for torture, then kill him mercilessly, it's the fate of traitors..." Juli began to cry at the possibility. Koren stood up to leave and bowed to the healers before she left explaining that Juli didn't want her there. As she left she offered the same explanation to the soldiers, who regarded her with a little bit more distrust this time, but remained silent nonetheless. Returning to the bath in her chambers, she gave back the clothes she had taken from the maid, who suspiciously eyed her as she dressed. Returning to the queen's chamber, she sat quietly in a corner looking out the window to wait for more news to arrive. Lenna came up to her and gave her a hug, as if grateful to her for sitting there so still.

"Are you feeling better now?"

"I'm much better, thank you Lady Lenna. Anything new?"

"Everything is over now, the soldiers have captured the hall and put an end to the siege. The majority of the delegates are either maimed or dead. The king has lost some of his knights, and as you know Palea is dead. Kloe had her arm ripped off, but she will live..."

"That's horrible!" Koren gasped.

"We just heard a few seconds ago that the Vice-Queen has passed away, and her eldest son too, they found his sword on the battleground. Althea had attacked him, but she thinks you finished him off."

"Me!" Koren jumped from her seat at the suggestion, then remained calm thinking it was best that everyone thought Orion was dead. It was possible that Althea had seen her create the inexplicable blue sphere, and thought that it was in self-defense.

"What about the queen? Has Althea seen her yet?" Koren inquired.

"Yes, she came by when you were bathing. The real reason why the queen was so ill is because she is pregnant, the stress probably affected her so." Lenna shared the news smiling.

"At least there are some good news today…" Althea saw them and approached them, still wearing the hideously bloodied garments she wore in battle. Upon seeing her Koren could not help but let go of the tension, crying bitterly.

"Dear child, I'm sorry. You must be traumatized with so much ugliness, the things you have come to witness today you should've never seen. I just wanted to know how you were feeling and thank you a thousand times for courageously saving the queen's life. The whole kingdom of Bandah is indebted to you. We now know that Juli was acting with Orion, we don't know their intentions and we will never know. They are both dead… It is possible that they sought to overthrow the government of Bandah. If he had succeeded killing his father and the majesties, he would have become Viceroy of Cyrus, and a powerful contestant for the throne of Bandah. Anyway, it's all speculation, thank you for saving Violet."

"I just did my duty."

"You did well. Why don't you eat and rest a bit, there is still much to do ahead of us. Tomorrow we will perform the Death Rites on the departed, including Juli. Don't worry we are not doing an elaborate ceremony for her, just for the ones that deserve it. The following day we will crown Prince Atle, to put an end to this nightmare and return home." Althea told her as she sat on the ground, vanquished.

"What about Palea?" Koren said sadly.

"Her and all our other warriors will return to Bandah this dawn in a special carriage, their bodies will be prepared for ceremony in Bandah, not here. The queen wants them returned to their families and mourned as heroes of the crown." Althea struggled to get up, her eyes reddened and sunken into her face.

"I'm going to change and soak in hot water for a few hours, find me if you need me."

"Althea, all this commotion has me feeling strange. Do you think it would be okay to get some fresh air?" Koren asked before the witch had gone.

"Certainly, the grounds have now been secured and I don't think there is any more danger. I think fresh air and a good walk will serve you well." The woman gave her a tired smile and left.

"She seems overwhelmed, I can't believe all that has happened. I'm not sure I'll be able to sleep tonight; all I can hear are the horrible sounds of the audience hall, the screams, and the pleas… I also don't know what it's going to be like walking past Palea's empty room…" Lenna cried bitterly, Koren held her briefly; she couldn't stay next to her any longer. Her soul was numb with so much tragedy, and she didn't want to deal with it anymore. Leaving Lenna and her misery behind, she went to the only place where she wanted to be, next to her beloved prince.

Guards were everywhere, reaching the stables without arousing suspicion had been an incredible feat of invisibility and speed. The royal garments she wore served as immunity, allowing her to move freely between the patrolling soldiers. Taking great care to sneak into the stables unseen, she walked inside and looked around for Zaur's stall.

"Zaur, I'm here." She spoke in a whisper, closing her mind as best as she could, so that the other Pegasus couldn't access it. Zaur didn't reply, he trotted to her and kicked the ground softly with his front legs, while pointing with his muzzle to the back part of his stall. There was a tall pile of golden hay, where she could assume Orion was hidden.

"Orion, its me. Please tell me you are fine…" The hay began to stir and from the golden spears Orion's body surfaced.

"I'm almost fine, a healer has found me earlier and tended to me begrudgingly. She told me my mother died…" He said almost losing his breath due to the pain his wounds still inflicted on him.

"Yes, she has died. They will perform the rites for her tomorrow."

"I must see her then, it is all my fault she has died, I dragged her into all this mess…" His words gave away the heaviness of his sorrow.

"You can't see the rites, they'll catch you… You might have an opportunity to escape… Come dawn, they are taking the dead back to Bandah, they won't do the rites here… you must depart with them. You cannot stay in Cyrus…" Koren supplicated trying to make him reason.

"Pray tell, how am I going to do that?" He replied flatly.

"I will come back tonight with more details, I swear." Gently squeezing her prince's hand she looked intently into his eyes, trying to see something other than lifeless stillness. Securing him again under the hay, Zaur accompanied her to the exit, where he kicked the ground again, but this time emphatically.

"I have to help him." She said defiantly and left.

The king and the remainder of his knights were at the queen's chambers when Koren got back. Apparently having just returned from dealing with the aftermath of the attack, since they still wore the same outfits as earlier. All of them looked as if they had just stepped out of a hideous hell. They sat sullen, exhausted and silent, missing their three dead comrades. King Papo kneeled by the queen's bedside; holding her hand tenderly and directing his adoring gaze at her.

"Everything is in order now, the bodies are wrapped and prepared to be put in the carriages tonight." Koren overheard the conversation.

"Oh, my dear king, this day has been unexpectedly disastrous. We were absurdly taken by surprise, we must be thankful we are still alive." The queen cried.

"Please calm down, its not good for the creature in your womb. Lets make it believe that it is coming to a world full of love and hope…" He kissed her hand softly.

"Don't leave me. Stay. Stay forever, never again do I want to be separated from you…" The queen sat and threw herself at him.

"As you wish, your highness." Papo hugged her fiercely, while his semblance found solace in her proximity. Althea left the room, possibly to start making arrangements to accommodate the king, which would imply finding different accommodations for the rest as well. Koren left the room, distraught by the scene and the mission she was trying to carry out. The other ladies left as well, allowing the monarchs some privacy, heading to the terrace nearby. Koren followed remaining silent, staring blankly at the horizon. Kloe lay on a chaise nearby, her gaze calmly lost in the clouds, as her hand caressed the stump on her left shoulder. A grotesque angry scar shone bright red under the day's clarity, making Koren feel sorry and repulsed at the same time. Only the breeze imprudently disturbed their peace as it played about the shivering leaves.

"Palea should have never joined the fight, she had the least experience... she was good and happy cooking..." Marussa broke the silence.

"It was her decision, she has died an honorable death." Talma replied.

"Honor? What is that? She is no more dead that one of those Lagartunes." The nymph spat out.

"You are right, but the evil creature died to satiate its desire for violence and flesh. Palea died to defend the innocent and the throne of Bandah." Pumzi butted in the conversation.

"Stop arguing, no one had expected the possibility of an attack in there. No one can foretell the outcome of these situations, we made a decision on the spot and fate was cast." Kloe spoke her gaze still afar.

"I don't think her body should be with the others in the shed, we should demand her body is with us until we depart..." Marussa suggested.

"That is nonsense, we are not leaving for a couple of days, not a friendly time frame for a corpse. We would be unsettling the queen even more than she already is. Palea is gone, what is left behind is merely a residue of what was. I'd rather remember her the same way I saw her last, with her impetus and delicate grace intact... Not stiff and lifeless." Anari spoke on the verge of tears.

"I'm sorry. I should let it be..." Marussa apologized affected.

"I think I'm going to walk some more, I have been restless and fresh air helps." Koren stood up before the others could say a word, leaving the terrace at once. She walked aimlessly, lost in thought, until she realized that her wandering steps had inevitably led her to the stables.

"Zaur, it's me again... I have heard they have the bodies in a shed, but I can't figure out which one..." Orion started to come out of hiding after hearing her voice.

"You need to identify yourself better... I think I know which shed they will put the bodies in. The healer came back and left me some dragon's blood. I'm stronger now... I know it's a temporary solution, but it would give me enough magic to transfigure myself and go about the castle without being caught." He sat next to her on the ground, folding his long legs to his chest. She was barely able to look at him, nervous by his proximity.

"I will leave you my coat, you can take my form and go about, the guards have seen me all over, they won't suspect. Once you reach Bandah you'll have to leave the castle grounds immediately, hide in the forest. Ask anyone to guide you to the stream that surrounds the castle on the north; it's smaller that the main river and it leads to a cavern system. There you can hide, I will come find you as soon as I get to Bandah..." She offered timidly.

"My fate is in your hands, I'll do as you say... I have no choice. We had planned to kill the kings of Bandah and my father, so then the Major Kingdom of Astra would have to take over. It would have then given to me the throne to Cyrus due to traditional succession laws and I then would make a claim to Bandah as well. When I realized that we would not claim the lives of Queen Violet and Papo, I just wanted to die there… Now here I am… Just as good as dead and waiting to see what becomes me." He sighed.

"Don't lose hope, I'll do everything I can to make sure you are okay. We share now the same burdens… treason is death." Koren looked him in the eyes, knowing that even though they had now bound their lives, a future together was impossibility. If they were discovered they could only pray for a swift death. Worse yet, Koren's love for him was an aberration, since her loyalties lay with the queen. These facts floated about in their subconscious, although their mangled love tightened its grasp on them, rendering them helpless. Orion found her hand and squeezed it tenderly.

"You are so young, perhaps you don't know what's good for you, I can't make you part of this. Today you feel a certain way, but years may come to pass and the burden won't relent… guilt is a powerful enemy. Also, it is best if you find someone worthy, to hold your heart and cherish it once it's ready to love…"

"Don't treat me like that just because of my age, I'm not that young! I'm not a person that cannot think or feel. If it hadn't been for this "girl" you would not be here, I saved your life. When would it be okay for me to love you? Tomorrow? The day after? Ten years from now? Why is it that a child can sit on a throne to rule a kingdom when someone dies, but it cannot rule its heart?" Her voice was upset.

"I'm sorry, milady. I didn't mean to hurt your feelings or be condescending. I wanted to let you know that I would understand if you changed your mind about all of this… and me. There might be a time of retrospection on your part, and you could regret having met me."

"The future only belongs to time. I have no regrets." She said defiantly, not only to him, but also to the vicissitudes that hey had already conquered. Orion smiled tenderly, in awe of her passion and resolve, aware of the fire in her. She sat closer to him, wanting to feel his warmth, scent, and body. They both knew that they were surrounded by helpless uncertainty, that perhaps more ill would befall them; time the biggest of them all. They would only steal time from that moment on, they both knew. Even so, they regarded each other with happy smiles, knowing that the mysterious bond of love at least gave them the comfort of one another.

"I have to return to the castle. I swear that the first thing I'll do when I get to Bandah will be to find you…" Koren broke the silence, dissipating any illusion of peace.

"Koren, I just want you to know that I'm sorry. I didn't think this would be a blunder of such magnitude, I thought I'd carry out my plans without so many innocents losing their lives. Now I've lost everything, my mother, my home… I have nothing to offer you. I also have this magical wound full of negative energy and who knows what I'll become." Were the only words he could say before sorrow drowned his voice.

"There is nothing left to do but keep going. You better learn that it is of no use to do something good or bad, if you'll only regret it later. My mother told me that." They both stood up, awkwardly standing too close, not knowing how to bid their farewell. Koren desperately embraced him, taking him by surprise.

"I'll see you soon." Orion whispered in her ear, wrapping his arms around her. She lifted her face full of tears trying to find the essence of the forest once again in his eyes. He let himself go in the effervescence of her turquoise irises, and he tenderly deposited a soft and delicate kiss on her yearning lips.

Chapter 4: A fallen prince and a magic lesson

Koren awoke again with the lively birdsong braiding itself in the fresh morning air. For a moment she thought that she had had the strangest nightmare, although a tightness in her chest and an unwelcome flood of grotesque images told her the truth. The reminiscence of the day past assaulted her virulently, mercilessly, up to the point when she had kissed her fallen prince. The sounds of others came as an indication that the day was already on its way in the castle. A new maid came to her the minute she stirred from the bed, offering a warm robe. Koren briefly thought about the last maid that had served her, but was sure that she would not be anywhere near her. They walked to the bath hall were a large wooden tub awaited full of essence water.

"Is everybody else awake?" Koren inquired.

"No, milady, Lady Marussa still sleeps. The ladies are in the terrace, except for Lady Althea, she is tending to the queen."

"Why? What happened to her?"

"Her pregnancy is turbulent, milady. The poor woman cannot bear a bite, she has been vomiting nonstop." The maid informed as she poured hot stones into the water to heat it up.

Koren allowed the hot water to melt away the tension in her body, enjoying the scent of jasmine that rose from the water. The maid rubbed her body with a soft cloth, reviving her achy limbs and reminding her of her mother's care. The though of Mistress Flora brought a deep feeling of homesickness along. She took her time in reaching the terrace, guilt weighing down her steps as she wondered how she would face the others. The secret she carried in her heart was hers to bear, a penance for daring to love the outcast. Her thoughts inevitably fell on him... What had happened to him? Did he escape after all? If he were captured it would be known that someone had helped him. Would he betray her? Koren felt as color drained from her face, she was about to turn around to her room when the others noticed her.

"Good morning." Lenna greeted her amicably, making her feel relieved. They would not be so nice to her if the truth had been discovered.

"Good morning." Koren wished everyone as they returned her greeting.

"You will find our group a little morose, but it is to be expected, morale is low." Pumzi declared flatly.

"I know, I feel depressed too, can't wait to get back home."

"We are all feeling the same way, I hope we never set foot in this wretched place again." Lenna added gathering some unwelcome glances from some of the others present.

"This place is not at fault, it all has been that soul less bastard, Orion. I hope his soul is wandering miserably on earth." Talma was rabid. Koren felt uncomfortable, fidgeting in her chair, the weight of her treason crushing her. Silence fell upon the group and Koren thought that was probably the best to ease the tension. A maid came after a short while to let them know that the Death Rites were about to be carried out. The ladies returned to the castle to change into the traditional white robes that represented the beginning of the dead's spiritual journey. They filed into the queen's chamber to find her much too pale and afflicted, even though she gave the order to proceed. In spite of it all, Koren felt a sense of excitement for she had only heard about Death Rites, but had never been to one.

The group came upon an open field were a beautiful and small wooden temple had been erected. Ten priestesses, naked except for a thin white sheath of fabric that responded to the soft breeze, sat quietly in its interior. Their long hair was loose and their feet completely smeared in mud that had slightly begun to dry. Right in the middle of the field there was a gigantic pyre, with the promise of fire ready to burn the flesh of the dead. Close to the pyre other large tents had been erected and decorated with many beautiful flower bouquets. Each tent had a carriage inside similar to those which had brought the soldiers from Bandah only days ago. Trumpets ruled the expanse of the field, signaling the beginning of the ceremonies. A small crowd of people gathered in the field, broken into smaller groups discernible by the color of their garments. A melodic song emerged from the priestesses' tent, their soft and complex voices impregnating the air. They grabbed flower garlands from the floor and placed them on each other's necks as they walked from the tent to the pyre. The women lifted their arms up in the air from which intensely dark flames suddenly burst out, lighting some torches at hand. Koren felt a sudden unease as she stared at the black flames, as if they were part of a sickening void whose heat swallowed mercilessly. The priestesses walked to the pyre and leaned their torches on the wood finally arousing it. A gigantic ball of black fire shot out from the heart of the pyre, raging ferociously as blinding bright smoke erupted from it.

The first one to make a move was the Viceroy of Cyrus, who seemed to have aged a century in a span of hours. Plutarco walked in to the shed where the bodies had been amassed in the company if his son. Atle also seemed to have aged overnight, his crest sullen, as he held his father's arm for moral support. They approached a small wooden carriage with a gurney attached to it. The gurney had the body of a person completely wrapped in white linen. Atle and his father led the swan-like bird pulling the carriage to the funeral pyre, followed by a small escort of guards. The priestesses greeted them in silence and immediately grabbed the body thrusting it into the flames. A spectacular array of bright colors tinged the black flames, and suddenly the image of Juli appeared projected before the blackness. She seemed pale, confused and scared; there was fear in her eyes. The visible burns she had suffered before her death, obviously not the reason of her agony at that moment. Juli walked close to where her husband and son stood by the fire, her supplicating arms reaching out to them, saying something only they heard. As if fearing something the others couldn't see, she turned away and ran screaming. The Viceroy and Atle, visibly disturbed by the encounter, walked away to sit at their place next to the queen and King of Bandah. Another cart carrying a gurney approached the pyre promptly, allowing for another family to bid farewell to a loved one. The process repeated itself endlessly throughout the morning until dozens of families said their good byes. Koren watched as some let go with silent tears, while others wailed bitterly. Her thoughts wandered to Orion, wondering what he would feel if he saw the pain his ambition had sprouted.

There was a brief pause after the morning rites, which every one welcomed. The long hours sitting to witness the pain of others took an indescribable toll on everyone present. The food presented by the maids went mostly ignored and talk was at a minimum. Everyone settled in their seats once again to welcome the next group of families to take part in the ceremonial last rites well into the night. Koren felt beyond exhaustion, having cried endlessly throughout the day, deeply affected by all the untimely departures. The children clamoring for a dead parent and the parent looking back from the flames full of longing had broken her heart. Every so often, the only one excused briefly from the ceremonies had been Queen Violet, who had to vomit in a deep golden dish, dutifully held by a hapless maid. Towards the end of the affair the queen was so pale, that she could pass for one of the dead in the pyre. After all the bodies had been cremated, the priestesses began to chant, this time getting closer and closer to the dark fire. Koren watched in a trance, hypnotized by their melodic song, until she suddenly snapped up horrified at what she saw. The women seemed intent in throwing themselves into the fire; she let out a scream as they walked into it placidly. No one else watching seemed to react or think that the priestesses' apparent suicide was out of place. She stared at the fire noting how it intensified briefly, then suddenly extinguished, as if it had never existed. Standing in the center of the large fire pit, in a circle and holding hands, the priestesses stood unscathed. Stepping over embers, which still glowed with the remnants of a strange black light, the mud in their feet had now turned to clay. As they walked, still holding hands, the clay broke off. The priestesses returned to their makeshift temple where several trays of fruit and goblets full of sweet wine awaited their arrival.

Queen Violet immediately gave the signal of dismissal, allowing Talma and Althea to help her back to the castle, where the king awaited so that they could retire early.

"The queen looked terrible, do you think it's a good idea we leave tomorrow?" Anari commented to the others.

"Althea thinks it's best that her highness returns to Bandah, that way she can be cared for by our healers and midwifes. Its probably the best, she wants to go home too." Kloe informed.

"I had not idea that having a child would be such a horrifying endeavor, I'm glad I'm not human." Marussa told the others.

"It is not always like that." Kloe gave her a dismissive look.

"I hope it's a girl, then she won't have to go through the whole thing again." Pumzi added.

"It doesn't matter what it is! Of course a girl is preferable, but the queen has expressed that she would like to have a large family." Kloe spoke a little exasperated by the others.

"I have a large family, we are many sisters." Lenna offered smiling.

"Oh well, that's not a feat, you fairies just appear for no apparent reason. If a flower blooms, there's a fairy, if a start twinkles too bright... fairy. If a baby is born, another... That is just ridiculous!" Pumzi joked as the others joined with laughter, much to Lenna's mortification.

"Don't tease her like that. Life is a wonderful miracle however it comes about." Koren spoke on Lenna's behalf, which rewarded her with a grateful smile.

"You have no sense of humor." Marussa replied flatly. The group finally arrived at the chambers where their personal armada of maids awaited to offer their attentions. Koren waved the maid away and just climbed in bed, feeling a deep need for comfort. Once she closed her eyes she tried desperately to ban the fleeting images of the dead floating in the pyre from her mind, sleep eluded her. Outside the moon and stars shone brightly, and it was their twinkling glory that finally lulled her to sleep.

Movement coming from the other ladies' rooms finally awoke Koren the next day. The preparation of their belongings to be packed away for travel had already begun. They would return to Bandah that afternoon, in the back of dragons this time to make for a swift journey. Koren was excited to go back home, although reluctant, knowing that she would have to face Orion. Worrying thoughts of his location, safe arrival and the possibility that he was aware of who had killed his mother ran amok in her head. Seeing him again would bring back the memories of the sorrow she had witnessed, sorrow that came to pass by his doing. Reminiscing on his words of regrets did little to ameliorate the outrage she felt, however much she thought she loved him. The thought that they would not travel by Pegasus also bothered her, she would have liked to speak to Zaur and thank him for his loyalty. Zaur had made her feel safe, and the flight on him had been pleasant, just thinking about the scaly skin of a dragon gave her chills.

A maid came to alert her that the ladies were to meet at the queen's suite. There was still a matter to be resolved and it would be carried on rather quickly that morning. Tradition called for a sumptuous ceremony in the coronation of a Viceroy, however Atle would have to be crowned in a simple ceremony by the ruling kings of Bandah. This particular arrangement seemed fit due to recent events, the queen's delicate condition and her desire to return home promptly. Viceroy Plutarco accepted the arrangements gladly; he was still mourning his disgraced wife and son, both loved by him in spite of their treason. The coronation would take place in Plutarco's office, witnessed by the few delegates that survived and the majesties of Bandah and their people.

The office was exquisitely beautiful, the shelves had been ornately carved, and the books in them appeared to bejewel their existence. Wooden statues abounded and tapestries of picturesque forest depictions graced the walls. Those present sat in silence, while the Queen of Bandah approached without the usual ceremony, followed by the king. Plutarco reached for his crown with trembling hands and held it out solemnly to the queen, as if by doing so serenity descended upon him. Prince Atle approached them, looking ghostly pale and kneeled so that the queen could place the crown on his head.

"I now present to you, the Viceroy of the kingdom of Cyrus and all its subjects." Queen Violet kissed his forehead, and then gently tapped his shoulders with the scepter she held in her hand, nearly causing him to lose his balance. Two delegates came to his side and placed a beautiful golden cape, composed of tiny hummingbird feathers, on the young man's shoulders. The new Viceroy stood up and smiled at everyone, then kneeled in front of the kings of Bandah, to kiss their hands properly. He rose and held his father tightly, letting him know with teary eyes how much he loved him. The old man held his son full of pride and sadness, wishing his wife had witnessed the moment, even if her treason had been such a burden on Atle. The delegates proceeded to hand Atle the official seals of Cyrus as tradition called for. Queen Violet congratulated him once again; wishing him a long and fruitful reign, then announced her departure. King Papo wished him well in his new tenure and said his farewells, as they all left the office to let the young man and his father begin a new monarchy.

"I think it was lovely, event though it was a simple coronation. Atle seemed regal and ready to accept the crown." Anari commented.

"I agree. I can only imagine what was going through his head. Having to accept the crown in spite if having lost half his family." Kloe added.

"I think he looked very handsome. I smiled at him the whole time trying to catch his eye... he will need a queen... I think he is too shy though." Lenna laughed at her words.

"Oh Lenna, only you would think such silly things. The boy has more important issues in mind right now; tomorrow he'll have to start replacing the lost delegates and the cabinet members. He must act quickly, the Viceroy is taking the lead of a very unstable kingdom right now, he is vulnerable." Kloe pointed out.

"I fell in love with the cape they gave him..."Anari tried to ease the tension.

"Yes, it was stunning." Pumzi agreed as silence reigned once again in the group.

The remainder of the day unfolded quietly, as preparations for travel were arranged properly, every so often a walk through the gardens was mandatory to ease the unrest. In the afternoon the royal suite was ready to depart, waiting for them, groups of dragons lined up in the same field were the death rites had taken place. There were no trumpets or glorious ceremonies of farewell, a somber aura surrounded the group, furthered by the queen's frail appearance. Violet walked slowly to Talma, once again a gargantuan black beast, which she climbed onto with great effort. The king mounted a smaller green dragon, while the rest of the travelers followed suit, sometimes up to fifty or so per beast. The biggest dragons carried the group's belongings and the rest of the soldiers. Koren rode a grey dragon with the other ladies, excluding Althea who still preferred to travel by herself, this time minus the broom.

The queen raised her scepter and ordered departure, her dragon becoming airborne immediately, followed by the king. Koren grabbed the leather harnesses that held her in place tightly, uncertain that this mode of transportation was safe, given the simple furnishings that served as seats. The dragons had large leather and metal straps around their necks, from which numerous leather ropes fell into a pliable platform, similar to a cover on the dragon's back. The cape was secured in place tied to the dragon's hind legs with thick leather ropes, and it was in this platform that leather seats were set up for the passengers. The dragon seemed to squat briefly to get an impulse and with a strong flap of its wings suddenly became airborne. Koren closed her eyes, waiting for the jerking movement stemming from the thrust, yet it didn't materialize. They flew placidly in a matter of seconds; Koren couldn't believe the smoothness of the flight, the movement of the wings almost imperceptible. A magical force shielded them from the wind; the only way to confirm that they were moving at all was looking down at the passing earth. The blur underneath scurried by with such velocity that it was nearly impossible to discern any clue as to their whereabouts. Every so often the dragon would let out a huge blast of grey fire, which vaporized the clouds on its path, sending a drizzle of warmth to the passengers. This delighted Koren, she enjoyed the refreshing steam to combat the dryness of the magical atmosphere in which they traveled.

The flight didn't seem to last long at all, although the day was about to end when they arrived at Bandah. The outskirts of the forest surrounding the castle became recognizable making Koren's heart skip a beat. It was very possible that Orion was there, hiding in the cold heart of a cave… The dragon began descending, almost as if it were a feather falling onto the ground, and landing gently. At the open clearing, Queen Violet waited for the ladies' arrival to retire at once to the palace, the king standing by her side patiently. Talma had already switched back to her human form after having been freed of her travel harnesses. Althea arrived in the middle of a mist, her hair in disarray and her cheeks flushed by the wind's relentless attack. Koren dismounted the dragon along with the other ladies and followed, looking around to see if she could spot Zaur.

"From now on the king shall reside in the Queen's Tower. You will no longer have free access to my private chambers; only Althea will remain as my Lady-In-Waiting. More details will be given to you later. You will see the knights come and go through the tower, as they will still need to confer with Papo their daily matters, other than that it should all be the same as usual. Please don't feel alienated; be certain that you all will have the same access to me as before." Queen Violet addressed the women with a faint smile.

"I just hope you feel better soon, your majesty." Anairi said tearfully.

"Oh please don't cry. I will be fine, the witches and midwives will care for me. Now it is time to retire. Anyone else has something to say?" The queen replied.

"Your majesty?" Koren's voice surprised her as the queen turned to face her.

"Yes, Lady Koren?"

"Oh. I would like permission to spend a few days at home with my mother…" Koren was unable to meet Violet's eyes.

"My dear child, no need to feel embarrassed by your request. Of course you need to be with your family after what you have endured. You may stay at your home as much as you desire, but you must not neglect you palace duties. Come to the library in the mornings and skip the afternoon meetings, leave anything for me with Althea."

"Yes, your majesty, I will do so. I only need a few days off to rest a bit. Thank you." Violet caressed Koren's cheek affectionately and smiled, before heading to the palace. Koren kept the pace with the others feeling a strange heaviness in her soul. Guilt was starting to burden her, knowing that she had to make up so many falsehoods. Getting close to the main courtyard by the palace she couldn't bear to take another step forward and bid farewell to the ladies. She had only walked a little ways before seeing a pair familiar figures standing in the path. Koren ran to her mother's open arms that anxiously tightened their grip around her. Her father embraced them both unable to hold back his emotion.

"Word came this morning about what happened in Cyrus... How horrible! My baby, so innocent, you have had to witness such atrocities." Mistress Flora cried bitterly.

"Can we go home now?" Koren pleaded breaking free from their embrace. The trio headed home surrounded by the quiet and darkness of the forest, which was only interrupted by Flora's loud sniffling. As their little house came into view, Koren felt an immense relief, even if her heart pounded when she looked up the trail to the river. Flora was the first one to enter and sat her daughter by the fire, getting her a delightful cup of warm soup. Master Lorean sat in a comfortable chair nearby, observing his daughter quietly and enjoying the warmth.

"Thank you mother the soup is delicious, but if it's okay I'd like to retire now."

"Of course, dear." Mistress Flora smiled and grabbed the cup from her hands. Koren didn't say anything else and retreated to the heart of her little home. Her parents might have thought that she was headed to bed, when in reality she scurried to the pantry. Carefully and silently she searched for readily available edibles in the dark, stashing them away in a linen sac. After grabbing a loaf of bread, jam, dried meats and fruits, and a bottle of wine she hurried out to her room. All the goods were stashed safely under the bed where she knew they would escape her mother's sight. Koren went to the toiletry armoire trying to find something that might be of use to Orion if he was injured, although she didn't know in what condition he might be.

"What are you looking for?" Mistress Flora startled her.

"Oh, I had and injury... and I was looking for... Do we have dragon's blood?" Koren hesitated a bit.

"What? Dragon's Blood! What kind of injury do you have? Let me see! I'll call your father..." Mistress Flora exclaimed in panic.

"No! Don't! It's all right now, it was merely a magical burn, but it was tended to already. I had a few drops of dragon's blood in some tea at the castle and it made me feel really well, so I thought it would be a good idea to have it handy..."

"I can make you some linden tea. Dragon's blood is a very potent remedy and quite expensive just to have lying around. I've only seen flasks of it in the castle's infirmary. But I'm sure your father can take a look and make it better... Or I could talk to Lady Althea tomorrow."

"NO, mama, please. I'm fine, really, I only thought it was a common remedy. You know, a little bit of your tea will be more than enough to make me feel great." Koren pleaded as she grabbed her mother's arm affectionately.

"Fine. But if I think anything is out of sorts I will go to the palace without delay." Mistress Flora spoke firmly.

Koren retreated to her room in silence, shutting the door behind her to have some privacy. It would make matters worse if her mother saw her preoccupied face. Orion besieged her thoughts again and again, like a malady intent on never healing. The uncertainty of his whereabouts and well being made her heart beat anxiously, impregnated by anguish and fear. Was he alive? Could she help him? What could she possibly do about Orion? The knowledge that the last time she had seen him he had been in possession of dragon's blood comforted her. He had enough to last for a while, besides he was a strong and courageous man who would not relent in the face of misfortune. Was that a good thing though? What plans would he make now? Would he return to Cyrus for revenge? Would he stay in Bandah? The answerless queries went roundabout in her mind, submitting her into a restless sleep.

Daylight peeked in through the windows in shimmering filaments to caress Koren's skin with its warmth. She woke up startled, realizing that she hadn't even changed the clothes from the day before. Her eyes immediately focused on the forest spreading past her window, which hid in its heart the man she loved. Gathering herself as quickly as possible, heart racing at the possibilities that lay ahead, she ran out of her room. Mistress Flora was in the kitchen, fact that surprised her and left her sullen. Having to deal with her mother's meddling that morning had not been in her plans.

"Good morning, mama."

"You are up and about early! I decided to stay for a little longer to see if you needed anything. Your father is already gone, I have sent word that I will stay with you if you like me to..." Flora offered smiling.

"No. I don't need you here. Really, I'm fine. I just wanted to spend more time at home, that's all. I'm actually going to take a nice long walk in the forest before heading out to the palace. The queen asked me not to forget my duties." Koren spoke casually, trying to hide the nerves that crept through her body.

"Very well, I'm glad to see that you are doing fine after the things you saw, although it may hit you later. The whole weight of it, that is. You know where to find me if you need me, or if you need to talk, or whatever you need just ask, my love."

"Thank you. Oh... You know what? I forgot to tell you a secret, but you must not tell..."

"Tell me!"

"The queen is with child!" Koren let out the news with a shriek, enjoying her mother's reaction to the surprise.

"About time! Oh, I do hope it's a beautiful little girl..." Mistress Flora smiled appreciating her own daughter with tenderness.

"The bad thing is that she is having a terrible pregnancy, very afflicted with ills, mama. Althea waits on her all the time."

"That can happen sometimes. At least it's for a good reason, finally an heir to the throne! Everyone wants this monarchy to keep reigning. It is time to have the little footsteps of princesses and princes heard all over those stuffy palace halls. I'm glad that there is good news in the middle of all this Cyrus mess. Anyway... I'll be going now, I'm sure Lady Althea must be looking for me to work out a special diet for the majesty." Flora deposited a kiss on the girl's forehead and left to work.

Koren stood in the threshold watching her walk away, as soon as Flora's figure disappeared from sight she ran back to her room. Grabbing the hidden goods, and looking around for anything else of use that she could take, Koren headed out into the cold. After taking a few steps, the idea that perhaps a wool blanket and her pillow would be nice things to present to him, made her return. Out of the house the cold morning air came out in gulps of steam through her mouth as she raced through the familiar paths. Somehow the distances seemed longer, the earth wetter and the air colder than she remembered. Heading towards the stream usually meant a nice respite in the middle of the forest to enjoy the singsong of the running water, but this time she paid no notice. The main entrance to the caves and caverns lay hidden behind dense foliage at the larger part of the waterway. A small pond of clear and cold water pooled right at that spot, which made it unappealing to enter the subterranean landscapes beneath it. Koren looked around for clues and traces of someone having been there, but everything seemed untouched. Knowing that Orion would not leave any tracks behind, entering the cave seemed to be the only option. The water slapped her legs hard, the cold stinging as she felt like a fool for not removing her boots before wading in. Her anxiety was not letting her think things through clearly, fear too. At least she had the common sense to hold the bags of goods she brought over her head, and not ruining them. The thought that Orion had not made it to Bandah began to squirm in her mind uncomfortably.

The large cave was cold and dark, seemingly empty. The dank air inside quickly overpowered breath, as if its mere heaviness would drown. The river sounds were amplified inside the cave's dome, and the shrills of some unseen creatures, permeated the otherwise unnerving silence.

"Orion?" Koren ventured feebly, afraid that her voice would break havoc in the cave.

"Koren…" A faint call came out of the heart of the cave.

"Where are you?" Koren asked trying to make out his figure somewhere in the dark. Walking forward, frustrated by not been able to see, she raised her hand and ordered her to light the way. The thought was so desperate that a white flame surged from the palm of her hand, illuminating the cave and disturbing the sleeping bats, which started to flap about aimlessly. Orion came to sight, curled up in fetal position on the ground, squinting at her. Koren ran to him to embrace him, he barely moved, letting out a cry of pain as her arms reached for him.

"What's wrong? What happened? I thought you had dragon's blood to last you a while…" His paleness alarmed her.

"I did. When the flying carriage was approaching Bandah I knew I had to jump out, or risk being discovered. The mist of dawn was perfect to cover my escape… I saw the castle's outline at close range, so I calculated my fall upon the forest as best as I could. The second the carriage started to descend, and the forest was clearly visible, I jumped… The landing was horrible; I'm not sure why I'm still alive. My legs and arms were broken when I hit the ground; I'm surprised my head was not bashed. I'm just awed that I lived… I drank some of the dragon's blood to restore my magic enough to be able to heal myself as best as I could. Unfortunately, the flask was shattered. I have no more… Again I'm left to face the claws of the magical wound the witch bestowed upon me…" He groaned.

"But if your body is fine, why can't that wound also heal?" She demanded to know.

"Don't you know? It's black magic. The witch's intention was killing me; this kind of magic destroys in unspeakable ways. It's probably still feeding on my own negative energy… Who knows? Luckily, you absorbed most of that black magic; your intention to save me had enough white magic to neutralize the attack. And you survived it too… a scary thought." He tried to explain.

"Why is that scary? … It doesn't matter…. What you say is horrible; you'll be tortured forever. I will go to the palace and find some fresh dragon's blood for you. I give you my word I'll do anything possible to make you well." Tears blurred her sight. Orion made a superb effort to seat and embrace her.

"You are the reason I lived… There is no other. Thank you for helping me, everything that has befallen me has been by my doing, but knowing you are on my side gives me great hope." She raised her gaze to meet his, whom in spite of his paleness and unshaven face was still beautiful. His state made him look vulnerable, making her love him even more. Koren searched for the thick woolen blanket and wrapped it around his shoulders, were it was received with deep gratitude. The simple food absorbed him entirely for the best of a half hour, his stomach delighting on the blessings of nourishment.

"Maybe you should go outside and get fresh air, I can help you. Don't worry about being seen everyone thinks you are dead. Also, no one ventures out this far into the forest."

"They really think I'm dead?" He asked incredulous.

"The official assumption is that I killed you. You see, after Althea attacked you she didn't know my intention was to save you. When I used magic she just assumed that I was finishing you off, that you disintegrated." Koren explained as she hoisted him up to walk out of the cave. They sat close to the entrance, thinking that it was no good getting all the way out and having to cross the cold water.

"That is excellent! No one will ever suspect me again. I can use another name, change my appearance and start my life anew. Of course, I'll need more dragon's blood…" Orion spoke to himself out loud.

"Where will you go?" Koren asked feeling a knot forming in her stomach.

"I can't live in a cave all my life… I'll travel north, it's what all the desperate end up doing anyway." He declared flatly.

"I know you are right. I didn't think it would be any other way… I will help you in anyway I can." Koren hung her head.

"I swear I'll come back for you… Now it's not the time…" He spoke tenderly. Koren was afraid to ask which would be the right time when a relationship between the two could be a reality. Deep inside they both knew the truth.

"I have to go to the palace, after carrying on my duties, I will find you the healing blood and bring it. I'll also bring more food you had quite the appetite. Should I gather wood to make you a fire?" Koren offered solicitously.

"Just make a magical one." He responded casually.

"I haven't been completely honest with you… I had just begun working for the queen before our trip to Cyrus. Prior to that my life was very humble, this forest was my playground and I just ran about with the other castle children. I'm not of noble birth or trained in magical skills. Up to this moment all I've done has been by instinct." Koren confessed with aplomb.

"If those are your confessions we have nothing to worry about. You have done quite well magically; certainly you must at least be aware of how powerful you are. Imagine all you'd be capable of if you had full use of your skills, you'd be invincible. I don't care whether you are noble or not, as a matter of fact, I happen to detest nobles. While I'm recovering here I'll teach you some skills, I was the best of my class." He announced proudly.

Returning to the inside of the cave, Orion picked a good location for the first magic lesson he would impart on his beloved.

"We'll make a fire. First, you need to have a perimeter in mind; this helps you to visually focus. Pretend these rocks right there are the base of your pyre. Now think about flames… luminous, hot and sturdy. You know fire, you've seen it… now build it in your mind and place it there. Believe that this is reality, one that you chose." Orion spoke as she focused on the place he had pointed out. Her thoughts revolved around fire, yet nothing was happening. Frustration was creeping in after a few futile attempts at lighting anything, when she noticed that Orion could barely stand any longer. His body was trembling and his effort to be by her side was making his paleness return. The only wish that crossed her mind was to warm him up, wanting more than ever to make a vibrant fire. A little white flame burst intrepidly between the rocks on the ground surprising her. Another flame seemed to follow, and another, until an exquisite smokeless fire comfortably warmed up the area. Orion smiled broadly, and then slumped on the ground covering himself with the blanket, as he laid his head on the pillow she had brought.

"Mmm, this pillow smells like you…" He hugged the pillow to his face.

"Too bad we can't change our reality that easily…" Koren spoke in a trancelike manner, staring at the fire she had just created out of nowhere. Silence descended momentarily on the cave, until Koren realized that Orion was about to fall asleep.

"I'll be back this afternoon, or as soon as I have secured the blood." She whispered to him, kneeling by his side to kiss his cheek.

"No. Don't come so often. Tomorrow will be fine don't arouse suspicion. A day more, a day less, who cares?" He shrugged and smiled.

"I care, you crazy man!" Koren laughed as she kissed him again before leaving.

Reaching the palace seemed to take no time for Koren, as she had been lost in though. Remembering that her mother had mentioned that there was dragon's blood at the infirmary was auspicious, but she didn't have a clue where the place was. Heading to the library she resigned to finish the librarian duties before embarking on her mission. Morning slipped away tediously before her first stroke of genius of the day finally descended upon her. Walking over to the dormant library window, and knowing no one to be there at that hour, she ventured her plan.

"Welcome, Lady Koren."

"Greetings. I need a map of the palace, the most recent one. Make sure that the infirmary is in it. Also, I want only one title that is most useful for learning magic… And a book about dragons, thank you." As Koren requested items they appeared. She grabbed the light spheres out of the window and raced to the area nearby, to settle once again in the same chair she had used on her last visit. The hope that the same treats that materialized last time would make a reappearance. Seemingly, the library system was slacking off that day, for no preferential treatment materialized.

She sighed profoundly to focus on her reading, as the lights transformed into books on her lap. The first selection to inspect was the map, where she could see the entire palace plans. It was amazing to discover all the chambers and halls she didn't know existed in its interior. The infirmary seemed to be a large section, located underneath the area in between the queen and king's towers. Certainly that place would have dragon's blood, she thought. Memorizing the path to follow, she traced the route, which would likely get her there without attracting too much attention. Moving on to reading about dragons, and finding them a fascinating subject, brought Talma to mind. Finally, a thin manual that seemed written for children was all that was left to be read. Strangely, it had yellowing pages and a musky smell. Perhaps it was one of the special books Lenna had referred to, of which they kept the hardcopies, because they were very important. The title read: "Fundamental Principles of Magic" and no author was listed, which augmented Koren's curiosity. The work seemed to be too simple to be of any importance, but if the magical librarians had picked this for her, they must be on to something. The first page read:

-Fundamental Principles of Magic-

1. All beings are magical beings. No exceptions.
2. Imagination if the foundation of magic alongside intent.
3. The magic inside you begets the magic outside you.
4. Only we are capable of liberating our full magic potential.
5. Magic is not a mystery it is a natural phenomenon.
6. Letting go of beliefs helps conquer our magical limitations. "Believing is limiting the possibilities."
7. Practice magic until it becomes an ordinary event for it to become an extraordinary event.
8. Magic to do well is more powerful than magic to do harm.
9. Magic must respect the natural order of life.
10. Magic is the ability to have affinity with life and the creative universe.

Koren stopped reading at that point realizing that she had spent more time than she had expected in the library. Returning the dragon book and map to the window, she walked away putting the little magic manual in her pocket. Although the piece had not seemed so impressive, it was simple and practical, which she preferred. Running through the desolated halls, and knowing that it was teatime gave her confidence to carry out her quest. Stopping to look around at strategic stops and ensuring she had not been seen by anyone, Koren continued moving silently. Upon reaching the main entrance of the infirmary she heard a group of female voices. The women sat sharing lively stories in a small waiting area, in front of a large magical window that allowed plenty of sunlight to come in. A breeze also seeped in mysteriously bringing fresh air to the room. There were too many healers there to go past them unnoticed; Koren's heart sank at the prospect of retreat and surrender. The flowing breeze sparked an idea... the memory of winters cold. The window trembled as a gust of icy wind full of lovely snowflakes, barged into the group of startled women. They scrambled from their seats at once to address the magical mishap, giving her the opportunity to race to the infirmary. Purposely avoiding the areas where the sick lay recovering, she headed straight to the medicine laboratory, aware that she might bump into someone.

The doors to the laboratory were wide open, uncovering a large repository, where rows of tall shelves were lined with flasks. It was a colorful spectacle of sorts, the things contained in the glass amazed Koren as she walked past them. The unnerving shrieks of live creatures came from the back of the place making Koren's skin crawl. Curiosity beckoned her to explore the contents of all the flasks and jars at hand, however she remained resolute in finding what she came for. The sooner she found the dragon's blood the likelier it would be to escape sight, so she ran swiftly through the rows. Every item in the place seemed to be categorized meticulously, classified by name and healing properties. Koren was unable to recognize any of the substances, her frustration growing at what seemed a futile endeavor. Glancing around, a large glass armoire caught her eye; she went to it and discovered that it was an elaborate and functional piece of art. Its visible contents were elegantly placed in lovely jars, some of them encrusted with precious stones. One particularly ornate bottle sitting in the upper shelf had a gold label declaring its content, Dragon's Blood. Koren smiled triumphantly.

The armoire didn't seem to have an actual door to open, the glass panels appearing to be hermetically sealed. Koren touched every corner and crevice trying to find a way to get hold of the flask, to no avail. It was obvious that the use of magic would be required to gain access to anything in there. Desperation was building up inside her; she mutedly pounded on the glass, tears streaming down her face. Her only thought was that Orion needed the dragon's blood, and she was so close, so close... "Please I need to save someone..." Koren whispered pleading with the glass to recede. She reached desperately with her hand for the flask, and surprisingly this time, the hand went through the glass without effort. The motion was similar to having the hand go through a curtain of water, as the fingers wrapped tightly around the dragon's blood. Fear had her wondering if she would be able to retrieve the flask as she pulled away, nearly ready to faint. The moment she had her hand out, the glass returned to its original state, a solid panel. Her heart pulsed so intensely she was afraid it was going to explode in her chest, as her legs made haste to carry her swiftly to the main entrance regardless of who saw her. Koren paused briefly to see if the healers were still by the window, but they had all probably moved to a more comfortable location. The floor still bore the remains of the melting snow after all. A jubilant sense of triumph overwhelmed her, easing the tension and allowing a more casual stride. Once again she would see Orion's magnetic grin and tan skin. Almost out of the palace doors she bumped unto Lenna whom immediately noticed her state of exuberant joy.

"I went looking for you this morning, your mother said that you had gone to the forest. I even went to your house and around, and I didn't see you. Where were you?"

"Oh… I ended up not going to the forest after all. I went to visit my papa instead, at the stables. I don't like the forest that much anymore, it's boring." Koren lied. Lenna observed her frowning sensing something was amiss.

"I can't argue with that. But, are you all right? You seem kind of strange right now. What's that you got there?" Lenna inquired pointing at the bulge in her pocket.

"Oh this, it is nothing. Mother requested some botanical infusions to make a special tea. I'm fine… it's just she wants this right away and I was racing over. I like to run… I better go now." Koren began to walk away hurriedly.

"I can come with you, I'm done with my duties. I appreciate what you have done and I admire you, plus you are nice to me. The others treat me like an idiot…" Lenna whined as she tried to follow.

"No! No… Maybe some other time we could do something together. How about tomorrow? After I hand this to mother I want to go home and lie down, I've been… having headaches." Koren replied getting away from Lenna as fast as she could. The fairy stood open mouthed unable to say what she had intended, a little miffed by Koren's rejection. Accepting defeat Lenna spun around and walked to the palace to find something to occupy her.

When one goes with a purpose the way seems endless, and for Koren this was no exception. Thoughts focused on Orion, she failed to notice the fragrance of the roses floating in the garden, the echo of the fountains, or the sun's magnificent brilliance. For her the world had turned into a singular scenery, the one which life had forged upon the face of a fallen prince. The forest welcomed her back full of life and familiar sounds, mostly by the creatures that hid away to see who ventured in their territory. The stream was clear under the sunlight, going about with melodic songs of water and stone clashing rhythmically. Koren stopped momentarily to remove her delicate slippers this time, smiling as she felt the water's icy caress sending shivers up her spine. Carefully stepping on the stones, she reached the exterior of the cave, taking great care not to make too much noise. To her surprise the fire she had made earlier was still going just as she had left it.

"Hello!" Koren announced her arrival with a mix of joy and insecurity.

"You should knock before you enter… I haven't made myself up yet." Orion's weak voice joked. The girl ran to kneel at his side, immediately presenting the flask she had brought. The young man opened his eyes widely, delighted to see the tonic that would restore his strength.

"You are wonderful." Orion whispered making her blush ferociously, relishing his admiration. With trembling hands the prince opened the delicate flask, careful not to spill its precious elixir. Dipping his little finger in the contents, he pulled out one luminous drop of ruby red blood, and sucked it dry. The change was instantaneous, color miraculously returned to his skin, his body radiating again youthful virility. Orion's eyes came alive with the familiar intensity and sparkle that Koren ached for. She watched the transformation in a mist of awe, stupefied by love; observing him come back to life was similar to beholding centuries of romance and rebirth in one moment.

"Thank you, milady." Orion came close to her and took his time leaving a sensual kiss on her cheek, making her legs tremble. He stood up and stretched his limbs, awaking them. Orion sprung to action and left the cave, Koren following his lead, to greedily breath in fresh air. Without hesitation he flung himself into the cold water in the pond, swimming with abandon as he laughed heartily.

"What are you waiting for, Lady Koren? Jump in!" He motioned for her to join. Koren stripped down to her undergarments, smiling excitedly before jumping in. The pond water was freezing cold, yet to the splashing and wading youth who joyfully played, there could not be a more perfect place. Soon enough both began to shiver, escaping to sunbathe in the warm rocks by the pond. Koren continuously glanced his way making sure that he was real, surprised at the turns life had taken to bring them together at that precise moment.

"Lets go back to my lair fair maiden, lest you die of exposure. Your lips are purple, and the fire which a powerful enchantress built in my cave still burns fiercely." Orion said in mocking gallantry, instigating a race to the inside of his hideout as they both laughed happily. Sitting by the fire, they shared a meal of bread and cheese that seemed too fancy for the occasion. Orion tried to have her eat more, yet she refused.

"No, you eat that. I haven't brought you anything else. I wont be able to return until tomorrow, this is going to have to last you until then."

"Don't worry about me, now that I'm all good I can hunt and find food in the forest. Remember that I sort of grew up in one?" He winked at her as he playfully tossed a piece of bread in his mouth.

"What are you going to do now?" The words inevitably escaped her.

"I'm not leaving yet, I'm in no hurry. I need to come up with a plan, maybe go back to Cyrus, or to the sea... Before all this happened I had a quest in mind, perhaps I should pursue it." Orion answered after a brief pause.

"What quest?"

"In the northern mermaid kingdom, out at sea there is a small island, home to a small temple. This temple houses a seashell, but it is no mere seashell, it's called Ossida. A magical artifact whose possession will bring great fortune, for it has the power of the sea. With one single wave it could destroy battalions of men, a flood to wipe up armies in the blink of an eye. It can also manipulate non magical water to your bidding, making it a powerful weapon..." Orion explained exhilarated by the notion, his eyes wide open and his hands shaping wild gigantic waves.

"What good is it to you now? Your brother is the Viceroy, you don't have an army..." Koren reminded him. Orion remained silent without daring to look her in the eyes.

"What do you have in mind now? Kill your brother? The royals of Bandah would never recognize you as ruler. Please, stop leaving so much pain behind your ambition... I was at the funerals; I witnessed your family's grief after sending off your mother to the black flames. And she wasn't going in a good state! Children lost their parents and other loved ones... You want more of that?" Koren spoke airily standing at once.

"Don't give me that look of scorn, things didn't turn out as planned, it was not my intention to have so many casualties. You don't understand, you are too young... Sometimes we have to fight for what we want in ways we never thought possible." He replied defensively standing to face her.

"I have done just that!" She glared at him pausing for a moment.

"You knew there would be deaths involved... Stop referring to me as if I were a little girl, at this point is nothing but a lousy insult. I may be young, but I know that even if you want something it does not give you the right to take another person's life wantonly... I could have been a casualty that day!" Indignation rang in her words.

"Then you should stop playing innocent, your hands are not so clean... I know you killed my mother. Besides, I tried to warn you!" Orion responded curtly.

"I did my duty to my queen... Your mother tried to kill Violet! What does that have to do with anything else? You are trying to find some crazy seashell, goddesses know with what end in mind!"

"I don't want to argue with you... If you are feeling this way, it is best that I leave right away and never return."

"No! No... It's not that at all. Please, I beg of you, just recapacitate on this. Start your life again elsewhere, everyone thinks you are dead... please." Koren begged tearing up.

"I implore you to stop, milady... I'm not worthy of your sorrow. What am I supposed to do? Do you think I'm going to be a fisherman? A hunter? Become a merchant in some far trading post? Koren, sooner or later someone is bound to recognize me... I am a prince. I grew up being different than just any other person, every one has their place in the world and mine is to rule... " Orion explained beseeching her understanding.

"We can run away together... live away from the world, happily. If not, then you must take me on your quest; here I'm nothing but another servant for the queen. If you go, my peace goes with you..."

"You can't come with me... You are too young to face the outcast world I must travel in from this moment on. It's not like you can pass unnoticed easily, even if you did, there would be a manhunt on your behalf. Every stone would be upturned; this would put me at risk... Spare yourself the disdain of a vagabond life... I'll have to spend many nights in undesirable places, with undesirable people; I cannot willingly expose you to that. But I swear, I swear! If you love me, Koren, I will come back to see you whenever I can, until the day when I can finally tear you away from this place and make you my wife... Even if I have to topple the whole kingdom of Bandah..." Orion reached for her hands gripping them tightly. Searching for her eyes and opening his soul to hers, so that she could see the resolve he carried in his heart.

"Don't leave me here..." Koren pleaded heartbroken, her body letting go of composure as her tears flowed bitterly. Orion leaned closer to hold her in his arms, refraining from an intense desire to kiss her, feeling that she was indeed just a girl. While she held back the same desire, but for not knowing how to kiss...

"I want you to excel in the study of magic, you will have greater skill than the most accomplished witch." Orion spoke trying to ease the silence, forcefully drowning the sorrow in his voice.

"Do you really think my life will be normal from now on?"

"You are right... we have done and seen events that intertwine our fates more so than any other two people could. I will be forever loyal to you... For the same reason that you saved my life... I will come back to you." Orion embraced her to himself possessively.

"Of course, you go and leave me here... pitifully waiting for the day you'll return, if you return..." She replied, her voice bitter.

"There is no other way... I promise I will return."

"There are many other ways, you just don't want to..." Those were the last words that fell heavily upon them before silence overtook the cave. Koren broke free from his arms, and then walked to the exit, not before turning to look back one more time. The intention was to sear his image in her mind forever, since something inside her felt that it would be a dreadful long time before she saw him again. Orion smiled at her tenderly trying to ease the heaviness which both would have to bear from that moment on. A piercing ache pricked her heart, as tears blurred her vision, she fled the forest in a haze. The way home was exceedingly short since she ran away with all her might from a situation beyond her maturity. Mistress Flora and Master Lorean were away at work sparing themselves the sight of their heartbroken daughter. Koren locked the door to her room forever safekeeping the flood of tears that furiously wanted to leave her body. It was a sad state in which sleep triumphantly whisked her away from sorrow. Crying had left her body exhausted, although even in her dormant reprieve her rage and impotence made her body tremble.

Morning arrived full of gloom, the dense fog seemed to be a dark presage of ills to come. Koren left her room feeling that she had slept a hundred years, for her body was heavy and achy. Her parents had not bothered her slumber, for what she was immensely grateful. The thought of having had to sit through an evening bottling her sentiments was unwelcome. The house was silent; her parents were sleeping in, giving her the perfect opportunity to head back to the forest unnoticed. Fear pulsed through her veins; the sensation of an impending emptiness pounded her chest fiercely, almost taking her breath away. The forest sounds suddenly became sinister cackles and the usually clear stream had become a grey serpent ready to strike. The mist had not relented to the sun, its thickness a burdensome veil whose wetness made friends with the painfully cold air. Approaching the cave, a second wind of hope made her run as fast as she could, forgiving the elements. Koren was at the entrance, where merely by noticing the absence of a warm fire, her worst fears were confirmed. The devastation of reality sank in collapsing her knees to the ground. Orion had disappeared without a trace, as if his stay at the cave had been an imaginary blink of the eye. The all too familiarly furious and impotent tears were unleashed at her abandonment. Feeling as if she hated him a bit for letting go of her so easily, a crushing weight descended upon her soul. A part of her tried to understand and assimilate the situation, it was better for both that he had left at once. Another part of her trembled with the desperate hurt of truncated love interlaced with lost illusion. Once again, that cave would be just another place in the forest. Devoid of the promise of finding hidden within it the lovely green eyes of the most beautiful man in the world.

Koren was unaware of time, remaining crumbled in a trancelike state, until her defeated soul told her it was time to go home, or anywhere else for that matter. The forest had shaken off the morning mist allowing the sun to percolate between the foliage. Air seemed to cleanse with its purity, which Koren's embattled nose due to incessant crying, greatly welcomed. Instead of heading home she kept walking towards the palace, the thought of facing her parents made her sad, they would know something was amiss and make demands. She didn't want any of that, speaking to anyone was not in her plans. Lies would have to be told again and again, since she could never speak freely of that secret love hidden in her heart.

The palace was up to its daily routine and business. The irony of life's ability to unfold in spite of people's sorrows was not lost on her. The workers saluted her with courtesies as she walked on by, and the women smiled timidly as they went to their stations, uncaring of the empty smiles she returned. Koren went up to the queen's office intent on finding Althea to let her know she was coming back to the official routines of court. The ladies and the queen were congregated there when she arrived.

"Koren! You had us worried. We had an important meeting this morning and we were not able to find you anywhere." Althea informed relieved to see her, although mildly upset.

"My apologies. I went to walk in the forest early and lost track to time. I noticed that I had been gone for a while, so I came back here directly. It wont happen again."

"Fine, and as soon as we are done here go see your mother. She was very worried..." Althea scorned.

"As you all know, Violet is still indisposed, her condition is not momentarily the best. We hope this improves, but I'll have to remain completely in charge of the lot of you. We will convene here in the morning as usual; I think it's best to keep things as close to normal as possible. It has not been the same without Palea, but we must go on. We are allowing easier entry to the knights in the tower, turns out they have to seek the King's Counsel more frequently than I thought. You will come upon them more often and I expect that you respect formalities, also that those gallant men don't make you misbehave. As a matter of fact, Marussa, please refrain from enchanting them, if they got lost in the tower it would be embarrassing." Althea couldn't suppress a laugh after her words of caution. The women shared complicit glances and giggled. Koren was the only one devoid of a reaction, since her heart only belonged to one man, regardless of his absence.

"One more thing, it has come to my attention that in a couple of days it will be Koren's celebration of life. We have all had such miserable times lately, that I think a ball fit for a lady of Bandah's court is in order." Althea announced excitedly as the other ladies shrieked with delight. Koren couldn't be more chagrined, but had to suppress her disdain with smiles of pretend joy. From that instant Koren lost track of what the others said, although arrangements for her party seemed to be going full steam ahead. The unexpected thought of having to invite her parents and some of her friends from her past life popped into her head uncomfortably. All she wanted was to be left utterly alone, and here was life seeking more opportunities to torture her. The meeting ended as Koren was lost in retrospection, thinking about all the events that had come to pass in very few days. Her life had been so simple before then, she had not known death, pain and love so closely that they touched her. The memories of her days in the forest came back, the playground games with her friends at the castle, and the carelessness that she gad grown accustomed to.

The image of a girl her age sprung to mind as if it were the specter of a memory, yet she knew it to be real. Omira, her childhood friend suddenly reappeared out of nowhere, to remind her that there were people somewhere else whom she cared about. Koren knew exactly where her friend would be at that moment, seeing the repeating routines she lived so many days, replayed in her mind. The castle's youth would be out of their lecture halls running wildly, dirtying their clothes and leather boots, through the castle's markets and walls. Gripping nostalgia commanded her to walk the castle's maze to reach the place where she new her friends would be. Just as she had foreseen, a group of kids of different ages had gathered to run about, chat or play games on one of the castle's courtyards. Koren approached them silently, observing their antics with envy, thinking about all the things she could no longer enjoy. Not one of them had seen a body dismembered in battle, or have had to kill, nor would have to wear heavy and constrictive clothing. None of them would have to suffer an insolite love.

"Koren!" Her friend noticed her and ran to embrace her. Instinctively Koren tried to protect her clothing from the dirty girl, taking a few steps back. Omira stopped her effusive welcome embarrassed by her appearance, although gleefully smiling at the nice surprise.

"Hi, I wanted to come see you." Was all that Koren could say before finding herself surrounded by the inquisitive glances of the group. The girls admired the beautifully crafted dress Koren wore, regarding the distinguished lady her friend had now become.

"You've come to play with us?" A boy from the crowd jeered.

"No... I have better things to do than dirty up. I only came to see my friend." Koren replied with newfound arrogance, when indeed what she really wanted was to join their boisterous games. Omira smiled and looked around with pride, feeling very special for having closeness to a lady from the court.

"Why? Do you need a servant? Funny, a servant for the servant..." A girl nearby mocked Koren causing the eruption of laughter amongst those present, and making Omira blush with shame.

"I guess what defines a peasant is its lack of manners. Luckily, in the palace we are taught how to treat lesser people." Koren condescended, inciting offensive hollers from the youths in general. A tall girl broke apart from the group, coming face to face with Koren, where she made a small gesture with her hand. The magic took Koren completely by surprise; it was not very strong, but very effective. She felt the earth suddenly glide under her feet, landing with a hard thud on the ground. Omira ran to her side to help her sit, while clumsily trying to dust off dirt from Koren's delicate gown. Koren incorporated furiously, her eyes and cheeks burning with rage. Shoving Omira to the side, she held her hands in front of her without stopping to think about what was about to happen. A potent light sphere sprung out of her hands completely engulfing the figure of the girl before Koren in flames. A piercing scream paralyzed everyone present, and as it continued, the children started to run about in every direction screaming in terror. All the girl's body was covered with an intense fire; her desperate cries for help were testament to the pain she suffered, as she tried in vain to put out the flames with her hands. Soon the girl collapsed to the ground squirming with terrifying spasms and ready to lose consciousness, her body unable to take anymore. Men had been alerted and had returned with buckets of water to put out the fire, only to stand in disbelief at the terrible scene playing out in the courtyard.

"Koren put out the fire, she's going to die!" Omira yelled a desperate plea. Koren couldn't hear her, overtaken by the perfection of her magic. A small crowd had begun to gather around them in order to help; yet the bucketfuls of water that people dared to toss at the tortured girl were of no use. Soon they started to yell at Koren, insisting she relent, yet afraid to come near her. Soldiers immediately responded to the cries for help amidst the chaotic scene, some of them racing to the palace for help. One confident soldier tried to put out the fire with his own magic and failed, then he pointed his finger to the sky producing a ray of red light pointed upward, to signal distress. A sudden burst of color appeared in front of the crowd, raising more shrieks of alarm.

"What is going on?" Althea's authoritative voice boomed as her impressive figure commanded attention. People stepped away, some crying and gasping in despair, as the young girl vomited and convulsed on the ground. Althea ran to the burning figure recognizing it to be a magical fire, and then placed her hands upon the body making futile attempts to stop the attack. Terrified and surprised she looked around to find the author of such despicable magic. Althea's eyes fell on Koren, who stood observing the burning in a trancelike state. Omira stepped out of the crowd to address the witch.

"It was she!" The girl pointed at Koren in tears.

"Koren! Only you can stop it, do it now!" Althea ordered with a hiss, making Koren come to her senses. With a swift gesture of her hand, the fire disappeared as if it had never been there. The flames had extinguished like a soft whisper, as the girl gasped for air on the ground, unaware that neither her clothes nor body had burned at all. Those present gasped at what had transpired in the hands of a young girl, glaring at Koren as they finally departed.

"Take her to the palace infirmary at once!" Althea ordered the soldiers, who did her bidding immediately. The remaining soldiers dispersed the rest of the crowd and sent the children home to their parents. Omira approached Koren to say farewell, but only found rejection from who was at one point a good friend. Koren pushed her away forcefully, upset that Omira had pointed her out to Althea. The girl didn't say a word, only walked away from Koren with her head sadly hung.

"I don't know what to say." Althea walked to Koren full of ire.

"I only defended myself, she used magic against me." Koren declared flatly.

"That was no self defense, that was torture! I fear for you, how could you use such powerful magic in such a way? I don't know if we could teach you what you need to learn in the academy... we can merely guide you. From tomorrow on, report to class at midday. I don't think it is worth the risk of not properly educating you about magic." Althea seethed.

"I'm sorry, Althea. After I did the magic I was frozen, I couldn't believe I did that." Koren pretended remorse, when in fact; to her surprise she had thoroughly enjoyed herself.

"Each of our actions is a valuable lesson; today you have lost and gained something. Pray you don't forget. I'm glad to see remorse, but I think it's best that you remain secluded in the palace for a while... until this shameful episode is forgotten. Lest people demand that you be properly punished." Althea walked hurriedly grabbing Koren by the arm.

"Punishment? Like what?" Koren asked alarmed.

"The use of black magic is a crime, you would have a trial where you'd get a fitting punishment. However, most of the time it involves torture and death, and you are too young and ignorant to face that. Lets hope your youth and inexperience also convinces others of the same, and they assume it was a youth's game gone awry. I will speak to the queen about this, but I warn you; this is the only time you will be spared. I will have no more black magic from you…"

Koren didn't notice any indication that word of the incident had spread in the palace; people didn't seem to regard her differently. Walking over to a nearby garden close to the fountains, she sat to enjoy the delicate rose scent and the lull of the flowing water. Inevitably revising the magical event that had come about by her doing… Aware she had lied to Althea after denying she didn't know what she was doing at the time, when in fact she did. All along her intention had been to torture the girl, too see her roll on the ground begging for mercy… humiliated. The experience had been cathartic for Koren, her own pain subsiding to witness the one of another. Pride welled up inside her with the secret knowledge that not even Althea, proclaimed to be the most powerful witch, couldn't overtake her magic. Omira's image came to mind, bringing with it a profound sadness. The relationship that they had once shared had inevitably and irrefutably been severed forever. Emptiness fell upon her, tears rolling down slowly to anoint the loneliness she felt. The harrowing thought that in the span of one miserable day she had lost her only love and her best friend wounded her heart. This way and so early in life Koren began to know solitude, which could be further felt in times of suffering. The turmoil in her life had her in such a daze that she failed to notice someone approaching.

"Good afternoon, milady." A masculine voice startled her, making her swallow her sorrows at once. Trying to be seen presentable, she wiped her tears away before turning to the visitor.

"Good afternoon, milord." She smiled politely.

"Are you well? I don't mean to intrude… I was walking and saw you here…"

"No, I'm fine. I have just been affected by the blooms…" She explained.

"I have recently joined the king's men, I'm new to the palace. On top of that, now we have to operate in a new area, it's making it harder for me to get to know anyone." The young man offered.

"Welcome to the palace. I'm new here as well, although I think I've seen you before with the other knights… And really, I'm fine." Koren spoke timidly accepting the handkerchief he took out of his vest.

"I'm the youngest of the knights, just like you are the youngest of the ladies… we already have something in common. Furthermore, I know who you are… the lady that saved our queen. My name is Kanek, and I come from Astra." He kneeled requesting to kiss her hand, she obliged charmed by his antics.

"I guess you know I'm Koren. I was born and raised in Bandah, right in this castle. My mother is the Head Royal Cook and my father works at the stables." She replied taking her hand away from his calloused ones.

"My dear parents are the military chiefs in Astra, my mother trains the soldiers in martial arts and my father leads them to slaughter." He chuckled.

"Quite a violent breeding you have... I'm surprised you didn't join their ranks over in Astra." She mocked him amicably.

"I told my parents I wanted to see the world, then my father talked to a friend of his, that heard through a friend of his and so forth, that the king of Bandah had lost some men recently... Surprisingly, the king offered me a place in his court, just like that. Of course, I had to show off my amazing military skills in a ridiculous joust, but here I am."

"You are funny, and I'm glad you are here. What is Astra like? It's so far away..." Koren was curious to know.

"It's a little different than here, much colder and white. We have lovely cities in the clouds, of orb like nature, overlooking the main city. We also have a magical forest; it is quite the adventure to go in there. I'm no good with words I can't describe Astra properly. Even though these two kingdoms were founded about the same time, I tend to think of Astra as the more progressive one, when I got here everything seem a little on the rustic side. Of course, Bandah is not behind, it's just a matter of stylization." Kanek flashed a wide grin.

"Sounds interesting, someday I'll get out of this castle... I might dare to visit your faraway kingdom."

"Perhaps the day you do, I'll be glad to show you around." His words made her blush instantly. Silence prevailed as they looked away to different corners of the landscape, searching for a place to rest their gaze that wasn't one another.

"It has been a pleasure, milady. I best get back to the king, he might need the services of a dashing knight. If I'm not mistaken, I shall hope to see you soon." Kanek curtsied.

"Yes, actually... I enjoyed having someone to talk to." Koren willingly offered her hand to him, who kissed it smiling. Kanek left glancing over his shoulder a few times and smiling, his tall and agile body maneuvering the garden's paths effortlessly. Koren let her gaze wander to the firmament, trying to escape Orion's image, which inevitably came to her. He would already be far away, doing who knows what... Probably trying to survive or feed his dreams of power...

Her soul wrenched with the turpitude of power, then her thoughts fell on the queen and her royal gowns... The ostentatious nature of the court helped her understand Orion's regard for his place in life. They had all come to be nobles by a struck of luck, their title brandished by their bloodline, none more deserving than those they ruled. Orion's claim to power had been as meritless as any noble's, yet he was fighting for his place in the world. For better or worse, Orion was taking reins of his destiny. Mistress Flora had emphasized that if one wanted something badly, it was their duty to get it. Nonetheless, images of broken bodies and the bloody mist of battle complete with the clash of weapons and screams poisoned her reverie. Wondering if that was what fate had prearranged for the dead, or if it was Orion's sole responsibility to cut short their dreams. Some lived, some died... is it easier to believe it was fate?

The question as to what she wanted more than anything arose in her mind. The answer was unique and absolute, Orion. Fear gripped her after reaching this conclusion, for the consequences were astounding. Not forgetting that she was placing her happiness in the hands of a man who'd rather have a throne. This fact didn't faze her, love had vanquished, she felt the anguished tightness only obstinate adoration could impart. A more sinister though crept into her mind, this time asking to what lengths would she go for Orion's love. Once again, the answer was firm; she would go as far as she needed to, and do whatever it took for him. Finally rising from the bench, beset by a strange heaviness, she could barely grasp all the compromises her soul carried out for her beloved. Her leaden steps carried her to the queen's tower, where she entered her apartment with the intention of living there. Perhaps the new belongings and surroundings could offer some solace. Ringing the service bell, she waited to inform the maid that she would now reside there and expected to have proper staffing. Next, a bath was in order, followed by dinner in the main chamber, after which no further service would be requested. The maid prepared everything as specified and instructed the other servants their new duties. Koren ate in her room, aware that for the first time in her life she was doing so by herself. Her heart sank as she remembered having forgotten to tell her mother that she was fine, or that she would spend the night at the palace. Mistress Flora's smiling face appeared to soothe, however she set it aside, convincing herself that it was time to relinquish the maternal bonds and prepare for what lay ahead.

The following day Koren woke up surprisingly refreshed. Apparently her eloquent display of magic the day before had left her bereft of negative energy for the time being. Finding Althea would be easy at that hour, for the ladies would be getting to the queen's office any minute. As expected the witch sat with a look of preoccupation behind the large black desk, sifting through a pile of documents and frowning.

"Good morning, Althea. Excuse me, I'm here for instructions..." Koren announced her presence quietly. The woman looked at her and smiled, inviting her to seat.

"Good morning, and congratulations. All the papers and such arriving from the library are thorough and pertinent, it's a shame I can't read as fast Violet. You have done a good job. Oh yes, I did make arrangements for you to go to the academy today, head over at noon and find the East Wing. Erasmus, your professor will be on the lookout for you. It should have been my duty to personally instruct you, but as you can see things are a bit complicated for me right now... He is a wise teacher, make sure to speak to him loudly, he is missing an ear. Oh, and please, do not attempt to do magic while in there." Althea warned sternly.

"He is missing an ear?" Koren said as it was the only thing that had piqued her interest.

"Yes, he put it for safekeeping somewhere, just in case he went deaf from the other one. Of course, he then forgot where he put it. At least that is what he says..." Althea raised her brows insinuating there was more to the story, but without further comments went back to her work, dismissing Koren.

The walk to the library gave her plenty of opportunity to think about the little tidbit of information Althea had mentioned, thinking it was such a strange tale. The library duties made the morning melt away in a hurry and the announcement for the arrival of midday came too soon. Gulping some soup she had ordered from the unseen tenants of the library, Koren left at once to the Royal Academy feeling unbridled excitement. Stepping lightly she smiled at the thought of mastering the magic inside her, certain that she would excel above the others. The gigantic palace that housed the Royal Academy was a monstrosity overflowing with ornate windows that allowed light to come in from every angle. The walls were made of highly polished golden marble, which warmed the sight more than the touch. In the main edifice there were three large doors full of inscriptions, Koren assumed it must be some ancient language she had never seen. Wondering how could a simple human open one of those doors, she placed her hand upon one of them, and it gave way easily. Holding her breath, she spied a multitude of impossibly silent students inside the threshold. Large wooden signs with gilded letters indicated that to the right was the East Wing and to the left, the West Wing. Following a chattering group of students, the East Wing seemed to be the next stop.

A large hall, where a group of about a hundred students awaited engaged in civil conversation, preceded the East Wing. The majority of them seemed to be about Koren's age, while others seemed to be to old to be anywhere. As they saw her walk past, the students curtsied aware of her status in the palace, which made her stand out more than she would have preferred. A bench close to one of the windows seemed to be the perfect place to wait until summoned. Her dress was making her feel fatigued, she wasn't sure if it was because of her nervousness, or the large amount of bodies in the place. From now on she would try to remember to wear light clothing whenever she left the palace.

Koren felt a little let down when she saw the multitude of students; she had assumed that she would have private instruction with some sort of warlock. A cooling breeze refreshed the hall and brought everyone to attention.

"Welcome." A raspy voice announced from the back of the hall, and the group as a whole tried to seek the owner.

"We shall divide into groups to make things easier for everyone, preferably by age. Young learners up to the age of fifteen please stand at the back of the hall. Those sixteen to twenty five years of age come to the front, any one else stay in the middle. My name is Erasmus and I'm in charge of beginners, if you have any questions please wait and soon you will have the opportunity to find answers. The group on the back kindly head through this door and up to the first floor, the group on the front head to the second and the last on to the third. If you loose your way you are not qualified to be here! Now go meet your professors and good luck to all..." Erasmus evaporated into thin air causing a momentarily sensation of panic and chaos, the disoriented groups looking similar to angry ants.

Koren remained observing patiently from her bench, until most of the crowd cleared, it didn't seem wise to have to stress over a spot in front of the line if they were all heading to the same place. Her group went thorough another set of doors, this ones made out of red glass, leading to a spacious classroom full of comfortable chairs. Erasmus awaited their arrival smiling behind a podium at the center of the room. Once every student had found a place, he nodded pleased at the orderly way in which they had done so and smiled, showing a glimpse of very sharp teeth. Koren observed him more intently after realizing he was a dragon, specially the way he was covered from head to toe. A short black velvet tunic descended from his neck, barely covering leather pants of the same color, while his hands were gloved. His hair stood out as a wild fortress of matted hair on his head, although it was quite similar to a pile of cobwebs. Koren saw that indeed his left ear was missing.

"You have been chosen to be here due to your affinity with magic, and the first thing I will inform you is that we will teach you nothing. Only you can unleash the powers you possess, our only hope is to guide you in the journey to reach that potential. We hope your magic will help make a difference in the world... " Applause erupted from the enthusiastic students.

"You will find a revised manual of instruction in the side pocket of your seats with the lessons we will cover as we progress along. It is our duty to explore magic and make it grander!" Erasmus shouted with excitement.

"The first thing I will ask of you is to take a moment to think... One by one I will ask you to come here and show me some sort of magic. Or at least make an attempt at it. Obviously, it has to be appropriate to a lecture hall! I will let you know when time is up." Erasmus happily welcomed the boisterous excitement that surged from the students, although having to pound the podium to restore order. Koren looked around to see the rest of the group concentrating hard, their eyes focused on the ceiling, or out the windows. Some pressed their hands to their foreheads desperately seeking thought while other tapped quietly at their armrests trying to extract an idea. Nothing was occurring to her, although an intense desire to prove herself to others as a powerful being gave her a sense of urgency. Letting everyone know that not even the mighty Althea could trump her magic would have been a great start, but she didn't know what the decisive display ought to be.

"We shall commence." Erasmus words took Koren by surprise, given that her mind had upturned every idea she could conceive and nothing seemed practical enough. Erasmus long finger fell on a young boy in the middle of the room, indicating that he would be the first one to show his magic. The student was probably of about fourteen years, his face burning ferociously with embarrassment as he bravely walked to the podium. Erasmus towered over the nervous boy, but gave him a comforting pat on the shoulder as he stood next to him.

"What is your name?"

"Otes of Pandea and Munz."

"Otes, show your skill." The young boy hesitated for a second then opened the palm of his hand where a beautiful white rose bloomed to perfection.

"Excellent, child, what a beautiful manifestation you have produced. Have a seat, next is you..." Erasmus' finger selected another young boy. He introduced himself and when it was his turn to show his skill a violent gust of wind shook the hall. As the magical displays continued, Koren was taken aback by what she witnessed, feeling horrible and knowing that when her turn came up there would be no skill to show. She was well aware that her incursions in magic had been unintended and very dangerous.

"Now you." Erasmus words finally landed on her. Somewhat heavily she waded though a sea of curious glances, courtesy of her royal garments and beauty, towards the reviled podium.

"Your name, milady." Erasmus asked out of courtesy, since her royal garments betrayed her identity.

"I'm Lady Koren of Lorean and Flora, sir." Koren replied as her heart thundered.

"Show us your skill." Erasmus observed her intently. Koren looked around at the expectant faces, opening her mouth to speak, only to falter. Feeling humiliated, tears were threatening to barge in and siege whatever remained of her pride. The dragon raised his eyebrows questioningly.

"I have something to tell you..." Koren whispered inaudibly, her voice breaking. Erasmus, unable to hear her, realized something was amiss and turned with a funny gesture to present his good ear. The students laughed out loud as he put his ear almost into Koren's mouth. As she was about to confess that she didn't know how to use her magic well, a sudden burst of inspiration hit her.

"The ear you are missing is hidden inside a diamond in the lost cave of Muzka, where you slept for hundreds of years after your true love abandoned you. You took it off desperately trying not to hear her voice anymore..." Koren whispered the words so that no one could hear. Mysteriously, a large diamond appeared in her delicate hand, but there was nothing in it. She reached for Erasmus' trembling hand and placed the stone in it, making sure no one saw the move. Erasmus instinctively took his other hand to the left side of his head, realizing with a gasp that after going amiss for many years his appendage was in its rightful place. The dragon leapt away from her, making some of the students startle. However, given that no one had paid attention to his missing ear, its sudden arrival went unnoticed. Confused looks started to surface amongst the students, along with the suspicion that the girl from the palace had no magical skills.

"Well...good, I... I will be back in a minute..." Erasmus babbled confusedly, as Koren returned to her seat, ignoring the imprudent stares of others.

"Don't feel bad, for some it takes time..." A girl nearby tried to console her.

"Oh, yes... I know. Thank you." Koren avoided facing the other students, focusing instead in the scenery out the window. Erasmus returned to the room a little afflicted, as if he had lost his inner peace. Again he took his place in the podium facing the eager learners.

"Lets proceed with the magical skills presentations. You there... come on." A young girl was next, and she showed how she could make a little squirt of water come out of her hand. The very last student to show a skill impressed the class by turning his skin a variety of intense colors.

"Unbeknownst to you, you have already passed the first basic lesson given in this class. The reason you came up here was not to show your magic abilities, but to show your courage. Courage is fundamental to great magic, for it is directly connected to your self-confidence. Magic must be certain, hesitation can lower your guard and your strength, thus reducing the effectiveness of whatever you intend to do. This could have dire consequences, as you can imagine. I cannot emphasize enough the importance of believing in your capacities. The only one who dictates the outcome of your magic... is you. Questions?" Erasmus paused to accept inquiries.

"So what happens if someone is more adept in magic than us? Not everyone can do the same things..."

"You are right about that. We have different aptitudes, but part of your self-confidence is knowing your strengths, it is those that will help you succeed. We will do some exercises to find your fundamental strengths; it will help you find the proper skills to build upon that. Even though one magi seems more powerful than another, if he has greater mental agility, or appropriate mastery of his strengths, this could balance things out in any situation." Erasmus replied and continued speaking to the class.

"In the back of the room there is a basket full of stones, please grab one. All the stones are equal and their magical powers are neutralized. Consider those stones your practice boards, for upon then you will attempt your magical lessons. Some of you might be bored to tears with the basic principles, but please go through the motions, we must all be moving at the same pace. We cannot build a house without a foundation, and when we practice the same concepts over and over they become a natural part of our actions, as magic should be." He motioned for the students to get their stones.

Koren felt prying eyes on her, but everyone seemed to be concentrating in the menial task of picking a stone. Suddenly turning, she surprised Erasmus staring at her, who turned away quickly as if being caught partaking in a hideous offense. Returning to her seat stone in hand, she defiantly looked him in the eye expecting to hear something, although nothing happened.

"Now that you all have the stones, place them in your dominant hand, it is easier to focus your energy on something rather than deciding at the last minute how to else to release it. With time this will make no difference, just follow instructions. Now hold the stone tightly, you may close your eyes if you wish, and think about your first magical manifestation. If you haven't had a full one yet, concentrate in something that satisfies you. It could be reading, running, cooking, clouds... there are no limits. But it must be proper; this is only a practical lesson! The stone will take the form of your fundamental magic. This only implies the channeling of a primordial force to your advantage, through your best outlets, we all have many forces inside us." Erasmus paced the room, hands placed on his lower back, overseeing his student's efforts. A young woman jumped out of her chair, soaked from head to toe, when her stone turned into a plentiful stream of crystalline water.

"You have the power of water. Remember this, it will be your strength. Water is a powerful element, which nourishes and destroys life. It will respond to you, it will make you stronger. When you use your magic think of it as a stream, let it flow and it will take the proper course." Erasmus explained while he made the water disappear, returning the stone to the girl. A young man began to wrestle a vine that had sprouted from his stone and was trying to entangle him.

"You have the power of vegetation, plants are your friends, except perhaps for this one. I assume its behavior it's due to some unrelated issues, come see me after class." The dragon made the plant retreat into the stone, while the student panted glad to be safe from it. Slowly, most students began to find their powers, although most were a repetition of others. Erasmus raced about the hall controlling the magical mishaps released every so often.

"Those of you who can see a reflection of yourselves, do not worry, you are not narcissistic. That is the manifestation of being able to see into the future, or reading the minds of others." Erasmus continued his lesson.

Koren squeezed her stone thinking hard about the first time she had used magic; undoubtedly it had been in the palace, ever since she had burned the queen's gown. The stone began to heat up, and as Koren thought about fire, it began to turn an intense orange color. A white flare burst out of the stone similar to a diminutive burning gust of wing, setting her sleeve on fire. In spite of its intensity the fire didn't seem to cause her any harm. Erasmus ran to her after seeing the propagating flames menacing to take over the hall. He quickly put it out taking the stone away from Koren.

"Dragon fire of such purity, impossible!" The old dragon exclaimed outraged uncaring if the others heard him. He stared into Koren's eyes mortified when he was unable to read her mind.

"I have not seen a creature like you, white fire belongs only to white dragons, the most feared of us all. Althea warned me about you, but this is unbelievable. You must leave; the others are in danger if you practice here. Come to my study after suppertime, I think an hour or two of training in the evenings will be sufficient for you. You can go to the palace or stay here to watch, but I cannot let you join us." Erasmus offered regaining his composure. Koren stood up straight and returned the hot stone to Erasmus, who had to appease the heat with some appearing water. She departed with her head held high, for now there would be no doubt about her power. Delighted with the looks of admiration and respect cast on her, she savored the triumph of being more than a pretty face.

Koren decided to go see her mother after having neglected her for so long. Entering the kitchens and their comforting familiarity made her smile happily. The welcome of the tinkering pots, the chatter of the cooks and the swishing sounds of blades on cutting boards were music to her ears. Going by the bakery, she dared to steal the customary treats, while the baker turned to see who was putting their hands on his beautiful trays. The man turned beet red and frowned.

"You again! I have told your mother that I don't like you coming here and taking anything you want from my station. This is not a sty, it is a royal kitchen!"

"Master Obreu, I would hope you use some caution when you speak to me. Must I remind you that I'm a noble lady at her majesties' court, your impertinence could cost you dearly." Koren purred taking a delicate bite of a sugary confection. The man sealed his lips firmly about to explode with fury, yet he curtsied as protocol called for when greeting a noble.

"Besides, these desserts are disgusting, they are all burned." She said calmly. Upon hearing these words the baker rose incredulous, offended by the terrible accusation. Quickly, he went to inspect the trays bearing his culinary works of art, to ascertain that they looked just as he remembered. To his surprise and horror, every single treat had inexplicably burned to a cinder.

"No! That is impossible! I worked all night on these, they were perfect just seconds ago…" The man screamed ready to faint, burying his face in his hands, and weeping bitterly.

"I guess you have more work to do." Koren smirked and moved on to her mother's station. The baker's wails thundered in the bakery as he tossed the trays in anger, clamoring for his assistants to come at once.

Mistress Flora, who was calmly slicing the fillets of a large fish, heard the scandal and raised her head to come face to face with her daughter.

"Koren! Where have you been? Have you forgotten you have a mother? A father? We had to be notified by a guard that you stayed in the palace! What is going on?" Flora exploded angrily impaling the fish with her knife.

"I'm sorry, mama. I didn't think about it..."

"How could you not? Your father is looking rather ill thanks to you; you better go see him soon. Apologize for you wretchedness, Koren!" Flora took a deep breath and exhaled heavily, calming herself down, then walking over to embrace her daughter. Koren took a step back seeing her mother full of fish blood and other unsightly decorations, rejecting her affection.

"Mama, you are going to ruin my dress!" Flora's eyes looked hurt, she took a few steps back and returned to her fish.

"Yes, you are right. I will ruin your beautiful clothes... And what is with all that noise coming from the bakery? Hope you didn't have anything to do with it."

"No, I don't know what's the matter. That baker is insane."

"Don't ever speak ill of others, you were not raised like that. The poor man has been having a hard time lately, his youngest son is dying from a work accident, and the healers can't help him any more." Flora informed her.

"The less of them the better." Koren shrugged as she sat on a nearby stool.

"What is wrong with you? I have never heard you speak such poison before; you better start minding your words. You are now a young lady and inappropriate behavior is not pleasant, ever. Just tell me what you have been doing lately..." Koren briefly related her recent occurrences, editing information as she saw fit. Flora was unpleased with the news that she would have to study with Erasmus after supper, thus moving in permanently into the palace.

"You knew it was going to happen someday, the moment I accepted the queen's invitation the palace became my home. My apartment is wonderful and I have my own servants, there's even enough room for you and papa to live there..."

"We'll never leave the forest. We belong there." Flora emphasized the last words.

"Also, they will hold a royal ball in my honor, to celebrate my birth!" Koren exclaimed gleefully.

"But we always celebrate at home, together as a family. Remember I always make you your favorite wild strawberry tart?" Her mother said with sadness in her voice.

"Oh mother! I'm not a child anymore; there will be a ball in my honor! The whole court will be there, even the majesties, to celebrate me! It will be a beautiful event, Anari is going to make me a special gown, unique..." Koren explained to her mother as she ignored her crestfallen countenance.

"No one had told us anything..."

"Maybe Althea hasn't had a chance to. She has been busy with the queen's affairs; it was her idea in the first place. I'm sure you will be invited." An uncomfortable silence stood between them. Both were thinking about the possibility that an invitation was never intended. Koren realized that this prospect didn't bother her at all. The thought of her mother, obese and flushed, wearing a wildly colored tunic caused her disdain. So did her father's antiquated leather attire. They would embarrass her in front of everyone with their peasant presences. The thought that perhaps Althea hadn't invited them for that reason surprised her, it would be unlike the witch, for she prided in being just and fair.

Koren remained in the kitchen for a couple of hours complaining about having to assist to the banquet hall with the other nobles too regularly; a special feast for the knights had been planned this time. It would be the first one where the ladies and knights were to be formally introduced to each other in a more social context. Given that until recently they had led separate lives in different towers.

"I had seen the knights before, but I met the youngest one recently in the garden. We will be able to socialize a lot more, although it doesn't matter, they all seem too serious to have interesting conversations with. The young one was nice, though..." Koren commented casually.

"Appearances can be misleading, of course they have to be serious. They are not the jesters! The knights' carry on official royal affairs, we have lost many over the years. They must be reputable men, they act as envoys to his majesty, traveling around the land in his name. Imagine if a drunkard came to visit in the name of the king, disastrous! Although, it has happened..." Flora nodded at Koren's disbelief.

"A drunkard! And then what?"

"What do you mean what? The dungeons of course, he's probably still there... drunk as ever." Flora let out a hearty laugh. Shortly after Koren left her mother's side in a hurry, hoping to visit Erasmus and have enough time to come back for the planned events later in the evening.

The Royal Academy was eerily silent, missing the heat of the living. Koren wondered if she was supposed to go to the lecture room where she had been earlier, or wait for the dragon there. Erasmus firm steps' answered her question echoing down the hall as she turned to face him.

"There you are. I wasn't sure you were coming with all the activity in the palace... Lets go to my study it's more comfortable there." Koren followed him aware of the vibrations her steps sent through the empty hallways. His study was cavernous, cold, and yet mysteriously welcoming.

"I really don't know what to do with you... I imagine all you are missing is figuring out the proper use of your magic at will, and the rest will happen naturally. I have been seeking information about your particular magic, and there have been but a handful of documented cases of humans with white dragon fire. I can safely assume you also have elven blood."

"My father is half elf, no one knows though." She responded.

"Nor they will, it is best that it's not known that he is half dragon as well. You know the matter of mixed races; some people can be profoundly ignorant when it comes to that. Some dragons in particular, like to keep the purity of our breed, being of the opinion that only wisdom deserves power. Thanks to our longevity wisdom usually comes to favor us. These dragons also believe that humans are not worthy of dragon magic, they see them as lesser beings. Regardless of all that, who are we to judge? Who am I to judge? No one rules in the heart, if one of your grandparents was a dragon, consider yourself lucky." Erasmus grinned.

"What if it was an enslaved dragon?" Koren offered trying to excuse her ancestors, not because she agreed with the dragon's ideals of breed purity, but because a more sinister reason could exist.

"You know too much. But you could be right; someone looking to have powerful descendants could have enslaved a dragon to procreate. But enslaving a dragon is no easy feat, any dragon can defend itself ferociously, even a young one."

"Yes, but a dragon can easily become a slave before its fifth year, they cannot control their powers as well." Koren thought out loud.

"How do you know this?" Erasmus observed her.

"I read it at the library where I work, anyone has access to that information." She replied casually.

"You are wrong, only people with the Royal Seal have access to that library and its secrets. Keep this in mind; it is your duty to protect that information at all cost. Someone with the wrong intentions could find unimaginable power by accessing a lot of those books..." Erasmus paused briefly then added:

"Imagine what a horrible act it is to subject a child, be it human or dragon into slavery. Who can rip out a child's heart?" Erasmus declared with such force that Koren jumped from her seat in alarm.

"My apologies, I didn't mean to startle you. I think it is best we go on with the practical lessons before we run out of time." The old dragon declared more to himself than to her. Time raced by, and progress was made quickly, for Koren showed great aptitude to instinctively learning magic. When it was time to go, Koren had already managed to hold rein to most of her powers. Once she figured out the affirmation that magic was similar to a tool, she could bid it at will.

"There are no secrets when it comes to magic, as you have noticed. Just clearing the mind of beliefs and limitations is enough to embrace the idea that magic always resides in us. Always." Erasmus bid farewell to the girl with those words. Watching her joyfully skip away to the palace, he sighed fearing the power he had just released upon the world. Koren was still thinking about the recent discovery of her father's fantastic lineage. The humble man who spent his days at the stables taking care of beasts had secret magical powers beyond what she had imagined. Curiosity overcame her, wondering incessantly about her grandparent's identities. Her father never spoke of his family, or his past, everything she knew she had heard casually from her mother's mouth. After a warm bath she went to bed to ponder those queries at leisure, but sleep had other plans for her.

The following day, Koren was anxious to speak to her father. Her duties at the library seemed extraordinarily long and tedious, making the morning drag. On top of that, she was sure that Anari would come find her at any moment to make her try on another formal evening gown for the night. The thought would normally please her but it would mean another distraction that kept her away from talking to her father. Heading out of the library, she bumped into Lenna, who carried in her hand a lovely bouquet of purple blooms.

"Koren, it's been a while since we talked. I know there hasn't been the opportunity we are so busy. Look, I'm working on the floral decorations for tonight. Our nightly events are taking a toll on me… Congratulations, I heard from Marussa that you are training with Erasmus; he's one of the oldest dragons in Bandah. Maybe even in the world!" Lenna shared, her agitated wings thrilled with emotion.

"Yes, he is very wise. I'm lucky he is my mentor. Can I keep the flowers? They are beautiful; I've never seen them before… I'm somewhat excited about the banquet too; do you think the queen will go?"

"Of course, she barely gets out of her chambers. You missed when we took the mermaids to her room to cheer her up it was a lovely concert. The midwife says that it could be anytime before Violet improves, she has seen worse cases. I hope she gets better soon, I miss the old routine and Althea is on the edge. We are deambulating though the palace bereft of our queen! Except for Talma, she's got a lot in her hands right now." Lenna confided.

"Why?"

"Of course, you didn't know. Talma has a daughter, just starting to spout fire. The servants refuse to enter her apartments, which is partially burnt, so Talma spends her day with the girl. It's only temporary, control will come to her soon, if someone can get results it would be a dragoness."

"I had no idea. Funny, Erasmus and I recently discussed young dragons…" Koren was pensive digesting the new information. She was aware that every twenty-five years dragonesses without a mate would automatically have offspring, an evolutionary tool devised to ensure procreation of the breed. The young dragons would remain with their guardian mother until the age of five, more or less. Once the dragonlings gained mastery of their magical powers it was usual for them to be released in a magical forest to fend for themselves in life.

"You should visit them sometimes, the girl is adorable and Talma is glad to have someone to talk to." Lenna suggested.

"Maybe I will. I got to get going…it was nice talking. Need to visit my dada he is not feeling well, and the library has taken too much of my time. Thanks for dropping that on me."

"Better you than me." Lenna smiled, stuffing the flower bouquet on Koren's hand and walking away. Koren was relieved to see her go without having to dismiss her the way she had had to the last time she saw her. There were no more interruptions on the way to the stables, where everything was quiet. Master Lorean was away sitting in a clearing close to the stables, feeding two magnificent unicorns some fruit.

"Papa!" Koren called as she saw her father's languid frame. Lorean's face brightened at the sight of his daughter and he walked to her to embrace her.

"Oh, so you have appeared. If it weren't for your mother's updates I'd never know you no longer existed." Lorean recriminated as the unicorns curiously gazed at her, their manes flowing silkily in the breeze.

"I have been busy, I am a lady after all. Also, I have been studying magic, albeit briefly, with Master Erasmus… " Koren proudly informed.

"Yes, I heard about that, you mother mentioned it. How is that going?" Lorean asked visibly uncomfortable.

"Turns out I have Dragons' Fire. White..." Koren decided to tell him the truth without hesitation, knowing that he would know the significance of those words.

"So you know then..."

"That you are half dragon too? Now I know, but I want to know more. I want to know what you are capable of doing. I want to know about my grandparents." Koren demanded.

"I suppose it's time that you know your bloodline, but I must emphasize that no one should discover the truth. Some dragons would persecute us, since they believe that only pure dragons deserve their power. I have lost all my siblings this way; you had two uncles and two aunts. All their families were also savagely eradicated; I only escaped for looking more like the elven kind. My mother never spoke of my birth... When I was very young she left me to the care of a humble human family that took me in as their own. We lived close to my parents whom I visited frequently with the pretext of learning the care of magical beasts. They had a beautiful castle in the outskirts of Bosia. My parents were persecuted until their last days, and even though my father a ferocious warrior, he had let go of his immortality to age with my mother and was easy prey. They decided to let go of this world, to reunite with the universe... Before they did they brought me he here to this castle, where I'll always be protected." Lorean's voice was burdened by the past.

"Why will you always be protected here? Why couldn't come here too?" Koren inquired only a couple of the million of questions that her father's relate had unleashed in her mind.

"They gave up... I will always be welcome here because I'm a member of dragon royalty, even if some won't accept it. This is quite the conundrum for humans, since the royal bloodline of dragons supersedes that of mortals, or even elves. Although so many years have passed that no one remembers or cares about me, or my family. And I prefer it to be this way..." Lorean explained. Koren felt he was holding back much more to the story, as she observed him in awe.

"Papa! You could be the king!" Koren yelled about to explode, her thoughts bingeing on uncontrollable revelations. What she had heard made her look at her father in a different light, and herself too, for she was a real princess.

"I do not want to be the king. I have never wanted to. I have told you I lead a simple and happy life here, working in the stables. Living in my lovely home with my beloved wife and daughter. I'm not afraid of being killed now; I can live a peaceful existence... I want not for riches or power..."

"Can you turn into a dragon? Can I? Do you spit fire?"

"Yes to all... Now listen to me! I am Master Lorean, the beast caretaker; I'm not a dragon, or a wizard or anything of the sort. And you are... Koren. The girl of uncommon beauty, that grew up in a little house in the heart of the forest. Is that clear?" Her father asked emphatically.

"Sure... Who were my grandparents then?"

"My father was Arund-Dena, from the most ancient and revered dragon family. He was the heir to the throne of the Arund family, until he met an elf maiden by the name of Oma. They fell hopelessly in love, causing a furor amongst their races, for both do like to keep purity of the blood. Arund-Dena forsook the throne, causing a war amongst the royal dragon families to establish themselves as supreme rulers.

Our race was decimated by the senseless wars, most surviving dragons lost interest in political affairs, while some hibernated possibly forever. Still, there were those intent on regaining power and restoring the race to its glory. Arund-Dena's existence and connection with an elf made him a sizable thorn on that path. He began to fear the possibility that he could be enslaved, a prospect worse than death, so he asked Oma to rip out his heart. My mother accepted and kept it hidden in some secret place, safekeeping it from the enemy. He didn't mind being mortal, as long as he was with her…" Lorean held back the tears the loving memory of his parents was bringing back.

"I'm sorry papa, I didn't wan to make you suffer." Koren embraced her father.

"I only want you to understand that there are reasons why the past must stay there sometimes. If the truth were found out, I don't know if I could defend you, or myself, dragons are creatures of great and incomprehensible power. Whether they are good or bad. I want my life to go on as it has for the last centuries, calm and quaint."

"Don't worry, our secret is safe with me. I've seen what dragons are capable of and I have no intention to have one come after me." Koren laughed trying to ameliorate the tension. Master Lorean agreed and smiled, stomping his boots on the ground to clean some of the grime in them.

"Papa, what are you doing? Look at all this dirt you are putting about!" Koren was mildly angered by the dirt frying in every direction.

"Oh yes, mind the pretty lady. I think you better head out to the palace I need to finish here. I hear you have a lot of prettying up to do, your celebration is tonight and you should rest. Althea came to invite us this morning, so we'll see you there."

"Oh, that… You know every night there is something going on over at the palace. They have to make a special something for a special somebody of a special place… At least I get to have a place by the queen and a special dress. Lenna has found some fantastic flowers to decorate the halls, and they have brought in mermaids." Koren spoke with elation, giving him a quick hug before departing. She was on her way to a quick library visit, with the hopes of finding additional information about her ancestors, when a masculine voice made her jump.

"Hello, Lady Koren."

"Kanek! You scared me." She said recovering from the impression.

"Please excuse me, it was not my intention. May I walk with you? I'm bored. The bad thing about times of peace is the insufferable idleness for people like me." Kanek smirked.

"So you'd rather there'd be conflict? I'm sure the king can find something for you to do. Aren't knights supposed to assist to the government councils to be up to date with the political affairs of the kingdom?"

"Yes, you know too well… But it is not mandatory. Besides, I get all the information from the others. I'm the youngest one, my opinion is rarely requested and Aken is the king's assistant. He's is the one that needs to be at the official meetings. You ladies run the castle and have more executive power than we do, all we are good for is fighting." He complained.

"That is boring." She agreed.

"It makes no difference, all castles operate by the same rules. Sometimes I just have to escape to the city. Bandah is quite enjoyable, it has great markets and the architecture is lovely…"

"I've never been to Bandah." She declared.

"No, that is a shame! Why don't you request permission to go with me next time? Tell Althea, I'm sure she won't mind you taking time off. Besides, you will be thirteen summers of age and you are old enough to travel on your own." He offered excitedly.

"Oh, so you heard of the ball in my honor…" Koren blushed.

"I'm looking forward to it. Tonight I will wear my best outfit just for you." Koren didn't reply, lowering her head with embarrassment. They soon realized they had inadvertently walked over to the garden by the palace, where she abandoned the idea of visiting the library for fear that he would come along too.

"In a couple of days I was planning a visit to Bandah, and I'm very serious about my offer to with you there." He blurted shyly.

"I think I will talk to Althea, but I should go now, I better be rested you know how it is…"

"Yes, life at court could be exceedingly taxing. I hope that at least you will confer upon me the honor of a dance, or two, or three…" Kanek smiled broadly. She smiled back and watched him wander off, suddenly feeling an inexplicable turmoil in her. Unable to sort her sentiments yet, she was indeed glad to have found a friendly diversion at the palace. Up to that point she had not felt any desire to strike a friendship with the ladies, mostly due to the guilt she felt for being a traitor. Perhaps Kanek could offer a respite from all the incessant novelties that seemed intent on plaguing her life in unbearable ways.

At her apartment a group of maids, decorated the place with colorful garlands and flower bouquets. An incredible delicate cover of soft grass replete of wild blooms had replaced the carpet on the floor. The laborious women stopped briefly to greet her.

"Good day, Lady Koren."

"Good day, it is. Thank you for making my dwelling so beautiful."

"Lady Anari awaits for you at her atelier as soon as possible." One of the women informed her. Deciding to go to the workshop at once, seemed like a fitting idea, rather than watching the women decorate. It was sort of strange to watch how adept in magic the maids were, almost as much as any of the members of high office. Although it made sense to allow them to use magic, the majestic upkeep of the castle demanded it. Koren walked at leisure through the upper halls, then tapping with sharp clacks the marble steps on her descent to the tower's third floor. There she noticed an increase in activity, as hurried assistants scurried about carrying large rolls of fabric. The outer courts of the floor were noticeably vacant, devoid of the usual activity. The large doors to the theater were invitingly open and the glorious melodies of a string instrument ensemble filled the air. In spite of wanting to stop and take in the music, Koren moved on to the clothing workshop.

The exquisite gowns were already standing in attention at the fashion hall, displaying the colors for the night, turquoise and gold in honor of Koren. A dress with a wide train caught the girl's attention, its delicate embroideries of pearls and thread of gold against an intense turquoise, were breathtaking. It was similar to the many depictions of the shimmering sea that she had swooned over for many years.

"I'm glad you finally made it over here. I wanted to know if you liked your dress..." Anari spoke.

"Is it this one?" Koren asked full of excitement.

"Of course, not. Don't be silly, that is for the queen. Yours is right over here..." Anari led the disappointed girl to another dress, that although majestic paled in comparison to the other.

"What do you think?" Anari said taking pride of her creation.

"It's beautiful, thank you." Koren replied pretending to be excited, when it fact she was bothered that even when it was supposed to be her night, the queen still would be the most important person in the hall.

"I picked the colors thinking about the loveliness of your eyes."

"That is very accommodating of you, I never dreamt I'd own such a lovely piece of art." Koren acquiesced.

"Excellent! I'll have it sent to your chambers, try to be ready by the afternoon, it will be a long affair. I heard that even the queen of Astra and her king are coming..."

"What? I can't believe it!" Koren was genuinely surprised.

"Of course all the Vice kingdoms were invited too, it is customary to send an official word, but to have a visit from Astra's royals is amazing..."

"Sounds big." Nervousness invaded her, for she had never thought of herself important or noble, and the reality of her new position finally sunk in.

Koren was hiding away in her room, reading some non-impressive reports about the kingdom when a maid rushed to her.

"Lady Koren, you must come! The guests are arriving! The Nubian Dragons are about to land!" The woman was about to faint from excitement, gasping for air as she relayed the information. Koren stood up calmly, allowing the maid to lead her to the place where they could spy the arrivals unseen. For some reason no one had thought to visit the observatory to watch the sumptuous arrivals. Koren realized that it was possible that everyone else in the castle had seen the spectacle before, leaving her alone to watch with the maid. From the side of the observatory's terrace one could clearly see the landing clearings, as long as one didn't mind the steep altitude from where they observed. Koren leaned out as far as she dared to admire the large congregation of witches and dragons that had just arrived. Amongst them an ancient woman of long white tresses descended from a beautiful white dragon.

"That is the queen of Nubis." The maid pointed out.

"She's very regal, but my, she looks extremely old."

"Oh yes, it is rumored she is past eight centuries old. She is an elf, and knowing how little they age, she must be older than time." Koren and the maid shared a laugh at the thought.

"How come there's no one else here to watch the people arrive?"

"Every one has seen this before, but I never tire of watching. There are too many fancy affairs going on at the castle, you'll get used to it. I fetched you thinking you'd like to see this, but if milady is bored we could go back inside."

"I figured..." Koren shrugged her shoulders and continued to watch the clearing. Seeing the amount of dragons transfiguring into humans to join the queen of Nubis left her surprised.

"That queen must be very powerful, there are a lot of dragons with her. Do you think they are all slaves?"

"The horror! That is unspeakable! The dragons are there because they chose to. Enslaving a dragon is a terrible thing... You should never speak so casually of it, specially here in the castle, milady." The woman warned sternly.

"I'm sorry, I didn't mean to offend you..."

"No need to apologize, you didn't know that it was not proper to talk about it. Just beware, there are many dragons around us and it is best to be on their good side. Dragons feel like they don't serve anyone, they are only friendly to other races. I think since they've seen the results of conflicts, they want a peaceful coexistence with others. They do prefer tranquility after all." The maid explained. Thunderous calls of approaching horns gathered their attention, as another large group arrived, this time by land. An army of people riding bison like beasts spread slowly through the grounds, as large caravans came to the forefront.

"Oh, the Amazons have arrived! It is the vice kingdom of Yesén, all the way from Astra. I didn't think they would come, perhaps they've here to visit Violet as well, due to her arduous pregnancy. They rarely leave their land... That tall woman full of muscles at the front is their queen, Ylana." The Amazon queen stood out by her stature and sculpted physique, her hair was long and green. In her hands the woman carried a large silver bow that seemed to weight as much as a farm horse.

"I better go get ready, I'm afraid I had underestimated the whole event." Koren gulped as she stepped away from the edge of the stone railings.

"You still have plenty of time, there will be more arrivals, and their pomp makes them take their time." The maid chuckled.

"It doesn't matter, I want to be alone. You can stay here for a while if you like." Koren offered and walked away without waiting to hear a reply. The truth was that she couldn't bear the sight of Cyrus people arrive, knowing that she would be affected at the sight of them. The flood of memories would definitely swallow her and drown her for the night, knowing that it would not be Orion arriving with pomp. Atle would arrive, an unbearable thought at the moment.

At her apartment it was easier to occupy the mind with the preparations for the ball. The maids would come promptly at the sound of a silver bell, yet they remained uncalled. Koren dressed herself in spite of the arduous task of managing the fancy gown singlehandedly; her desire to be left alone was that much more important. Regarding the image of a beautiful young girl staring back form the mirror left her breathless. Her face betrayed the roundness of her tender age, with velvety skin not kissed by time, and ferociously turquoise irises that spoke of immaturity. Soul searching in those eyes, she felt lost seeking for the idea of the girl that she once was. Had her destiny been written on her face it would have made things much easier, for she wouldn't have to know uncertainty. She had the face of a queen, but would she ever be one? Orion had promised... Queen. The word circled her thoughts hissing poisonously, with the knowledge that she had more right to throne than the current occupant. If that were the case, no longer the inferior dresses would be sent her way, and no longer she would follow... she would lead. Ironically, she was part of one of the most honorable and ancient races, and there she was serving a lesser one. Closing her eyes to quiet her mind, and trying to send the erratic thoughts to the heinous pit they had ascended from to torture her, was futile. Something inside her aroused from a long dormant state thrashing about her soul like a frenzied beast. As her eyes found her again facing back from the mirror, the discovery that peace had abandoned her forever leaving instead ambition, glared at her. Perhaps she did not have an army, but with her cunning she could get to the throne faster...all without having to completely denounce her dragon blood. The knowledge that in her power were the secrets of the Royal Library illuminated in her mind, the answers must be waiting for her. She accepted the fact that somehow she would be the queen; the affirmation left some calm behind, similar to that felt by those who have stopped searching for something precious. Greeting and welcoming the Koren who would carry on this new destiny without looking back, there was no hesitation or fear...

Lady Koren sat in her study quietly staring out the window in her finest garbs, waiting to be summoned. Thinking someday she would hold balls for the distinguished guests and the preparations would be different. The thought of the crown of Bandah sitting upon her brow also made her smile; she would be a glorious and beloved queen. These thoughts didn't seem strange or foreign anymore, after acceptance comes the contentment of settling without prejudice or doubt. Once she became queen, she would find Orion and give him a royal pardon, so that they could be together forever. Blushing at the prospect of being kissed over and over, of sharing sensual caresses as lovers do while discovering each other, made her tremble. She would finally hear the proclamations of love that she longed for. For a moment she was ashamed of such sentiments, knowing that she was too young in the eyes of others to be a lover to anyone, but there seemed to be no ill in secret fantasies of love.

The maids finally came to call on her, advising that it was time to meet with the rest of the ladies at the queen's main office. Pretending to be calm, in spite of the thunderous emotion banging in her chest, she filed elegantly past the maids. Lightly elevating herself from the ground to gain some speed, the fabric of her gown floated like a delicate veil in the mist. Pumzi was the first one in sight at the hallway, a living doll made up for a fancy magical stage.

"Watch out! You are going too fast, Althea is going to knock you out again." The dwarf joked amicably.

"Nerves. I can't wait for it all to get started, the buildup has been unbearable." Her words were true, for other unspoken reasons.

"I can imagine it's your party. I do enjoy all these festivities and productions. It is nice to see you, how long has it been? I miss seeing everybody, the queen better get herself together soon."

"I sort of like it. It's good to have the liberty of going wherever I want and not have so many meetings. Come to think about it, the way it was, was rather a bland palatial routine." Koren commented.

"What? You are already bored of the palace? I've been here much longer than you and I'm still fascinated by it. You have to find a way to enjoy life here, there is a lot to do and the meetings are only but a fraction of your time. I travel a lot in official trips you should explore that option. Marussa and I recently escaped to Albah it was stupendous. Perhaps we could all get away together!" Pumzi suggested full of excitement.

"Sure." Koren replied noncommittally, pretending to like the idea. They reached the office and found that the majority of the ladies were already there. Althea and the queen were the only ones missing. Koren realized with dismay how much her dress resembled those of the other ladies, therefore not standing out at all. The discovery bothered her tremendously, for she had contemplated the glory of being special that night. It didn't matter, when she became the queen she would always be the center of attention. The thought brought along a deep sense of shame and guilt, her mind becoming a treacherous path of ambivalence. One moment she knew she would be the queen and the next she was horrified for thinking such a thing. At least her mind was safekeeping those thoughts from others, for if they realized the ambitions seeded in her, they would brutally dismember her with their hands. Talma would possibly swallow her whole...

The light chatter in the office was interrupted by the arrival of the queen. Violet's constitution was still seemingly frail; her skin was ashy and her body thin. There was no visible bump in her gown to indicate a pregnancy. Forgetting all her thoughts of glory and power, Koren ran with the other women to joyfully greet the queen.

"Your majesty you look fabulous!" Pumzi joked.

"Oh thank you, I know. I wouldn't have missed our lovely Koren's celebration for nothing in the world. I don't think I can make it through the whole event, but I will try. I don't feel guilty not showing up at banquets and such, but this is a special ball." Violet spoke softly, visibly making an effort to stay animated. Koren wondered if the healers were not telling the truth, perhaps there was something else wrong with the queen and they had to keep it a secret. Violet still looked stunning in spite of her ailments, the fragility of her semblance gave her an ethereal character reminiscent of dreams.

"My dear Koren, you have now lived thirteen years and enter a new stage in life. It is a difficult one, for these coming years mark the transition you will experience into full womanhood. Most of the time you will be frustrated by the limbo you'll inhabit. Stuck between the worlds of adulthood and childhood, one barely crediting for your ideas, the other boring you to death. The only thing I can advice you is to be patient. Life is an evolving process and everything you undertake from this point on will help to shape you into the woman you will be. Don't let go of your childish illusion, but don't lose yourself to it either. The world is always different to what we perceive there is unexpected despair. You have the advantage to carry within you immense power, which I hope you will use for all our sakes and good." The queen spoke tenderly holding Koren's hands in hers, silver eyes fixated on the girl's. The ladies approached, some tearfully, reminiscing youth and relating to the moment. Marussa embraced Koren, trapping her under an aroma of garden flowers with her strong ebony arms. All the ladies followed suit, embracing her with joy. Althea was the last one to hug her, and after she did so she presented her with a small wooden box.

"It's a small gift from me." The queen smiled as Koren accepted the box. The girl opened the gift in a hurry, to discover a beautiful bracelet in its interior. The jewelry was made of clear precious stones that shimmered more than luminous stars. Koren was breathless beholding the stunning acquisition.

"Thank you, this is incredibly beautiful." Koren declared as Violet helped her put the bracelet on. The other ladies chattered admiringly and remembered the joy of celebrations past.

"I think is time we make our way to the grand hall. The guests are there ready to celebrate." Althea interrupted. The queen nodded and stood in place, while the others lined up in formation behind her with the exception of Althea. The witch came to Violet's side to assist her as she walked. The queen had refused adamantly to be carried into the hall regardless of how fancy a small carriage could be made.

The queen's entourage paused at the threshold of the grand hall allowing the pages to announce their arrival properly. Koren began to perspire and her heart didn't let up on its boisterous excitement. The sight of the grand hall exquisitely decorated, the multitude of important invitees and the glow of the chandeliers formed a knot in her stomach. Searching the hall her gaze fell on her parents, sitting at a table close to the queen's. Astonishingly they both wore clothing suited for the stature of the event. Mistress Flora wore a chestnut tunic that complimented her skin and her hair had been coiffed elegantly. Master Lorean wore an elegant black outfit similar to those the high-ranking officers of the castle would wear to fancy events. He stood out majestically from anyone in his proximity, obviously incommodated by the lack of anonymity. His elven blood and then some were impossible to hide; curious glances were already eyeing him with suspicion. Koren felt great pride in him, secretly knowing that he had more royal blood that any one person in that room could possibly imagine. Pushing the thought aside she faced the crowd taking her place in the procession. The queen sat in her imposing throne as the king sat in a smaller one next to her, the ladies continued to be seated at a table on the left facing the guests. The trumpets flared to announce the beginning of the ball after the chancellors had an opportunity to address the crowd and welcome them to her majesties' palace. After that, every dignitary and their groups would present a gift to Koren after paying their respects to the queen. Each would bring something more beautiful or more amazing that the previous, leaving Koren in a state of utter bewilderment.

The queen and king of Astra were a sight to behold and they gave her a chest full of diamonds, and a diamond-encrusted tiara, which Queen Risa of Astra gladly placed on her head. The woman smelled like the freshness of the open prairie, and her sparkling white gown accentuated the long golden curls that framed her lovely face. Queen Risa complimented her on her beauty, kissing her cheek to wish her happiness and prosperity. King Olan gave her a light sword of unquestionable value, and then he kneeled to kiss her hand, making Koren feel faint. The second largest group of visitors also came from Astra. Koren thought that since the monarchs were there this was no mere coincidence, for it was the Amazon warriors from Yesén.

That entourage had impressed her like no other from the moment their large drums began to overtake the hall. She had been entirely fascinated. About twenty Amazons marching in perfect formation walked in, five women per row playing the drums. The women played an exhilarating military song that stung the ears but electrified the hall. Half way through the song the group split in half and yet another group of twenty women came forth with their weapons at hand. The movements of the platoon were precise and sharp, the blank faces of the women intensely focused on the military exercise as they reached for their large bows in unison. Each woman grabbed a silver arrow, which they unhesitantly pointed at Koren and those next to her. Koren stared in horror at the sharp points of the lethal arrows aiming at them, screaming in alarm as the women released them. She instinctively flinched waiting for the painful and swift death that was certainly soon to follow, only to be met with an intoxicating smell of jasmines. Koren opened her eyes in awe realizing that a new group of Amazons was headed towards her, and that the arrows had become large bouquets of flowers spreading all over the floor. She gaped at the women approaching, for each was enchanting in their own way. The women were tall and robust regardless of age, and each stage of a woman's life was represented. It struck her as odd that even with all the differences the women seemed like a large group of sisters. The most common hair color amongst the Amazons was the forest green they were known for, which shone intensely as the forest leaves do. The elder women stood out for the purity and abundance of their white hair that they carried in dreads and braids tied to their bodies. The Amazons wore simple clothing, the most ubiquitous a light brown suede tunic that was reminiscent of faded leaves. Some wore a simple linen tunic and leather pants.

The Amazon warriors stood out by wearing a light chainmail tunic, which fell delicately over their visibly beautiful breasts. They wore leather pants of a mossy green color and leather gloves that made for a tight grip on the arch of their bows. Koren appreciated the details with enthusiasm impressed by the existence of such a group of people. The Amazon queen came forth, easily recognized by her royal demeanor and poise. The woman's stature was astounding as well as the defined musculature visible in her lithe body. She had long hair of a deep green color whose braids strangely wrapped her limbs, similar to the ivy plants. Queen Ylana wore a simple gold crown that matched the glow of her skin, and a necklace of gold and precious stones. The necklace showcased the fullness and beauty of the lactating mother's bare breasts. In her arms, the queen carried a naked baby girl that clung to her mother shyly. Whatever else the queen wore was similar to the warriors, with the exception of a sharp golden dagger that hung from a belt at the hip. A young woman standing by the Amazon queen and wearing a gold tiara came forth with a small metal crate. Queen Ylana made some strange gestures to the girl and the girl offered the crate for Koren to take.

"It is your present." Queen Ylana smiled.

"This is my sister Cirya, she's deaf mute. It is an honor for us to be here and present you with this feline; these cats are valuable warrior companions in our land. They are highly intelligent, excellent trackers, ferocious and loyal." The queen continued as Cirya took out of the crate what seemed to be an inoffensive and fluffy kitten. Feeling liberated the cat stretched out its limbs and roared with surprising strength. Cirya got closer to Koren, placing the small animal in her arms, which then unhesitantly climbed on to Koren's shoulders. The cat stayed there quietly purring as Koren tried to peek at her new companion. She saw the animal had long and soft white fur with brown hues; its whole tail was the color of dark bark.

"You are her owner now, she has accepted you." Ylana informed her nodding in agreement. The Amazon queen made a small gesture with her hand startling the drums to life once again. With precise movements the group gathered into orderly rows ready to depart, it was then that the Amazon men's existence was noticed. Like their women counterparts the men were of impressive physiques, however, they wore simple suede clothing and seemed unarmed.

After all the presents had been given and all the pleasantries said, the ball officially began to the delight of those present. Tables were brimming with delectables in such large quantities that it would have been impossible to try every single dish. Smiling witches tempted the guests with bubbling drinks while fairies the size of hummingbirds spread mists of euphoria on the crowd. The mist feel upon their heads in a sparkling drizzle, which upon touching the skin made people feel the kiss of the summer sun. Koren walked delightedly amongst the people, having briefly spent time chatting with her parents. Mistress Flora had surprised her by ordering wild strawberry tarts be made for all the tables and Koren was very grateful for her favorite treat. Master Lorean was quiet and feeling out of place, refusing to talk to any one for fear that they would want to know more about him. As she thought what to name her new animal companion, Koren saw Kanek bee lining to her with a smile on his face. The thought of running away momentarily invaded her, but she resigned to his company.

"You look lovelier than ever, milady. The queen must be pleased to have such a precious jewel on her crown... Anyway, I wanted to see the little critter the savages have brought you." He joked as he tried to reach and pet the cat. The animal responded by hissing and presenting some surprisingly ferocious claws in an unfriendly strike.

"I believe she is not pleased with your comment about her people... Isn't she beautiful? Her fur is incredibly silky." Koren retrieved the cat from her shoulders to cradle her tenderly in her arms. The kitty stayed put pleasantly all the while keeping a suspicious eye on Kanek.

"I think I'll name her Neroli. I've always liked the sound of that word; it's so exotic, just like her. Kanek smiled trying to fall in good graces with the cat, which started to purr and look around.

"Neroli is an excellent name. Do you think she would let me take you away for a dance?" Kanek extended his hand invitingly nodding towards the dance floor.

"I've never really danced…"

"It doesn't matter, tonight you set the standards. There is always a first time for anything and it would be my honor to dance with you. We are close acquaintances now, let me whisk you away." Kanek reached for her hand, which was still petting Neroli, and the cat showed him sharp teeth.

"It is alright Neroli, it is my ball so I better dance. It is no use to turn down an opportunity, and waiting for things that will not come to pass…" Koren spoke confusing Kanek. She said the words out loud for she had thought the reprehensible idea that any moment, in some corner, she would find her prince. Wishing that he would surprise her motioning to come over for a forbidden kiss in the garden, after having risked everything to be at her celebration. The passing of each minute had sadly convinced her that her hopes were nothing but silly ideas. Orion was far away from her, possibly not sparing her a thought.

Once within the dancing crowd, the fabric of the colorful gowns grazing each other, the laughter and the music forgetting was easy. Koren gave herself entirely to merriment, setting aside the feeling of sorrow that had briefly possessed her. The tower bells finally announced the pre-dawn hours to the few remaining at the hall before being heeded. The queen and king had made an early exit, while the rest of the crowd slowly drifted away to their beds. Koren's feet were unbearably sore as she liberated them from her leather slippers. Neroli followed her silently towards an outer terrace with a balcony facing the gardens, where she could enjoy some solitude. Her parents had gone back home happy and exhausted, having danced more in one night their whole lives. The cat purred in her lap as her gaze greedily swallowed the beauty of the night sky. The blackness enveloping the world was similar to a cape embellished with star brocades. Giving in to the hopeless desire of having her prince close to her, she beckoned his deep green eyes and tender smile. Upset when his image was not sharp, his memory seemed to be dissolving slowly. Repeating his name over and over in her mind, and intent on fanning the waning embers of memory, her lips could not take it anymore. Orion was the word with which her lips exploded, releasing at once the angst that piled in her chest. It was a sole magical proclamation of love, unexpected and uninhibited. It laced itself with the wind traveling to reach a far away place and landing in the hazy mind of a broken prince. Orion was at an island in the middle of a tempestuous sea, facing death once again. Having failed his mission of retrieving the magical seashell from its demonic gatekeeper. The prince opened his eyes recognizing the soft call of her lulling voice, renewing his desire to live, knowing that somewhere far away she needed him… and loved him.

Chapter 5: Slavery, death and tears.

After her birth celebration, not many days seemed to differ from the ones that passed. Koren found herself in the constant company of Kanek, fact that she wasn't sure she liked or disliked. On a bright sunny morning he sent word with her maid that he had made preparations for a due visit to the city. To her surprise Althea confirmed the plan when they saw each other at the queen's office. The funny smile Althea bestowed upon her made her feel somewhat uncomfortable, especially when the other ladies gave her teasing smirks. Violet had ordered that before leaving to the city Koren must visit her chamber, the queen had been placed in bed rest due to her advanced pregnancy. Koren was delighted by the request since she hadn't seen the queen for a while and was getting used not to. She went full of curiosity to the majestic suite where music filled the air, and the ever present smell of jasmines attacked the senses.

"My lovely Koren, I'll be brief... there have been several requests for me to allow you to leave the castle with one of the knights and I have agreed. Protocol would have the members of our courts separated, but I don't believe in those arcane rules. I see fit that you make friends with a young man close to your age, and Kanek is a well-educated noble. It could be a prosperous relationship for you..." The queen spoke sipping from her tea. Koren felt the need to clarify the extent of her relationship with Kanek then decided against it; perhaps it was to her advantage.

"We are only friends, he is aware of this."

"Oh, I know. I'm just giving my whole hearted approval, that is all." Violet answered with the same little smile that Koren had noticed earlier in Althea.

Koren left the room bothered by the situation, not able to understand the furor amongst the ladies that her friendship was causing. What she didn't grasp was that for the other ladies, living alone and wishing for a partner, the concept of falling in love was extremely appealing. Althea waited in the hallway and chatted the whole way to the palace's exit where Kanek stood ready to go. The man standing there was surprisingly unfamiliar; there was something in Kanek's demeanor that suggested there had been a change. He wore the official regalia of a proper king's knight, which was a black leather military jacket adorned with silver insignias and the king's crest. His black leather pants complimented the handcrafted riding boots he wore to make up the whole outfit. The darkness of his outfit seemed a fitting compliment to the depth of his ebony eyes and hair, while the silver accents of the garments complimented the golden warmth of his skin. Kanek was standing next to her Pegasus beaming at the thought of leaving the castle in her company.

"Oh, I hope you have a great day touring the city." Althea declared overtly giddy dispelling the silence that had tried to descend upon them. Immediately she turned and disappeared from sight as if wanting to unhinder some unforeseen event from taking place.

"I'm astounded at all the pomp just for a silly trip to the city. You'd think they were letting me go to some foreign land!" Koren exclaimed smiling at him for the first time since her arrival. He let out a sigh of relief and smiled.

"You have no idea all the promises I had to make just to get you past this threshold. Let there be no doubt milady, that I will defend you with my life if necessary." He rolled his eyes dramatically, which caused her to giggle.

"Zaur, I'm glad to see you." Koren approached the Pegasus who tenderly caressed her arm with his nozzle without saying anything else.

The trip to Bandah was brief, no more than a half hour, accounting for the leisure in their pace. The riders explored the world under the Pegasus' wings and pointed to many distinct details that stood out. Koren enjoyed the aerial view, full of lush green landscapes and beauty. The land was plentiful of little villages and farming plots, and as they neared the city larger settlements were visible along the magnificent city wall. The Pegasus' descended by the wall's entrance in the middle of a large avenue full of riders, carriages, carts and other beasts of burden. The chaotic scene came to a sudden halt after the arrival of emissaries from the castle was noticed. Their royal garments gave them away as important members of the court causing unbridled excitement on those present, who immediately wanted to see the visitors up close. Everyone alike succumbed to curiosity, falling on their knees as they realized that one of the visitors was one of the queen's ladies. The courtesies caused a bigger problem since mobilizing the crowd at that point seemed an impossible task. Koren blushed embarrassed by the situation their arrival had caused, unable to fully accept all the reverence that was being bestowed on her, but liking it very much. The lucky few who came in close proximity were left paralyzed by Koren's impressive beauty. Word had spread that one of the ladies in the court was the most beautiful maiden in the kingdom, but seeing her in person left people speechless. Kanek made way for them directing the Pegasus' towards the main entrance, trying to move things along and snap the city folk out of their trancelike state. Slowly, the pace of the crowded way returned to normal and people chatted excitedly about the royal encounter. They gave way to the newcomers without taking their eyes off of the beauty, even as children ran around telling what they had just seen. The news spread rapidly and the desire to see the beautiful maiden brought small crowds of curious onlookers throughout the streets. Koren instinctively shied away trying to hide her face, but Zaur gave a slight jump and made her straighten up.

"Do not hide yourself, you are who you are. It is their problem for not knowing what to do. It is not your fault that they can only stare imprudently." Kanek positioned his mount as close as possible to Zaur smiling and waving handsomely to the onlookers, seemingly unaffected by the situation.

"You have caused a commotion, milady. I assure you it won't last long. You have to understand that you are probably the most beautiful thing they'll ever set eyes upon..." Kanek teased.

"Very funny. I'm not a thing... I hope the novelty wears off soon, this is not going to be any fun if they keep staring at us as if we've come from another world." She complained.

"We are from another world! It is very likely tat they have never visited the castle. It is not commonly open to visitors as you can imagine."

"Indeed. I do remember how amazed I was about the castle and all its inhabitants it all seemed so wonderful. To think that now it all has become so mundane." Koren said relaxing and smiling at people, most of who salted with a friendly wave of their hands.

"We'll reach the city's garrison soon, we can leave the rides there and continue on foot. If you dare… Although it might not be a good idea with all the fancy garments you are wearing." Kanek observed her gown with a raised brow. Koren wore a gray silk dress with delicate sky blue lace, which was more of a formal dress than city garb.

"We always have to wear this stuffy clothes. It is all Anari's doing… She is always coming up with fashionable wear for each hour of the day, for every imaginable occasion and season. Of course, the queen allows her to indulge. Sometimes I think about all the material used for our luxurious clothing and wonder how many industries are we supporting in only one endeavor." Koren commented and smiled.

"That is severely unjust! We only get a few attires. We have our daily uniform, which you have seen me wear and this, our official outfit. Our gala uniform, you saw that too at your celebration and finally our burial regalia." He informed chuckling.

"Burial clothes? Are you serious?" She asked incredulous.

"Yes, traditionally when you become a knight you are warned that there is a high mortality rate due to all the conflicts we must engage in for the sake of the crown. Everyone gets their burial clothes, sort of as a reminder that we have forsaken our lives to the kingdom."

"Ha! Not even in death you can chose your fate! What are they like?"

"You only get to see the design, they have to be made to fit what's left of you when you die…" Kanek replied and looked away uncomfortably.

"Oh." Koren felt a sudden pang of despair at the thought of losing her dear friend.

The garrison finally came to view after they had weaved their way through the swarm of people and the daily routine. Kanek courteously saluted the sentry guard, who immediately replied with a formal salute and bowing his head at a nobleman. Another guard came to them hurriedly approaching the Pegasus' with great caution intent on assisting with the rider's dismount. Kanek gave the young soldier a curt glance making it known that he didn't need any assistance. The embarrassed young soldier immediately turned his attention to Koren, freezing on the spot as he saw her face. He tried to reach towards the bridle with trembling hands, trying to help her dismount and ready to offer his assistance. Kanek smirked at the young man derisively slightly pushing him aside to extend his hand to Koren and help her get down from Zaur. Koren laughed at the absurd expressions manhood on display and effortlessly dismounted unassisted.

"Gentlemen, it seems I've managed. Let's carry on." She announced triumphantly. Kanek did not conceal his contempt towards the young soldier, who noticed his unwelcome participation and wisely left right away.

"Sorry, I guess nothing inspires men to behave foolishly more than the presence of a beautiful woman." Kanek shrugged his shoulders.

"Nonsense. I do think men should have deep regard for women's delicate natures. Not because we are weak or anything of the sort, that is ridiculous, but because it shows that we are seen as something special."

"I see you as very special." Kanek declared looking away and blushing. Koren pretended not to hear his last words, although they raised an alarm in her mind. The fear that her relationship with Kanek was beginning to take a turn into something else began to materialize uncomfortably. In spite of the prying eyes of the city dwellers their passage through the city's streets and markets was free and enjoyable. Koren loved exploring every corner of the city with the fascination of a curious child. Loving the sight of the old structures curated by the esthetic eye of time and the polished cobblestones of the streets. It was a pleasure to observe slate color of each cobblestone, similar to the scales of a moving serpent reflecting the light, and the color of its transient population. Every so often a friendly person would approach them to present Koren with a bouquet of fresh flowers or regards for the queen. Koren would smile and accept the flowers only to give them away to people she passed.

"Are you hungry?" Kanek inquired as they approached the main plaza in the heart of the city.

"I'm starving. Where should we go?"

"You get to choose. Usually, I go and eat at the garrison; it's free food for all members of the military. I'm not sure the grub would be to your delicate palate's liking. It's food at its simplest."

"What? You have come here so many times and only eaten at the garrison?" Koren exclaimed in dismay.

"Well yes, I'm practical. I don't see much use of the waste of money for street food, when there is some available to me elsewhere. Besides, we eat daily like royalty at the palace, it is not like I'm left wanting."

"You have a point, but you are not right. Part of being away from the castle is experiencing what other people do, including how they eat. My mother is the royal cook, I've eaten the best meals in the world throughout my life, but still I'm curious as to what regular food is like. Lets eat what people would eat when they are out and about. I saw some food stands close to here and we could try it out."

"You win, lets do that. Let it be noted that you'll pick where and insist upon it." He laughed as they headed to the main plaza, which was full of activity. The markets were full of shoppers and the street food vendors were dishing out steaming plates of food, which people carried to communal tables nearby. People enjoyed the music of plenty of musical entertainers, while others read or chatted animatedly. A few brave ones would try to carry on a conversation close to the roaring fountain in the middle of the plaza that created a thick mist in its vicinity. Children ran about unbridled spreading joy, laughter and mischief in equal parts on the plaza as parents sat to take a break from their daily rut. Koren walked over to a small stand whose smell of freshly baked bread and roasted meat beckoned the senses. There was a line but people courteously made way for the young noble couple as they approached.

"What are you serving?" Koren inquired smiling. The cook stared in disbelief and briefly hesitated before answering.

"Milady, we have roasted goose, bison meat form Kaniba and local fish. Plates are served with a loaf of bread and fresh leaves." The man uttered in what he thought was a dignified matter.

"Sounds great! I'll have the bison roast, make it a generous portion." Koren winked flirtatiously nearly making the man faint.

"How about for the Sire?"

"Same. And some ale, the best you have."

"And the lady? What would she like to drink?" The man could barely look at her for fear of his nerves.

"Anything with berries in it. Please." Koren reached for her pocket to pay, but Kanek stopped her immediately.

"I will pay, it is my treat. Besides, I don't think that man has seen one of those coins in his life."

"What do you mean? It is good money, Althea gave it to me before I left." Koren commented confused.

"There's nothing wrong with your money, it is just too valuable. To get one of those this man would have to work day and night for a few years." Kanek whispered in her ear. Koren thought about it for a moment, realizing that she had no concept of money's worth since she had never had the necessity of using it. A server brought their food in metal plates full to the brim and large wooden cups with their drinks. Kanek gave the cook and the server some coins and they both grinned apparently pleased.

"Keep the change." He said and turned away. Koren followed him to a small table where they could sit to eat quietly. She experienced a pleasant feeling of freedom unlike any other she had ever felt, fascinated by the daily life of the city and its seemingly uncomplicated disposition. Koren felt such elation that when Kanek gave her an adoring smile she didn't check herself and returned a complicit one.

Nightfall covered their departure to the castle where they headed to the stables. Master Lorean received them happily to take the beasts to their stalls and formally meet Koren's charming friend. The old man and Kanek spoke amicably and comfortably, so much so that Lorean asked Koren to invite the young knight to their home one evening for supper. She tried not to pay attention to her father's open approval of Kanek, cutting their visit short by yawning incessantly. Lorean hugged and kissed her before sending her off to the palace as he made his way home for the night with the promise that she would return soon to chat. Kanek walked with her in high spirits, visibly giddy of having spent such a wonderful day in her company. Althea magically appeared at the palace's entrance, scaring them tremendously, as if she had been anxiously waiting for them. Koren wished Kanek a good night and headed straight to her apartment denying him the satisfaction of admitting that she had had a great time. Althea walked alongside hearing with interest about all the fun activities in the city, delighted to know that Koren had enjoyed the trip. Althea thought that it had been a while since she had left the castle and perhaps it was time to do so. In her room, Koren fell in her bed exhausted ignoring the maid's attention or the hot tea by the bed.

The following days evaporated in a blur of anxiety when the news came that the queen was about to start labor. The castle was suspended in a state of stillness every time Violet let out a sigh or a sign of discomfort. Koren and Kanek took advantage of the situation and the little attention paid to formalities to do as they wished. They would go on daily walks and neglect their palace duties, visiting places that they saw fit to entertain themselves. Together they would hunt, swim, read and explore the castle grounds uninhibited. Koren took him to her home in the forest, to show him where she had been raised, although never disclosing the existence of the caves, thinking that it was probably better if they remained secret. They walked carefree on a lovely forest trail, when suddenly Kanek came to a halt and motioned for her to be quiet.

"What is it?" Koren whispered alarmed.

"There is a strange smell in the air, I don't think we are alone." Kanek murmured scanning their surroundings.

"I don't really smell anything out of order, perhaps a little smell of something burning..."

"Precisely. There is no smoke and no visible fire, only one thing can smell like that... a dragon." He declared searching intently with his eyes, while she began to look as well with a new sense of urgency.

"Look! Those bushes..." She pointed to some vegetation that seemed to have burned suspiciously.

"Reveal yourself, it is an order! We are envoys of the majesties!" Kanek shouted the order with authority. Koren stood threateningly, knowing that Kanek would not have any defense against a dragon's attack, but she would have a chance. Unhesitantly, she formed a ball of fire in her hands ready to strike with lethal force, proving to the invader that she could stand up to a dragon. The tension increased when the bushes rattled ferociously. Koren was ready to strike when the figure of a small creature burst out of the foliage. This was no mere dragonling; the girl in sight was familiar to Koren, who recognized the pure pearl skin and baldness. She relaxed and let out a sight motioning to Kanek that it was okay to let down their guard.

"Kalani! What are you doing out of the palace?" Koren yelled with astonishment.

"If your mother knew you were out here she'd be furious! Its is dangerous for you to be out here!" Koren reprimanded the silent girl. Kalani hung her head sadly, looking very frail, especially with the humble chainmail tunic that hung from her petite frame.

"Do you know each other?" Kanek asked the obvious mainly to spare the little girl from Koren's fury.

"Of course I know her! She is Talma's dragonling. She's supposed to be locked in the tower; she has not matured yet, and has no control of her powers. Her presence puts all of us in danger, not to mention that she is vulnerable to attacks." Koren informed him visibly upset.

"Please don't tell mother, I'll return to the palace now. I'm just so tired of being locked away..." Kalani's soft voice pleaded.

"You have to understand it's for your own good, and for others, that you're put away. You will have many opportunities to get out once you are ready. Be patient, your mother is working hard to help you. Remember that you are not just like any other dragon." Koren was reproachful not caring about the tears in Kalani's red eyes.

"I know, I know, but what can I say! I didn't think I'd get caught out here..." The girl shrugged and wiped away a tear.

"Fine. Come along with us, we'll go back to the palace together. Kanek will have to follow a few paces behind us, lest you have an episode and turn him to cinders." Koren laughed letting go of her original upset.

"What about you?" Kalani demanded.

"I'll be fine. I will let you in on a little secret that you both must keep to yourselves forever. I have dragon blood, and not just any kind; I'm a little bit like Kalani. I have white fire... As you know, there isn't half a dragon, or a quarter dragon, you are either a dragon or not. I'm one, perhaps not as powerful as a pure one... but still. I hope the secret is safe with the two of you, the consequences could be fatal if you said anything..." Koren confessed.

"You hadn't said anything!" Kanek burst out surprised and offended.

"It is a secret, Kanek! Although I was going to tell you..."

"Is that true? You were going to tell me?" He replied very pleased with the information.

"Well, why don't you visit me more often?" Kalani demanded.

"I can't people would notice it and the secret would be out!" Koren exclaimed frustrated at the lack of understanding in the situation. The conversation became pleasant as they made their way through the forest dispelling any previous tension.

"This is not bad at all, maybe we can gather here in secret to talk..." Kalani offered shyly.

"That's not a bad idea, we can be like a special task force for the queen..." Koren smiled at the thought.

"As long as you both agree not to cremate me..." Kanek added with exaggerated concern.

"We better get close to the castle, if the bells toll it means that the queen is in active labor and I must be there." Koren informed.

"You are so lucky to be there when a baby human is born, mother says it is magical." Kalani spoke tenderly.

"I heard it is a disgusting affair..." Kanek laughed.

"I think it will be a girl, King Papo will not disappoint. He will give the kingdom a strong and intelligent queen, just like Violet." He continued talking with his chest full of pride.

"It is a boy." Kalani mocked him.

"What do you know?" Kanek confronted the dragonling offended.

"There are a lot of people that already know what the queen is bearing, but it is prohibited to speak of its gender. You know that a boy would not bring as much happiness as a princess would. The queen has chosen not to divulge any information." Kalani clarified.

"Then it is a boy." Kanek stated astonished as if the thought had to sit in his mind for a while before being fully assimilated.

"I don't. I only said that to mess with you." Kalani joked making the group laugh for a while.

The trio slowly continued on to the palace where they parted ways to their respective places. Koren was saddened by having to face solitude again, feeling that the castle was more of a prison for all of them than anything else. She found herself questioning her servitude to the queen; her youth would have been better spent in the freedom of the forest and common life. Feeling somewhat emotional Koren went to the stables seeking for her father's attentive ears and words of wisdom. He was in the back of a large stall struggling to mend the gash on a furious Minotaur's leg. The enormous beast roared with pain as Master Lorean tried clean out the grotesque wound. Koren decided to leave at once, always thinking poorly of the atrocity that a creature of such a beastly nature could have a humanlike body. She wandered around for a while pondering whether to try to visit her mother instead, but she hadn't been able to return to the kitchen after she heard of a particular baker's untimely death at his own hands. Suddenly she found herself going back to the forest summoned by its magical spell. Once there she felt like following the path to the caves trying to recapture some of the memories she tried to leave there. Almost close to the cave's entrance she noticed a figure crumpled at the waterside. Running to help the fallen person in such poor state, she pulled at the limp body, which was partially submerged in the cold river.

"Sir! Sir?" Koren moved the man to make him respond, but he just moaned. Pulling him to shore was not hard for the man's frame was emaciated, his clothes tattered and the boots torn. The man was probably a poor beggar who had too much too drink and lost his way in the forest. His face was caked with dirt, grime and an impenetrable beard. The man tried to open his mouth to speak but no sounds escaped.

"Sir, you are in horrid condition, I will take you to the palace guards and they can assist you. Do not fear you will be tended to; the castle is there to help the queen's subjects. I'm a lady of the court, you are in good hands." Koren spoke trying to soothe the man who tried to move and couldn't. When she tried to levitate him, the man reacted by forcefully shaking his head emphatically and reaching with his bony hand to grab her arm. He tried to speak once more and failed, then open his weary eyes. Koren felt the ground tremble under her feet, as a flood of emotions suffocated her voice, noticing the intense green eyes pleading. Squalid tears began to flow from Orion's eyes as she threw herself at him. She wanted to hold him, protect him and feel his body in her arms again. The reality of his presence was still absurd and hard to grasp. Koren kneeled by his side, crying as she tenderly caressed the grimy visage full of love. Orion managed to give her a weak smile, his eyes rolling to close as he fell in a comatose state. Koren shook him and pleaded to awaken him, and no response came. She knew he was in a delicate state, the place where life and death met for every person, and one definitive step was all that was needed to go either way. Her heart thundered with the familiar despair of losing him, this time forever. Thoughts hammered her head frantically and erratically searching in vain for a solution. Taking him to the palace would be a mistake; there was no other option but to try to heal him somehow. Unfortunately, she didn't know how. She did know however, that she would not stop fighting for his life.

With a wave of her hand the entrance to cave was cleared of vegetation, and carrying his limp and weightless body in her arms was effortless making for easy passage. Thankfully she had never spoken of the cave's existence, thus no one would search for her there if she were being looked for. Orion's luck had not run out, for it was her that found him lying by the water. To think that it could have been Kalani or Kanek that found him gave her chills. He was safe with her now; once again the cave was a haven for her love. Fully working her magical skills she created a comfortable chamber for him, complete with a warm hearth. Trying to make the place as masculine and grandiose for a prince as she could, hoping that when he came to his senses he would want to stay for a while this time; or maybe forever. This concept was too abstract for both and she knew it, especially under the circumstances. There was never a more inappropriate time to think of the future, but having him so close gave her hope. Orion had returned to her side, and that was all she cared about.

Koren prepared a hot bath for him, full of lavender and chamomile to soothe and bring warmth to his body. She held him to her chest again, crying at the sight of his wasted body, and incredulous of his proximity. Nothing mattered, her love had never ceased to exist or diminish in his absence. Koren undressed him tenderly, removing the worn and tattered leather boots, which no longer protected the bleeding feet plagued with suppurating sores. These were not the boots of a prince, but of a man that had experienced severe misfortune. Whatever was left of his clothes she removed, vestiges of what was once a wool coat and a cotton shirt easily peeled of in shreds from his back. Koren was horrified as she saw his battered torso full of lesions, sores and scars accentuated by a cruel thinness in which his skin was merely a veil upon his bones. His long limbs lay deflated, sporadically covered by symbolic tattoos she had never seen before.

Barely seeing through her tears, the growing ache in her heart was becoming unbearable as well as the fear that she could not save him this time. Placing her trembling hands on the rope he used as a belt, she struggled to untie it realizing that for the first man she would see a naked man. Reproaching her thoughts, she focused on the task at hand, removing his pants so she could wash him. It was necessary to inspect his body for open and festering wounds that would speed his demise. Pulling down his leather pants while she blushed, and afraid to look, she soon discovered that the rest of his body was in as bad a shape as his torso. The long legs had lost their musculature and there was a large gash on his thigh angrily oozing fluid. Koren didn't study the rest of his anatomy wishing to do so under better circumstances... Carrying him in her arms to immerse him in the hot water, she dedicated the better part of an hour to scrub away his skin until clean. Burning off with her hand the despicable beard, she was glad to see that at least part of his body was soft. His hair had to go as well, for she couldn't find a way to untangle the large knots or deal with the critters setting shop in there. It took about three changes of water for the bath to clear and he was washed to her satisfaction. Koren removed him from the tub gently, he seemed as if he were made of rice paper and would melt away in any moment. A woolen blanket was created to wrap him up in the bed by the hearth, where blue flames glowed dimly. Koren sat by him holding his hand brokenhearted, not knowing what to do next. Orion lay unconscious, and she was afraid to leave him as easy prey to death. Yet knowing that she would have to return to the palace soon. Her cat Neroli came to mind, and she focused intently on her. Concentrating hard to let the feline know her location she summoned her to the cave with urgency. Shortly after a loud meow was heard in the outside of the cave and Koren opened up the cover she had created to let the animal in. The cat came swiftly to her side uncaring about the fact that they had company.

"Neroli, you must stay here. I have to return to the palace and pretend to retire for the night before I can get back here to care for this man. This is Orion, my mate. He is your master too and I want you to care for him as if it were me." Neroli meowed softly and leapt to Orion's bed, where she bundled up next to him.

"If he were coming to his senses notify me at once. It is unlikely but if he attempted to leave this cave you must stop him at all cost, he might not be thinking straight..." Koren ordered petting the cat under her chin. The cat purred and stretched her paw comfortably, watching intently as Koren departed before settling in with the dormant man. Sunset had given up to darkness and Koren was certain that Althea would begin to worry about her if she didn't reach the palace before dark. Flying was not her preferred mode of transport, but it seemed the appropriate option to get there fast.

"Hi! I'm looking for Althea, I'm afraid she might be wondering where I've been." Koren was almost out of breath when she ran into Pumzi in the garden.

"Girl, you didn't have to race here! You look ready to faint. Althea is at the queen's chambers her pains intensified today, I'm sure we are going to be summoned to the birthing ceremony very soon." Pumzi shared elated.

"What? A birthing ceremony?" Koren asked surprised, still uncertain as to what part the ladies would have in the process.

"Oh, you will see. Go fetch Althea now, before she raises the alarm that you have gone missing." Pumzi laughed and shook her head. Koren ran in a hurry to the queen's tower where she found Althea anxiously pacing the hall by the queen's suites. The witch muttered words out loud which Koren couldn't understand.

"Althea, I came to say good night."

"Good night, dear girl. I'm just mentally preparing for Violet's labor, I'm a little nervous. It will happen any moment now!" Althea grinned.

"She must be desperate to meet her child." Koren smiled too.

"We are all excited, imagine how the king is feeling. It will be quite the event... You go and rest now; you must be focused during the birthing ceremony. We will fetch you..."

"Fetch me? You mean I literally have to be in there?" Koren was aghast.

"Of course, you are a lady and you must be there to witness the birth of the royal heir." Althea announced with pride, while Koren felt faint. She would have to remain in her apartment the whole night instead of going to Orion's side as she had planned.

"Do you have an idea when you'll send for me?" Koren faked curiosity.

"Well these things are never timely, babies arrive whenever they please, and nature takes care if it we just wait. It could be in an hour or in a couple of days..."

"I was wondering if I could spend some nights at my parent's, but this is more important. Although, I could leave Neroli in my chambers, she can fetch me at home if necessary..." Koren suggested casually.

"That should be fine, I'll instruct the maids to have the cat find you if you are not around. It's no use for you to be cooped up in the palace, I happen to know that you are enjoying Kanek's company..." Althea smiled and winked at her.

"We are good friends." Koren replied and walked away grateful that things had turned in her favor. She immediately went to the palace's infirmary taking advantage of the impending news of labor and the chaos it was creating in the palace's inhabitants. The infirmary was a mess thanks to all the witches, healers and midwives at hand and ready to assist with the royal birth if necessary. Koren didn't want to attract unwarranted attention to her and turned her dress into one similar to the simple linen ones the sick often wore. Deciding to change her appearance as well, her hair became a brown shade and much shorter than usual. Almost invisibly she made it to the area that she had visited before searching for dragon's blood, knowing that it was Orion's only hope. Trying to look calm she searched in vain cabinet after cabinet, but there was no dragon's blood to be found. Pocketing some mermaid's fat that would be of use for sores and wounds she headed out somberly. It was possible that the flask of blood she had taken before had not been replaced yet since the healing blood was not frequently used. If there were any, it would be in the queen's suite as a safeguard to possible complications in labor. Koren left in despair, having failed and wishing she were a full-blooded dragon.

Neroli was in the same spot where she had left her; as a matter of fact nothing had changed in the cave's interior. Koren ran to Orion's side fearing the worst, placing her cheek close to his nose to feel if there was still air coming and going. Being so close to him allowed her to appreciate his scent, the same one that had made her tremble from the moment they first sat next to each other. His breath was nearly a sigh, yet it was still there, it was a relief. She unwrapped him carefully to rub the mermaid grease on his battered skin. He didn't move at her touch, even as the skin lesions began to disappear and improve, it would take time to bring back his body to a normal state. Small scars plagued his body as it healed, leaving a constellation of bumps on his skin. Koren's tears invaded her sight again, full of sadness, bitterness and frustration. For a brief moment the temptation to give him her blood arose, knowing that she had some dragon blood, yet she was aware that it would be a grave mistake to do so. She would condemn him to a different living hell by turning him into a blood-sucking creature. Koren had read how mortals seeking immortality had mixed their blood with dragons in unnatural ways, or how mortals with dragon's blood had given it to others and damned them forever. The mortal blood would perish, and would need to be replaced frequently with its own kind. Koren wept wrapping him up in the blanket, then trying to force a spoonful mermaid fat on his cracked lips with the hopes of nourishing his body.

"Neroli, go back to my place. Stay there and come for me when they order you to." Koren was barely able to find her voice. The cat meowed loudly and sped away, not before climbing to Koren's shoulders and liking her face affectionately. Left alone Koren felt empty and desperate, her soul crushed into a pulp. Analyzing her options one by one, and each one less appealing than the following, Koren decided that she would die with him. Not content with an early demise, the thought of finding dragon's blood came to the forefront once more. Her father couldn't and wouldn't help, no matter how much she pleaded; besides he was not a full-blooded dragon. Erasmus came to mind, he would ask too many questions, just like Talma. When she thought of Talma the image of Kalani came to mind... Hope built up inside her chest like a fortress, with the certainty that her new friend would not ask too many questions. The visit to Kalani would have to wait until the next day; Koren resigned and laid to rest next to Orion's still body. Not a long time had passed before a loud meowing aroused her from her sleep. Startled, Koren incorporated and let the cat come in the cave.

"Just my luck, what a disaster... My true love is dying and the queen goes into labor. Unbelievable!" Exhausted and sleepy she had no choice but to leave Neroli to watch Orion while she was gone. The cat found a comfortable spot by Orion to watch his sleep, as she closed hers to catch her own. Koren flew to the castle, hating the way the humid wind made her hair stick to her face, dried her eyes and made her flap about sometimes. Reaching the queen's chambers she saw the other ladies there with sleepy faces too. Althea smiled, her hair unusually messy.

"We are all here now, lets bring this creature into the world. The other witches and the midwives are there, lets go in." A sharp scream emerged from the queen's room dispelling the drowsiness of the ladies at once.

"There's no wasting time, undress and put on these..." Althea ordered as she passed around a thin linen tunic for each. Koren dropped all her garments to the floor just like she saw the others do, not wanting to stare at their nakedness. She felt she had dealt with enough naked bodies for the day, until she spied Marussa's glorious figure and had to admire it briefly. The tunics were a symbolic gesture, since they offered no practical purpose as clothing; their transparency did little to abate the cold.

"Walk with me. Clear your minds, and think only pure thoughts of life, beauty and love." Althea ordered as they entered. The queen's suite was dimly lit; the glow of candlelight was warm and soothing. There was a strong smell of mint and sage, diffused in the air by a mysterious breeze. Violet painful moans sporadically shattered the silence making Koren forget all the other events unfolding in her life at the moment. There were two witches and three midwives surrounding the queen al of them completely naked and anointed with fragrant oils. Althea walked to the queen's side, she was also naked except for the beads of sweat that covered her body. The witch signaled for the ladies to have a seat in some large cushions nearby, while one of the witches gave them small bouquets of fragrant leaves to fan in the room.

Koren noticed the witch must have at least hundreds of years if age, for her breasts were as long as her life, almost reaching her belly button. The old witch's body was severely wrinkled, covered with tribal tattoos which looked more like doodles than symbols due to time's passage over them. The old woman had white hair, but Koren noticed that the hair in her pubic area had been dyed a scandalous purple color, which made her regard the witch with more respect. Koren sat in a corner trying to avoid staring at the strange women on display. The queen was lying on her side as a midwife massaged her back and another her swollen womb. Violet squirmed in pain letting out yelps of pain and moans, blood starting to soak her legs as one of the witches cleaned her with warm cloths.

"Papo… Bring Papo here…" The queen ordered clenching her teeth.

"Your majesty, men are not allowed in the sacred rites of birth…" Althea reminded her tenderly.

"I don't care! I am the queen of Bandah and I order for him to be present. Any commoner can chose who attends the birth of her children, why not me? … Get him now!" The queen shouted. Koren saw how her midsection strangely contorted making her scream from pain. Althea whispered something to one of the midwives who then came to Koren to ask that she go fetch the king. Koren jumped to her feet, relieved to be gone from such a terrifying scene. She raced to the king's tower storming to the audience hall where some knights were idly engaging on a card game. The men rose to their feet to greet her and bowed, nearly knocking the table full of cards over.

"I have been sent here to summon the king to the queen's side, She has ordered for him to be present." Koren blushed realizing that she was practically naked in front of them. The men ran into a different hall and returned with the king who seemed pale and anxious, his eyes wide open.

"Lady Koren, what has happened? Is something wrong?" Fear besieged his words.

"No, your majesty. The queen has ordered that you must be present a the birth, you must come." The king didn't reply, his legs carrying him as fast as they could to the queen's tower. Koren ran surprised at his speed and at his ease when he entered the room. Papo pushed the women aside and embraced his wife. The queen sat on the bed looking frightfully tired, with bloodshot eyes and cracked lips. A witch tried to offer a drink, but Violet knocked it out of her hands.

"My love, please be strong! I wish I could help you bear this pain, but this journey only you can walk. The task has fallen on women to bring life forth, that is why you are all sacred…" The king spoke softly, shedding tears of sorrow as his wife clung to him. Papo sat next to her in spite of the bloody mess on the covers and began to rub her belly with great care.

"How is the labor progressing?" The king asked the eldest witch.

"It has been difficult, the first time tends to be harder, but she has had more of a hard time. The channel of life is opening properly, I have felt it, and this will not last much longer." The witch replied. Violet screamed again, as furious contractions assaulted her body. The king held her and kissed her forehead looking utterly lost.

"Prepare a hot bath." A witch ordered and a midwife raced out of the room. The queen screamed again and again, showered with sweat and tears for the sake of her heir. It was at that precise moment that everyone's fates were sealed, for a plan formed in Koren's head. A plan that was possibly infallible, yet so sinister in nature that its very existence was frightening. Koren looked around to the others fearing that her thoughts would have been known, but they were all focused on the queen's labor. An idea of how to make herself queen had suddenly presented itself in the unlikeliest of moments, an opportunity to pardon Orion and be with him forever had opened up. It would just be a matter of patience… the plan would require time. It would also require that the child being born was a boy. Koren concentrated in Violet's womb searching for the baby's heartbeat, only to find out that there were two in there. Twins! Koren opened her eyes astonished at what she had just found out, and then concentrated again to find out the babies genders. The little heartbeats were distinct from one another in spite of their short existence. There was a subtle beauty in one, which divulged the character of a girl and the other of a boy. There was no way to be certain, but Koren had to take a chance. The girl could not be born, or it would certainly ruin any hopes that she had placed in her plan. The decisive moment in her entire existence had arrived, she had to act now or waste the only viable opportunity she could think of as a way to the throne. Closing her eyes and focusing with all her might, the image of a small creature arrived in her mind, a small girl curled up inside her mother who must not live. Koren wanted to stop the girl's heart... The rhythms of a couple of heartbeats pounded in her ears similar to thunder, as she willed that one would cease... and then there was only one left. Koren knew that she had accomplished her goal, one child had died, hopefully the princess. Her act had been so despicable that she knew that from thereon there was no looking back, her soul had partially died.

"Argh!" The old witch screamed falling to her knees.

"What?" The king demanded with fear in his eyes.

"Something is terribly wrong, just seconds ago I heard the heartbeats of two babies, now..." The witch tried to explain and her voice failed. The witch incorporated and whispered something to Althea who suddenly became somber.

"What is happening? I order you to tell me!" The queen screamed with her hoarse voice.

"We must induce labor immediately, or open the womb to retrieve the child." Althea announced sternly trying to remain calm although her lips were quivering. The midwives disappeared and returned with several flasks on their hands, pouring some of their contents in a goblet, which they offered to the queen. In a matter of seconds the queen began to experience intense contractions, which elicited sharp screams. The old witch made her squat on the bed to push assisted by the midwives. Her fruitless endeavors were difficult to witness and some of the ladies wept silently. Violet collapsed on the bed about to lose consciousness as the king held her hand full of despair. He searched the other's faces helplessly as he cried.

"Your majesty, you must push or we will lose the remaining baby." The old witch announced with authority. Violet raised her head to fix her eyes on the old woman who remained stern. Althea and another witch grabbed Violet's legs folding them into her belly to widen the birth canal; the king sat kneeling behind the queen, grabbing her by the armpits to support her upper body. The queen pushed and screamed repeatedly until finally a small head began to appear. Koren watched in a trance, crying unabated because she knew that she was the culprit of the sorrow still to come. The queen would birth her children with great pain only to be devoid of the happiness of receiving both of them alive. Koren would have rather died that watch the heartbreak; if only she could turn back in time and take back what she had done... her repentance had no weight against death.

The senior midwife reached between Violet's legs towards her womb with her long fingers to pull out the firstborn. A saddened midwife covered the limp little body with a soft wool blanket. Silence fell on the room laden with the crush of the infant's death, until the queen let out a sharp wail of despair that made those present cringe. Violet had expected the cry of a newborn, only to watch the silent little body whisked away.

"Violet, you must gather strength from your heart, you are not done! There is another child and it is alive!" The old witch's raspy voice commanded. The queen took a deep breath with new determination, seizing every new contraction with relentless angst. The midwife reached again for the baby's head, pulling it out with ease. The old witch grabbed the child and placed it on his mother's naked chest, and for a moment it looked as if the baby would suffocate. The infant spit out some fluid and gasped for air, beginning to cry with all its might thereafter. Violet smiled at her baby holding it tight against her body, crying for joy this time. The king moved closer to peek at his son amazed by wonders of life, leaning to kiss the little forehead as he wept with joy. Althea walked over to where the stillborn lay, uncovering the tiny corpse to observe it briefly with the other birth attendants. They tenderly wrapped it again and took it to the mother for a brief farewell.

"It was a girl. We don't know what went wrong, she was fine until shortly before her birth. There are no visible defects on the child and it's not worth to study her body, sometimes Mother Nature deals an unsuspected fatal blow. I'm afraid it will remain a mystery..." Althea handed the stillborn to the new parents, who bitterly cried as they saw the baby girl who seemed placidly asleep. The infant boy began to cry for attention, Althea took the dead child away and handed her to a midwife. The woman would then take it to the priestesses who would perform special death rites for the tiny princess. The king gave the order that news of the birth could be shared, requesting that no mention be made of the stillborn princess. The queen requested the celebrations be kept at a minimum since there was no girl heir to present to the people. The old witch approached the bed to finish helping the queen in her labor, for the residues of the birthing process still had to be pushed out and carried to the kitchens to be cooked. The placenta would be made into a special dish and fed to the new mother. Violet carefully wiped her baby clean with soft cloth and led him to her breast as a witch oversaw the latching process, ensuring that it was done properly. A midwife showed her how to massage her swollen breast to feed the baby boy. Koren felt so horrible she could not watch the scene, trying to convince herself that she had nothing to do with the princess' death, even though the truth stung wildly. Crying full of despair, her stomach turned and she had to run to vomit on a corner of the room, violently shaking.

"You have seen enough... It is unfortunate that you had to witness a stillbirth. Life and death walk hand in hand, and the birth process can unexpectedly bring sorrow. It is sad, but these things do happen, sometimes a mother or a child is lost. We must focus now on the beautiful prince that has arrived in our lives, we must cherish him too." Althea help Koren stand up and kissed her forehead, trying to wipe her tears away. The witch held her close trying to comfort her unaware that Koren cried for reasons she could never imagine possible. A panicked midwife interrupted their embrace, so Marussa and Lenna helped Koren sit and gather herself.

"There is a problem, the queen is bleeding unstoppably!" The woman announced full of desperation, as Althea returned to the queen's bedside. The old witch gave Althea a sad look, letting her know that the queen's womb had been affected during labor and that if the bleeding didn't stop it would be a death sentence.

"Hurry! Bring my instruments and dragon's blood!" Althea yelled out the order washing her hands in a nearby basin. The king watched in horror as Violet began to lose her color and her state of consciousness. One of the midwives gave the queen some sort of thick beverage that seemed too bitter to swallow.

"We have no dragon's blood!" The returning midwife proclaimed with disbelief. Althea turned to face her full of rage.

"What do you mean? There was a full bottle in the infirmary. That blood was extremely rare and quite precious, it is not easily retrieved from its cabinet!" Althea shouted angrily scaring the woman away. Talma came to them in a hurry.

"Give her my blood." Althea stepped aside so that Talma could get close to Violet, while slicing with her fingernail the tip of her thumb. Two bright red drops of blood fell on the queen's mouth and the change in her was imminent. Minutes later the old witch declared that the bleeding had stopped. However, she also announced with sadness that it was very likely that the queen would be barren from that moment on, and only time would confirm her suspicion. Koren stared at the scene perplexed, there was no dragon's blood for her to have and save her prince. It was now evident that she had taken the only available supply from the palace and she would have to wait until it was replaced who knows when. Anari was the first to leave the room, obviously affected by the birth and the dreadful turn of events. Marussa followed her with the same affliction as she sniffled away her sadness. Koren thought it was the perfect moment to depart, that way she would be shielded from looking at the queen face to face. Once in her quarters she was frightened by some strange noises coming from the waiting room, fearing that Neroli had returned with bad news.

"Don't be afraid it's me..." Kalani poked her head from behind a little side table.

"You scared me! What are you doing here? You darned dragonling!" Koren scorned.

"I wanted to know news about the birth and mother hasn't returned yet..."

"She won't be back for a while, there have been some unfortunate events at the birth. You really should wait to hear what happened from your mother, it is not my place to tell you those things. Besides, you will get in trouble for leaving your room, and trust me, now is not the time for mischief." Koren said impatiently, collapsing into a comfortable chair and thinking about getting back to Orion.

"Please, just tell me what happened! Mother won't tell me, she always keeps things to herself. And no one has seen me come here, I can already make myself invisible." Kalani pleaded. Koren stared at her for a moment, wondering if she should offer to tell her what happened for a small amount of her blood. Deciding to start the story to raise her interest, she began to relate in detail the birth ceremony. Slowly she threaded the story as if she were weaving thorns into cloth, reliving the night was a burden knowing that she had murdered an innocent child. Her chest felt oppressed by that heaviness, the one that never lets up when it comes from guilt.

"That is horrible! It sounds like a terrifying thing to have a baby. I would have fainted right away, it happens to me every time I see blood!" Kalani interrupted Koren's tale at the mention of the bloody mess in the queen's bed. While the dragonling's words were casually said, they struck Koren sharply. A nefarious idea took shape in her mind for the second time in a span of a few hours. It overpowered any sense of morality or emotion that Koren had left, if any.

"What is it you say? That you faint at the sight of blood?" Koren said flatly as she planned in her mind step by step what she was about to do. It could be a dangerous move, but at that point there was no return... Recently she had committed one of the most heinous crimes; if she did another it wouldn't make any difference.

"Oh yes, it's the silliest thing. Mother says it will go away with time. One of the chambermaids was frightened and dropped a jar, cutting her finger. I went to see what happened and when I saw the blood... Thump! I was flat on the ground."

"That is bad. And how long where you out for?" Koren asked innocently.

" I don't know, a few second I guess. Mother slapped me back to life." Kalani laughed remembering the episode. Koren was solemn, without hesitation she turned her nail into a sharp claw and made a sudden gash in her forearm. Bright red blood flowed freely into the ground from the fresh wound as Kalani stared at her friend confused and surprised. Her eyes rolled to her head and she fell face first on the ground. Koren jumped to kneel at the dragonling's side breathing heavily as she turned all her nails into terrifying claws. Having read how a dragon was enslaved was one thing, but trying to do it was another. Kalani's tiny limp body seemed so defenseless that she thought she would not be able to hurt her. Resolve welled up in her as she turned Kalani to face up and tore the little metal mesh frock that she wore. Kalani's chest expanded and collapsed rhythmically under the pearlescent glow of her velvety skin. Koren concentrated hard, thinking that her claws were made of the strongest material on earth, also the hottest so much so that they began to hurt. Raising her hands to gather strength she plunged them once and for all in the small chest. The skin didn't give way easily, Koren frantically slashed with her might releasing white fire to break into the cavity and reach the heart. The white fire burned this time with and intensity that was almost unbearable, and she bit her lip with such force that blood squirted out. Digging through the chest she finally grabbed the tiny heart that was pulsing with extreme heat, like a ball of fire. It had been merely a few seconds when Kalani came to her senses feeling the intense pain and realizing the evil that had descended upon her. The little dragon took out her claws intent on fighting back... but it was too late. Koren ripped out her hand at once and gave her the first order of her slave hood.

"Don't make a sound." Koren said emotionless. Feelings had left her soul for good; it had now fully become a dark swamp of foulness. There was nothing there except anxiety, death and emptiness. Kalani observed her new master thorough teary eyes, devastated and heartbroken by the vile act of treason that Koren had carried on. The hole in Kalani's chest slowly sealed, leaving behind a grotesque scar, similar to a silvery spider. Koren found a small satchel where to put the beating heart, which was not bigger than a rosebud. Hiding the heart in the inside lining of her gown for safekeeping, the bulge it created was barely visible. Kalani let go of her pain and cried bitterly.

"Stop crying. It is done... Soon you'll understand why I have done it. I know you'll never forgive me, but you are much too powerful to let such an opportunity pass. You should have listened to your mother and stayed in hiding..." Kalani was silent trying with all her might to swallow her tears.

"You will never tell that I have your heart or where you saw me put it. You are my slave now; if you try to escape I will order you to murder everyone that you care for.

Understood? I want you to make yourself invisible and follow me in silence." Kalani nodded, aware that both knew she was magically bound to obey. Koren stood up and left as Kalani disappeared from sight. She left the palace quietly averting all the sentries and flying to the forest as fast as she could. Upon reaching the inside of the cave Koren allowed Kalani to make herself visible once inside. Neroli opened her big eyes and hissed at the dragon, sensing her presence even though she could not see her yet.

"It is fine Neroli, this dragon won't hurt you." The girls came close to Orion who was still in the same position in which Koren had left him.

"This is the man I love, he is half dead and that is why you are here... to save him. Get close and pour some of your blood in his mouth." Kalani heard the order and approached the man timidly. Biting into her index finger and looking away she let a few drops fall on his parted lips. Koren sat by him, placing her face next to his to hear his breathing. Suddenly, his lungs gasped for air with great greed and expanded fully restarting life in his chest. Color began to return to his face as his body warmed up. Koren laughed giddily knowing that he would be all right, with her eyes full of tears as he opened his. The glowing green spheres that she had ached to see again shone with intensity.

"My love..." Were the first words that Orion uttered, his voice dry and raspy. Koren fell on him to embrace him with all her might, making him moan with pain.

"Watch out, you are too strong..." Orion warned smiling.

"I didn't think I could save you this time... You had me worried. I can't believe I just happened to be there at the forest when I found you..." Koren caressed his face tenderly as they both exchanged with their eyes stories that their lips couldn't word. Neroli came to sit by the couple purring happily. Kalani was the sole outcast, standing miserably in a corner and embarrassed by her presence there. Orion noticed that they were not alone.

"Who is that?"

"It is a gift... for you. A dragon, but not just any dragon, a white dragon..." Koren beamed full of pride.

"What are you talking about?" Orion asked incredulous and confused by her words.

"That there is Talma's daughter, one of the ladies for the queen. You might remember the mighty dragoness that came to Cyrus with us, that is her mother. I have to tell you so much... it is a long story. Lets just say that everything that will change your life forever happens in one day."

"You have to tell more than that, I don't get it!" He exclaimed lost.

"She is my slave, I have enslaved a dragon... The opportunity came up, so I did it." Koren declared flatly shrugging her shoulders. Orion was flabbergasted when he heard the words, jumping to his feet in a state of panic.

"What have you done? If it were not because you are a lady I would curse at you! Have you lost your mind? Enslaving a dragon is beyond evil; I did not wish that for you, ever. I would have chosen to die, Koren!" He shouted pulling at his hair as tears fell down his face.

" You have lost your soul… You have lost your mind! It is my entire fault! Give her back her heart and perhaps you can still be saved, let her kill us both… at least we'll perish together!" He pleaded pacing the cave frantically and yelling in disbelief.

"No. I won't give her her heart and you will stop your frenzy. And believe me, I have done worst things, no one can save me now… perhaps not even your love." Koren declared reaching for his hand, letting him know that only time was the true enemy and they would have to battle it together.

"Tonight I killed the princess of Bandah…" Koren confessed. Kalani let out a wail and crumbled to the ground. Orion was silent for a moment.

"From the moment I laid eyes on you, I knew that you were my equal… fact which deeply scared me. Now I know for sure that we are the same and that is why life brought us together." Orion smiled and came to kiss her forehead.

"I'm also your slave… You are more powerful that I could have ever dreamt of." He continued as he reached for her face.

"I know you will leave again soon… But I have a plan now, so that you can come back to me for good… We'll discuss it later. How long were you lying on the river before I found you?" Koren changed the subject.

"Probably for three days, I'm not sure."

"You are a mess, I can only imagine what you have gone through all this time. Look at you, all bones!" Koren scorned.

"Yes… It was a horrible failure. I did go north, further than Stella Maris. Trying to find in vain a group of men to start my own militia, the lack money made it all impossible. I ended up selling the dragon's blood that you gave me to buy the services of a few mercenaries. I got work for my men and me on a sailing boat, which I then stole by killing the captain. Then I was able to get more men to find the isle where the damned Ossida shell was hidden. We spent many days at sea, suffering the wrath of tempests and marine beasts, most of our crew was lost before we even set foot on the cursed island.

The death demon that guards the shell descended upon our group mercilessly right after our arrival. It eviscerated the men with its claws, tearing out their hearts through their mouths and stripping the flesh of off their bones. It was terrifying. I fought and tried to run away like every other soul, although I'm certain no one else escaped. I can't still believe I made it out in one piece… but I know I have to thank you for it. I was facing the demon, lying on the ground defeated and waiting for it to tear me apart, when I heard your voice in the wind. The demon must have heard it too and thought that there was someone else on the island that had escaped its wrath. It saw that I was weak, apparently deciding to finish me later, and went to search for the owner of the voice. I could barely stand, so I crawled with all my might to shore wanting to drown rather than face the demon again. I floated for a few hours before I lost consciousness, my last though of your beauty and that of the stars above. I sort of remember a face staring at me, which now I believe belonged to a mermaid; she must have saved my life. I came to my senses in the cliffs north of Stella Maris, hungry and thirsty. A group of witches celebrating some sort of maritime ritual spotted me and came to my aid. They fed me and gave me a bottle of wine then send me away, so I decided to come back here. I lived on the charity of others, begging for food and clothing getting weaker by the day due to my condition and lack of dragon's blood to heal myself. Well, and somehow I made it... here you have me. A failed and broken man." Orion shed dry tears that barely left a salty trace on his face.

"No, my love, don't say that. You have run out of tears... and just as well. We will be together you will see, we just need to be patient. I don't think that it is a coincidence that life keeps bringing you back to me. There is a fate for us..." Koren embraced him.

"The plan came to mind today... during the queen's labor. I had too much on my head, wondering what I would do if I couldn't find any dragon's blood for you. And being there in her room, staring at all the blood and thinking about the babies in her womb... For there were two, a boy and a girl... I suddenly had a flash of inspiration. If the majesties were to die, the baby girl would be the immediate heir to the throne, but if the girl died then the boy would be next in line. That is the plan... I killed the girl so that there would be a male heir. Somehow we will kill the queen and king, and then I will marry the boy prince at one point, there isn't any law that forbids it. Given that I would be his wife and older, I would reign until his sixteenth year when he would come of age and decide to ratify the marriage contract. Of course, we would wait until he is the king officially so I become queen before we kill him too. Then I'll be a widow and a queen, ready to marry you and pardon you..." Koren explained excitedly as Kalani's whimpers filled the cave.

"You are insane. We are doomed... you have perpetrated all this madness thinking we actually have a shot at this incredibly implausible plan?" His face fell to his hands in despair.

"Do you have anything better?" She demanded, and then continued to talk airily.

"Why are you staring at me like that? Are you upset? Have I done wrong in trying to save our love?"

"No. Nothing of the sort... you are the strong one and have done nothing wrong. I'm looking at you admiring your perfection. I understand the magnitude and vision of your plan; it would be hard to carry on, but truly a genial machination. You have told me that you have murdered a child princess and enslaved a dragon... all in less than a day. Then you tell me about this plan that defies all convention... And what have I done? Nothing. It is now my duty to pull my weight on our fate and be a man, carrying this plan to fruition. I will not let you down." He held her tight.

"As soon as you are fully healed, you must leave with Kalani. Use her to get an army; I'll have her do your bidding. Make sure you go far, they will be scouring the kingdom and surrounding territories for her. We can communicate thorough her and when you have a decent army we can coordinate an attack on the palace, after some sort of distraction. I will take care of the queen and king they trust me. Once they die, we will need a priestess to marry us... you'll have to find one that is willing. I know you will be careful."

"Yes, yes, I understand. Now that I think about it, I'm getting some ideas and we might just be able to pull it off. I think it will take me about two years to gather a sizable army, probably made up of mercenaries and ogres, although that is pretty much the same..." He commented.

"What? Two years! That is too long! I'm fed up with life at the palace. The only good thing about that place is Kanek..." She whined.

"Time will fly because now we have a mission, you'll see. Who is this Kanek you talk about?" He inquired curtly.

"He is only a friend. One of the knights, young like me so we tend to spend some time together." Koren explained without noticing Orion's tenseness.

"Kalani, you may speak now. You will leave with Orion and protect him at all costs; you will also do as he says as if the order were mine. Just don't forget that I am your real master." Koren spoke to the dragonling.

"Why don't you give me Kalani's heart?" Orion demanded.

"Don't think I'll surrender her so easily. I enslaved her... I earned her. Let's be clear, only because you are older I will not follow your lead as you please. The world doesn't regard me as an adult yet, which I think is an insult since I'm capable of anything, don't you make the same mistake." Koren warned.

"You are absolutely right... you are not the innocent girl that you seem. I also want it to be clear that even though you think you are not a child, I will not touch you until you come of age. I want to respect you as any proper man would, you deserve no less." Orion informed feeling her too close to his body.

"Certainly, the immoral have morals. How fitting..." Koren said with sarcasm getting away from him and walking to a nearby chaise. He was silent.

"There is mermaid fat soup, have it so that you are restored. The sooner both of you get out of here the better, the search for Kalani will start right away. If Talma finds you, she would tear you to pieces, right after she is done torturing you mercilessly. It would be known that someone else enslaved Kalani and I'd have to do something, which would ruin all our plans." Koren spoke without emotion.

"I can't believe you are so evil..." Kalani's voice surprised them. Koren glared at her while Orion observed her intently.

"Why don't you have hair?" He inquired.

"I don't like it, it is white when it grows and I look like a hag." The girl replied. She understood the horrible situation in which she found herself, yet she felt some sort of excitement at the prospect of leaving the palace for good. The irony was not lost on her, so many years feeling trapped by her mother but she was truly free.

"Can you change your appearance? Look more grown up?" Orion demanded.

"Yes, I can. Mother suggested I look like a girl to let others know I was still training with her. It is the custom..."

"Make yourself look older then, that way I won't feel like a wet nurse." Orion suggested. Kalani closed her eyes briefly and morphed into a beautiful young lady. Koren rose from her seat to get a good look at her, taken aback by her loveliness. Kalani could possibly be the most beautiful creature in the kingdom, possessing an ethereal beauty that surpassed Koren's. Her red eyes were similar to two intense drops of blood on pure white marble, and the golden dawn of her skin glowed radiating warmth. Kalani's carmine lips stood out perfectly from her chiseled oval face, where her high cheekbones defined her glorious image.

"No, she can't be like that. Look at her! Everyone will notice!" Koren complained with a little bit of jealousy.

"You are right, we'll have to cover her up somehow." Orion stood straight, his weakened muscles still trembling a bit. With his hands he managed to turn the woolen blanket that covered his body into a comfortable outfit for himself.

"Oh, it is so nice to have my powers again." He expressed with a smile as he approached Kalani. He made a black cape appear and tossed it over Kalani's shoulders.

"There you go, cover up." Kalani obeyed, trying to get lost in the cape.

"That's not going to work. Kalani, turn into a horse. It would be more practical…" Koren settled the matter. A beautiful white stallion replaced the lovely maiden and Orion raised no objection to the change.

Orion turned to Koren, getting close and accelerating her pulse with each step he took. He stopped right in front of her, their bodies barely touching; yet close enough to feel each other's breaths. He grazed her face with his, inhaling her scent to bury it deep inside his being. Koren stood on her toes trying to be at his level, an impossible feat due to his imposing height. As their cheeks met, their skins mutually electrified and Orion trapped her in an intimate embrace.

"I love you." Orion's deep voice declared in a whisper, making her chest tighten. It wasn't a tightness that choked, or anguished, rather an indulgent sensation of being wanted and loved.

"I love you too. You are in my thoughts day and night. I do good and bad for you… It hurt to miss you, it hurts to know you are leaving me here again…" Koren sought his eyes as her own filled with tears, more as a recrimination than a complaint.

"I know. I feel the same way. I would give anything to go back in time and surrender the throne to Atle without a fight. I know we would have found each other no matter what… we are two hearts, but one soul… forever. Without my ambitions you would have been my only goal… to have you, to wait for you and make you happy." Orion spoke tearfully.

"Do you think so? I don't know if everything would have been the same, although it is worthless to think of what could have been, it has been denied to us. You are in my life now and I'm not focusing on the details on how you got there. I just want time to speed up so that we can be together. Although… We can still make a run for it, Kalani would protect us." Koren tried to persuade him.

"They'll look for you and her just the same. I'll be dead soon enough and if they figure out you have her heart it will be only a matter of time before you follow. There are too many things against us. Your plan is the only card we can deal fate to trump it…" Orion brought her closer to him. Koren let go of her angst crying ferociously against him, allowing the intense bitterness a release. He supported her trembling body struggling with his own sorrow by remaining silent. Then he spoke bitterly.

"I will never return… Please forget about me and lead your life without having to commit any more atrocities. I can't bear to keep hurting you… I love you, but I can't be your damnation."

"No!" Koren yelled at him breaking free from his arms.

"You are already my damnation... don't be a coward. If you leave me I will kill myself to avoid this anguish. I will give Kalani her heart and let her get revenge." Koren threatened with glaring eyes.

"Don't say that! I know you would do it... but can't you see, I'm the worst thing that has happened to you."

"You have already happened, and this is what we've got. Make up your mind about us once and for all because I can't stand the uncertainty." Koren declared furious. Orion stared at his love with sadness, seeing her coming undone, and her eyes prey to the swollenness of grief.

"Forgive me. Who am I to give up so easily when you have done the unthinkable to give us an opportunity? I will never, ever, leave you or threaten to leave you again for good." He threw himself at her feet and she crouched immediately to help him stand, just so that she could return to his arms. Their faces met at one point, ever so close as she searched for a neglected kiss and he wanting to give it. He couldn't overcome the roundness of her youth, though not of a child, it wasn't of a woman either. She pulled away letting her frustration be known.

"I'm sorry." Was all that he could say.

"I think you should depart at dawn." Koren said expressionless.

"We will head to the plains. I should be able to find a tribe there that would welcome us; they tend to be secretive and don't ask much. I'll gather men as fast as I can, I need a small group that is strong enough to carry on an attack on the palace and small enough to go unnoticed."

"How long do you really think it's going to take?" Koren asked flatly.

"Possibly a couple of years, it is not easy to come up with an army..."

"Time is such a boring irony... We can't control it, we can only suffer it." Koren replied dramatically.

"We will stay in touch all the time, Kalani will facilitate that. Time will fly; I promise you..." he tried to console her.

"Sure, that's easy for you to say. You are leaving and doing things as you wish, while I fall back into palatial complacency. It's just a lovely prison, for us the nobles, life in a castle is just servitude."

"I know, you already told me that, but there is nothing that I can do." He said exasperated.

"You have to come visit when you can, don't let too much time pass." She begged.

"It is too risky, Koren."

" We could meet in Bandah, I have been there with Kanek and I could start going on my own to avoid suspicion." She suggested stubbornly.

"This Kanek, the so called friend, why is he all circling you so much. I'm sure he is trying to woo you."

"Are you jealous?" Koren tried to provoke him.

"Certainly. You are beautiful, very beautiful, which man wouldn't want your eyes to favor him?" he reached for her hand and kissed it softly.

"Perhaps he is less scrupled and can see me as a woman..." Koren teased more unaware that her words would have deathly consequences. Orion was silent, kissing her hand again, and then he spoke with seriousness.

"Make no mistake, no other man shall have you. I am yours and will not hesitate to vanquish anyone that poses a threat." Orion fixed his eyes on her, letting the words sink in. they remained in place for a spell until she decided that it was time to clear the items in the cave.

"Stop doing that, come here." Orion summoned her to his side in a comfortable chair that he was now providing. Had anyone spied upon them they would have seen a young couple madly in love, unaware that they had in conjunction carried on abominable crimes, against life and nature. He pulled her close and they remained enjoying their proximity for as long as they could. Koren could smell the manly aroma that he exuded, while his healing body began to flourish again. She felt an incredible urge to run her hands all over him, to touch the thick wiry hair on his chest, and let go of the want in her body. The arousal of her body surprised her by its intensity and unfamiliarity. Her pulse quickened while her body felt warm, inside and out, wishing that he would touch her everywhere. She wanted him to feel her reactive skin. In the back of the cave Kalani trotted back and forth impatiently, trying to avoid looking at them.

"I must return to the palace... I've been here long enough. Kalani's absence will be noticed soon..." Koren stood to leave. Orion did the same and trapping her in his arms one more time he slammed her into his body. His breath was intensely denouncing a pent up desire as he resigned to place an anguished kiss on her forehead. Koren looked at him with a hint of resentment, and possibly a little bit of hate as well. Unforgiving for the emotional and physical exile he was imposing on her. Without a word, walking firmly and not a glancing back, Koren left the cave. Had she failed to do so she would never have the fortitude to leave his side. Somehow she made it to her chamber, to her bed... where she laid crying bitterly and undone. Thus, sleep found her.

Chapter 6: Farewells and loneliness

Koren woke up to bright sunlight peeking through the windows. Taking a moment to digest all the events from the night before prior to setting foot out of bed. Knowing that it hadn't all been a dream, the images inevitably flooded her brain leaving her in a daze. Her mind replayed the queen's arduous labor, the acquisition of Kalani's heart and the painful farewell to Orion. He would already be far from the castle, seeking the army with which to fight destiny. Outside her room there seemed to be unrest, there were voices and steps storming the outer hallways. She was certain that Kalani's absence was known and the frantic search had begun. Neroli purred at her side, her ears flattened as if aware that she should keep her guard up.

"Are they looking for Kalani?" The cat meowed and did something unexpected, scratching Koren's arm to rouse her.

"You naughty cat! What is the matter?' Neroli raised her paw and hissed, letting out a strange yelp. Making Kanek's image suddenly pop for some unknown reason into Koren's mind.

"There is something else... with Kanek?" Koren asked surprised and alarmed at the same time. The cat hissed emphatically showing its sharp teeth. Koren jumped out of bed, ringing the service bells desperately while a growing knot tightened in her stomach. The maid came in flushed by her race to the room.

"Good morning, Lady Koren." The woman would not look her in the face.

"What is happening in the palace? Why is there so much noise?" Koren demanded to know.

"Milady, you must speak to Lady Althea..."

"Tell me what you know! Now!" Koren yelled feeling anger in her voice.

"There has been... It is a disgrace, milady. Sir Kanek has suffered a brutal attack in the middle of the night... They tried to save him... He has just died." The words fell upon Koren heavier than a thousand years of misery, knowing in her heart that the only person behind such a horrible crime was Orion. It had been his farewell and a warning... Guilt crushed her soul, regretting the jealousy she had elicited from Orion, even thought she never though any harm would befall Kanek. Running in her sleepwear she raced to the king's tower, taking down mercilessly whoever happened to stumble upon her path. Storming into the tower's main hall she found a group of knights, breathing the same somber air within their ranks. Halting, she finally noticed that Althea, Anari and Marussa were behind her. The knights turned to face her in silence, until one finally spoke.

"Lady Koren, we had expected your visit. Please walk with us to the king's office." Blassa, a dragon of intense yellow eyes and red hair, tried to hold her arm and lead her.

"No! No! No! Then it is true! Where is Kanek?" Koren screamed desperately as truth stung her soul. Her friend had died... Anari walked to her to embrace her, but Koren shoved her away.

"Get away from me! I want to see him!" Tearful sorrow began to pour choking her voice.

"You will not see him. He is being prepared for Death Rites…" Althea calmly explained, observing with sadness the ache in Koren's heart.

"I want to see him! I want to see him!" Koren shouted feeling her body burn with rage and ready to explode.

"Everybody leave now! Get away!" Althea yelled to the others present, sensing that something was about to happen, and then ran for cover. Intense flares spewed out of Koren's body in every direction, destroying everything in its path, including a few walls and windows. A frightful tremor shook the palace causing general panic, making all the emergency plans for evacuation to be set in motion. Koren fell to her knees, surprised by her force and by the pain that had released it. Somberly she realized, a little too late, that perhaps she had also loved Kanek. He had represented all the good things that a relationship could give… friendship, companionship, adventure and calm. Closing her eyes she saw him smile at her, how his eyes had always lit up when he spoke…Kanek. Nothing could take the pain of his death out of her mind, not even if she forced herself to think of Orion…

The dragon knights, Talma, Erasmus and her father were the only ones who dared to approach her, aware of the danger. Master Lorean held out his hand, tearfully leading his heartbroken daughter to his comforting arms.

"I'm so sorry, my love. I know how much he meant to you… But you cannot see him, he was attacked by a dragon and…" Lorean's voice failed him. Koren could sense what her father wasn't saying, that Kalani had been enslaved and ordered to attack Kanek. Still, seeing his dead body will make it all real, and she would be able to tell him that she was sorry for killing him.

"I really want to see him, papa. I want to say good bye…" Koren cried into her father's chest.

"I'm not sure you can, they are taking him to Astra so that his family can be there for the rites." He sadly informed her.

"Please, let me see the queen and talk to her. She can talk to the king and allow me to go with the knights to Astra… Please, I beg…" Koren turned to face Althea supplicating.

"Lady Koren, I'm the Senior Knight and if the queen allows it, we can find a solution. You may travel with the knights… We all knew how much he cared about you. As a matter of fact, he made your ladyship his heir at the moment of his death."

"You were able to talk to him? I wasn't summoned! You damned bastards!" Koren shouted a reprimand, eliciting gasps from the other ladies.

"Milady, he was barely able to speak, we found him near dead. The healers tried to save him… I think it is best that you meet with the king, he wanted to talk to you." Blassa spoke calmly and full of sympathy. Althea walked over to her and held her arm lightly leading her away to the queen's presence.

Queen Violet was at the Royal Nursery with her son cradled in her arms, while the king sat sullen on a chair nearby. Seeing the family together caused a stir of mixed emotions in her heart, knowing that they were short a member by her doing.

Koren sat where Althea took her to, glad to get off her trembling legs. Violet came to her and embraced her tenderly...

"My dear child, I'm lamenting all the terrible events you have suffered since your arrival at the palace. You have lived in less than one year that which others luckily may never experience in a lifetime. I don't know what to say, such misfortune is terrible to explain. Kanek's loss is insurmountable, and we are sure that we have lost Kalani too. She has been enslaved and used in the attack. Talma has confirmed it, and we know that only a dragon could inflict such damage. He was tortured and left right at the junction where life could not walk through. The person who ordered his death sent a clear message, we are alarmed. We have raised security at all levels..." Violet's words whipped Koren's ears; she tried not to listen anymore. Bitter tears came up to accompany her in her disgrace.

"He loved you. He had already told us all that when the moment came, he would ask for your hand in marriage. His dying wish was that you be given his sword and this... They were his most prized possessions." The king came to kneel at her side, extending his hand to give her a small object. The image of a shiny object came through the blur of tears to reveal a lovely golden ring. Koren grabbed it and squeezed it hard in her hand, letting the hardness of the metal hurt. Her foolishness struck her again; knowing that Orion was a dangerous felon, Kanek should have remained anonymous. The king walked over to grab Kanek's sword and presented it to her.

"Your majesty, I know he will be taken to Astra. I would like to go along to bid farewell, please." Koren addressed the queen weeping softly.

"We thought so, you may go. The decision to hold the rites there was in favor of his family, they would like to bid farewell too. Given than time is limited to hold the ceremony, you must prepare to depart with the funeral committee at once. Only a few knights will be able to go, we cannot leave the castle vulnerable or unprotected. The fact that Kalani has been enslaved under our own noses points to the severity of the security breach. We don't understand why Kanek was singled out, or why no other sign of attack has surfaced... We have no clues at all, we do know that whoever carried on the enslavement of a dragon and such an abominable murder, is someone to be very afraid of." The queen spoke holding her son close to her chest defensively.

"Leave by midday. The dragons will take no time to reach Astra, barely a half hour... I'm sorry this has happened." Koren heard the queen's voice as if she were far away, as if reality had suddenly become a vacuum. Holding Kanek's sword in one hand and the ring in another, she walked away silently without properly being dismissed.

The maids avoided her as if she had some deathly pestilence, lowering their gaze as she entered the living quarters. Apparently not knowing how to deal with the girl's grief. Gathering strength, Koren locked herself in her room, where she put her hand on Kalani's heart.

"Kalani." She summoned.

"Mistress, I hear you." Kalani's voice clearly responded.

"Tell Orion I will not forgive him for killing Kanek."

"He says that he is yours, but you are also his… that you don't forget." Kalani's voice responded.

"I will get back at him and he will regret this, you tell him that!" Koren roared.

"Don't get like that, he says. How can you say that, he asks…"

"You tell him that Kanek was my friend… That I don't forgive him for taking away the only thing that made my life bearable and colorful. He was the only person able to soothe the abandonment, which Orion condemned me to. And that is it, Kalani, I don't want to hear another word from him." Koren hissed. Aware that Kalani would not give her any more messages Koren fell on her bed engulfed by misery. Taking a deep breath she got up and headed to the king's tower. There was a lot of movement in the hall; workers were fixing the considerable damage that she had inflicted earlier. Without facing anyone or their curious glances, she went directly to the king's office. The dragons Puzo, Blassa and Talma where there with the king apparently expecting her arrival.

"Everyone seems ready, you must depart at once. Blassa and Puzo will carry the remains. Talma can take you." The king informed Koren.

"I can fly there." Koren said firmly.

"Are you sure? You will all travel at full speed, we have sent a message earlier to have everything ready once you arrive." The king informed.

"Yes, your majesty. I'm fully capable of flying there myself." Koren reaffirmed, although not too happy with the idea of flying. Not only because she hated it, but because her close proximity to Talma brought the risk that she could sense Kalani's heart's location. The group walked in silence to the garden, where a beautifully carved wooden casket bearing the royal symbols of Bandah awaited. Koren ran to it, knowing that Kanek's lifeless body rested in there. Blassa acted quickly to grab her arm forbidding her from opening the casket. Puzo came close and smiled sadly, also standing between her and the corpse, understanding her grief. Koren felt like pulling him away by his long braid, but resisted the urge. The braid roped around his neck similar to a dark vine and then dropping down his back, the traveling custom of dragons to keep their hair away during flight. The dragons took each side of the coffin and became airborne effortlessly, disappearing from sight in seconds.

"Keep an eye on me, so you don't get lost. Just in case, have this magical compass; it will take you wherever you ask. Ask for Astra!" Talma explained with a half-smile.

"Thank you." Koren replied unable to look her in the eyes. Talma ascended and Koren jumped to get an awkward impulse. Earth fell away rapidly; or rather she lifted quickly to the firmament, focusing on Talma's lead. The trip was over in what seemed to be the blink of an eye and soon the scenery drastically changed. Shapes of edifices appeared in between the clouds, and the visiting group began to descend, coming upon a magnificent castle made of the whitest marble. Talma led Koren to a landing clear right next to an incredible forest. The sheer height of the trees almost overshadowed the castle's existence. There was a small battalion of soldiers dressed in formal military wear accompanied by several priestesses prepared to receive them. Koren spotted a group of people to the side, which she assumed must be Kanek's family. Trumpets flared with a sad hymn making some of those present begin to cry. Blassa and Puzo landed elegantly, delicately placing the casket on the soft grass. Talma set foot on ground and immediately straightened her hair to look presentable. Koren tried as best as she could to land carefully, but inexperience robbed her of her balance, and made her tumble indecorously on the ground. A few men ran to her aide, and she stood up embarrassed, refusing their help. A man dressed elegantly in brown velvet and gold accents immediately approached her.

"Milady, welcome. I'm General Fabius Dais and Berh, I salute you." Koren mimicked all the courtesies that the officers extended and followed the group through the clearing. A woman that wept bitterly threw her body over the wooden casket upon seeing it, wailing disconsolate. The general who had welcomed Koren raced to the woman's side to embrace her comfortingly. A lovely maiden in military garb and a young man that could have been Kanek's double joined them.

"The majesties await to commence the rites." General Fabius informed out loud to lead everyone into the place where the Death Rites would be performed. The familiar pyre lay on top of a small hill nearby, and Koren's chest tightened, as she got closer to it. The official colors of Astra were a vivid turquoise blue and dark brown, accented with gold, which made the funeral seem more of a festivity than a solemn event. A couple followed by a large entourage of knights and ladies came to greet the visitors. Koren assumed they were the monarchs of Astra, unbelieving that they were so simply dressed that they looked like commoners.

"Welcome to Astra. I'm desolate that you are here under these circumstances. We knew Kanek since he was a boy; he ran through our palace as he please, such a happy child. We saw him leave seeking adventure with great sorrow and now our sorrow is greater." The queen of Astra said unheeding formality.

"I'm King Olan, in service of Risa the Queen of Astra and her subjects. We hope you enjoy your short stay, regardless of the reason for your visit. Please, do not be afraid of asking for any comfort you can think of." The king spoke to the newcomers as they kneeled to the monarchs. Each of them presented themselves formally to the queen as their Bandian protocol required.

"Oh, formalities are not necessary here. We have a bad habit of doing without those here in Astra." Queen Risa chuckled. Koren thought the queen's name had a happy singsong sound to it that perfectly matched her personality. Risa was beautiful, vibrant and refreshing. The group continued on to the pyre, and once they were spotted by one of the priestesses, the black flames were lit. The black fire powerfully roared, sending chills to the crowd who knew of its magical nature. As the priestesses started their walk into the sinister fire, Koren fell in a trancelike state, unable to hear a sound. She stared intently into the undulating black flames, knowing that at any moment Kanek would surface. The fire rustled and intensified, as streaks of color began to splatter in its midst. Suddenly Kanek's figure appeared as clear as if he were alive. Koren wanted to go to him…

"Do not touch the fire, or you will become part of it." A priestess warned sternly, as she detained Koren by the edge of the pyre. The exchange startled Kanek who looked around confused at first, then sullen as he saw his mother cry.

"Mother! Don't cry… I'm relatively fine, I don't feel anything and I'm not afraid." Kanek joked at the ridiculous idea of being dead.

"Kani! Kani! My baby boy, my love... Why you? Why so soon? Who has done this to you my child?" The woman wailed falling to her knees.

"Mother, hold your grief, it is of no use. The one who did it was following orders... At least death came to me in the hands of a friend...She cried desperately the whole time and begged for forgiveness. I knew the dragoness that killed me, she is a slave now, but I don't know to whom. That person is the true killer..." Kanek spoke clearly trying to comfort his mother.

"I'm sorry, son. Farewell, I will miss you so much. Don't be afraid and follow the path to the unknown now, you always liked adventure. We are very proud of you and that you were our son..." Kanek's father said trying to remain unaffected, yet the quiver in his lip was giving him away.

"Thank you, father. I'm not sure what's coming, but I'm not worried for some reason. It is calm, quite colorful and I can see everything clearer than before. It's hard to describe. There really aren't shapes, just energy... good energy. I know that I should be sad for your sadness and my death, but I'm not. I sort of remember being alive, but now I'm not feeling anything... It's strange." Kanek then turned to his siblings to bid his farewell, trying to think of valuable last words to leave them. The priestesses interrupted him to warn that time was running up, he would have to depart soon. Koren faced him trembling watching float in between the world of the living and the dead.

"Hello..." Was all they could say to each other, and then Koren began to cry.

"I guess now that I'm dead, this is the only opportunity that I have to tell you all the things that I didn't have the courage to say before. I love you. I. Love. You. The first time I saw you, I think I loved you. All this time I dreamt endlessly about the day that there would be a sign that you felt maybe a twitch on my behalf. There was nothing that I cherished more than the time I spent with you, and I wanted to do that forever. I wanted to be yours and to make you happy..." Kanek said tenderly.

"Kanek it is all my fault, I'm so sorry... I should have never been your friend. You were the best thing that happened to me at the palace and it will not be the same without you. I can't fathom the idea of walking the garden without you, without my arm in yours, or the laughs we shared... I'm sorry you had to die for me to realize how much I truly care about you..." Koren tried to choke her cries to talk.

"Koren, don't cry for me. I don't want your pain, all I want is for you to remember the good times we shared. If you ask me not to leave you, I won't. I'll walk right out of this fire and become a ghost for eternity, as long as I'm by your side." Kanek sincerely offered.

"No! I don't want you to do that, it is not right. Besides, you don't know who I am... or how dark is my soul. I have hurt you enough to then condemn you to wander a living death, unable to touch, feel or escape. Kanek, you would hate me if you knew the real me..."

"Milady, what nonsense you speak! No ill can come from you... I'm witness to your smile; to the way you cherish the sun's warmth and the garden flowers. That's why I loved you, it wasn't for your beauty... it was the way you affected everything around you and then let it into your self. You are a good person, and your soul is akin to the purity of life. Just ask me and I'll remain here, until the moment you walk into the black fire to see you go unto the unknown, perhaps even go with you..."

"No... I thank you for your words and for the illusion of me you carried in your heart. I want you to go on, you are going to a different place. I could not make you happy in life or death. I really am not what you believe, and I'll apologize again and again, because you didn't deserve to die. You were the most wonderful man I met and I couldn't even recognize that. I did love you..." The words escaped her lips, as the prisoner that flees the dungeons, and upon seeing light it is surprised by its existence. Orion was her true love, yet her love for Kanek was all that was calm and pure, and with him it would perish.

"If life is cruel, death is unbearably so... you finally said the words I longed to hear! Thank you for having the courage to let me have them. I feel no emotion now, but if I could, I'm sure I would have died of joy anyway. Don't be sad for me, I don't feel any sorrow for you or for the life I'm leaving, literally. I'm gladly taking your declaration of love as the best memory of this life. I'd give anything to be alive and be able to touch just one more time..." Kanek smiled.

"Stop, I can't take it anymore..." Koren begged; her soul shattered.

"Farewell, milady. My love. I wish you happiness forever, may your smile never cease to brighten the world. I saw you put on the ring I left for you... It was mother's. Well, at least I got to see you wear it." Koren let out a sorrowful moan, suffocated by the emotional turmoil inside her. Vertigo attacked her viciously, and without being able to control herself, she passed out.

Koren came to her senses waking up on a large room with a magnificent view of the forest. Talma sat on a large chair observing her quietly.

"You had us worried, you've been out cold for a couple of hours." The dragoness spoke amicably. Koren sat up straight in a hurry tapping her body instinctively to verify that she was wearing the same dress she wore earlier. Sighing with relief she relaxed after feeling that Kalani's heart was still undetected in her clothing.

"I don't recall anything other than everything going dark and falling..."

"You were lucky that there was a priestess close to you to push you away from the fire... It was almost as if you were one of those black flames that swallowed life... Of course that would not be possible, they are made of sheer negative energy. Anyhow, you were spared from joining your lover friend to the unknown."

"Oh... Kanek. Its all over, right?" Koren asked sadly.

"Yes. He is gone." Talma confirmed with sympathy while Koren slammed herself back in bed, hoping that the mourning light in her soul would go out soon.

"We will return home tomorrow morning, there is nothing left to do here. Tonight you have been invited to join Kanek's family for dinner at the place where they are staying. They didn't want to stay in the palace; they are staying at a small inn nearby. I told them when they left that I would let them know if you would go."

"I will go, it would be rude of me to decline their offer. Besides, I have something to return to Kanek's mother."

"I will send word. You should eat something now and take a bath; it will make you feel better. If you need me, have the maid look for me at the queen's offices. Later I will be in the garden, this place is unbelievable..."

"Talma... How about you? I mean, how are you doing?" Koren inquired avoiding her eyes.

"Terrible. Kalani is in the hands of an evil person, and I hope we can save her soon. The moment we return I'll rejoin the search... I think you now know what it is like to lose someone you love... now imagine it's your daughter." Talma got up slowly as if her body ached tremendously; she tapped Koren's shoulder lightly, and kissed the top of her head.

"Rest now." Talma said as she walked away, leaving Koren gasping for air after the intense fear that she might feel Kalani's heart on her.

Koren paced the room nervously, still disturbed by her declaration of love to Kanek. Certainly pain had made her do it; no one could elevate her soul like Orion... Or could they? Demanding to know why she blindly loved him, the realization that Orion had never done anything to earn her love stabbed at her mind. Why had destiny chosen such a tortured love for her? Why had she? Or was she merely obsessed by the idea of loving him? Eyes shut tight and recalling his image, Koren retraced the outlines of his lips, his cheeks and the intense green of his eyes. Orion was perfection and passion personified... And yet if they were strolling together and speaking of mundane things; what then? Those theoretical questions were absurd and pointless, Kanek was dead and he had taken any hope of discovering other paths to love. All that she had done until that moment made her undeserving of being loved by a pure soul. Even if she decided to walk away from Orion and find someone else, how could she lead a simple life when her soul already bore the darkness of evil? Another man would just rightfully look at her with spite and reproach. The time when she was a humble human being had past, selfishness and ambition had made her violate the laws of humanity and nature. The shocking part was her continuing willingness to go on, never pausing to ponder about good or evil, or what defined them. It didn't matter, those concepts suddenly seemed like opportunistic options in relation to a person's circumstances.

Koren left the room and walked aimlessly until reaching a beautiful hall full of hanging tapestries. The palace was strangely empty; there was no service or chatter in the halls, and no nobles strolling without reason. Finally she came upon a group in a lovely outer courtyard by the gardens. Talma and other knights animatedly joined the group in conversation.

"Good afternoon." Koren greeted.

"Good afternoon, Lady Koren, it is a pleasure to see you." Blassa smiled.

"Kanek's family will be here in an hour to come for you, we have decided not to come, to allow for some intimacy." Talma announced.

"Thank you." Koren sat with them as she nodded a greeting to the others present. The conversation resumed, as the differences between Astra and Bandah were engagingly explored by the candor of the speakers. Astra was presented as a land eternally in springtime, where nourishing soil and lakes sustained plentiful agriculture. Bandah had to its advantage multiple geographical zones that were host to a diversity of microclimates. Koren decided to walk away shortly, having had enough of the contest of kingdoms unfolding. The garden had a surprisingly large variety of fauna and botanical species, which encouraged exploration. Tiny hummingbirds, large butterflies and fairies the size of crickets confusingly fluttered about the colorful flowers creating a colorful chaos. A group of fairies delicately placed a crown of flower on Koren's head as they splashed her with the mist of sweet nectar. She smiled grateful for the treat and the lovely present heading out to the forest to explore further. The trees were impressively tall, and their green foliage so intense that it seemed impenetrable. Koren was lost in the scenery when she heard some footsteps approach. Turning to see the intruder she let out a yelp as her heart skipped a beat, thinking that Kanek's ghost was coming to her.

"I didn't mean to scare you, milady. Please accept my apologies. I was told that you would be here in the magical forest. I've come to accompany you to dinner with my family." The young man explained grinning widely.

"Greetings. Yes, you scared me, I thought you were..."

"No need to excuse yourself, I understand. My brother and I used to think we were twins born years apart. I'm the eldest one, though. I must properly introduce myself, my name is Sir Romulo, but please call me Romulo. I'm sure you already know how informal we are here in Astra."

"Yes, the likelihood is amazing... And I'm Lady Koren." Koren extended her hand to be kissed. Romulo kissed her hand gently and they began to walk back to the castle. Every so often their eyes would embarrassingly meet as their shy smiles eased the tension.

"I had spoken to my brother recently, and he mentioned you. He was such an arrogant oaf that I never took his words seriously, but this time he was right. He said that the was no fairer maiden and I agree..." Koren blushed embarrassed by the bluntness of his compliment.

"Milady, please forgive my rudeness! I didn't mean to make you feel uncomfortable. I'm such an idiot when I'm nervous..." Romulo added apologetically.

"It's alright. I'm used to the stares and the comments, I don't care anymore." She smiled shrugging her shoulders. The group in the garden came to view and they still chattered animatedly as before.

"Lady Talma, I'm taking my leave with Sir Romulo. I will not bother you when I get back. I'll go directly to my room and sleep, if you don't mind." Koren told the dragoness who seemed a little tipsy from the sweet wine.

"Oh, that is great! Make sure you tell the guards when you get in, they'll let me know your are back."

"I will do so. Good evening to all of you." Koren waved and curtsied to all. Leaving with Romulo they made small talk as they went to get their horses, chatting about the pleasant weather and picturesque landscape of Astra. At the stables they mounted gigantic steeds, which gallantly took them through the castle and the surrounding green fields. They reached a large avenue of slate cobblestones that presumably led to the city of Astra; the road was impeccable and quite vacant.

"Where is everybody?" Koren asked full of curiosity.

"These roads are barely transited, no one comes to the castle. It is a world apart, isn't it like that in Bandah?" Romulo replied.

"I guess, usually people fly over to the castle for official matters. Our castle is self-sustaining too city folk rarely visit. Kanek and I liked going to the city, though." Koren commented feeling strange at the mention of the name.

"Nice. I've never been to Bandah it seems too far away. I can tell you though, that you would like the city of Astra. It is colorful and vibrant... I would say festive. We are staying in the outskirts of the city, you won't get to see it this time, but you should return someday. We are originally form the Great Plains, from Kaniba. These beautiful horses are from there too; it's a spectacular area. We like to live out in the open; it is fitting for all the military practices our family business requires. My family has been in the lead of the Royal Militia for years, you can see I'm part of it..."

"Kanek had mentioned his military pedigree, he was truly an amazing knight."

"Didn't seem to help him much against a dragon. It was a white one though, who survives that?" Romulo looked away as Koren remained silent and full of guilt. Rage building up inside her towards Orion's misuse of Kalani.

Not only was Kalani strong, but also she was a unique dragon. Each dragon spewed fire the color of their skins, thus the white dragon's fire was the culmination of all the colors together, making it incredibly lethal. Furthermore, it would go unnoticed in daylight, giving the dragon an unprecedented advantage during an attack. The only other dragon that had this stealth mode of attack was the black dragon, which could attack at night with its dark flames unseen. Not surprisingly, only a black dragon could bear a white one and vice versa, making their rarity more valuable. Kalani was a precious acquisition not to be flaunted improperly.

"I don't even want to think about his last moments..." Romulo kept going.

"Please, can we talk about something else? Kanek meant a lot to me, it hurts to know he found death that way. It was an act of cowardice and sheer evil. I don't want to cry right now and come undone before your family."

"Forgive me. I haven't had the opportunity to talk about my brother's death with anyone... We will be at the inn in a quarter of an hour, we can gallop a little faster." Romulo gave a swift kick to his horse that immediately sped up as the second horse followed suit. The inn came to sight tucked into a small hollow where forest fauna ran rampant.

"Look at all the deer! And the critters! This place is magnificent, everything is so perfect." Koren exclaimed pleased.

"Thank you, Astra is indeed magnificent. Although this place pales in comparison to that forest you saw earlier. It is an ancient magical forest, full of wonders we haven't fully discovered yet, it is the driving force of our kingdom. Next time you visit, you must explore it." Romulo suggested.

"Wonderful! This place is more fiction than reality, had I not seen it, I would doubt its existence. No wonder Kanek thought Bandah was homely and rustic..."

"Is that really how it is?"

"Yes and no. I grew up in the castle, so I can't really say a lot of what Bandah is really like. The castle is sort of austere and not as flowery as yours, it is darker than the white purity your castle exudes. The city is lovely, the architecture is sharp and there are a lot of turrets involved... But you would have to see for yourself."

"I have seen some depictions of Bandah and my impression was that it was a dark and romantic place." He commented courteously.

Kanek's mother waved at them from the outer courtyard of the inn greeting them happily.

"Greetings, Lady Koren, and welcome. We are so honored that you have accepted our invitation. We return to Kaniba tomorrow and were hoping to see you before then." The woman spoke as she led them to the inn after they left the mounts at the stables. The inn was simple but welcoming, constructed entirely of a light colored wood and wildly decorated by brightly hued blooms. In the middle of the main hall a large hearth glowed intensely purple and welcomed guests with its enjoyable heat. Koren joined everyone at the large communal table where dinner would be served, and feeling comfortable without the formalities that she had grown accustomed to at the palace. She waved at Kanek's sister and father who welcomed her with a smile, strangely thinking that they could have been her family if only...

"I'm glad that you have joined us, milady. I'll start by proposing a toast in Kanek's name, who is probably now enjoying new adventures..." General Fabius raised his goblet and the rest followed suit.

"I toast for the happy years he lived and enjoyed. To all the times he held me giving me love, and making me proud. He was a fine young man." Kanek's mother proclaimed loudly.

"I toast for all the times we raced in the prairie, for the patience with which he taught me how to ride a horse and for all the chores he did for me when I was too lazy to do it. For the times he kissed my head softly and promised I would find a man as good as him." Kanek's sister visibly stifled her desire to cry while remembering her brother.

"Cheers to him that was the best game partner, fight contender, rider and adventure seeker. I will never forget the luck I had for having had him as a brother and a friend." Romulo shared. Silence descended on the table as they waited for Koren to speak, unaware that she didn't know what to say.

"I toast for him having taught me in such a short time the value of a friend." It was all that Koren could say for fear of falling apart publicly.

After the toast the servers brought different dishes full of food to sample, so that they could decide which one would be their dinner. They settled for a bird roast with a wine sauce, and boiled vegetables, much to Koren's delight. At one point during the meal Koren felt as if she was being stared at, ignoring the feeling at first but then looking about without noticing anything amiss. Although the somber figure of a man hiding his face with his cape by the hearth caught her attention. It had to be Orion; the way he stood was distinctly familiar. The food lumped in her stomach making her feel ill, she pushed her plate aside unable to take another bite. Her hosts continued to chat amicably in spite of the sudden change she experienced, unaware that she was barely paying attention to what they said. Koren announced she would leave immediately after the others had dessert, saying she preferred to ride back soon to rest for the early return home the following day.

"Thank you for your company, if you ever come to Kaniba please visit us." Kanek's father offered courteously.

"I'll keep that in mind, although we rarely get out of the castle."

"Have a safe return to Bandah, we are all worried about the white dragon... It was a pleasure to finally meet you." Kanek's mother, Janna, gave her a hug.

"Likewise. I also have something to return to you." Koren removed the ring she was wearing in her hand.

"Oh no, you should keep it. It's yours… Kanek had wanted you to have it." The woman smiled and tried to refuse the ring.

"I know, but it's a family heirloom and perhaps Romulo could give it to someone, or Sarissa could keep it." Koren motioned to the young people at the table.

"Besides, I have his sword, there is no greater gift or honor." Koren added and placed the ring on the woman's hand, closing it to ensure that the ring would remain there. Janna smiled and accepted the ring in silence.

"Good night everyone, and if you visit the palace please have tea with me. I can find my way to the castle." Koren turned to leave.

"Nonsense, I can ride with you." Romulo replied indignated.

"No, I'd rather ride alone. I want to…" Koren said decisively as she kissed everyone good-bye and walked out right away lest the tears took advantage of the situation to seek release. Walking over to the stables she tried not to show any emotion, aware that Orion would probably be watching her every move. Hurrying and with her heart pounding she mounted her horse and got on the road, mortified of the increasing nervousness. Orion would appear at any moment and she was resolved to deny him the satisfaction of knowing how much he affected her. Shortly, in a solitary stretch of the road, the masculine voice she expected materialized at last.

"I have been observing you." Orion rode his horse next to hers.

"I know." Koren answered non-chalantly turning to face the green eyes that made her tremble. The weakness that was threatening to turn her into a weeping fool was hard to contain.

"Kalani said that you don't want to hear my words."

"It's true. I asked her not to tell me anything else. Why are you here? Have you come to enjoy my suffering?" Koren asked curtly. She didn't want him to think he would be easily forgiven, especially after the horrible day she had endured by letting go of Kanek.

"I came to see you, and to talk to you. We followed since your group left from Bandah."

"I'm glad to hear you are thinking clearly by exposing yourself and Kalani to capture. What is it that you wan to say that is so important? … That you are mine? That I am yours and that is why you killed my friend?" Koren's fury gave her strength.

"I was jealous… the thought that someone else could have your love was terrifying. Thinking that someone else could kiss you or touch drove me insane… Knowing that he would be with you day to day when only I could dream of it sent me over the edge…I wasn't thinking straight…" Orion explained supplicant.

"I cannot forgive you. You know how much I have done for you, how I have given my soul for you without questions or demands. For you, I have destroyed and reconstructed the twisted fabric of life and you devalue my love with a jealousy attack!"

"I know. I know. I'm a failure… It was a low blow to you. If I could undo it, I would. Please, I cannot go on without your forgiveness. I carry this weight wrapped around my neck like a metal chain, a chain made of bitterness for having let you down." Orion's sorrow and repentance were visible in his eyes.

"Unfortunately, you can't bring him back, and you killed him so brutally. How could you use Kalani for that?"

"I wasn't thinking! I couldn't go into the palace to beat him up or something, so I sent her in. I only asked her to make him suffer, I had no idea that she would do or how she would do it." Anguish hampered his words.

"Leave, go away. I don't want to see you. Look at you, you miserable idiot. I'm not ready to forgive you. Do whatever you want; it's what you end up doing anyway. I'll think about Kalani later..." Koren said dryly, kicking her horse to gallop away without looking back. Once she felt alone, crying was inevitable; the bitter tears she was growing accustomed to singeing her face. The cold forest air dried up her tears and revived her a little, the scenery serving somewhat as a distraction to the revolting spiral into which she was falling. There seem to be another rider in the distance, but she knew who it was and decided not to look at him.

The following morning was fresh and luminous, the wild bird's harmonious orchestra winding its melody through the morning breeze. Koren took her time getting ready feeling certain weariness in her body and requesting that the maids let her be. Kalani's heart safely put away in her clothes tempted her to ask the dragoness what Orion was doing, but she resisted. Deciding to walk around in the halls to explore the palace, led her into Blassa who seemingly was doing the same out of boredom.

"Good morning, milady. Did you sleep well?" He inquired courteously.

"Good morning, Sir Blassa. I slept very well, thank you, and you?"

"We should stop the pleasantries, it does get ridiculous. I'm rested and the palace is nice. Although it seems too slow and uneventful for my liking, our palace would be hustling and bustling by this time. Ready for the trip?" Blassa commented as they walked together.

"Yes, it's too short anyway..."

"As you know, some of us are aware that you are part dragon after your outburst at the palace. You come from a strong bloodline if I'm not mistaken. You are one if us, don't forget that, we'll look after you." Blassa said in an overly friendly manner. Koren knew that his gesture was a generous one considering most dragons' dislike for racial mixes.

"Thank you, although I hope the event is forgotten soon."

"Don't worry, precautions were taken to keep your secret. The official story is that the damage in the king's tower was a result of the same attack that killed Kanek. I was wondering if once we are in Bandah we could see more of each other, perhaps for tea, or a walk through the garden... Now that Kanek is gone, I'm sure you'll like some company." Blassa smiled with his sharp teeth visible.

"Sure, why not. I'm always busy, but I could spare some time..." Koren replied out of courtesy, not having any intention whatsoever of doing what she said.

"I have discovered a beautiful art gallery right down the hall, would you like see it?"

"Yes, I would like that very much." Koren accepted the offer noticing that the dragon was overly trying to act gallantly. Blassa led her to a large and airy hall whose walls were covered by exquisite depictions of colorful landscapes. There was the exception of a wall in the back of the room, which displayed the portraits of past and present rulers of Astra.

"This is impressive! The gallery in Bandah seems so bland in comparison."

"True, they do have a flair for color in this kingdom." Blassa chuckled nodding his head affirmatively. Koren was not amused by his charming behavior, and rather focused on appreciating the art at hand. In spite of having seen him occasionally at court events, Blassa was a complete stranger to her and his attentions unwelcome. She glanced at him without being noticed when the opportunity arose, to study him more. Blassa was not young or very attractive, which was of no consequence for a dragon could change its appearance if it so desired. He seemed poised and handsomely outfitted... yet it was his hair; the color of red berries that reached his waist, which was a shock to the eyes. Not to mention the cinders that inevitably flew out every so often from it. Further unsettling was the yellow intensity of his eyes that seemed to read a person with one glance.

"Here you are!" Talma's voice overpowered the silent gallery.

"Good morning. Where you lookinf for us?" Koren greeted her smiling.

"The queen would like us to have breakfast with her this morning. I have been looking for you both for a while, we are starving, so please come grace us with your presence at once." Talma chuckled.

"Forgive us, time is still here while admiring all these beauties..." Blassa smiled and threw a glance at Koren as he said the last words. Talma eyed them suspiciously, particularly as Koren shrugged her shoulders. All of them departed together to reach the great hall where they would eat. The spread was delightful; to the point that Koren thought that Astra was a more refined kingdom than Bandah in every aspect. A brief encounter at the garden post-breakfast served as a nice opportunity to chat with the majesties. The queen sending her love and regards to the majesties of Bandah for the birth of their son, announcing that she would soon visit the palace to bring the customary presents for the prince. After the charming encounter Koren and Talma walked together in the garden to wait for the time they had set to depart. Talma's proximity was unnerving for the girl who tried to walk as far from the dragoness as she could without raising suspicion.

"There is something I must talk to you about..." Talma said increasing the tension in Koren's mind.

"Yes... What is it?"

"I think it is obvious that Blassa has placed too much interest in you... he likes you. He won't be the only one. You are growing up and soon enough you'll make a lot of decisions on your own and such, but... It's your beauty... It could be a curse. Men will want to win your affection however they can... They know that soon enough you'll choose a partner, or partners. Of course they'll want to be the ones..." Talma paused briefly.

"You see, not all of them will want to become your partners, some of them might just want to posses your beauty and entertain themselves with you. Dragons in particular would want to use you to breed… I'm not saying that is what Blassa is after, but it is a general warning about male dragons. A dragoness takes a very long time in bearing a dragonling, close to five years, while a woman or elf can do so in less than a year. The offspring would still be very magical, in reality there is not that much of a trade-off to preserve the purity of the dragon race. Mortality is not so much of a curse according to some dragons… I mean, you are less than half a dragonling and still very powerful, you could have very powerful drangonlings."

"Great. I'll keep that in mind. I'm not really thinking about relationships right now, I'm too young and I just lost a friend… I really don't feel like being in a relationship of any kind."

"I'm glad you can see things clearly, take advantage of your mortal youth in educating your mind and then fill it with passions. I didn't mean to lecture or be nosy. I look upon you as if you were my daughter too… Now that I don't even know if Kalani will ever come to my side again, the thought of not being a mother kills me. I was looking forward to all her life stages… I certainly hope that you'll allow me to be more in your life. You have brought youth and beauty into what otherwise would be an aging court…" Talma shared as she placed her arm around her shoulders. Koren tried to remain calm and smiled in return.

Talma and Koren returned to the castle grounds were the other Bandian contingents were waiting ready to depart. The monarchs of Astra were also there handing several wooden trunks to the dragons to take to the queen of Bandah.

"Hope that we see you soon!" Queen Risa bid farewell to all. Koren kneeled to kiss the queen's hand and turned to the king to do the same. Blassa and Puzo were the first to take off after the pleasantries were exchanged.

"Do you still have the compass?" Talma asked readying herself for flight.

"Yes, but don't worry I'm not going to need it." Koren smiled as she levitated in unison with the rest. Earth slowly fell behind and the incredible sensation of lightness that preceded flight filled her in spite of the wind's pressure. Having a large trunk tied to her back she felt every bit a dragon, especially since she wore the clothing that usually set them apart. Her flight gear was all made of comfortable black leather with the official insignias of Bandah in silver, cut to fit. Her hair had been tied up in a braid and roped around her neck similar to a scarf, also emulating the dragon's tradition to do so. Fog intensified shortly after their take off making their flight formation tighter. Through the thick clouds a blinding light suddenly flashed swallowing Blassa and Puzo who suddenly dropped from the sky at high velocity.

"We are under attack, descend now and seek shelter!" Talma's voice boomed inside Koren's head. The dragoness immediately landed as Koren followed, spotting the others' bodies hitting the ground causing an explosion and a dust cloud. Talma ran to the bodies to inspect them and then halted in horror.

"No! NO! It's Kalani! We have to get out of here now!" Talma shouted grabbing Koren by the arm to drag her away, since she froze at the sight of the calcinated dragons. Blassa and Puzo had been literally burned to ashes, which continued to glow with a strange white candor.

"Koren, move! We must return to Bandah at once!"

"Why can't we fly?" Koren asked her mind raided by the uncertainty of what Orion was plotting now.

"It would expose us, right now we are easy targets on land or air. Have you ever transported yourself anywhere?"

"Just appear somewhere? No, I've never had..."

"I know it's not the right time for a highly skilled magical lesson, but it's our only hope of escape. I need you to concentrate on any part of the castle that you remember clearly." Talma grabbed her by the shoulders forcing her to think.

"I don't know. Like what?" Koren asked helplessly.

"Think of your room, or your home in the forest. Think clearly!"

"I'm thinking about my room..."

"Close your eyes and focus on being in it. See yourself in every detail there... touch something that you familiar with, you are not here, think you are already there..." Talma suddenly became silent, aware that they were no longer alone. The dragoness turned to come face to face with a beautiful white stallion spouting white flames through its flared nostrils.

"Daughter..." Talma's voice failed as she raised her hands to attack Kalani, but was unable to. The knowledge that Kalani was not acting on her own volition paralyzed Talma, for dragons would not attack one of their own in those conditions. Also, Talma couldn't attack Kalani, simply, because she loved her.

"Talma go on without me! Save yourself!" Koren shouted knowing that Kalani would not hurt her, yet Talma was a different story altogether.

"Please let my mother live..." Kalani's voice infiltrated her mind pleadingly.

"What does Orion want?" Koren demanded to know, unaware that she had spoken out loud in haste. Talma stared at her confused.

"He asked me to kill all the dragons..." Kalani replied.

"Why?" Koren shouted upset. In that moment Talma screamed in fury as she realized with certainty that Koren was indeed communicating with Kalani, the truth piercing her heart. The scream alerted Koren to the imminent danger in which she had placed herself now, for judging by Talma's contorted face of hatred, it was clear that the dragoness knew who had Kalani's heart.

"Kill her." Koren gave the order without flinching or wasting time. Kalani's lethal ball of transparent fire swallowed Talma in a burning spiral as Koren ran for cover. Peeking to see what had happened, she only got to see Talma's body fall in a rain of ashes to the ground.

"I'm so sorry Kalani... I mean it. But she would have killed me." Koren approached Kalani with tears in her eyes.

"I hate you beyond words. You made me kill my mother..." Kalani yelled falling to the ground unable to withstand the pain. Koren didn't order her silence, understanding what she must be feeling at that moment.

"Orion killed your mother. I killed her too..." Koren cried bitterly.

"Where are you?" Koren screamed out loud to the surrounding seemingly empty forest.

"Here I am." Orion stepped firmly on the ground coming from behind a tree nearby.

"What is the meaning of all this? You have killed these dragons and Kalani's mother! Yes, you!" Koren reprimanded in a fury.

"I've come to give Kalani back to you. If you can't forgive me how can I go on?" Orion declared coming undone before her.

"What am I going to do with her? Now more than ever she'll shred me to pieces! You are such a fool, throwing everything away over a lover's quarrel. You are truly making me think you are worthless, you are a brat... worse than a child!" Koren scolded in a rage.

"Come with me now... Right now. Lets leave everything behind and go to the barren lands, we can join a merchant tribe that knows nothing, or asks nothing. We can live there together and make our life away from crowns and power. I don't want any of that if I can't have you. I want you..." Orion fell to his knees before her.

"No, I don't want to live like a beast. I don't want to hide. If I go now, we lose the only opportunity that we have, if I'm not at the palace we can't have the upper hand. I want to be the queen, do you hear me?" Koren spoke staring at him blankly.

"At least give me your forgiveness. It will be a long time before we see each other, and who knows what ills can befall me. Don't let those be the last words you say to me..." Orion dropped his shoulders, defeated.

"Forgiveness is earned. Lets make it clear that I'm not yours. I belong to me and I'm merely allowing you to share a part of me." Koren declared with newfound clarity and firmness, with a confidence that she had never felt before in her life.

"Get up, I need you to hit me." Koren told him.

"Hit you? Are you insane?" Orion exclaimed disturbed.

"How do you think that after such an attack I'll return to the castle unscathed?" Koren inquired casually. Orion stood frozen.

"You will have to hide the bodies properly, they'll search the place thoroughly for them. Talma must not have the death rites; she knows I have Kalani's heart."

"You are right... about everything. You are truly amazing..." He observed her adoringly.

"You better man up, we cannot have any more outbursts or mistakes from now on. Now hit me!" Koren ordered.

"I can't do that, have Kalani do it." Orion answered firmly.

"Kalani, get over here. Punch me in the face." The stallion rose from the ground swiftly transforming into a beautiful maiden whose face bore the traces of hatred and disgust. Taking aim, Kalani struck with such force that Koren fell a few paces back, squirming in pain on the ground. Blood gushed from her mouth and nose, as she spit out several teeth. Koren began to cry from the intense pain of having her face crushed, and raising her eyes she saw Kalani's white nakedness ready to strike again.

"One is enough!" Koren glared at Kalani, glad that dragon slaves couldn't kill their masters or she would've been finished swiftly. The dragon returned to her steed form and trotted away to a clearing nearby.

"I hope they can fix this at the castle..." Koren wept and laughed spraying blood as she tried to talk.

"Don't worry they fix everything... besides even with your face smashed and bloody you still look beautiful." Orion smiled and helped her to her feet.

"I better go now, this hurts. See you soon..." Koren said coldly, rejecting his embrace when he tried to hold her in his arms. Orion lowered his gaze in silence as she turned to leave without saying another word.

"Kalani, I'll keep in touch. I'm sorry about your mother... honestly. I want you to let me know as soon as Orion establishes a close friendship with anyone, particularly a woman. Do you understand?"

"Yes, mistress."

The magical compass allowed Koren to navigate the fog on the return to Bandah, although she was curious about the mode of transport that Talma had suggested earlier. Figuring the attempt would be time consuming, and less pleasing than the flight. The best part of traveling sometimes, was the actual travel. It didn't take long to reach the castle where a group of guards were in the clearing expecting the group's return. Koren could make out clearly Pumzi and Marussa in between the retinue. They visibly became alarmed the minute they saw her appearance upon arrival and the absence of the others.

"Koren! What has happened? Where are the others?" Marussa asked worried as she relieved Koren of her travel belongings.

"We were attacked midflight... I saw the first ones fall and then Talma ordered me to land. It all happened too fast, I spiraled down and lost control. Landing badly knocked me out, when I came to my senses I couldn't find anybody else, there was not trace of them!" Koren faked anguish as she told her gripping tale.

"That's awful! Hurry, alert Queen Violet at once! Marussa ordered. The knights and soldiers ran about in a fast pace spreading through the castle to gather the proper officials. Pumzi held Koren's hand and led her to the palace's infirmary.

"Poor girl, it seems that you can't recover quickly enough from all the events you experience. Look at you, it's a miracle you didn't die!" The healers descended upon Koren like a swarm of efficient bees suffocating with their care. A drink was offered to immediately soothe pain, while potions eased the swelling in her face. A young witch made her drink a chalky potion that was bitter and made her choke in between gulps.

"It's so that we can give you teeth again, you'll have them by tomorrow. They will be small for a couple of days, you won't notice nay difference by the end of the week."

"Thank you." Koren said feeling the inflammation of her face receding, letting her speak clearly. There was commotion in the outer hall and Koren looked up to see what was the matter, only to see the queen approaching with her baby in arms.

"Koren! My dear girl, I have been told what happened!" The queen came to her side and tenderly held her hand.

"I really don't know what happened... we were attacked and I woke up after..."

"Hush, you must rest. No need to say anything about it now. I sent word for your mother. How long had it been that you left Astra before the attack? That could give us a clue to know where to search."

"It had been about a quarter of an hour, maybe less. There was a lot of fog and we couldn't see our attackers... I'm glad I had the compass Talma gave me to get back here." Koren commented with fake sorrow.

"That's enough, no need to say more. I'm so glad that you came back to us, we'll try to seek more answers later." The queen walked away to address the guards and officers congregating in the main hall.

"My baby! My baby!" Flora's desperate yells reached Koren as she stormed the room.

"They sent for me urgently, but they wouldn't tell me anything. I thought you were dead!" Flora wept.

"I'm fine, they have put me together nicely. I was lucky..." Koren dug herself into her mother's arms seeking the comfort that she knew resided there. Strangely the peace she thought she would find escaped her.

"Your father has joined the search party, they don't expect to find much. The fact that only you made it back points to a bad omen."

"I'm sure they are dead... I can't believe it. We were flying and suddenly the light came through the fog, it was probably the bodies of others lit on fire..."

"Stop, don't think about it now. You are here safe and alive that is what matters to me." Flora kissed her daughter's forehead.

"Mama, I don't want to live in the palace anymore. Please... I want to quit. I want to forget about all of this and go home..." Koren begged in a moment of repentful lucidity.

"Don't be a fool. Just because you've had some bad experiences you can't walk away from your title. You are now an official member of the court..." Flora tried to calm her down.

"Yes, you mean I'm the queen's slave. You have sealed the fate of this kingdom, mother!" Koren furious words erupted.

"No, dear, don't say those things you are in a confused state. You are part of the queen, of what she represents, and you were chosen from many to have the honor to serve the kingdom. You have demonstrated with your courage that you are an asset to her majesty's court and you stand out by many other reasons that your uncommon beauty. You saved the queen don't you remember that? We all have a destiny and I think yours is in the palace."

"What if I have an evil destiny in store?" Koren asked curtly.

"Oh, child! The things you say!" Mistress Flora rolled her eyes dramatically losing patience with her daughter. Koren turned away from her mother, hiding the tears that had now begun to descend freely from her bloodshot eyes.

"I'm done talking now. Leave." Koren ordered flatly.

"Please, don't be so callous. I only want you to realize you have just gone through another bad moment and you are overreacting. If you feel like it, come home for a while..."

"Overreacting? Mother, you are incredibly stupid. Go now. It is time that I grow up and accept that which is for me to live..."

"Don't you dare talk to me like that! I will not tolerate any more insolence from you. I'll ignore it this time because you are in a haze, but not again, unless you want a sound thrashing!" Mistress Flora rose, wildly upset.

"I said go away. As a matter of fact, don't ever return."

"Koren! What are you acting like this?" Flora demanded deeply hurt.

"You heard me. Go Away! If you don't get out, I'll summon the guards to have you kicked out of here at once…" Koren warned while Flora stood agape. The woman was bereft of her voice as she retroceded, deciding not to cause a scene. Flora thought that her daughter was traumatized by the earlier events and that she would come to her senses later. The reality was that Koren was heeding her mother's advice in fulfilling her destiny at all costs; she needed to grow up and renounce weakness. Koren realized she must leave behind anything that affected her, including her mother. Mistress Flora walked away unaware that she would never see her daughter again… not until the day she died, when her last thought was of Koren.

Sleeping uncomfortably, the arrival of a new day was refreshingly welcome. Koren suspected that she had been given a sleeping potion to help her rest. Seeing her travel clothes still on was sight of relief, Kalani's heart was still with her. There was a light knock on the door as Anari announced her arrival.

"Good morning! You look better than yesterday, how are you feeling?"

"Perfectly fine. Any news?" Koren greeted.

"Yes, they found the area where you were attacked, but no bodies. They were probably pulverized by Kalani's fire… we had suspected as much. It's just so horrible to think that Talma died by her daughter's hands. I can imagine she didn't try to defend herself…" Anari's voice trailed off.

"Oh no! That's terrible!" Koren exclaimed feigning surprise and shock.

"It is a miracle you survived. You must have escaped unseen thanks to the thick fog. The king thinks that the attack was truly targeted to the knights, and Talma just happened to be a casualty. Perhaps the assailant is trying to weaken the king's entourage since it is in charge of military affairs. After all, Kanek was the first one to die and he was also a knight, a well trained one to that."

"Really? That's what they think? Of course… it makes perfect sense." Koren nodded digesting all the information, and agreeing.

"So far that's what we've got. The healers sent word that when you feel like it you may go to your chambers, just make sure to go see the queen first."

"I'll go there now." Koren stood up ready to leave the infirmary.

"There is no hurry, we are all aware that you are recuperating." Anari gave her a friendly smile.

"I'm fine, really. I'll go freshen up and wear proper attire to meet with the queen."

"I'll let her know you'll be coming soon, but like I said, there is no hurry. I'm really glad that you are well. Welcome back."

"Thank you." Koren nodded again. Anari left and Koren made sure to tell the healers she was leaving too before heading to her place. A pleasant surprise greeted her at her flat, for the maids had taken every effort to welcome her back properly. The place had been decorated with flowers at every corner, while the air had been scented with lavender. Neroli jumped to her shoulders right away affectionately purring as Koren stroked her silky fur.

"It is nice to see you too." Koren rang the service bell to summon the maids.

"Prepare the bath." Koren ordered as the women got to work immediately. Koren smirked thinking of how easily she could do it all herself with a blink of her eye. The pettiness of menial tasks seemed so absurd... she sat to observe the women contemplating the idea of what would become of them if magic took acre of everything. Had magic taken over every aspect of daily life it would probably be a stunning failure, for people would come up with useless magic things to do. There was a necessity to enjoy life's banal pleasures. Magic was just an extravagant waste of the true luxury of being alive.

"Your bath is ready, Lady Koren." Koren smiled and put Neroli down to go freshen up, aware that she enjoyed being served more than using magic.

The visit to the queen's suite was brief and casual. The queen was more absorbed in the care of her infant son than in Koren's presence. Violet told her that she was glad to see Koren well and that nothing had been found regarding the attack. The news that the prince's formal presentation in court would happen under maximum-security measures was also shared. Koren took leave and went to the library to spend the rest of the day there. She didn't accept any invitations to tea with the other ladies, feeling like a castaway in the palace. That feeling took ground in her being and remained there for the following days, weeks and months that followed.

The library became Koren's refuge, until she discovered the daily legislative sessions and audiences. Figuring that it would serve better to get acquainted with the practical ruling of a kingdom. Koren wanted to prepare for the day that she would be the queen; the kingdom would continue to prosper under her rule. Her excursions taught her the inner workings of the castle and how decisions where made. The kingdom of Bandah was run justly by a well meaning king and a wise queen. The king was the queen's representative in all affairs of state and he was in charge to make decisions of lesser importance, such as keeping peace between territories, setting trade and enforcing the law. After king, the Supreme Chancellor ruled and his main role was to control the legislative branch, deciding which matters to present to the majesties for consideration. Koren was fascinated by the orchestration and organization, which with they operated to control the kingdom. Each vice kingdom of Bandah had two demanding delegates in every session whom seemed intent in securing all the benefits for their respective crowns. Koren preferred the afternoon meetings where the audience hall was opened to the queen's subjects to directly appeal their problems to the king. The audience that she favored most was the one when a desert merchant had brought in several of his gigantic beasts. The man wanted to show the king that such beasts required a costly upkeep and the newly imposed taxes on the possession of beasts of burden was unfair. The king had to admit that such large beasts required a lot of upkeep and reduced the tax to what it had been. As the merchant happily wandered off one of his beasts let out the foulest fart possible causing the cancellation of all audiences for the rest of the day. It also caused a new decree be announced, no large beasts allowed in the audience hall from that moment on.

The ceremony to present the royal prince of Bandah at court proceeded mostly unnoticed by Koren, having succumbed to a strange stupor. The festivities and the opulence to celebrate the boy didn't alleviate the tumescent state in her soul. Not even the affectionate greeting from the majesties of Astra aroused her from the trance. Koren watched absentmindedly as the queen and king announced the name if their firstborn, Eligius Maximus, to the sound of thunderous applause. Not even the fantastic ball that followed was tempting enough for Koren to remain there, and feigning illness she retired early. Somehow life was draining from her, feeling an unnerving lack of emotion and will. Her soul was wrenched in a suffocating vacuum formed by the evil she had carried out and would have to continue to. The worst part was suffering the illness of time for things to finally come to fruition. Orion plagued her thoughts constantly, as much as the temptation to call Kalani and ask for him. Her pride stifled her desire to reach out. Long forgotten was the sadness of Kanek's death and forgives had borne in her towards Orion, but she still wanted to make him suffer.

Days kept rolling on full of tedium, Koren expecting their end to try to patiently wait for the next one. A year crept away fumbling into foolishness, and the sole diversion in the castle was to chase the queen and her offspring around. Koren was tremendously annoyed by the adoration the little boy elicited from everyone. Eligius, who ran amok in the hallways letting his giddy cackles resonate on the walls, smote the ladies. Koren was not able to join in the cherishing of the prince like the others did, distancing herself from him as much as she could. Finally she caved into her desire to know about Orion and contacted Kalani, learning that they had made a settlement in the inhospitable parts of the desert. Orion had been forming dubious alliances with some merchant warlords and mercenaries to establish a secret army. Kalani told of how they traveled incessantly searching the alliances of questionable breeds willing to fight, or just wanting to savor destruction. The dragoness spoke of an elf woman named Pagorah, who was providing them with illegal weapons and who was getting close to Orion. The news sent Koren into a rage. Ordering Kalani to keep a close eye on them, and if there were just a hint of something other than friendship, to be told immediately. Koren hated the way her soul felt day after day, the dreary emptiness that mercilessly pounded at her. More than once she entertained the thought that perhaps death would be more of a blessing than waiting for life to come.

Koren turned fourteen and told no one. Queen Violet did remember and congratulated her; surprised that Koren wanted no celebration in her honor. Mistress Flora also remembered, attempting like many times before to reach her daughter, only to be turned away by the guards. The woman would spend many nights crying and aching for her estranged child who no longer wished to deem her existence worthy of notice. Master Lorean was also turned away, understanding that his daughter's position in the castle gave her the right to shun her parents, but not liking it at all. Koren felt antagonized by others' attempts to make her celebrate her birth in spite of her feelings against it. Fearing that they would throw a ball against her wishes she approached the queen with the request for a leave of absence from the palace. Violet was taken aback by the request, not to mention preoccupied, but then decided to grant Koren permission to travel. The queen thought that Koren was becoming a woman and perhaps she needed to find herself, loneliness and introspection were conducive to that. Seemingly that was what Koren was looking for. Koren wasn't sure where she wanted to go, and having always wanted to see the sea, her destination was ultimately Stella Maris.

"We will give you a proper entourage, you are a lady of the court. Traveling by yourself is not a thought I'd like to entertain." Violet warned after hearing Koren's travel plans.

"Your majesty, I'm grateful for your generosity and attentions, but I'd rather travel unnoticed. I'm capable of defending myself and the main reason I want to embark in this journey is to find solace in tranquility. With a proper entourage I'll have no peace, for people will want to see the palace oddity in their midst." Koren explained calmly resolute in her requests.

"I understand, however the idea that a lady of the palace is to be out and about in the world like some unfortunate transient is unsettling. You know that there have been random and unexplained attacks to royal envoys. You survived a terrible attack once, but what if next time you are not so lucky?"

"Precisely, if I remain anonymous no one would know I come from the court. Besides, if the attackers are set on killing me there is not anything I could do to stop that, they have Kalani." Koren reiterated her position.

"How do you think people will not know who you are? They only have to look at your face to know your identity..." The queen reached out for Koren's face and caressed it softly.

"I will cover my face. I will travel the back roads until I reach the sea. The magic compass that Talma gave me is still in my possession, getting there will be easy. I will camp on some isolated shore..." Koren pleaded her case.

"You may go. Pleas be careful and do try to go unnoticed. Return to the palace at once if anything turns out differently than we have discussed. How long will you be gone?"

"A couple of weeks, I have made arrangements to have my duties in the library looked after. I'd like to leave this afternoon, if possible..."

"So soon? I guess there is no point in trying to change your mind. Go, then. If you need me you know you can reach me..." Violet smiled as Koren leaned to softly kiss her cheek.

Koren left the queen's suite experiencing a crushing weight on her shoulders. If only the emptiness in her was an absolute emptiness, so there was nothing at all allowing her to feel. Neroli paced the room anxiously aware that there was an impending departure. Koren had a small travel sac with a few belongings that she thought would suffice while away. Taking Kanek's sword made her feel that he was going with her on an adventure.

"Time to go, Neroli. Say good-bye to all your life of luxury. I have asked for a horse, we won't fly. Aren't you excited?" Koren scratched the feline's fur playfully.

Once Koren tossed the sac on her back the cat jumped to the door and looked at her expectantly. As Koren walked away the image of a young woman coming from a mirror nearby caught her by surprise.

Her body had changed. The curves of her hips and breasts denounced her body's slow ripening, while the roundness of her youth gave way to the definition of womanhood. From the day she had begun to bleed regularly Koren knew that the transformation into a woman was on its way, but she had neglected to observe the results. Althea had been the one to inform her of what was happening to her body and why. Looking at the young woman in the mirror, the girl she thought herself to be did not exist anymore in the physical or emotional realm. The days of military training at the palace gave her a defined and strong physique, while her lean and long legs gave her the perfect height. Koren had always known her beauty, yet the subtle changes had accentuated it and she was pleased with what she saw. The next time she came face to face with Orion he would not see her as a girl... Orion... His name infiltrated her thoughts again, this time burying deep in her mind the expectation of a physical encounter between them. Unfamiliar warmth filled her body making her blush, knowing that a want had aroused her body and soul, and needed to be sated soon.

Koren swiftly left the castle; avoiding everyone for fear that they would try to impede her quiet departure. Knowing all the nooks and crannies of the castle made a getaway easy to where her mount waited. Skirting the forest she couldn't help but look to the path, which would take her to the little home that once, was the center of her universe. Koren scolded herself for thinking such silly childish longings. Neroli explored their surroundings at a short distance, happily enjoying the outing and keeping an eye on her owner all the while. The decision to take a leave from the castle seemed to be the proper one, a change of settings might not diminish the sense of loneliness but it would at least provide new scenery. Getting off the horse, she let her legs wander freely for a few hours without any precise path to follow. Night was creeping in slowly, preceded by the colorful array of pink and gold hues that the sunset sprayed on the grey sky. The fog was rolling in with the menace of cold and dampness, so finding a clearing to set camp would have to happen soon. Koren placed her tent in a small cove surrounded by the comfort of trees and silence, where for the first time in months she felt her mind at ease. Silence was an illusion, for the forest's sounds thrived in the night. Neroli came in the tent purring contentedly as she lay next to Koren. In that narrow space between dream and consciousness, curiosity struck Koren and made her summon Kalani.

"Mistress, I hear you." Kalani saluted coldly.

"I just thought about you, I wasn't meaning to call you... Where are you now? What have you both done?"

"I'm in my tent, Master Orion is in his. We have finally found the perfect shelter in the desert. You see, when we first got here the sandstorms made it difficult to establish a garrison. Looking around for weeks we came upon a grotto that led to some subterranean caves hidden from sight. It is the perfect place to build an army unnoticed, there is a river that provides water, and there are enough caves to provide plenty of room for all. Finding this place would be impossible if one didn't know of its existence, the use of a compass is strictly enforced for some men have already been lost in the desert. Orion already counts with twenty-five men; not a large contingent but it's a start. I must say they are all a bunch of undesirables… it has been hard. Master has to be forceful to control the men… He has visited some of the ogre clans, but they all remember his failed attempt to siege the throne of Cyrus, and refuse to become his allies. Master Orion keeps to himself a lot, silent all the time unless he must speak.

He trains us all in military arts for grueling hours every day and has named a few officials… About a week ago, we had a group of coquette witches stumble upon our encampment and the men led them in the cave, it was a depraved event. Master Orion didn't join the men in their orgies, he retired full of disgust to his tent and remained there until the following day, when the witches moved on. He ordered me to stay with him so that no one would bother me, he mostly read the whole time and wrote in his journal. I have to admit that he has been kind to me, always making sure I'm treated like a lady. During the week we get a lot of visits from renegade elves that work for a woman named Pagorah, the one I mentioned to you a while back… They bring food and weapons, although I have to hunt a lot to feed the men. In a day or two we will go south to visit more clans… and Orion wants to bring presents…" Kalani's voice trailed out.

"Presents? Why do you say it like that? What kind of presents are you referring to?" Koren inquired alarmed.

"Human flesh." Kalani's answer sent chills through Koren's spine, although she had sensed the answer. It was common knowledge that ogres considered humans a delicacy, preferably of young age.

"How are you going to do that?" Koren was afraid to know the answer.

"There are a lot of villages bordering the desert, south of here. They are close to the vice kingdom of Polaris. We will attack at dusk and take the children… Please, please, I beg you… Don't let Orion make me do that! I don't want to take part in such despicable actions, please!" Kalani's voice supplicated heavy with emotion and anguish.

"Kalani, you don't get to chose what you are ordered to do. I put you at Orion's bidding and you will do, as he deems necessary. I'm not sorry for you; you are not more a slave than I am. I'm the queen's property, I can't even leave the castle without permission."

"Yes, but you went there willingly… Please, allow me to tell Orion I don't want to hurt the children, his men can do it, they don't care." Kalani begged.

"You will do as you are told." Koren stated curtly as Kalani wept.

"This elf woman, Pagorah, what is she like?" Koren continued.

"Pagorah is different form the other elf kind women I've seen. Not so delicate or beautiful, I say she is rather masculine. She is always trying to seek conversation with Orion, but he treats her like the others, with aloofness. Although, she happened to bring some hunting falcons recently and they were gone for a long while. I don't know where they went; I asked to remain in the cave. Hunting bunnies is not my preferred hobby."

"Like I said, let me know if he gets close to anyone." Koren reminded.

"What do you plan to do?" Kalani sounded worried.

"Mind your own business... I will avenge Kanek's death. Keep our conversations a secret like before, and if Orion asks if I've contacted you, remember to say no." Koren laid her head on the pillow and without noticing sleep whisked her away briskly.

Koren received the cold and humid morning with a smile. Enjoying the new sounds that overtook the forest indicating that the day had begun already for many unseen forest dwellers. Eating some bread and cheese before packing and heading out, Koren felt no hurry. A few hours of pleasant riding led her to a clearing where she came upon a group of men. Koren greeted courteously from her horse and moved along, but one of the men of the group approached her. Neroli instinctively hissed at the man, yet he seemed unaffected by her threat.

"That's a grumpy cat you got there, milady... How come you are leaving so quickly?" The man gave a forced smile. Koren could sense his intentions were not good, accompanied by a wave of negative energy stemming from the other men, which had also stood to approach. Koren smiled at the irony of the situation, remembering all the tales where there always seemed to be a fair maiden in distress. The desire to wipe them off the face of the earth crept furiously inside her.

"That is a fine horse you mount, I dare say that such a fine beast can belong to a noble. What is such a lovely lady doing by herself in these parts?" Another man inquired as they all came too close for comfort. Koren's horse took a few paces back startled by the harassment, as she tightened the reins to make it stand firm.

"The lady is deaf-mute, or perhaps we are not worthy of her voice. Are we too ugly for your ladyship?" A third man jested, as the man who initially spoke to her took hold of one of the reins. Koren let him grab the rein and leaned forward to take a closer look at the man.

"You are certainly ugly... It's not that I don't want to talk, it's just that I'm busy entertaining thoughts of how to kill you all." Koren declared seeming exceedingly jolly. A tense silence overtook the group, and the men began to show their weapons uninhibited. Koren remained calm, smiling with a lethal gleam in her eyes. Those poor bastards could not fathom what a terrible end would come to them.

"Let go of my horse. If you do what I say I may show some mercy." Koren warned the man, and he didn't release his hold on the rein, staring intently at her. Swiftly and in the blink of an eye, Koren unsheathed Kanek's sword, and with an elegant movement let it descend upon the man's forearm. The limb was cleanly severed, although the hand grotesquely remained holding the rein, unaware that it had been separated from the body. The man stared incredulous at his dismemberment, and screaming in terror as the blood began to spurt. With another assertive movement of her sword Koren decapitated him effortlessly. The man's head dropped at his feet as he body collapse showered by his own blood. The other men stared in shock at what just transpired taking a few seconds to react, then raising their weapons to attack her at once. Koren jumped down from her horse and met the four men with a joyful grin. She knew she could pulverize them with a fireball, but that would rob her of the pleasure of a fight and slaughter. Kanek's sword was light and elegant, swerving in the air as if were an artist's brush. Koren was the painter spreading red blotches on a canvas. Every man tried to attack with might, yet she casually deflected their strikes, making them angrier and more frustrated by the minute. She enjoyed the clumsiness, which their anger provided, making it easier to cut off pieces of their bodies with every strike. Letting out cheerful laughs as body parts fell to her sword, she took ears, fingers and noses. Except for the man whose leg she cut at the knee only to see him stumble forward and hit the ground face first. The men were exhausted, bloodied and hurt as they foolishly tried to continue their assault. Koren had lost interest in the show and decided to put an end to it.

"My friends you seem tired... I'm just bored." Koren smiled, not feeling any sign of tiredness. The men responded by throwing their weapons down.

"Oh, if there is one thing I can't stand it's cowards. Brave men fight to death!" with these words she pounced on the men who tried to scramble, only to be quartered to death. Finishing off her task, she mounted her ride again enjoying an unbridled sense of power and will. Gulping in the fresh air and taking in the sky's blue, her chest felt full of a pride she couldn't explain. Knowing that what she had done was an aberration against social and moral imperatives did nothing to assuage the desire to do it again.

Coming to a principal way heavily transited by merchants and their wagons, announced the vicinity of a large city. Gargantuan beasts pulled large metal containers alongside carriage horses. Koren weaved her way around people covering her face with a large grey leather hat, able to spy upon the other transients with ease. The diversity of the beings surrounding her was astonishing, it provided a visual sample of the many races she had only heard of. Ogres, witches, elves, giants, fairies, trolls and more had for a moment something in common. The city of Manssa was the closest destination, welcoming everyone through large gates, which remained widely open. Filled with renew enthusiasm she made her way to find a place to stay and get a warm meal. Going through the city gates she had a hard time not being distracted by everything that was around her. Manssa was a smaller city than Bandah, yet it had lots of character thanks to its brick buildings that had been meticulously painted pure white. Metal balconies and gates of intricate design accentuated the stark contrast of colors that large vases with fruit trees provided. In spite of the cold, the buildings' vibrancy and spark made the visitor feel cozy. An inn caught her eye; it was painted the customary white, yet it had sapphire blue accents that beckoned.

A girl with golden hair came to the reception area, halting when she saw her, bereft of words. Koren smiled kindly familiar with the effect her looks had on others.

"Is there vacancy?" Koren asked waking up the girl from her trance.

"Yes! Yes, there is. You may leave your horse by the side of the building if you are riding, our boys will take care of it at the stables. The cat you cannot carry around, it would have to stay in your room for the safety of others. You must understand that it is no ordinary animal..." The girl eyed Neroli with caution.

"I understand, and that won't be a problem. I'll pay in advance." Koren placed a gold coin on the counter.

"I'm afraid I don't have enough change for that. You have to go to the banker and pay later." The girl told her trying to avoid staring imprudently at her.

"Alright. I will pay when I leave then. I want your best room and a bath be drawn for me." Koren motioned to her dirty garments, although no one would have suspected that the red stains on the leather came from several different men's blood.

"Here is your key, milady. You can have the large room at the end of the hallway. It's the most silent and comfortable one, it has a bath of its own which you can prepare or I can send the maid over. It will cost extra, though." The girl informed hesitantly.

"I have many more of these coins, spare no luxury." The receptionist nodded and bowed her head. Koren grabbed the key and headed for the room, finding it appallingly small in comparison to her palace accommodations. At least the room seemed clean enough, she thought. A knock on the door announced the maid's arrival and Koren let her in. The woman prepared a warm bath for her using some of the perfumed oils Koren had brought to scent the water. The maid helped her undress trying not to stare at her physical perfection, as Koren sank into the tub to relax. The bath refreshed her and made her feel ready for a short exploration of the city. Changing into more comfortable clothing and the leather hat that kept her hidden from the world, she headed to the bank.

The city's market was easy to find thanks to the large crowd assembled there, it was thriving. Finding directions to the bank, she called on the banker who advised just to change one of her coins. It would suffice for several stays in the city, he informed her. Koren was amazed at the value her coins had, and more so at how little money people had in general. Heading to the nearby stands surrounding the large square, she curiously visited each. Tucked away in a corner of the square, there was a stand with a black tarp visibly announcing the sale of magical items, and being tended by a witch with unbelievably purple hair. Koren came over fascinated by all the trinkets and potions on display, to be surprised that the majority of things for sale were considered black magic artifacts. She also saw familiar items like amulets and mermaids' hairs, as well as exorbitantly priced dragon's blood.

"Most of your wares are illegal in our kingdom." Koren commented smiling at the witch.

"Says who? The queen? The king? I don't know those clowns, so I could give a green pig's snout about what they say. I'll like to see what their incompetent soldiers can do against me!" The witch gloated attracting the attention of shoppers nearby.

"You are not afraid of the guards?" Koren contemplated the concept with surprise rather than curiosity.

"Afraid! Ha! Fear only exists to make the enemy powerful. The soldier that tries to get me will find itself short of a head! No one can send me to the dungeons!" The witch continued to vociferate and smile at everyone, showing some strangely filed teeth. Koren shrugged and kept looking at the displays until a delicate pearl ring stood out to her.

"What is that ring for?" Koren inquired.

"Oh, THAT ring. It is from a special collection of items that I have enchanted myself. That pearl is really the lid to a large trunk, when you take it out of its frame it opens a magical hole, which swallows many objects. You could even put a large harp in there!" The witch declared full of pride.

"How many things can you fit in it?"

"Well, just one. But a large one... If you put too many things it wouldn't be so practical, you know. Besides, I couldn't figure out how to make it accept more than one thing, there is a wizard out of town that could probably do it." The witch commented with a complicit wink.

"How much does it cost?"

"Girl, you don't have that kind of money. A jewel of this caliber is out of your reach." The witch said flicking her wild hair out of her face.

"How dare you say that, you have no clue who I am ... I'll fashion a ring myself!" Koren announced annoyed as she walked away. Bothered by the witch's poor treatment Koren snapped her fingers sending a spark at the stand, quickly setting it on fire. People began to run away from the flames as the hapless witch tried in vain to control the intense fire. The woman resigned to watch how her livelihood was elegantly turned to ashes while the rest of the market stood unscathed. She sat on the ground pulling at her hair and moaning at her misfortune, when her eyes found Koren's.

"You! Rotten bastard daughter of a sty, you did this! I didn't do anything to you!" The witch yelled dejected. Koren gave her a little smirk and turned to continue her trek at the market. She went to a jeweler and bought a ring similar to the one she had seen at the witch's stand, with a dark pearl that she liked better. The ring fit perfectly and the jeweler assured her that it would always do so, for it would adjust to the ring bearer's finger at all times. On her way back to the inn she came across a boisterous crowd, which she joined out of curiosity. The spectators surrounded a troupe of performers and actors. There must have been about a dozen people in a makeshift stage where some troubadours sang some double entendre songs to the crowd's delight. Dancers in colorful dresses moved in unison as some acrobats tried to get attention from passersby. Koren was used to the perfect formality of palace performances, yet thoroughly enjoyed the raw intensity of the acts. Her eyes felt an immediate attraction to a guitarist who seemed to be casting a musical spell on all the women present. The man had beautiful dark eyes defined by thick eyelashes, his dark wavy hair was casually tied up with leather ribbons, and his skin told tales of abandonment in the sun. Koren observed him enjoying the anonymity that the crowd provided, just as an actor showered the audience with tiny paper flowers making everyone move, thus leaving her exposed. Her hat also fell to the ground, and even though she picked it up hurriedly, when she looked up again the guitarist had his eyes fixed on her. Trying to focus on the showcase she ignore the stares and smiles that the man was obviously bestowing on her. The audience applauded wildly at the end of the show, and Koren joined sad that it was over for she had enjoyed it more than she would like to admit. The acrobats had been standouts, their bodies amazing the crowd with their incredible flexibility and jumps. While the belly dancers with the flutters and hip movements had captivated everyone's attention during their performance. Skilled witches who displayed and array of spectacular fireworks that enthralled the audience, eliciting more applause, performed the grand finale.

Feeling joyful Koren headed back to the inn to have a proper supper before going to bed. After ordering the food she sat at the communal table to wait when there was a commotion in the back of the eating hall. Turning, she found that the same entertainers she had seen earlier where staying at the inn, and performing for the guests.

"Ladies and gentlemen, distinguished guests of this lovely inn, The White Bear… Allow us to provide some unforgettable entertaining this evening. If you are pleased by our incredible talent, please generously fill our coffers!" The man with the intense dark eyes announced out loud eliciting loud applause.

"I am Pau, master musician and director of this very talented ensemble. It is my sincere hope that we can bring joy and merriment for you all." He added as he picked up his guitar from the ground. Koren sank into her chair trying to hide, the suspicion that the troupe's arrival to her inn was not coincidental raising an alert in her mind. The music was enjoyable and being able to observe the guitarist at leisure was a plus. People rose form their seats to dance and the crowd went wild when the dancers did their belly dance routine. Koren decided that they had earned a sizable tip and left a valuable coin in their coffer.

"Thank you all for your attention, our function has come to an end, but I must remind you that your generosity is greatly valued. Our musicians will continue to play for your enjoyment, get up and dance!" Pau took a bow cherishing the audience's response before leaving the spotlight. Koren saw him talk to a waitress then return to the hall looking for a place to sit. She tried to look away, covering her face with her hat, knowing that she had been spotted. His steps approached and she tensed.

"I won't bite you… unless you wanted me to… I hate dining by myself, and it appears that you are alone, lets sit together." Pau sat by her and extended his hand to hers.

"My name is Pau."

"My name is Koren." She replied shaking hands with him.

"You must be the queen of Bandah…"

"I'm not! Why do you say that?" She inquired amused.

"It is said that the queen of Bandah is the most beautiful woman in the land and I don't think that anyone could go higher than the pedestal in which you stand." Pau said seductively.

"Nice words, but if I'm not mistaken, last time I saw her the queen still was the most beautiful woman in the land."

"Oh, so you do come from the castle… I could tell you were a noble from far away. What is a lady of your stature doing in these parts?"

"I'm traveling north, you can call it a vacation."

"By yourself? Without friends?" Pau seemed genuinely curious.

"You ask too many questions. Besides, I don't have any friends, except for my cat… " Koren was amused by the questioning.

"I'm sorry if my prying has offended you, I don't want to bother you. Yet if it weren't for these indiscreet inquiries, how could I ever know anything about you? People waste so much time in pleasantries and shallow banter, I prefer to be open." The waitress cam and placed a large plate of wheat berries and vegetables in front of him.

"Don't worry, I'm not upset by your inquiries. It is true I have no friends, though. I live in the palace and even though people surround me, I feel quite alone. My childhood friends stayed there, and the ladies of court do not offer what I seek. I had a friend, but he died in a tragic accident..." Koren explained feeling a pang of sorrow.

"I'm sorry, about everything. I mean I'm sorry you have no friends. It seems to me that it is hard to find any at all... interpersonal relationships are so transient that I could probably also proclaim myself friendless." Pau raised his glass and smiled, toasting to some silent memory that came to him, making Koren guess that the honor was for a friend long gone. They sat in silence as Pau ate, Koren trying to keep herself occupied with the musicians and the dancing crowd.

"We shall be friends, then..." Pau's voice declared taking Koren by surprise.

"Right now, yes. I will continue my path and you, yours."

"Everyone has to follow their paths, being tied to anyone is nearly impossible, unless you are one of those tangled creatures." Pau laughed at the thought.

"What kind of friendship could I offer you? You are many years older than I, and we live in different worlds."

"I do not measure people by their years, but by their words, gestures and experiences. Something tells me that you are not like other young women I've met, and trust me I've met many... The fact that you travel alone tells me that the palace trusts you immensely. I dare say that you are to be feared... in more ways than one." Pau's voice was again a soft caress, his eyes intense and burning making Koren's legs inexplicably start to tremble.

"Then you better be careful." Koren smiled as she delivered the warning.

"I wan to show you something, lets get out of here." Pau stood and gulped the rest of his wine. Koren followed suit and left with him uncertain if doing so was a good idea. Pau led her through the streets, dodging the evening crowds as they moved out of the city. Koren tried to ask him where they were going, but the noise cancelled out her efforts. He kept going and looking forward, searching for some mysterious destination. Getting close to the forest, he finally slowed his pace.

"Now you can tell me where are we going?" Koren asked impatiently.

"There is this lovely clearing in the forest that I want to show you, we are getting close. I come here often when we visit these parts and I need some tranquility." Walking through a maze of paths they finally came upon an open patch of green grass and wildflowers that seemed out of place in the forest.

"It is lovely!" Koren exclaimed taking in the glow of the moonlight on the whispery blooms and sitting on the soft grass.

"We can talk at ease here..." Pau sat next to her, too close for comfort, yet she didn't move away. Koren could smell his masculine scent, a pleasant mixture of sweat, incense, leather and wine. Pau edged closer making her tense up as his head was coming close to her neck.

"I want to smell you. I have never been so close to a noble lady, and I find you intoxicating. I've had too many women smelling of oils and cheap perfume... But you, you smell like the glory of youth. So subtle, sweet and powerful." Pau whispered in her ear making chills race thorough her body, not sure if she liked what was happening. If anything was happening...

"How old are you?" Pau whispered.

"I celebrated my fourteenth year recently..." Koren was nervous.

"Don't be afraid, you are tense. I thought you were older... Your breasts are lovely and your wide hips seem ready to receive a man..." Koren moved away from him quickly.

"I already have a man." Koren informed indignated.

"I doubt it... That man hasn't touched you yet. I know by the way you trembled when I got close to you; by the way you tensed when I whispered in your ear... Don't worry I'll give you a chance to run away... "

"You wouldn't have touched me if I didn't want you to." Koren said curtly.

"You are mistaken, your arrogance blinds you. I could've put something in your drink at the table... No matter how powerful a person thinks they are, they are always... Always! ...Vulnerable... I'll lead you back to town." Pau said smiling. Koren was taken aback with the situation and was too shocked to reply or act, inexplicably furious for being seen as a girl in spite of the more troubling insinuations. Feeling already a woman, she knew that she could carnally please any man if she set her mind to it. Pau led them back into the city avoiding any further conversation, while Koren fumed in silence. Once at the inn, he bee lined back to his troupe where it didn't take long to have a solicitous maiden on his lap. Koren sat in a corner feeling dejected, upset that she had been so foolish to trust such a man and humiliated by the encounter. Deciding that it was not worth a swift vengeance, she went to her room to sleep away the deception that a guy she had casually met instilled. Her heart comforted her with the knowledge that the day would come when Orion would sate all her wants and sexual desires. Lying in her bed she thought about his green eyes, his strong arms and his scent, feeling her body respond. Desire rode her like a flood of uncontrolled passion until the moment she gave herself the pleasure of release.

In the morning, Koren grabbed her things in a hurry, feeling sort of depressed. Wanting to leave the city behind as soon as possible, she didn't even stop to get breakfast for fear that she might stumble upon Pau and his crew. Neroli was glad to be out of the room and was happy to climb every tree in sight, her acrobatics dissipating Koren's woes. The day passed slowly as the scenery changed with surprising frequency. An ample road could be seen through the hills announcing the arrival at the outskirts of Phaenides, the last city before reaching the north coast. Oddly, Phaenides was not surrounded by a great wall, as would have been expected. The city sat atop an imposing mountain where it could be openly admired. From far away visitors could observe the buildings and dwellings, lapping the side of the mountain in a beehive formation. Koren could hear fairy music in the air, and found that the main courtyard in the town was alive and cheerful. Fairies welcomed travelers with their music and ethereal dance accompanied by the roaring water of a gigantic fountain. People gathered cheerfully outdoors to enjoy the music and city life, making Koren realize that Bandah was perhaps the dullest city in the kingdom. Memories from the palace were austere and solemn, even the celebrations couldn't compare with the festive feeling that she was witnessing. She smiled at the thought of the ladies letting go of formalities to be in such a state of joyful abandon as those present were. Dismounting and seeking a place to spend the night, she came across a small inn that was to her liking. Once refreshed she headed to the marketplace, enjoying the fresh air and company of others. There didn't seem to be particularly appealing items for sale at the stands, although she purchased an elegant dagger to gift to Orion at some point. Sitting to observe people seemed a perfect way to spend the rest of the day, especially when they all seemed so curious. Fixing her yes on a couple walking hand in hand, she envied the way they looked into each other's eyes and smiled. Then on a group of maidens, whose boisterous laughter attracted the attention of some young lads nearby. Across from her on the street, a group of men and women of advanced age, toasted cheerfully to daily life and friends. Children ran in wild packs sharing their infectious laughter and yells up and down the street. These familiar images of daily routines seemed to play over and over everywhere, except in her life. Sadness clouded her reverie, feeling an outcast of the world. Her childhood friends had continued their lives in the village, doing the simple things simple people do. Some would work with their families, or apprentice somewhere, then have families of their own. After a hard days work, they would come to a warm hearth, to a family and to a meal with people who cared for what they had to say. Koren felt desolate… neglected in every possible way a person could feel. Bereft of friends, family and a future, and aware that the man she claimed to love was far away from her in every sense. A tear rolled down menacing to bring a flood with it, thus she ran away to the solitude of her room compressing her emotions, so as not to come undone in front of strangers.

Neroli came to her side, soothing her loneliness, and together they remained in bed until the following day. Koren spent some time coming up with the proper enchantment to turn the ring she had bought into the perfect hiding place for Kalani's heart. Keeping it in her clothes had proved dangerously foolish and it was best to deal with it then. The ring was satisfactorily enchanted after a couple of hours, and the heart placed in it for safekeeping. Koren was tremendously pleased with her accomplishment, for her magical skill exceeded that of even the wisest witch. After a light breakfast she departed with the intent of reaching Stella Maris before nighttime. Traveling at leisure was agreeable, and not having to think about her palatial duties more so. Lenna had fumed when asked to take over for her during the absence, but a promise of a fitting souvenir appeased her. The queen would be informed of the happenings of the kingdom, there was no doubt about that. It wouldn't matter at all, since the queen's sole priority was her son, who was the recipient of her adoring attentions and those of the court. The ladies fawned over the little prince doting him with nauseating intensity. Koren missed the library though, the pleasure of daily reading and the greetings by the ghostly voices. Of all the things in the palace, the only one that she cared for was the library, the place of peace and quiet. It was place that gave her everything without asking for naught in return. Books were the only place where she could hide and learn. She could explore the world through different eyes, and live a life where good and evil didn't exist, only words. There was heaviness in her chest as she continued her travel, wondering whether people felt that way too, or if it was just she. Althea had said that it would be normal to feel out of sorts as one transitioned from childhood to adulthood; there was a place of torment in between where feelings and character got figured out. Why did Mother Nature felt the need to torture the young? Wasn't it hard enough already to have to live?

The road to Stella Maris was poorly transited midday making for fast passage. Koren's heart began to race as she sensed the proximity of the ocean. Having read about it, her mind wanted to witness all the incredible things that were said about the sea. The city of Stella Maris came to sight at last, it was rather flat and extended like a concrete mantle upon the coastal terrain. There was no sizable city wall to enter this time, and those arriving would have to follow a red brick way, which elicited the clack-clack of trotting beasts. As usual people were the ones carrying the burden of activity and their comings and goings were a welcome to the city. The sensible thing to do at any city was to find the main gathering place, and Stella Maris was not an exception. The plaza was airy and counted with three majestic fountains decorated with marine motifs, such as seahorses, shells and mermaids. The middle fountain was imposing, forcefully spouting water by the top of a mighty shell, presumably in honor of Ossida. Koren immediately thought of Orion, of how he must have come and seen the city's beauty upon his arrival too. His image was fading, tried as she might, time was besting her efforts of reminiscence. Afflicted by this revelation of the cruel limits of memory she moved along with more dread than she had brought. Wandering listlessly through the streets she found a place to spend the night since she didn't want to see the ocean just yet, the proximity to it was exhilarating and she wanted to extend the sensation. A young man was at the reception and greeted her with a nod, after the shock of seeing such a beautiful face.

"What are you?" The young man asked abruptly.

"Pardon me?" Koren replied not knowing what he was referring to.

" I've never seen anyone like you... You don't look like the mermaids, or the fairies, or the witches..." He explained timidly.

"I'm just a simple human girl." Koren declared feeling that those words carried with them heavier connotations that the young man could ever fathom. She didn't know what she was, or who she was; she only knew what she had done... The receptionist kept to himself embarrassingly nervous in her presence, sighing with relief as she wandered off on foot into the heart of the city. Koren walked at ease shedding her hat and exposing her face openly to the gasps and stares from people on the streets. Eating on some of the food stands whenever something smelled appetizing was a good way to cover the city's expanse and observe people in their element. Spying others was rewarding, their menial tasks demystified by their industrious hands. Women and men tidied their homes, did their laundry and cooked, filling the streets with a multitude of pleasing scents and sights. Lacking were the maids and servants who were ubiquitous in the palace. Watching the mothers run after their wild offspring made her think back to the days in her little home in the forest. Her mother had cared for her lovingly, and she had grown dreaming about the palace and its mysteries. How she wished that magical illusion had never been shattered...

Just as the merchants were about to close their stands for the day, Koren came by to take a peek at their wares. The place was still full of a diverse multitude of people, although the mermaids and mermen stood out by their large numbers. They had tall athletic bodies and broad shoulders that indicated their affinity to the water. Their skin shone with the oils they had to smear on to protect themselves from the sun and air exposure. Both genders exposed their magnificent torsos and wore a wide belt adorned with coral beads or shells. Under the belt a kelp skirt covered their scaly legs, which were incredibly thin and deformed. Luckily, the lower limbs would turn into a well-built fin once the merfolk returned to water. Koren thought the race to be in possession of incredible beauty, giving substance to all the tales involving the merpeople and their mysticism. She ended up buying several pieces of coral jewelry to take back as presents, as well as some black coral earrings to wear. Dining outdoors was mandatory at night; the ocean mist brought saltiness to the air that was soothing. Neroli paced their room anxiously sensing Koren's excitement as she went to bed. The copper rays of dawn invaded the room arousing Koren from a restful sleep. Not wasting any more time she gathered her belongings and left to the ocean at once. The vegetation seemed to be similar to what she had seen during her travels, the expectation that it would soon change was latent, furthered by the stickiness the salty air deposited on the skin. The sun tried to vanquish the morning's coldness, arriving in a full array of warm colors and brightening the day. Koren eagerly expected the first glimpse of the ocean, having heard the sound of waves crashing. Suddenly the vision arrived, a magnificent blue expanse laced with white sea foam that cradled the horizon. Heart pounding wildly, Koren forced her horse into a swift gallop to the nearest shore, eager to remove her boots and feel the sand.

The grainy coldness of the sand caressed her feet as the cold ocean water rhythmically massaged them. Breathing deeply she felt ready to sink in the waves and swim far away, halting her desire to do so when she noticed that there were others at the beach. Fishermen and beachgoers enjoyed the sea alike, unabated by the water's unwelcoming temperatures. Deciding to seek a place away from civilization she rode her horse for hours, until feeling satisfied. Large trees gave an intimate shelter near a cove, which was the perfect place to set camp and go unnoticed. Koren sat by the sea, kissed by the waves and their eternal drift. Silence, and the vastness that faced her, combined to pry the anguish in her soul to light. Dark, scalding and bitter tears surfaced from her; lethal poison that left deep scars behind. The foul drops landed on the water's edge soiling it with the stench of depravation, causing fear in the marine creatures nearby. Hundreds of merfolk came to the surface to see which unfortunate creature exuded such disgrace, surprised that it was just a young girl.

Koren relived in a few moments the events that had caused an impact in her short existence, wanting to study them one by one. Memory inevitably took her to the first time she set sight on Orion, the man who would make her feel such intense emotions. The one who led her by the hand directly to hell... Only to leave her there, or allow her to escape, bringing back a thousand demons. Blood, screams and death smeared her recollections... How was it possible that so many horrible things came to pass? Her willing part in every nefarious act was undeniable, starting with the death of the unborn princess. Not forgetting the enslaving of Kalani or the killing of the men in the forest, which she thoroughly enjoyed. Orion was not to blame for those things; she committed every wicked act out of her volition. The sudden understanding that in life there were people born to do good and others to do bad struck her, recognizing that she was part of the latter. A vexing dispute over what separated good and evil took place in her mind, wondering about their subjective nature. What was good for some was not good for others, perhaps good and evil where not so different from each other. Merely a view from different angles...

Morning was perfect for a walk; it was healing to be near the ocean. Neroli had wandered off, yet Koren wasn't bothered by it, allowing the cat to return whenever it wanted. The sensation of not having anywhere to go and no one to answer to was exhilarating. Loneliness assaulted her momentarily, tangibly existent in the lack of having someone to share adventures, or nonsensical banter with. All that she knew and had seen was stashed away without ever been told to anyone regardless of how important it might have been. Two days, three days, four days... they all moved on swiftly turning into weeks and then months. A long time had passed when Althea's voice shook the silence and interrupted the peace.

"Koren, how are you? The queen wants to know that you are well; you have extended your stay away from the castle disappearing without a trace. I have been trying to contact you for weeks..." Althea reprimanded.

"Oh. I paid no heed to the passage of time... The sea and its mysteries are enthralling."

"You must return to the palace." Althea announced firmly.

"I'm not ready to return." Koren replied surprised that she still knew how to communicate.

"How long until you are ready?" Althea's voice resonated.

"I don't know. But if you want me to return, you'll have to come get me." Koren declared firmly.

"Ah, what shall we do with you? The lady who has rebelled... The only one who leaves the castle one her own... The only one that does what she pleases!" Althea sounded exasperated.

"What can I say? I asked the queen for a leave of absence and she agreed. Take it up with her... If you excuse me, I'd like to return to my tranquility, you are ruining my day." Koren said tersely closing sealing her mind away from further contact. She would return when she wanted, that was certain. No other contact came, and only time refused to be ignored, eventually bringing in the freezing winter temperatures. Only then, when snow began to fall, did Koren notice that she had spent a half-year in her makeshift home by the sea. In spite of the sullenness that befell her, the return to the castle could not be postponed and she headed back. Sadly bidding farewell, snow feathered on the black velvet cape she wore. A light travel garment that shielded her from the elements but not from the sorrow that returned to her heart. The horse dragged its pace, sensing the reluctance of their return. Neroli rode with Koren to find warmth and shelter under her cape. The landscape had turned completely barren and white under winter's merciless attack. Koren didn't stop at any city to spend the night, wanting to revel in the remains of her absolute solitude. At night, the tent served as a shelter, which she preferred to an inn. The sound of the sea was already sorely missed, since it was a perfect lull to fall asleep to. It was with great sadness that she had turned away from the sea, fearing that it would be a long time before they were reunited. The thought of drowning herself at sea was tempting, but she couldn't bring herself to do it.

The return to Bandah seemed exceedingly brief. Her chest compressed as the forest thickened, its familiarity bringing nostalgia and an urgency to go home. No one would be waiting to welcome her; the thought didn't bother her at all. It was late afternoon and teatime; the ladies would be in the garden adoring the queen as usual. For the garden remained lovely in spite of the thick snowfall, thanks to large glass hothouses erected for the wintertime. Koren left the horse at the stables taking great care not to stumble upon her father, having no desire to have any contact with him. The animal fell to the ground grateful for the water and feed, and for being out of the inclement weather. Lorean was nowhere in sight and curiously, the shunning of her parents had not caused her grief; it was another dull cut in her already callused soul. With assertive steps she walked over to the garden knowing that it was best to get the greetings out of the way. The surroundings seemed surprisingly beautiful; her memory had been unfair to the exquisite elegance of the castle. Guards came to halt her as she tried to make her way through the grand hall, unable to recognize her.

"Get out of my way! I'm Lady Koren... I have returned." She demanded taking of her hat and revealing her face. The soldiers gasped, taken aback by the familiar yet different beauty that stood before them. A young woman had departed and full-fledged woman had returned. Koren didn't wait for a reply, shoving them out of the way, and aware that they followed her with their gaze. Passing through the area with the fountains, and the gardens the place was desolate. She continued her search on the second floor, going through the magical forest, which seemed to have changed quite a bit from the time she saw it last. Asking where could everyone be hiding, she decided to continue on to the queen's private gardens on the seventh floor of the tower. She walked in astonishment, having forgotten the magnitude of the palace, it was incredible to grasp how much timed changed the perception of places. Reaching the main garden, familiar voices and a child's laugh, drifted towards her. The last time she had seen the boy, he had barely begun to take a few steps, for sure he would be running around now. Koren approached in silence, observing the group and not knowing how to interrupt them. The ladies were playing a chasing game with the prince who wore a large woolen tunic, probably belonging to his father. The little boy had a wooden sword in his hand, and was hopelessly trying to attack Pumzi, who dodged the strikes with incredible speed. The queen sat watching the games placidly, encouraging her son's knightly behavior with applause and laughter. Koren despised the scene, wishing that she could turn around and leave forever. The prince noticed the stranger's presence first, freezing in place when he saw her. Koren's outline against the threshold seemed threatening, similar to an imposing premonition of the future. Her face, framed by the long braid around her neck, caught the light revealing her identity to the group. The women were left breathless by Koren's captivating beauty. They appreciated her strong and elegant body of considerable height, worthy of an Amazon.

"Your majesty, I have returned." Koren kneeled at the queen's feet and kissed her hand as customary. No one moved, no one said a word… Finally Prince Eligius came to his senses and ran to Koren to look at her closely.

"What a beauty! Mother, I want to marry this one!" The boy exclaimed with a grin unknowing that those words were the prophecy of his demise.

"Yes! She is truly stunning. You have changed and grown quite a bit, dear girl. It took me a minute to recognize you." The queen found her voice as the others reacted and gathered around Koren to welcome her.

"You certainly have changed, my goodness. I think you might have some nymph in you…" Marussa declared cheerfully.

"No, if anything she would be a fairy." Lenna interjected. Althea looked at Koren from head to toe not saying a word, giving her a half smile, which's meaning Koren couldn't decipher.

"I'm afraid I cannot say that I'm the fairest of the land." The queen laughed.

"I'm Bickett!" The prince stood in front of Koren bowing with a gesture of gallantry.

"Your majesty, I thought your name was Eligius." Koren forced a smile.

"No, my name is Bickett, I came up with that name and I prefer it." The boy informed proudly as Koren arched her brow.

"Pay no attention to his banter, he is very talkative for his age. His verbal skills are advanced beyond belief, I'm not sure if that is a blessing or a curse." The queen joked.

"Yes, he does talk a lot and quite clearly. I'm sure it is thanks to the magical gifts the fairies bestowed upon him." Lenna explained with arrogance.

"I have brought some gifts from Stella Maris." Koren said shyly. Opening her travel sac, which was dirty and mistreated by overuse, she dug for the items she had purchased long ago. A lovely pink coral necklace was the first thing to surface.

"Marussa, this is for you. I thought it would look pretty on your skin color." The nymph took the gift with delight and immediately put it on.

"I love it, thank you!" Marussa said. Koren retrieved a similar necklace but in lavender, which she handed to Lenna.

"Thank you, it is lovely." Lenna thanked her and also wore the necklace. Koren continued to produce jewelry for the remaining ladies, a red necklace for Althea, an orange one for Anari, a yellow one for Pumzi and a turquoise one for Kloe. For the queen she procured a lovely white coral bracelet of exquisite detail, which was put on right away as an appreciation for the gesture.

"Is there anything for me?" Prince Eligius asked expectantly.

"Of course, your majesty." Koren lied, since she had not thought about the prince. Finding a coral souvenir that was tucked in her travel sac she gave it to him ceremoniously.

"This is a magic coin, it has the symbol of Stella Maris. That is the Seashell of Ossida, which legend says gives the power of the sea to whomever holds it." Eligius held the coin as if it were his most prized possession.

"Mother, look! A powerful seashell." The boy ran to his mother to show his new acquisition.

"I see... That seashell is very real, and when you grow up to be the king you can go see it if you like." The queen smiled at her son.

"I want to be the king, don't have a girl!" The prince suggested with a smirk.

"Your majesty, I would like to take my leave now and go rest. I'll come down for dinner, I'm sure I will have a lot of catching up to do." Koren addressed the queen.

"Of course, you must be exhausted. Welcome back." Violet gave her a warm smile allowing Koren to retire.

The apartment seemed foreign to her, as if she had never set foot in it previously. Everything was as she had left it, although it was obvious that the maids had kept the place clean in her absence. After ordering a bath to be prepared she sifted through the dresses available with chagrin, nothing seemed comfortable or appealing to her. Randomly grabbing a gown she tried to put it on to discover than it didn't fit her, probably none of the clothes did. Perhaps she had changed more than she admitted, it had been months since she had seen her reflection or worn anything other than traveling garb. Running to her parlor full of curiosity, she sought a mirror. The woman in the mirror took her by surprise because she did not remember herself looking like that at all. The perfectly oval face and pronounced cheekbones complimented lovely red lips, which were full and inviting. Disrobing completely to study her body, she was pleased with what she saw. Perhaps she was too tall for her taste and her breasts not as large as she wanted, but she was happy with her womanly shape. A smug smile lit up her face as she imagined what Orion would think of her now, when the time came to share their bodies, certain that he would fall at her feet.

The maid came in to let her know the bath was ready, lowering her gaze trying not to stare at Koren's perfect nakedness.

"Please summon Anari urgently, I need her to come at once." The maid nodded and took off, returning with Anari in tow after a few minutes.

"Koren, did you want to talk to me urgently?"

"Yes, I literally have nothing to wear, nothing fits me. Can you have something made for me right away?"

"Oh, yes, I should've thought about that. You have changed a lot..." Anari blushed trying to avoid staring at Koren.

"I know... everyone keeps looking at me as if I'm some sort of oddity. I have grown up, what can I say? I can't change. Can you dress me or not?"

"Of course. I just need new measurements." Anari cleared her throat shyly.

"I could have made myself a gown... I really called you here because form now on I would like to have my clothing be a little different. Just to keep in mind when you are designing for me..."

"What do you mean?" Anari seemed confused.

"I'd like my clothes to be simpler, more comfortable and darker..." Koren explained.

"Darker?" Anari let out the question as if Koren had punched in the stomach.

"I love darker colors, specially burgundy. I have in mind a flowing suede tunic, cut to shape with long sleeves..." Koren suggested.

"The queen decides the colors that I can design with ... we can't pick. You know our clothes have to mirror hers..." Anari carefully reminded Koren of her place.

"You are right ... I'm such a fool. Being away made me forget that we don't do what we like, just what we are told." Koren spoke dryly.

"It hasn't been a problem before... All the other ladies are happy with it." Anari offered blushing.

"Just forget about it. Never mind that I mentioned it. Please try to make my gowns as simple as possible, could you? The flow of fabric is suffocating... And I'll need something for tonight." Koren said curtly motioning for Anari to leave. Anari sat motionless for a few seconds taking in the situation, standing to leave in a state of confusion and disbelief.

During the course of the evening's banquet people sent curious glances at Koren all night. The king had welcomed her back and made kind remarks about how her remarkable beauty would light up the palace. Koren noticed that Althea observed her pensively, which was unnerving. The large banquet hall was plentiful of officials and dignitaries who no doubt would comment out of the palace about Koren's looks. She could sense the admiration; the murmurs and the toasts in her name making her feel uncomfortable. Shortly after the food was cleared from the tables people dispersed into a social colloquium, which Koren didn't join, sitting in a corner to herself and pretending to be preoccupied with her hairdo. Althea came to her in spite of her efforts to disappear. Although it seemed better to find out what was up with the witch rather than to keep guessing.

"Forgive me if I have been a little detached. I must say I was surprised when you showed up the other day, unannounced. I sense that you have changed a lot, and I don't mean physically. I can't put my finger on it... Precisely my sister has nightmares about a beautiful woman with blond hair that burns people alive..." Althea let out a cackle, laughing at the absurdity.

"Your sister is crazy." Koren said curtly, thinking to herself that perhaps it was time that Lula disappeared from the castle for good.

"Yes, she is a little off. What I really wanted to comment with you was that the queen and I are aware that we will be getting many requests for your courtship soon. We think that you should take your time in deciding... but that you should be married as soon as possible since this will make your life easier. There are some vice kingdoms that have young sons in their court, of marrying age. You would be an excellent vice queen! The queen thinks she can help you chose, as a matter of fact, she has someone in mind. Prince Atle is ready to marry, he has proven to be an excellent ruler, and word is, that he is actively seeking a bride." Althea's words rained heavily on Koren, as she tried to digest the information the witch was pelting at her. Upon hearing Atle's name she was panicked.

"Why do I have to marry? No one else has!" Koren was visibly upset.

"I should have waited a little bit to tell you... I guess I couldn't help it. We just think that with your power it is best that we place you in a strategic position..." Koren couldn't hear what Althea was telling her after that point. Atle was her lover's brother and enemy, the memory of him in Cyrus came back to her bringing a nauseating feeling.

"I guess you like the proposal, you are speechless!" Althea declared in jest.

"I'm too young to think about these things and I wouldn't want to decide on it with or without the queen. I don't ever want to marry."

"You are being silly, power couples have been arranged from the beginning of time. You are not too young to be engaged and a marriage contract of that caliber doesn't come around very often. I can actually arrange it..." Althea gave Koren a pat on the shoulder leaving her close to passing out. Without bidding good night Koren ran away to her chambers and cry in despair.

The following days were an insulting repetition of the life that she profoundly hated. There was nothing to do but get up at dawn, head to the library, fulfill he duties and try to be invisible at court. She always looked for reports about mysterious village attacks, but nothing out of the ordinary was recounted. The only recommendation that she personally took to the queen at one point was a book of poetry. It narrated the story of a man that had fallen in love with a star, titled "What do I do during daytime?" Most books were boring, except for a practical one that stood out every so often, witches were good at writing. After the library she would visit the audiences as she had before. At one point she tried to return to the Royal Academy, but was impeded by Erasmus who suggested she did something else to occupy her time. Koren never shared anything when it was time to meet with the queen and the ladies, and was bothered by the lectures the queen and Althea gave her regarding her parents. Koren nodded and listened then discarded their words as soon as she turned away.

Months went away slowly and monotonous, in such a way that Koren thought she was reaching insanity living the same day over and over. Kalani would give her no news about progress and seemed to be just as frustrated by Orion's inaction as Koren. Apparently the garrison in the desert had turned into a small city full of misery, the men succumbed to violence and disorganization amongst their ranks, which deemed them unfit for an attack. Kalani retold the way Orion had a firm hand with the men, killing one or two in front of the others to keep them in check. Orion had become a hardened man, who walked away into the dunes for long periods of time, only to return with renewed spirits. The morale in the ranks changed every hour, sometimes the men were perfect soldiers and others barbaric mercenaries. Kalani mentioned that tentative alliances with ogres had been secured, now they had to start delivering on their promises of human flesh, for which Orion needed more weapons. The army had grown and Pagorah could not procure sufficient armament for all without giving the operation away. New shipments would have to be sent illegally from several parts of the kingdom so that an attack could be carried out at the end of the month. Koren asked Kalani if Orion ever asked about her, and was pleased to hear that he inquired about any communication daily. Knowing that he thought about her every day made her feel guilty for having held a grudge for so ridiculously long. More so after being told that he anxiously waited to hear from her. Kalani always bid farewell with a trace of sadness, in spite of the hatred she fostered for her captor, Koren was as close to a friend as she would ever have and her only tie to her past.

A week after her most recent conversation with Kalani, Koren was at one of the king's audiences when a commotion created a disturbance. A group of heavily armed soldiers were bringing forth three prisoners in chains towards the king and the jury. The malfeasants were two men of dubious character and a masculine woman of short stature, who reeked and looked extremely dirty.

"Your majesty, we have caught these ruffians in the outskirts of Gandem, carrying with them a large cache of illegal weapons." The soldier's accusation caught Koren's attention. She stared at the woman; seeing that she fit the description Kalani had given her of the elf collaborating with Orion. The woman had a poorly shaved head, and intense green eyes that seemed menacing. Koren didn't think the woman was beautiful, but she was definitely good looking, to which she reacted with tremendous jealousy.

"What is your name?" The king demanded.

"I'm Pagorah, an elf." The woman seethed.

"What do you have to say about the allegations against you?" The king pressed on patiently.

"That your soldiers are bunch of turds. These weapons are legal and they are mine. They were lawfully purchased from the merchants in Nubis, there is no reason for my detention." The elf spoke defiantly.

"Your majesty, she forgets to say that amongst the legally purchased weapons, there were many illegal ones hidden." The soldier declared.

"Yes, they are powerful weapons and you may consider them illegal. Yet according to the Millenary Agreement you have no jurisdiction over weapons forged by elves, and those I have. Must I remind you the position of your race against mine." Pagorah replied curtly. A silence fell upon the hall as the king conferred with his jury.

"You are in the right, however, as ruler of this kingdom and its land I will confiscate your weapons. It is your fine for not paying the appropriate transport tax for weapons of such nature, a tax agreed upon in the treaty that you mentioned in this audience." The king announced.

"That is idiotic! You just admitted they are not illegal and manage to steal them from me! You are a lout!" The elf shouted angrily.

"With what purpose do you carry these arms in the kingdom?" The king demanded, upset by her insolence.

"I sell them where ever I want, the subjects of Bandah have a right to bear arms. Apparently his majesty has forgotten the people's rights!" Pagorah exclaimed as the soldiers began to lead her away.

"Yes, as long as they do so legally." The king waved her away, dismissing the profanities that she continued to pelt him with. Koren saw how the soldiers took the prisoners outside and released them, the woman continuing her diatribe of hatred towards the king and his jury. Koren tried to leave without been seen to see where the elf would go to next, but by the time she left the audience hall Pagorah and her men had disappeared. At the end of the day, she cried in her room out of rage and frustration, the sight of Pagorah had filled her mind with jealousy and envy. That nasty woman had access to him, while she could only wish to see him. Skipping dinner to avoid the blandness of court socializing, her room felt like a haven. In spite of feeling crushed, night trapped her in its tranquility, as she observed the starry black sky. Sitting by the window she released an anguished sigh that invaded the hearts of the ones that lay awake, nearly scaring them to death.

Chapter 7: Love letters

The celebration of her birth was fast approaching, and yet Koren hadn't reached out to Orion. It had been more than a couple of years since they had spoken last and there seemed to be no progress at all in their plan, if it still was viable. Kalani gave news that a military offensive was imminent; the men were fully armed now. Orion was antsy to start attacking the villages and terrorizing the land. Kalani also suggested constantly that Koren should send word to Orion, yet she refused. Koren had avoided him for so long that her courage had waned and the right words to say seemed to evade her. Grief clenched at her heart when the news came that Pagorah was now eating dinner with Orion every night, and he seemed to enjoy it. Koren was furious but didn't act upon the novelty, fearing that a jealous rage might compromise a rekindling of their relationship.

Again, Koren requested that no ball be planned in her honor for she had thoroughly enjoyed the lack of one the year before. Koren didn't dare ask for a leave of absence since the queen had complained about the length of her stay away from the castle the last time, and because she didn't feel like doing anything at all. Koren just wanted for days to speed away, anything to make life more bearable while she waited for Orion's next move. In spite of Koren's request a formal feast was thrown to celebrate her, and she soon understood the reason behind it. Amongst the guests was the Viceroy of Cyrus, Atle. Pretending to be thrilled by the event she carried on with a knot in her stomach, barely able to refrain from bursting into tears. After the meal was sumptuously served, music filled the grand hall as her worst fears materialized. The gallant Viceroy of Cyrus asked her for a dance, under the approving eyes of the court of Bandah. Atle's resemblance to his brother made her shake uncontrollably, and the boy that she had seen a long time ago had transformed into a stunning man. He smiled as he held his hand out for her to kiss, unaware that her stiffness came from nervous tension. Beads of perspiration gleamed over her skin before even setting foot on the dance floor and her heart fluttered for the wrong reasons. Atle was a wonderful dancer who glided her effortlessly to display her loveliness to sound of the music. His tan skin and his deep green eyes were too similar to Orion's, causing a commotion in her soul. However his eyes were lacking of the ferocious menace that always seemed to inhabit Orion's gaze.

"Congratulations and happiness for your celebration, milady. I'm glad to be found here in your presence. The last time we were in proximity was quite unfortunate, this is better." Atle smiled.

"Thank you, your majesty. I do remember, my first visit to Cyrus was rather unpleasant... But it belongs in the past now. I hear you are a well regarded monarch, counting with the full support of your court and subjects." Koren replied feeling tense.

"Please, don't be so formal, or think we can only talk matters of state. I'm glad to be able to open up and have a normal conversation for once." Atle offered in good manner.

"I don't know what to say... Your highness is a stranger and a Viceroy, I'm used to follow formalities on both accounts." Koren babbled; her mind paralyzed by the situation. Atle's physical similarity to Orion was torturing; her heart ached when she looked at him, wanting to love anything that related to her estranged love.

"I'd like to stop being a stranger then, we could get to know each other. To be honest, Althea contacted me... Personally inviting me to your celebration. She also suggested you were worthy of the throne of Cyrus..." Atle beamed when he shared the information.

"She said that?" Koren was outraged.

"No. It wasn't like that at all, I'm just jesting. It is true that I was personally invited by Althea, there needed to be young blood amongst the guests, the rest I made up... No one warned me that I would come across the most beautiful lady in the face of earth, and that she is indeed worthy of any crown." Atle confessed blushing. Koren let out a loud sigh incredulous of what was happening.

"My apologies if I have offended you." Atle countered immediately.

"No. You don't need to apologize, it is I. I'm very nervous..." Koren regretted the words at once, for he would assume his presence was causing the emotional upheaval.

"I have been a brute, talking incessantly... I'm sure you are told the same thing over and over in regards to your beauty. How could I not fall prey to it too? I'm nervous too and I'm a mere mortal." He smiled broadly and danced with more zest. In spite of her inner turmoil Koren felt that Atle's presence was somewhat comforting, even calming. They danced the whole night away, talking about Cyrus, life at court and art. Koren had shoved her emotional discomforts away and found the company of the Viceroy not only pleasing, but also appealing. Atle was a mitigated version of Orion's passionate fierceness; he was the calm against the tempest. At the end of the night, Atle gently kissed her cheek and promised to see her soon, words that perturbed but she didn't reject. The guests departed and Koren went to bed feeling lighthearted for the first time in years, her feet sore from dancing for hours. Neroli greeted her with a strange yowl, alerting Koren that something was amiss. Koren searched her quarters and found nothing out of place, reprimanding the cat for giving her a scare. Koren was about to dive in bed when she saw that an envelope was on her pillow, and the bed was covered with lovely white blooms. Her heart pounded so ferociously that she was afraid it would burst, and grabbing the letter with trembling hands, she tried desperately to break the wax seal. There was only one piece of yellowed parchment made of papyrus, still smelling of sand and aridness. The sender's identity was obvious. Koren read out loud the words to make them more real...

"My beloved,

I humbly send you these desert blooms so that you know that you live in my mind and heart. Word came that a large entourage from Cyrus was headed to Bandah to celebrate a lady's fifteenth year and it could only mean you. Time has been a surly jest, yet the desert exile that I suffer is nothing compared to the desert you have barred me to. I don't know if you still hate me, or if you still love me. The uncertainty has been an insufferable punishment. The silent dunes tell me more than you... These flowers can only be found in the most barren and frightful parts of the desert. And such is my love for you, here were nothing thrives, I thrive for you. Sometimes I cry like child, fretting about the many things that keep me away from you. Or when your sacred image fades from my mind, or when the lovely sound of your voice ceases to ring in my ears. I'm an aberration of this world; I've always wanted that which I was told I didn't deserve. Perhaps I don't deserve you, but I want you more than anything else. I inhabit a mortal insularism of which you can only keep me afloat. My life, my soul, and my love I had already relinquished to you. Now I give you all that is left, my pride. I beg that you no longer shun me, kneeling at your feet I beg, that you bestow upon me the honor of your words. I hope more than anything in the world to be by your side the next time you celebrate your birth.

Orion, truly yours."

Koren repeatedly read the letter out loud as if it were a healing prayer that restored her energy. She cried out of joy, out of sorrow, out of heartbreak and out of love. The short and simple missive written by his hand was the most wonderful creation of the universe, and his impeccable calligraphy a testament to perfectionism. Lying in bed blinded by the puffiness of her tearful eyes, Koren resolved to contact Kalani the next day to end the cruel silence between them. The exhilaration was vivid in her the next morning; as she went on to perform her duties. The palace seemed to unsettled, guards were going back and forth with serious faces, while the maids scurried away in too much of a hurry. Koren stopped a young woman in the hallway to inquire about the happenings.

"The castle is in high alert, word has come that some southern villages have been attacked by a mercenary army. To make matters worse, Lady Althea's sister has disappeared." The woman informed almost out of breath. Koren raced to the queen's office where the chancellors, generals and the king were conferring.

"We must send troops to the area surrounding the attack to secure the area. We don't have any intelligence as to which group carried on the attack or what motives they had. We do know there have been many civilian deaths, your majesty." One of the generals present informed the queen. Koren sat next to Lenna who greeted her in silence, while she mimicked the seriousness of the others present.

"Yes, the news is devastating. Send as many soldiers as are required to control the situation and rebuild the villages. We must establish communication with the cities of Tulas and Balta to keep everyone in alert." The queen ordered. As Violet spoke strategies to handle the attack, Koren sent mental messages to Kalani to keep Orion informed of all the military's movement. The generals were dispatched after getting instructions, the king followed after kissing his wife good-bye.

"This is unbelievable, terrible... Koren, I'm glad you are here with all the commotion I forgot to have them alert you." Violet apologized to Koren.

"It is understandable, seems like this morning has been hard. Lula has disappeared and there has been an attack?" Koren inquired the obvious. Violet placed her hands to her temples squeezing hard, indicating that a headache was assaulting her without mercy.

"Yes. They have utilized Kalani in the most abominable way... The survivors say that she came at dawn, walking down the main road spraying fire in every direction and turning each home into a pyre. People fled their homes in panic and as they tried to escape fell into the hands of waiting assailants. The children were taken and the able bodied men were murdered on the spot. The surprise attacks and the fire overtook the villagers..." The queen's voice shook as she retold the story.

"On top of it we have searched the castle and Lula is gone. I don't think we'll find her this time..." Violet declared anguished. A deafening silence filled the office as the ladies felt sullen. Koren bowed her head pretending to be swallow in despair, although she was excited that the attack had finally happened. She was also relieved that she wouldn't have to deal with Althea's sister; it didn't matter where she had gone to as long as she stayed there forever. The queen sent them off to their duties with the warning that at any moment they could be summoned if necessary and to be alert to any suspicious activity in the castle. Koren ran to the library eager to read all the reports that surely would be arriving from different parts of the kingdom. Able to read the reports properly, Orion's despicable mission was recounted with great detail, which gave her a guilty mind by association. All the audiences had been suspended until further notice so Koren found herself with nowhere to go but her room, where the task of writing a letter awaited. Having only been writing official papers, she was bereft or words to write that would concisely convey all the things she wanted to say. She didn't want to bore him; she wanted to sound grown up, yet frustration was creeping, as the task was getting difficult. With great resolve she sat, promising not to get up from the desk until a proper missive had been written.

"My beloved prince,

I have received your flowers... your words... and I thank you for leading back the light into my soul. I have been foolishly stubborn. Lost in the pain and fury that you made me suffer, I forgot that your torture is my own. I love you. Every thought that I have somehow ends and starts with you. Time is not passing swiftly enough; I don't even know what it is good for... possibly as a measure to our misery. My days are monotonous, automatic and empty. I wander through this castle like an estranged soul because I don't belong here. I only belong wherever you are. I anxiously wait for the moment when I'll see you again, it has been two long and dreadful years, and memory is worthless. I have been in contact with Kalani, don't get mad at her, I ask her not to let you know. Don't think that for one moment I have forgotten about you. I pray that life protects you that everything turns out as planned so that we can be together for the rest of our days. There are many things I'd like to tell you, but I'd like to whisper them in your ear..."

Koren, loving you."

Closing her eyes she summoned Kalani who answered at once.

"What are you doing?" Koren inquired.

"We are in hiding in the desert surroundings, Orion decided to take the long route back that circumvents the mountains to avoid the royal patrols. You information has been priceless in knowing the soldiers' location. The children have been delivered to the ogres…" Kalani said weary.

"Is Orion close to you?"

"The master is here, he is meeting with his commanders to plan the mobilization through the desert at dusk. By the way I'm my human form again; master says I'm a terrible horse. " Kalani commented.

"That's funny! But it doesn't matter, leave the group unseen and come to the castle, to my room. I have something for you to take to Orion." Koren ordered. In a few seconds Kalani materialized in her room. Both women were surprised when they regarded each other; time had not wasted a moment to change them… Kalani turned herself into a stunning woman. She was still bald and delicate, but her frame was tall and muscular. The little chainmail tunic she wore as a girl was now a shirt, which she cinched to the waist with a large leather belt. Her black leather pants and boots gave her a renegade look that made her even more appealing to the eye. For her part, Kalani couldn't believe she was looking at the same person that she had known; Koren was a woman of incredible beauty.

"Koren! You look so different, time has done wonders for you…" Kalani blurted in astonishment.

"Hmmm, you are not bat at all either, you better watch out for those men in the desert." Koren smiled appreciatively.

"Here, take this letter to Orion, but don't tell him you have seen me." Koren handed the letter as the dragoness sat on the edge of the bed.

"Oh, how I miss this castle… The desert is beautiful, but so infernal. The men are always busy with military training, while Orion leads them. I'm just stuck there blistering in the scorching sun. I almost look forward to the wretched witches that spring out of nowhere with their depraved behaviors. It is the only time that the men laugh…" Kalani casually spoke leaning back into the bed.

"Get off, you are filthy! Stop complaining to me, you'd be here with a different agony trust me. Want it or not, we are all prisoners to our fate." Koren pushed her off the bed with her strong leg. Kalani rolled off to the ground landing with a thump, giving her a look of hatred.

"I also want you to give him this dagger… This is for you…" Koren handed her a pink coral necklace, which Kalani received with surprise.

"Thank you." Kalani put on the only piece of jewelry she possessed, smiling with gratitude. It was an awkward moment for they both understood that their relationship was unsalvageable; any hint of cordiality was merely an illusion. Kalani disappeared without any further remarks, leaving Koren to her conscience.

Chapter 8: Betrothal and war

Normalcy left the palace for good, for the kingdom was under siege by savage and random attacks. Kloe and Althea, the ladies of highest military standing were in service, sometimes patrolling and coordinating security for large areas of the land. No matter how well prepared or coordinated the Bandian military seemed it was always a step behind from the aggressors. It was as if the anonymous enemy could foretell the future. Koren kept Orion informed of every detail and plan that Bandah's military would carry on, giving him the upper hand. The alliances that he had sought had been solidified at last; he now had a full army aching for battle and power. Koren requested several times to be allowed to join the military expeditions, which the queen refused to do with the excuse that the castle should not be unprotected. The truth was that Violet wanted to protect the younger ladies from the battlefields and their horrors.

One afternoon, Koren was wandering in the garden when she felt some firm steps approaching, undoubtedly belonging to a man. Turning to face the visitor, the shock almost made her faint, for she momentarily mistook Atle for Orion.

"I was told I could find you here. Greetings milady, how are you?" He smiled.

"Very well. As you can see, trying to keep busy. The kingdom is under siege, but someone needs to sit and be pretty. How come you are here?"

"Matters of state drudgery... Also, didn't want to skip the opportunity to see you. I enjoyed our evening together at the ball..." He said blushing, walking next to her in unison.

"Oh... So which matters of state?"

"I guess we'll have to talk about it. I came to ask the queen to rescind the peace treaty between the people of Lower Cyrus and the Lagartunes. They have been quite rustled by all the recent attacks in the kingdom, daring to attack some neutral territories. I want to officially warn them that if they attack my people they will be killed... But I need the queen's permission for my edict." He explained with intensity that she didn't know he had.

"I can imagine... the kingdom is in chaos."

"My audience is not for a while, so if you allow me I could keep you company."

"Certainly, as you wish, your majesty." Koren smiled.

"I was told that you like to travel. I would be exceedingly pleased if you visited Cyrus for a season." Atle commented poorly hiding his nervousness.

"I don't think now is the right time, the queen hasn't even allowed me to go in military excursions. I doubt she'd let me set foot out of the castle, period."

"Maybe in the near future. I hope all these stupid attacks cease and we can go back to sanity." Atle sighed. They chatted amicably for a couple of hours, all the while Koren showed the array of beautiful flora cultivated on the castle grounds. Even though they had a pleasant time together, Koren was relieved when he departed. Maybe in another life Atle would have been the perfect prince that she should have had, but in this one she had found another.

The following day Koren was called to the queen's office the moment she woke up, something she found surprising, unless there had been new developments in the attacks. With a little trepidation she reached the office to find the queen expecting her arrival.

"I have great news for you, have a seat." Violet announced with a grin.

"News for me?" Koren sounded perplexed.

"Prince Atle, the Viceroy of Cyrus has formally asked for your hand in marriage." The queen beamed as she gave the news.

"Oh... Why? He has only seen me twice, he doesn't know me..." Koren could barely talk, feeling as if she had just been slapped in the face.

"Dear, love happens when we least expect it. Sometimes it just arrives with a first look upon our object of devotion." Althea spoke, startling Koren who had not seen her.

"Is it decided? Then what?" Koren was taken aback.

"Of course I have agreed, we have signed a betrothal. A union between the two of you would strengthen the bonds of our courts. If you are set against it, the contract must be rescinded, but I hope that you act accordingly." Violet suggested smiling.

"It is of no use, of course I'll have to agree to it. It would have been better if you had consulted with me first before agreeing to it. We all know that the queen's words are irrefutable." Koren violently rose from the seat shocking the others with her impertinence.

"There is not a better marrying prospect in the whole kingdom. Atle is a gentleman and you will rule a Vice kingdom, what else could you possibly wish for?" Althea tried to reason with Koren and alleviate the mounting tension in the room.

"I thought you would be pleased." The queen declared genuinely surprised and saddened.

"Were you forced into marriage?" Koren demanded with insolence.

"That was different... we fell in love. From the first moment we saw each other we knew we were destined to be together and the court formalities didn't matter. It is not always like that... Us nobles have a duty to continue to be in power to see our reign carry on properly." Violet spoke trying to placate Koren.

"Your majesty, I know you're only guarding my best interests. Thank you." Koren curtsied and kissed the queen's hand with reverence, knowing that she had to relent. It was obvious that the queen was pleased with the match, and had n mind that Koren would thank her later. Lenna and Anari were ecstatic as they congratulated her, wishing they were the ones the Viceroy had placed eyes on instead. Koren plastered a demure smile on her face, trying to suffocate the rage ravaging her insides. All she wanted to do was run away and leave behind the ladies, the queen, and all the stupid things in between them. The moment she was able to depart, her legs carried her without direction until their collapse. The irony of being by the cave that so many times she used as a haven for Orion was not lost on her. There was no hiding for her... Although she knew that there was no way in the world that they could make her marry Atle. They would have to kill her first. The creepy thought of him touching her naked body made her vomit violently, as her rage choked. Spewing fire from her mouth she incinerated part of her surroundings, grateful for the energy release. The feeling of not being able to take it anymore took hold of her completely. She hated the castle, the queen, the ladies... and herself. The impotence of not being able to do anything but cry made her feel utterly stupid. As night crawled in, Koren realized she had to return to the castle, defeated as always...

A long bath was not sufficient to ease away the tension. Koren descended to the banquet hall valiantly, aware that many congratulations would be given to her on her betrothal. The news of the absurd marriage to Atle had indeed spread with incredible speed, to her chagrin. Koren drank too much wine that night, when she went to bed the world was spinning out of control and coming out of her throat. Neroli paced the room anxiously as Koren vomited and cried out of sheer despair. After a while she stumbled to her bed still feeling dizzy and nauseous, wishing she would just die. Koren was half asleep when a tap on her shoulders startled her. Quickly opening her eyes to face the intruder, she relaxed after seeing Kalani.

"Forgive me for scaring you, mistress. Orion has order that I give you this letter right now." Kalani placed an envelope on the bedside table and immediately disappeared. Clumsily moving, Koren lit the room to read the letter, if her trembling hands allowed it.

"My beloved,

You gave me what I ached for. You breathed life back into my dying body and the clarity I needed to go on. I also wait impatiently for the day when I'll see you again. I miss your skin's fragrance, your soft lips and the silky hair that my brutish hands will try to feel. I'm a beast. The afternoons I spend walking away into the dunes, in order to exhaust myself. Nighttime is a treacherous labyrinth in which my lust for you tortures my flesh. I think that I have you lying naked next to me, your hair a golden field in which I want to lose myself. I become delirious. I wont lie I want you physically and emotionally, greedily.

Before I go to bed I write in my journal, but it's really for you. Thinking that some day you'll be able to read my silly love fantasies. I tell you about the desert, the men I so disdain, the weapons we have, the military training... and the long walks in search of solace. I tell you that I would like to gallop with you in the mountains, visit the sea together, visit the tribes in the prairie and stay up all night drunk on our happiness. I write you poetry and tell you all the tender things that I want to whisper in your ear before sleeps find you by my side. I resent not having had the opportunity to court you, as you deserve. You'll know that I'm worthy of your love not by some mysterious act, but because I have earned it. I swear that when destiny lies vanquished at our feet, I will make you happy...

Orion, truly yours."

Koren held the letter to her chest tightly, trembling with emotion from head to toe. Orion lusted for her... Knowing that he wanted her as much as she wanted him let her know that they both were looking forward to the moment when they could be intimate. Time was passing slowly and she was dying to sate that carnal want that was overtaking every waking moment. Nightly erotic fantasies left her wanting more, as she tried in vain to imagine his naked body. Reading the letter over and over, his desire was palpable... Her body was so aroused that she unintendedly burned the parchment in her hands. To her horror, the remains of the alcohol made her dream that Atle was making love to her in the garden, as she screamed afraid that Orion would catch them. She woke up sweating profusely, feeling unrested, and upset at her abhorrent dreams.

Orion's letters arrived with more frequency in the middle of the night, every one more intense than the previous. Koren didn't know until which point she would be able to bear the sexual repression. Months transpired between love letters, village attacks and a kingdom in chaos. Her sixteenth year arrived in silence as she took advantage of the unrest at court to escape a celebration. Unfortunately, her betrothed remembered and sent a fabulous ring made out of rubies and gold that elicited many gasps from the envious ladies. He apologized for not delivering the present personally, as Cyrus was now actively engaged in war with the Lagartunes. A state of panic was still reigning in Bandah, for the terror attacks had been castigating the land for a year now. There was also no hope that the attacks would be mitigated soon. The land was in revolt, furious at the crown for not being able to contain the atrocities being carried on by the mysterious army that had descended upon the land. The people felt it was a dark force that blanketed everything with unabated death and misery. Koren was pleased with all the events, not only because it meant the kingdom was vulnerable, but also because Atle was busy elsewhere.

Seriousness and austerity paced the halls railing the soldier's steps as they did their perpetual rounds. The queen never left her tower without a security team, headed by Kloe and Althea, who had returned from their military tours. Prince Eligious was never far from his mother and was never left on his own in spite of his protests. Koren came to be a companion and playmate for the boy, not minding it all for perhaps it was best if the prince trusted her. Queen Violet's preoccupation had aged her, her world had been turned upside down and her people suffered the ravages of crime and violence. Vice kingdoms were threatening to secede from Bandian rule, feeling that they had not been properly protected and preferred their men to defend their own homes. The deadly army still operated invisibly and effortlessly, not one of their ranks had been captured, and no prediction of their next move possible. Orion had planned everything carefully taking advantage of the intelligence Koren provided to create disharmony amongst the territories. He was taking advantage of the weakness brought upon by separation and discord, as well as the fear of the people.

Koren simply lived for the arrival of each letter, enjoying them thoroughly as the promise of love seemed ready to come to fruition. Her desire for Orion was unbearable, limiting her functions and stupefying her wit. Certain that he would not longer see her as a child; she wondered if she would be able to please him sexually. Orion had had other women in his past and she feared the comparison. Fortunately, the library had a large collection of sexual themed titles in which she completely absorbed herself. Reading obsessively, breathing heavily and exploring the illustrations in detail were key to give her an idea of sexuality. Books had everything that one needed to know about sex, to the point of intimidation. Sexuality was as diverse and unique as those who enjoyed it. Finding a potion for avoiding pregnancy was the most valuable discovery in the books, since it facilitated something she had in mind. That afternoon Koren sneaked into the infirmary's cabinets to find the herbs she would need... The only mission in her mind was preparing for the most significant encounter in her existence, the day when she could finally have the man she so desperately wanted.

Another letter sat on her pillow that night. Koren jumped into bed grabbing the envelope as if it were a life saving float, desperate to read the contents.

"My beloved,

We have returned to the desert for a respite and a needed regrouping, not for long though. We will carry out a massive attack in Polaris; it remains a stronghold that needs to be subjugated. There are too many royal guards concentrated in that area. Our army has grown sizably, that was to be expected, when things are not well there are always many trying to join the victors. I believe we have an upper hand at this point; the kingdoms are getting weaker by the week. We soon shall target Astra's interior, we have to weaken them too or they could aide Bandah. I don't think we'll mess with the Amazon territory; they usually remain neutral as long as their kingdom is not bothered. I will set up a perimeter around their territories to position my troops for attack if they send out battalions. We shall see what their Amazon queen decides to do...

I don't want to bore you endlessly with the military minutia. It is just that in a sense I find it very fulfilling, been born for it. Don't you think that all this makes me forget about you, not for one moment. The wait until the moment we are together is cruel, and it makes me sort of afraid. I had never felt so vulnerable in my life, you could banish me with a look of derision, or kill me with a rejection. To that measure your love affects me. My love is not like the sea, or the moons, or the sun that go on in their eternal reappearing acts... My love is grounded; similar to the soil that I firmly step on bearing the weight my feet, and that I can have in the palm of my hands. It is real, palpable... Last night I wept like a fool, feeling frustrated and wanting to have you in my bed. Animal instincts were violently wrenching my soul and my body. I can't say any more...

Orion, truly yours."

Koren shut her eyes tightly, feeling exactly what he must be feeling. The parchment pulsed with desire and angst, a testament to the passion he was also repressing. Looking for the herbs that would prevent a pregnancy, she made a tisane in a hurry. The nerve-wracking wait for the water to boil was insurmountable. Trying not to scorch her throat she downed the brewage in spite of the lump on her throat. The resolve to spend the night with Orion was firm, and her courage must not wean. That night would be the end of their physical separation, of the silence, and of the aching. Summoning Neroli and ordering her to keep guard of the entrance, instructions were given to impede entry to anyone, at all costs. The feline understood that Koren must be told if anyone approached, but that entry was prohibited, and she laid in a spot by the door.

"Kalani." Koren called the dragoness.

"Yes, mistress." The sleepy answer arrived.

"Come to my room at once." Koren ordered and Kalani appeared suddenly, in her nightgown.

"Where is Orion? What is he doing?"

"I suppose he is sleeping in his tent. It has been a long journey back into the desert, everyone is exhausted." Kalani yawned.

"It just occurred to me that I cannot teleport to where he is because I have never seen his quarters, and neither he mine... But you have been to both places. Take me to his tent I want to surprise him. Put me somewhere that he wont notice me right away." Koren explained trying to remain calm.

"Alright. Step right here." Koren stood by Kalani who wrapped her in a cold embrace. There was a sharp whistling sound and a sudden coldness.

"We are in the waiting area of Master's tent, he receives people here, and I have never gone past this point. Just go ahead, that is where he sleeps. I think he has an office in there too, but I wouldn't know for sure..." Kalani whispered as they both looked to the canvas flaps that led to the dormitory. It was possible that Orion slept for the place was eerily silent.

"Thank you, you may go to sleep now. I can return to the castle on my own." Kalani disappeared, leaving Koren to fend in the darkness, as her heart hammered away. Shaking uncontrollably she stepped forward, moving swiftly and silently. Gently moving the flap out of the way with trembling hands she peeked inside. The room was dark except for the dim light of a lantern sitting on Orion's desk. He was there intently concentrating on something he was writing, probably another letter for Koren. She came close to him unheard, while observing his hand wildly glide over the parchment. Merely a few steps away from him and clouded by darkness, her presence was sensed, causing him to pull out his dagger.

"Who goes there?" Orion roared ferociously. He stood to face the intruder, freezing at the sight of an elegant woman in her nightgown. Koren stepped closer to the light so that he could see her better, afraid of getting stabbed. He stared at her intently, perhaps thinking he was in front of a vision made by trickery. The thought that it was a deity from another dimension crossed his mind. Koren stood still, unable to recognize the man she saw. He was taller than she remembered, more corpulent. Orion's hair cascaded in knots to his shoulders while a thick unkempt beard covered his face. Whatever skin was visible was crusted with the desert grime that was probably inescapable to its dwellers. It was almost like standing in front of a wild bear, if weren't for his intense green eyes, she would've never guessed the creature was the love of her life. Orion widely opened his eyes when recognition struck him, that beautiful specter was really her beloved who had come uninvited. Koren hesitated and took another step towards him, feeling her face blush as her body heated ferociously. Orion took a step forward, suddenly lifting his dagger and pressing it to her exposed neck in a matter of seconds.

"Speak." Orion ordered dryly.

"It is I. Kalani brought me here." Koren barely replied affected by emotion and fear. Orion dropped the dagger to the ground and lunged to embrace her. Koren held him as if there was nothing else in the world to hold on to, getting lost in the thick furs that constituted his coat. Orion let go and held her by the shoulders observing her in detail. A white grin appeared in the bushiness of his facial hair, displaying perfect teeth.

"Why didn't we think about this before?" He blurted laughing heartily, yet not able to conceal his nervousness.

"Come, have a seat... Give me a moment, please." Koren nodded as he sat her on his desk chair. Disappearing momentarily he lit several oil lamps in the tent and began to tinker inside large wooden trunks to the back of the room. Koren could hear splashing sounds coming from somewhere in the tent, but couldn't see what he was doing. Sweaty hands on her lap and trying to distract herself by looking around the place, a feeling of faintness began to rise. Finally, Orion came back justifying his absence with his clean appearance. He had changed into his best military uniform, and disposed of the beard and matted hair. His skin was also clean. Koren couldn't help but notice how imposing he looked in his thick wool officer's coat, full of silver insignias that declared his rank. He had also polished his boots, which she found endearing. Orion carried in his hand a ridiculously small silver tray where a couple of delicate silver cups and a little kettle chimed thanks to his nervous hands. Orion offered a little teacup before placing the tray on the desk.

"I don't entertain much here..." He chuckled as he continued to hold the cup.

"No, thank you. I don't want any..." As much as she felt terrible for rejecting the courtesy drink, there was no way that she could stomach anything at that point. She feared she might vomit out of sheer nervousness. Orion didn't take a teacup either, disappearing again in the tent's interior only to return with a bottle of a strong ferment.

"I don't know about you, but I need a drink." Raising the bottle to his lips he drank greedily, and smiled setting it down. Koren smiled sheepishly unable to respond, ashamed that she felt so lost in the situation. She couldn't take her eyes off of him; time had brought maturity to the familiar face, making it more sensually appealing. Orion continued to be a handsome and elegant man. Koren felt like a fool for thinking for a second that there was a similarity between him and Atle. Unable to withstand the anxiety, she stood and came to him, allowing her hand to explore his face with tenderness. He closed his eyes greedily accepting the affectionate touch, letting his skin relish the sensation of hers. Their proximity allowed their bodies to sense their altered breathing, their eyes declaring in summary what they had kept inside for so long. In perfect unison they fell desperately into each other's arms, lips searching for the kiss that up until that moment was only a dream. The kiss that came to be was unlike any other ever given; it was intense, desperate and overwhelming. The energy release shook the ground with such power that the tremor was felt throughout the land. Holding her hand firmly Orion led her to his bed. Koren followed without hesitation, her heart beating wildly and her mind concentrating solely in what was about to happen. He sat her on the bed, taking her silk slippers off and then his boots, then sitting close to her. She was about to undo her braid when he halted her, taking the braid in his rough hands to release the hair. Methodically, Orion undressed her in slowly, silently admiring what he saw. Koren breathed heavily, tempted to tear her clothes away rather than wait another second. A magical fire burst to life in the heat stove by the foot of the bed, proving light and warmth.

"You are the most beautiful woman that has ever existed." Orion declared as he took off his shirt, revealing an ample and strong chest with a few scars. The worst scar being the one left in place by Althea's attack many years ago. He had not removed his pants, and Koren didn't let him. She wanted to undress him as well, but hurriedly, wanting to finally feel his body although she appreciated his tenderness. Orion noticed her anxiety and decided to let go, letting his instincts take over and consummate an act that they both had wanted for so long. The moment his leather pants came off, she didn't even pause to cherish his nakedness for they both felt their bodies come alive. More like beasts, they attacked each other's lips in a lustful frenzy their hands trying to touch every place at once. Koren tried to stifle a euphoric yelp as she received him, surprised by the pleasure and pain that came with every thrust. Orion smiled, crushing her body to his and penetrating fiercely, feeling like the world's most fortunate conqueror. Their moans chased silence away as their bodies contorted searching for each other. Wanting lips satiating their desire for skin, sweat and saliva. Orion didn't stop until he felt her powerful release, then he let go, grunting profoundly. Both remained holding each other tightly without thoughts or cares, only the complete submission to each other. Cherishing in awe and stillness, the survival of the emotional and physical tempest they had shared.

"Sorry about your bed sheets..." Koren laughed as her virgin blood smeared the covers.

"Do you really think I care? Thank you for the honor. I know that as a woman you have the right to share your body with whom please, and you didn't. I'm fortunate and I will do everything to ensure that you never want for more." He smiled. Orion proceeded to caress her exposed breasts, abdomen, legs and all the in between. They made love again, this time with less urgency. Orion whispered in her ear all the words she had longed for professing his love and his lust for her body. Koren thrived receiving him openly, squeezing his body and trying to explore every corner of his skin.

"Are you thirsty?" Orion inquired as they finally rested.

"Oh, yes. Water please… How do you think I've been here?" Koren asked curiously.

"Not long enough… I think a few hours, you should leave soon." Orion handed her some water.

"I'll leave at dawn…"

"That suits me well, but don't expect to see the sunrise here, we are in a cave." Orion returned to bed and to her open arms.

"Caves seem to be a critical element of our relationship." Koren laughed.

"Will you come back tomorrow night?" He asked anxiously hoping for a positive response.

"If you want me to…"

"Of course!" He kissed her lips, between smiles and words of love.

The following morning Koren woke up with lightness in her step and the sensation that her body had been aroused from a long sleep. Every smile and every thought she bore, directly related to the night before. Her body glowed in response to the sensual memories as she wished the day to pass quickly to return at once to her lover's side. The feeling of fulfillment, which the secret harbored in her heart brought about, was overwhelming. Koren radiated such forceful energy that upon passing some hapless souls they would faint on the spot. The ladies and the queen noticed the change of disposition, mistakenly assuming that Atle had finally found a way into Koren's heart.

At the library, Koren received all the reports from the kingdom, as well as the updated recognizance maps. She then proceeded to adjust all the intelligence to Orion's advantage, especially by making minute changes to the maps, in order to conceal the location of the caves where the garrison was established. Furthermore, she took extra steps to ensure that all the maps in the palace had the same information so as to avoid any conflictive illustrations. The location of the caves in the desert would from that moment on be a secret unless a person already knew their existence and location. Rolling the new map she immediately took it to the queen's office aware that they expected it.

"Your majesty, the updated map is here from the troops that have been canvassing the territory."

"Thank you, Koren. This is instrumental for us, we need to go deeper into the desert areas, they have remained untouched for too long. It is large enough to fit an army in there, and they are not anywhere else in the kingdom. Althea, have the generals come." Violet ordered examining the maps as the witch disappeared from sight.

"It is imperative that we find their hiding place… They have eluded us so swiftly for too long, how can that be possible? We must put an end to this evil plague that has led terror into our lands." The queen fumed, searching every corner of the large map.

"I know. It is strange the way they carry on unabated. It is always the same mode of attack, they pick a random village, send Kalani in to burn it to the ground, then their men finishes off the deed. The death toll is staggering..." Koren commented stating the obvious.

"What is their motive? They are trying to take the kingdom down in pieces, but never carry out a decisive attack... How big is the army? I guess it doesn't matter; they operate efficiently, not curtailed by any of the traps we have set for them. Having Kalani on their side makes them powerful, almost invulnerable, there's not a more perfect weapon... I cant stand the thought of all those children taken away, knowing that the ogres are feeding on them, our attacks to their clans seem futile, since we are always a step behind..." The queen lamented out loud with the certainty that she had spoken those same words more times than she had wanted to.

The king led a group of generals into the office, their heavy boots echo storming the sour air. Koren had seen the generals before, yet she continued to be in awe of their poise. General Mabius defended the northern territories while General Omán was in charge of defending the south. Mabius was an elder elf that wore his pure white hair in a long braid and Omán was a younger Amazon warrior allowed to serve out of his kingdom.

"This is the most recent map that has come to us, but I don't think it offers anything new." The queen laid the map for the men to look in detail. The newcomers stared at the map in silence studying it with great care.

"This is strange. It seemed to me that some old maps included the topography of caves in the desert area. They have even been aluded to by merchants and travelers of the region..." General Mabius commented somewhat puzzled.

"The desert is a large terrain, it is possible that the team that canvassed the area has not come to find the caves. We should send a convoy to canvass the area again and investigate, send them out tomorrow morning. Spare no men to search the area..." The king spoke wearily.

"It is obvious that they are trying to weaken the royal forces and they are succeeding at it. I think a decisive attack on their part is imminent. There are no longer any neutral territories remaining, we've had to engage in conflict with tribes that are now attacking our subjects." Mabius added.

"We have no other choice but to remain in high alert and wait for their next move. We have ordered a curfew in every territory and armed the cities and villages. Every willing magical creature has tried to assist us, but I'm sure Kalani is using her magic to help the dark army go undetected. We are now sending word to the Amazon kingdom asking for their help." The queen informed.

"Your majesty, we have had a lot of defectors in our ranks. The men are desperate and their morale is low, most have returned to their places of origin to protect their families and properties. The whole kingdom is intimidated by this burdensome threat, knowledge that a white dragon is on the enemy's side has deeply affected our men and civilians alike." General Omán tried to impart the severity of the situation.

"I know! I know... I feel so powerless. We must continue to search for the enemy army; they can't be materializing out of thin air. There will be a clue at some point that leads us to them. It is unbelievable how they annihilate our troops, taking them by surprise, how they kill and kill..." Violet pounded on her desk visibly frustrated.

"Our witch and elf trackers haven't found anything, but there was a report by some traveling witches that they had stumbled upon a mercenary settlement months ago in the desert. We searched the area and found nothing, unfortunately the desert changes daily, it will be nearly impossible to find the enemy if it has a stronghold there." Mabius lamented.

"I'm sure they have enchanted the area to conceal their location, the person who enslaved Kalani is powerful and to be feared. Kalani's magic will be at their disposal too... perhaps they are hiding in thin air!" The king paced impatiently running his hands through his hair.

"I cannot believe we are at their mercy, we are the mighty kingdom of Bandah! Their surprise attacks and warfare strategy are unprecedented... They lay in wait quietly to attack at their leisure, as if they are ready to wait out our defeat. I don't even know who to surrender to! I'd give up my crown to save the souls of my people, for they have been decimated by the sieges and I cannot bear the slaughter of innocents." The queen's shoulders fell as she let out a heavy sigh.

"Your majesty, we must reach an agreement with the dragons, they must attack Kalani. If she were not in the way the situation would be even. Not one dragon has come forth to attack her, allowing her actions to destroy the kingdom!" General Mabius declared upset.

"We cannot ask that. Their customs have stood for thousands of years and we must respect that. Kalani is not acting willingly, the dragons know that and won't hold it against her, even at their own peril." Violet adamantly reminded.

"But your majesty, the casualties are mounting and they surpass anything in your dynasty's history. The dragons must understand that their participation will save us." Mabius pleaded.

"They have already decided their role in this war. The dragons will help combat any mortals to defend the kingdom, but will not hurt one of their own that has been enslaved. I will respect that position." The queen slammed her fist on the desk.

"Your diplomatic efforts is costing lives, it will cost you your kingdom!" General Mabius replied curtly.

"This is not the first time in history that dragons have taken that stance, our fate rests in our hands not theirs. We must fight for our kingdom. If the attacks are any indication, the people behind them are ruthless and could care less for the fate of the subjects. I took an oath that I would die protecting my kingdom, and I will do so if I have to. I will not leave all the peace and prosperity behind without a fight." The queen announced firmly. General Mabius fell silent and bowed to her in reverence. Althea walked over to the window and looked out into the horizon, momentarily trying to escape to another place.

"That is all... In two months time I want to assemble a secret entourage to travel to Astra, we have to request more help from their kingdom even though they have provided it willingly until now. It might be best to officially go under Astrian rule if our kingdom is not able to support itself anymore. Although the attacks have targeted some of their major cities and left them scrambling. Also, the kingdom has welcomed a female heiress and we have to be there to pay our respects. It will be a secret ceremony. I must admit I'm looking forward to getting out of the castle and celebrating something." The queen informed as the generals saluted and departed from the office. The king stayed behind, holding his son lovingly and letting climb to his shoulders.

"You are getting too big." The king laughed as the boy giggled.

"I can't wait to get bigger, then I can go with you and fight those rotten bastards!" The prince exclaimed eliciting reprimands for his language.

"You will be a proud warrior of our royal family." King Papo put the boy on the ground and affectionately kissed his forehead.

"Can I go with you to the audiences? I heard that they have been reinstated..." Eligius asked excited.

"Ah, those are quite boring, and I can't pay any attention to you." The king smiled, looking to the queen for advice, but she just shrugged her shoulders.

"Koren can look after me, we are friends." Koren jumped when she heard the prince say her name, her mind had been busy sending messages to Kalani to give detailed accounts to Orion about the meeting.

"Do you mind to keep an eye on Eligius at the audience hall?" King Papo addressed Koren.

"I don't mind at all. I can sit with him and bring him to the tower when her gets bored or tired. I'm glad that the audiences have resumed, I enjoy them tremendously." Koren recovered nicely.

"Is that fine with you?" The king pressed the queen for a definite answer.

"Yes. Koren will watch him, I trust her with my life." Queen Violet smiled from her desk and returned to write legislative edicts. Koren took Eligius little hand and they followed the king out to the audience hall.

That night as Koren lay in bed next to Orion recounting the events of the day, she had a feeling of estrangement. As if reality had lost track of her and vice versa.

"All your information has been very valuable, they'll never find us. It is ridiculously easy to plot our next moves... Then Kalani makes it so swift..." Orion mused whispering in her ear.

"Can you seize the throne without me having to marry Eligius? Maybe we could just get it all over with, the queen said she would consider surrender..." Koren cuddled next to him enjoying his warmth.

"My army is not that big, it has been perfect and practical for all the guerilla attacks. If we openly engage in a military offensive they could overtake us, even with Kalani and their weak ranks. I doubt the queen would surrender if she knew the reality of the situation. Are you doubting our plan now?" He asked disconcerted.

"No. It's just that I do have feelings for the royal family... I feel bad for them. Bickett and I... Eligius and I have sort of become friends, he is a lovely boy..." Koren explained affected.

"That's just how it is. It's either them or us. Someday it will be our family occupying the castle…"

"Then it will be our turn to be the ones to perish if someone hatches a plan for the throne…" Koren declared wishing to have never thought of the prospect.

"Monarchies and rulers come and go all the time, we are just bidding out turn." Orion laughed.

"There is something I've been meaning to tell you… But you must promise not to throw a fit of rage when you hear it…"

"What is it?" Orion arched his brow suspiciously.

"I am betrothed to Atle." Koren blurted with dread.

"No! Never! He will never lay a finger on you!" Orion exploded furiously.

"The queen has decreed it, it was set up because she was seeking to place one of her insiders in Cyrus. Violet thinks it's a valuable union…"

"When are you to marry him?" Orion roared.

"I don't know. I have the impression it will be soon… Atle has been tied up in Cyrus, but I can't discard the possibility that they will send me to him. I would help lead his armies, and then marry him… Althea has been dropping a lot of hints lately, driving me insane with her comments of how lovely Cyrus is this time of year."

"Damn it! We must move faster then… Why you? Have you talked to him?" Orion demanded.

"Why? Don't do anything rash! If you send Kalani to kill him it would be too strange to dismiss a connection to me, as it happens that both my presumed lovers would be dead. I have seen him at court only; we barely have spoken to each other. I'm certain that all of this is Althea's doing somehow. I have the feeling that she wants me out of the castle; it's been a while now that she stares at me oddly and behaves as well. Her sister disappeared from the castle… I also think that is odd." Koren calmly spoke, unaffected by Orion's explosive temper.

"When did you say the queen was going to Astra?"

"In a couple of months… A small tour will leave on dragons to get there fast. While a large caravan will be sent to Albah to create a diversion for your army, they assume you will watch the castle's movements and attack it. It will all be soldiers, so ignore the diversion, or send Kalani to annihilate them. What do you have in mind?"

"I have to weaken Albah and Polaris prior to the trip, they are the ones supplying the most help to Bandah, but I think I can do several swift attacks. Cyrus is too tied up dealing with its inner conflicts… Nubis won't be able to help the Bandian entourage if we do something during that short trip; the mountains are perfect for a surprise attack… We have to kill the queen then." He was audibly formulating a plan.

"Just seize both kingdoms…" Koren offered.

"What do you mean?"

"Well, my love, I have studied a lot… and I know that there is an old treatise between Bandah and Astra stating that if one kingdom falls the other will absorb it until a new monarchy is established. It is mostly a reassurance that one kingdom will help the other, especially since the same families of royals tend to establish their rule on both kingdoms. I think it was originally intended to keep the peace if an heirless queen died suddenly, and that way the surviving monarchy would ratify the new one. Now that Bandah is weak we can strike Astra, killing the monarchs and their child, becoming the de facto rulers of both kingdoms…" Koren shared.

"It is not impossible, but the attacks must be effective and precise. Astra is not weak enough… I think it is best to concentrate on Bandah… We must carefully work on the particulars of our next move. Too bad I never captured that damned seashell."

"We should try to find the Golden Sword then." She said as she outlined his profile with her index finger.

"Nobody knows where it is."

"I do. It is at the Demi-goddess' temple in Albah…"

"You are beyond belief…" Orion climbed her, covering her body completely with his and letting his intentions be known. Both smiled enjoying their intimacy and an overwhelming sensation of power that was making them soar. That night Bandah's destiny had been rewritten, all that was would cease to be… a storm was coming.

A plan had been finally hatched and time was taking care of the rest, leaving Koren tense and nervous beyond reason. The slow years had led to the moment where the crucial part the plan had to be carried out. If everything went as planned she would soon find herself at the helm of two kingdoms, which caused a cold fear to run through her body. The idea that the plan would fail was suffocating, although there was no turning back; the moment to act was now or never. The impossible outcomes cruelly tormented her… as well as the possible ones. Every second was spent revising the actions that she would have to carry out in concert with Orion's. They had to take advantage of an opportunity that would be hard to replicate. According to the plan, when the entourage returned from Astra, Orion would attack the Bandians. Simultaneously, Kalani would attack Astra's castle with the intent to kill the queen and princess. An attacking group of ogres on Astra's grounds would facilitate Kalani's task. Orion would have another group waiting in the outskirts of Bandah to officiate a wedding between Eligius and Koren after the queen had been murdered. That part lay in Koren's hands… She had to kill the queen… and the king. Profuse sweat was testament to the suffering all those ramifications brought about, having conceived the plan years before; the thought of how hard it would be to carry out didn't matter.

Koren sat in company of the queen and the ladies unable to look them in the eye, trembling at the idea that she would have to kill them all somehow. Staring intently at each of her companions she was lost in reverie… Admiring Althea's fiery red hair, Marussa's glassy black complexion and her stunning violet eyes, Pumzi's doll-like hands and Lenna's translucent wings. Then there were Anari's enchanting smile and Kloe's stump where her powerful arm use to be. There was not a definite feeling of friendship towards them, but Koren's heart ached at the thought of their demise. They would all fight for the queen to death… Sitting close to his mother was Eligious, or Bickett, how he preferred to be called. The boy smiled beautifully unaware that fate would prey on him. He would lose his parents and his future in one strike, living as a prisoner on his castle until his premature death. Koren shut her eyes commanding the banishment of thought form her mind, letting out a deep sigh, and transporting herself back to the sea. She had been happy there. An image of Orion's naked body came to her, his supple lips, his green eyes... Peace was there. Koren knew she would that for him she would destroy the world if it were necessary.

"What do you think the princess will look like?" Eligius happy voice dragged Koren back to reality.

"All princesses are beautiful. This one will be tiny because she is a baby, but I bet you anything that she'll be perfect." Lenna replied lovingly.

"I can't play with her?" The prince pouted disappointed.

"You'll definitely have to wait on that." Kloe laughed roughhousing him a little with her existing arm, which he enjoyed. The cozy scene nauseated Koren, who hid in a corner trying to read a book and wanting to leave. The castle bells tolled the mid afternoon hour releasing Koren from the visit as she took leave to her quarters with the excuse of needing to be rested for the evening banquet. Nearly racing to her room, the castle became a dooming labyrinth of endless proportions. Soon everyone's destinies would change, not just hers. If the plan failed she would be discovered as a traitor and tortured to death. There was no going back now... having to descend to dine with the nobles required a superhuman effort, and every bite of food felt like gravel. Koren made small talk and smiled placidly, pretending that wrenching angst did not afflict her soul. At the end of the night, fleeing to her room, she found solace in the burning tears that she was desperately trying to fight back. The trip to Astra would take place the following day... The turmoil in her was driving her to insanity. Thinking of Orion, she went to him seeking the solace and comfort that his arms could provide.

Orion was sitting at his desk, writing military journals and studying maps.

"You have come quite early today." He greeted her smiling. Koren didn't reply anything but thrust herself into his arms weeping intently.

"Has something happened? What is wrong?" Orion inquired full of preoccupation.

"No." Koren was able to reply as he sat her on his chair, holding her face delicately between his rough hands.

"You can talk to me." He pleaded.

"It is nothing. I'm so tense and I'm nervous about tomorrow..."

"You must be strong. I know it's unfair for me to say that, because all the weight of this mission has fallen on your shoulders. It is normal to feel anguished, it will ease once we have the kingdom under control, I promise. We must try... we must. Everything is set up; I have found a priestess to officiate the marriage rite. You'll go down in history as the first queen that seized the crown without having to battle fiercely for it." Orion's voice entered her mind placating her unrest, hypnotizing her into a submissive trance.

Everything he said made sense, as if by speaking a word it became a reality, allowing their plan to already succeed. Orion took her by the hand and led her to bed, the only place that had given them the opportunity to leave the world behind. There they would open up their bodies and souls, as well as their desire. One thing that she knew for certain was that she did not want to live without him, that she would follow him until the end… To death… To insanity. In that moment they were nothing but intertwined beasts consumed by pure sexual instinct. Orion coupled her every orifice in a frenzy, desperate to absolutely posses her, wildly releasing her vociferous pleasure. Beyond their love the world wasn't real…

The following morning Koren woke up with a feeling that everything would come out as planned. A premonition deeply rooted in her heart that gave her tranquility. The secret preparations for the trip to Astra had been secured and they would depart that very afternoon. They would be split into two groups, one of a few dragons to scout the area for danger and the second to accompany the travelers. The queen, the ladies and the prince would be in a small carriage disguised as a cargo transport, pulled by Pegasus'. A small group of soldiers in Pegasus would follow with sentry witches flying about. The entourage would seem like that of a traveling noble rather than the queen of Bandah and everyone hoped that the enemy would not take notice. Koren was aware that it would still be hard to take down the entourage on the way back… but there was no other way. Grabbing some of her travel garments she headed out to where the rest were waiting, feeling extremely dizzy. The ladies were tense, everyone wondering if it was a good idea at all to leave the safety of the castle. They all took their place of travel and the trip to Astra was short and without trouble.

Koren felt a pang as they landed on the same spot that she had come to for Kanek's farewell. The memory of that day made her swallow dry as she forced herself to stay calm. The monarchs of Astra greeted them effusively and for one moment it seemed that the kingdoms were not under threat and that live was wonderfully amiable. The queens hugged each other seeking comfort in their long friendship, as the kings stood by looking solemn. The castle was just as Koren remembered it, beautiful and colorful. An orchestra of fairies, who played lively tunes to ease a little the sullenness of their souls, greeted the guests. The evening and the festivities to follow happened in spite of Koren's mental absence, for she was lost in a thick mental fog full of bad omens. She didn't even pay attention when the princess of Astra was formally presented, only seeing the tiny infant in her mother's arms later on. Throughout the night a feeling of nausea pervaded her experience, unable to swallow a bite or drop of the goods offered. She found herself thirsty at all times. The hours before the return to Bandah were eternal, heavy and full of agony. Koren threw herself in bed with abandon feeling her mind spin out of control with incessant vertigo, up to the point when she violently vomited several times. What she perceived as her weakness made her furious, reminding herself that once and for all her years of servitude to another would be in the past. By the next evening she would be the queen of Bandah and Astra, what else could she ask for?

Wishing more than anything to have spent the night with her lover she sank into a depression. She understood that he would be placing his men in their places ready for attack; there was no room for clandestine romantic encounters. Running the plan again and again through her head in detail, she knew there was no room for mistakes. No one could ever accuse her of not earning her crown… She was instrumental to the plan; it was her that would stain her hands with royal blood. Koren searched her heart for the truth, and it readily presented itself... No one was forcing her to do anything against her will. Her hunger for power, governance and admiration were guiding her and giving her the strength to destroy the world surrounding her. Surrendering to sleep, she disappeared into the innocent vacuum of bloodied dreams.

Dawn arrived bright and warm, announcing the arrogant sun with great pomp. The birds chanted harmoniously as dew bedazzled the land. Koren opened her yes feeling lighthearted, hoping that it had all been a cruel dream that her mind had fabricated. For a moment she thought that she would look around and find herself in the little house in the forest... that it had all been a sinister fairytale. Reality struck as she observed the image of a woman staring back from the mirror, the girl in the forest had remained there with her childish dreams. That ordinary day would be the day that would dictate the rest of her life, as well as Orion's... and the others. Heading to the breakfast table she greeted every one casually, although she was merely going through the motions. Eating was impossible; a terrible discomfort in her stomach was increasing by the minute, making her feel more anxious. Once the queen of Bandah began to formally bid farewell to her hosts, Koren's heart began to succumb to a frenzied state. She mindfully gave in to fate hopelessly trying to appease her worries. Kneeling in front of the queen of Astra to kiss her hand almost made her pass out, she avoided looking her in the face, lest she would not be able to kill her later.

The walk to the waiting carriage was tense, although all around her people chatted amicably. All she focused on was the formation of the traveling group to pass along the details to Orion. Nothing had been changed for the return trip; the dragons would head out first, then the king and his knights to protect the queen's carriage. The fifty soldiers and the witch sentries would follow close behind to ensure the back was covered. Koren gave Kalani a detailed account of everyone's position to make sure Orion would be ready to strike properly. Once everyone was ready and the first wing of a dragon moved, Koren knew that the main event was about to unfold. The queen's carriage lunged forward with a light pull, ascending to the sky with the constant tug of the Pegasus' that made the passengers jolt softly.

"We are airborne. In a couple of minutes we will reach sufficient altitude for the Pegasus' to allow the carriage to glide effortlessly on its own wings." Koren informed Kalani.

"Orion says that we will attack in ten minutes, by then you will be away from Astra and over the forest." Kalani replied. Ten minutes... The burden of such a short amount of time sat heavy on her chest as she looked at her travel companions. Queen Violet caressed her son's hair softly as he tried to peek out the windows with great enthusiasm and curiosity. Althea observed him lovingly, creating sparkling butterflies out of thin air to make him laugh hysterically. Kloe watched the clouds, her thoughts rooted in some mystery hidden there, while Marussa flirted in jest with the prince to garner his attention. Anari and Lenna were discussing the fashions of Astra at great length hoping to design similar gowns at their return to the castle. Pumzi listened intently trying to add her opinion as well. Koren could only think of the next move, which was to make everyone in the carriage fall deeply asleep. Sleep would deprive them of the opportunity to defend themselves, and ultimately their lives. She also had to plug her ears without being noticed to avoid being stunned by the Elán birds that would be used in the attack. The gigantic fowl originated from Cyrus, a place known for its avian diversity, much of which was familiar to Orion. The birds let out a powerful screeching shriek whose intensity left every creature nearby momentarily disoriented, sometimes even exploding the inner ears of the unfortunate.

"We have spotted the dragons… Make them fall asleep now!" Orion ordered via Kalani. Koren let out a fake yawn, letting out a yellow mist from her mouth that dissolved into the air. The insidious gas spread swiftly, unnoticed by the others as they immediately succumbed to a magical sleep. Koren observed them for a second to ascertain that they were indeed asleep as she put the special plugs in her ear, smiling smugly. The most feared witch in the entire kingdom had fallen easily to a basic act of magic; trust was an ironic enemy indeed. Turning her finger into a powerful claw she made a whole in the back of the carriage from which she could attack the posterior group of soldiers.

"We attack." Kalani warned. Immediately the carriage jerked from side to side with sudden jolts. Koren could visualize the ogres on the ground tossing the large nets reinforced with magical black coral from their catapults to trap the dragons and the king's knights. From another angle Orion's artillerymen targeted the carriage's Pegasus' without harming the carriage itself. About a hundred birds of Elán darkened the sky with their enormous wings overtaking the soldiers and witches with their screeches. Koren looked out of the carriage to realize they were descending swiftly and assess the situation. Fortunately, the people inside the falling transport were unaware of the peril. With lethal aim she joined the air attack, emitting fireballs to incinerate the disoriented soldiers and witches in midair. The unfortunate souls had no idea where the strikes were coming from as they were castigated by the bird's presence. A witch or a soldier would valiantly try to kill birds only to end up taking down one of their own in the confusion. Koren was becoming desperately frightened for the carriage seemed to be about to crash land, in spite of the knowledge that Kalani was supposed to grab it at one point to land it properly. To her relief the carriage came to a delicate sudden halt, to be placed gently on the ground. Koren jumped out to fall right in the middle of a ferocious battle. Dragons and knights had escaped some of the nets and were fighting with all their might. Koren told Kalani to drag the carriage deeper into the heart of the forest to hide it from sight of the desperate Bandian forces focused on securing the queen. In spite of the defensive, the attacking forces seemed to be at an advantage, the severed bodies of soldiers, witches, Pegasus' and dragons forming a grotesque carpet on the forest's ground.

"Kalani come now." Koren summoned the dragoness. Kalani immediately appeared and embraced her transporting her back to the castle in Astra. Koren opened her eyes once again in the clearing she had been at a few moments before.

"I have never been to the castle I can only bring you up to here…" Kalani explained.

"I know. Wait here for my signal, you know what to do." Koren said as Kalani flew to the castle and began pelting it with fireballs to create a distraction so that

Koren could go forward with the plan. Koren raced to the castle tearing at her gown seeking to look distressed, even burning parts of it to make it look credible. A soldier ran to meet her as soon as she neared the gardens.

"Help! Quickly! We have been attacked, take me to the queen!" Koren proclaimed with great alarm and desperation in her voice. The soldier didn't even think to stop and question the absurdity of her sudden lonesome appearance on palace grounds or the request to be taken to the queen. He recognized the royal wear of the ladies of the court and that was sufficient proof of her identity and authority.

"The queen is at the music hall, it is tea time! Follow me!" the man raced through the castle with Koren at his heels. She smiled recognizing the perfect location in which the monarchs were, she was familiar with the part of the castle and it was away from everything. Making her nails turn into sharp blades she impaled the soldier's back mortally wounding him. The man, taken by surprise, choked to death with his own blood collapsing to the ground. It didn't matter if they found him, by that time it would have been to late... Koren crossed the great hall towards the auditorium, as the music could be heard, plentiful of flutes and string instruments. Smiling, she imagined a group of refined fairies playing the music with arrogance. Silent steps took her into the hall, where she took notice of a group of ten musicians, the monarchs and their people.

"Kalani fully attack now." Koren ordered, and a loud explosion shook the castle. The music stopped at once and some cries erupted from the commotion, creating a momentarily state of chaos. Only a second was needed for Koren to carry out her evil deed, taking advantage of the reigning confusion. With all her might she turned into a human torch unleashing the full strength of her inner fire in the place. Death swiftly came to the hall to take the souls of the present. The walls began to burn and crack by the fire's intensity, even though the attack lasted a few seconds. The fully incinerated rulers of Astra lay on top of each other as if they had tried to protect something with their bodies... Suddenly Koren heard some muffled cries. Making her way through the cremated bodies, she kicked the queen and king's bodies out of the way to reveal that the princess had survived the attack unscathed. Koren was aware of the ramifications of the girl's existence, she was the true heir of Astra and Bandah. Forming a fireball to dismiss the child at once, she realized she couldn't kill her. Not knowing what to do she picked up the baby and took it with her, fleeing before Kalani finished off the castle.

At the clearing, Koren was able to observe how Kalani turned the majestic castle of Astra into rubble. The dragoness had taken her true form; becoming a ferocious dragon of such proportions that the highest tower in the castle seemed nothing but a seedling next to her. Her tail had terrible thorns that hammered everything in sight into pieces and the horns in her head thrusted violently at every structure defeating them effortlessly. The royal guard valiantly tried to stop the dragon's attack but she made game out of them by scorching them in a matter of minutes. More men arrived to defend the castle in spite of the absurdity of the situation; the desperation of the attacks was a clear indication that no one believed the queen of Astra was alive.

"Kalani, we have to go." Koren summoned her. The dragoness was back in a second with her human form.

"Who is that baby girl?" Kalani asked surprised.

"It's the princess. Her parents saved her life and I couldn't bring myself to kill her. I don't know why... Go, take her to the forest and lets have fate have a go at her. I'll wait for you here, hurry." Koren ordered. Kalani disappeared right away, lest Koren would rescind her instructions and made her kill the child. As a matter of fact, Kalani was wildly surprised that Koren had spared the child at all. Cradling the baby gently in her arms, as she reappeared somewhere in the heart of the magical forest of Astra. Kalani stared directly at the ground, as she made a soft mat of moss where to lay the baby girl. Closing her eyes sporadically so that if she were ordered to return, she wouldn't be able to have enough details to get there again. The child cried in desolation, aching for her mother's breast and warmth. Tears welled up in Kalani's eyes knowing that she couldn't do more for the girl, but hope to give her some magical protection. An ancestral song, without words just sounds, delicately rose from Kalani's lips. The girl ceased her crying to listen to the agreeable melody knitting magical threads around her. Birds nearby joined the chant and all the forest creatures left what they were doing to respond to the magical summon. Kalani opened her eyes briefly to see the baby's tiny beautiful face. Admiring with tenderness the delicate ringlets that glowed like golden silk under the sun. The lovely light brown eyes bedazzled with golden flecks captured her and reflected the child's destiny. Kalani deposited a loving kiss on the curious girl's forehead and closed her eyes for good.

"Please come save me." Were the pleading words Kalani let out before disappearing. The heaviness in her mind would have eased enormously if she had kept her eyes open, for she would have seen that there was someone else at the clearing with them. In between the animals that had come from the forest there was someone who had been for a very long time hidden and waiting for a signal. Signal, which had finally materialized that day...

Kalani came back to Koren after a couple of minutes that seemed eternal, to return to the battlefield in the forest. The fighting had been suspended in time; their short absence had not made an impact in the outcome of the battle. A stench of raw and burnt flesh permeated the air in a revolting manner. The eviscerated, mutilated or incinerated bodies that littered the ground repulsed Koren. Snapping back to her senses she ran towards the carriage, ordering Kalani to help finish off the king's men. Grabbing a sword from a dead witch she headed to finalize the act that would ultimately give her and Orion the crown.

In spite of the madness surrounding the carriage, there was eerie silence in its interior as the occupants slept profoundly. Koren looked inside to find the ladies, the queen and the prince serenely enjoying the magical sleep. Knowing that she must act quickly, she entered the transport with violently trembling hands and knees. Convinced that if anything a swift death was the best way to go. It would be a never-ending dream, no suffering. Approaching Kloe first, since she was closer to the entrance, Koren took a deep breath to gather strength. Closing her eyes she flung the sword and decapitated the Amazon without mercy. The head rolled on the carriage's floor making morbid thump sounds as the blood began to spray profusely from the neck. Numbing her soul she turned to Anari, who seemed to smile even as she slept, her hair a delicate halo golden strands falling perfectly over her shoulders... always ready for a big event. Koren administered the same sudden death with one strike, refusing to feel the heartbreak that threatened to weaken her resolve. The next one in the aisle was Pumzi; her inert little body had comfortably fallen asleep on Anari's lap, making a beheading difficult. Analyzing her options and actions, Koren wasn't sure why she had decided to decapitate them all, it had seemed like such a practical idea to send them off that way, but the excessive amount of blood was now repugnant. Without hesitation she chopped off the dwarf's head where it lay, severing Anari's leg while at it. Smiling to herself she remembered Anari hadn't much use for a leg anymore.

Koren turned to the other passengers, stepping carefully on the puddle of blood that was covering the floor. Althe was the closest one to the exit, always net to the queen, who had the prince in her arms. The boy was sitting in his mother's lap, his head comfortably cradled in her soft bosom, enjoying the up and down of her breathing. On the other side of the queen were Marussa and Lenna, who had fallen to the side where Koren had been sitting. She raised her sword to decapitate Lenna, but couldn't bring herself to do it; the fairy had been the only one to reach out to her all those years. Koren decided to leave her for last. Steeling her nerves she turned to Marussa, beheading her swiftly. Unexpectedly, along with the flowing blood there was an array of luminous sparks, which snapped, similar to a firework. The commotion aroused the sleeping women to Koren's utter dismay. Lenna screamed in terror at the sight of all the blood and her friend's heads in it, staring blankly at nowhere. Koren reacted immediately, reaching with a deathly touch for the queen, who surprisingly had been turned into stone. Realizing that Althea had turned her into a statue to protect her from certain death, have her immeasurable displeasure. The fear that the plan would be thwarted began to grow inside her; terror pounding at her chest for it would mean her demise, and Orion's. With all her might she turned to Althea, attacking her with a potent fireball focusing on her immediate destruction, failure was not an option. Althea made a protective magical sphere that saved her and the prince from the attack. Lenna had thrown herself out of the carriage by the window, trying to escape the horror she had witnessed. Eligius screamed as thick tears rolled down his cheeks, trying to desperately hold on to his mother's concrete neck, confused by the situation.

Althea counterattacked with a fireball of such power that it sent Koren flying through the carriage's wall and out, landing disastrously hard on the ground. Koren knew that the impact had shattered her legs, yet she sat to defend herself, willing to accept the consequences. Althea would show no mercy at that point for the truth was now in the open. The witch came out of the carriage in a blaze of fire intent on annihilating Koren.

"My sister was right about you, you are a demon!" Althea raised her hands aiming blasts of lethal fire at Koren. The young woman tried to absorb the attacking black magic with her own to make herself stronger or weaken Althea's attack, but her weakness was apparent by the second. Calling Kalani was not possible for she had to use every thought towards her defense. Althea increased the force stemming from her hands, as Koren felt every inch of her body consumed in terrifying pain, the end would come soon. Her bones were shattering from the sheer pressure of the attack and her mind was already beginning to haze. Unexpectedly, Althea stopped her attack and stared at her in shock.

"I'm sorry to have to take the life you have in your womb, but that is how it is." Althea's words resonated in Koren bringing a new breath of life into her; the news gave her the strength to fight back. The witch had made the biggest mistake of her life, for that pause allowed Koren to gather her might and use her full magic to make an offensive. Unleashing her dragon fire with deadly force, Koren was able to engulf Althea in a spiral of castigating flames. The witch screamed as her flesh began to be consumed by the heat, aware that she had lost the upper hand in spite of her experience and power. Koren's dragon fire was now operating at its full potential and she would be hard to defeat. With the last of her magic powers, Althea turned herself into a little mouse and scurried towards the forest unseen by her attacker. Koren assumed that Althea had been fully consumed by the fire and took a deep breath, more of relief than nourishment. Feeling exhausted beyond belief, she tried to heal her body as much as possible to stand and head to the battlefield. The devastation was absolute, not surprisingly though, only King Papo remained standing. He valiantly fought Orion as Kalani stood there, watching in silence as tears streamed down her eyes. The surviving ogres and soldiers from Orion's camp sat resting and tending to their wounds. Some of the men searched the dead bodies for valuable loot, uncaring for the sanctity of death.

"Kalani, Lenna escaped to the forest track her down and bring her here alive." Koren ordered as the dragoness ran away from sight to do her bidding. She walked slowly, making her way through the corpses and the triumphant living; who had never seen her but had instruction not to attack the beautiful woman with turquoise eyes. Reaching for a bloodied blade on the ground, she came near the fight. King Papo was obviously tired yet unrelenting on his sword attack towards Orion, who returned the strikes smiling triumphantly. The king noticed Koren and ran to her, standing to shield her body from Orion.

"Koren, stay protecting the others, I know you are powerful. I'll take care of him…" Papo shouted without turning his back to Orion.

"There is no one to protect. They are all dead." Koren destroyed his morale. The king lowered his sword and turned to face her, his face contorted by pain and exhaustion.

"Violet? Eligius?" Papo inquired out of breath. Koren shook her head in silence, taking away the vestiges of hope that he carried in his soul. Koren took a step towards the king as Orion set his sword down to see what would be her next move.

"I killed them." The king look intently into her eyes as his own became blurry, incredulous of what he had just heard; only to find himself prey to her sword. Koren impaled the monarch through his chest, although not as mortally wounding him as her treason. Not taking his accusing eyes off of her, the mighty warrior king of Bandah fell to his knees at her feet. Orion came close and kicked the sword in the dying man making him fall to the ground face first.

"You refused me the honor of killing the bastard." Orion complained in jest.

"There is something I have to tell you…" Koren declared seriously.

"The boy? Is he dead?" Orion asked panicking.

"No, he is still clinging to his mother…"

"Well, then lets go and get this done. We have to get you two married right away, lest there be a rescue effort. Time is of the essence…" Orion grabbed her by the arm, almost dragging her back to the carriage. The priestess was sent for immediately.

"Impressive." Orion muttered in awe as he saw the carnage in the carriage. Koren was indeed impressed that it was her who had carried such savagery, feeling completely devoid of a soul. Prince Eligius was still gripping his stiff mother as he cried unabated. Upon seeing Koren he began to yell in terror, falling prey to a fit of hysteria. Orion mercilessly took him by the arm and forcefully removing him from his mother's proximity, as the boy kicked wildly.

"Shut up and come along!" Orion yelled in a manner that the boy muted in terror. They walked back to the clearing where the intense battle had been fought to meet the woman who would officiate the marriage rites. The prince's eyes were wide open in terror as he grasped the macabre images of bloodshed and death surrounding him.

"Here they are, marry them." Orion gave the order.

"Just remembered what you promised, I will be the official priestess of Bandah." The woman spoke harshly.

"Yes. I have given you my word." Orion nodded with a hint of urgency in his voice. The old woman ordered Koren to take the boy's tiny hand in hers and bound them with magical thread to begin the marriage rites. The words were symbolic but didn't make the event any less real. Half ways through the ceremony Kalani appeared with Lenna in tow, they remained in silence for the remaining part of it.

"It is done. Lets go to the palace to announce it and establish the new ruler of Bandah and Astra." Koren declared without emotion. Orion's men wrapped the king's corpse in a woolen blanket as instructed by their general, as well as the queen's petrified body.

"What about Lenna?" Kalani inquired restraining the fairy by the arm.

"Lenna, it is up to you what happens next. Do you renounce your loyalties to Queen Violet and join my court in Bandah? Or perish?" Koren asked flatly.

"One queen, another queen, it is all the same. I'm merely a lady at court. I just don't understand what is going on… You are married to Eligius!" The fairy exclaimed in disbelief.

"All the queens and kings of Bandah and Astra have died. The only surviving official heir to the throne is Eligius. Unfortunately, he cannot fully rule until his sixteenth year of life. Now that he is legally married I, his wife, can rule on his behalf until that day. You are probably aware that this situation will have to be ratified by the council members given their loyalty to Eligius line and their desire to get peace again in the kingdom. Those wise men will side with the conquerors if they know what is best. If they chose otherwise, we will kill the boy… and war will be unleashed on the kingdom as the struggle for power arises. You know there are always a lot of powerful royals willing to seize the opportunity of greater rule." Koren explained briefly.

The triumphant troops of Orion's army mobilized as planned to the outskirts of the castle in Bandah, where Kalani infiltrated to toll the castle bells and calling for open council. Koren held Eligius hand as she forcefully led him to the great audience hall, followed by Orion and the priestess. Soon the members of the council arrived in alarm, heeded by the urgency of the bells and news of attacks. The men and women in the hall stared at the newcomers accompanying the prince and Lady Koren with much intrigue.

"Detain that man! That is Prince Orion!" A woman's voice yelled shattering the silence in the hall. At that very moment the large doors to the hall were thunderously slammed shut making everyone turn to see the feared image of Kalani.

"Chancellor Usor, please step up to the podium." Kalani's voice boomed, as people began to shake in terror. A short elderly man with a long red beard walked silently to the anterior part of the hall standing by the podium and the throne, which until that point had been occupied by King Papo.

"My name is Ma'ura, witch and priestess of the ancestral order of Ura in the northern part of Nubis. Chancellor, do you know this boy?"

"Yes, he is Prince Eligius Maximus of Bandah." The man answered not knowing what to expect. The large doors opened momentarily to allow the passage of a group of soldiers that carried something heavy in a woolen blanket. The men came up to the podium where they tossed the contents of the blanket on the ground, which were none other, that King Papo's bloodied and lifeless remains. The sight elicited screams and groans of pain from the audience. Prince Eligius ran to lie on his father's dead body crying desperately.

"Papa! Papa wake up! Please!" The boy yelled as the others witnessed the horror. Orion grabbed him to pull him into sight again.

"The monarchs of Bandah and Astra are dead. You can be provided of further poof to that effect if necessary. According to law, this boy is now the sole heir and ruler to both kingdoms." The old priestess let he voice float and sink into the audience.

"He is only a child, if its true what you say, the kingdoms will be at the hands of the councils in place that have ruled with the monarchs until he is of age." The chancellor roared eliciting ayes' from those present.

"That would be true, except that this boy has married lady Koren. I have officiated myself. She is of age to rule and can do so until he can." Audible gasps surged from the crowd, a woman fainted by the impression and the chancellor was in visible shock. A tide of murmurs began to cover the hall.

"There is no law in any kingdom that establishes a marrying age, this union is completely legal." The priestess announced.

"Any of you against this new monarchy, or that operate against it, will be sentenced to death for treason. As Bandian rule allows." Koren addressed the crowd for the first time. The murmurs increased as the council members concurred about the situation; some people tried to escape the hall but stopped on their tracks at the sight of Kalani.

"As you can see, it is in your best interest to ratify the union and establish Prince Eligius as heir and ruler. If not, you will all die right now and the kingdom will spiral into the vacuum of war. It is no secret that each Vice kingdom will want to assume complete power. By allowing this, you will bring the peace that the people have been clamoring for. " Ma'ura addressed the crowd again. The chancellor returned to discuss with the members of legislation and dignitaries, the possible options and outcomes.

"It is possible that the Vice kingdoms will not accept this new rule." The chancellor struck back.

"That remains to be seen. Most territories are weak and we have an army that has operated unabated, perhaps they also would fear more conflict." Koren spoke defiantly.

"Agreed. We will officiate Prince Eligius as heir to the throne and accept Lady Koren as Princess Regent. As long as attacks no longer ravage our land and the dragoness stops tormenting our subjects. We also demand that the Prince be always present at audiences and not be excluded from ruling or safety." The chancellor exclaimed.

"I will look after the well-being of the prince, my husband. Summon all the military generals here at once and have all the members of the castle gather at the main courtyard. Send envoys to all our territories, including Bandah and Astra in its totally to announce the new changes. Make sure that our allied forces are aware that we have conquered..." Koren spoke for the first time as ruler.

"From this moment on, I absolve Prince Orion of all the charges standing against him, and name him Supreme Commander of the Military Forces of Bandah. Ma'ura shall reside as the Official Priestess of Bandah from now on." Koren added stepping away from the podium. Orion followed stepping on the king's dead body as he made his way, while the old woman dragged the screaming boy by the arm.

"I want Lenna to be my assistant, find her." Koren demanded. Kalani came to join them without saying a word, taking the prince's hand in her own and giving him a secret smile. The little boy stared at her full of hope, squeezing her hand and sensing that no harm would come from the strange creature. They were both victims of a situation they couldn't escape.

"From now on, Eligius will reside in the queen's tower, seal it off, no one is to have access unless I give permission. Orion, a guard must be established at all times, lest there are rescue efforts in the future. Kalani, you keep him in sight all the time, if someone tries to take him out of the tower impede it. Make sure he comes to the audiences at least once a month, that should appease the chancellors." Koren said firmly.

"I will move into the king's tower..." Koren announced out loud.

"One of my men has told me that an ogre has recently lost a child, maybe we could have her care for him." Orion suggested.

"What? What if she east him?" Koren was appalled at the idea.

"We'll threaten to kill all her tribe if she eats him. You see, being that she is an ogre she'll have no loyalties to him, she'll never try to help him. It will be like giving the boy a guard dog..." Orion explained.

"Fine, if you think that it's a good idea. As long as I don't have to see him... he reminds me too much of his mother." Kalani went ahead with the prince, heading towards the tower that was once his mother's. The Priestess separated from the group to wait for new instructions, unaccustomed to palatial life. Orion and Koren finally walked together, still unable to fully savor reality and triumph.

"What was that thing that you wanted to tell me earlier?" Orion remembered.

"There was a survivor in Astra..."

"Oh no... Someone important? Is it going to change things?" Orion asked preoccupied.

"I don't think it will change things at all. Princess Kai'ri survived thanks to her parents. I couldn't bring myself to kill her, I'm sorry. She was so tiny and lovely, and got the best of me. I sent her Kalani to dump her in the forest, I doubt she killed her." Koren confessed.

"You should have brought her to me! I'd have no problem getting rid of her. With luck, she'll die of exposure, and even if she didn't, no one would know who she is." Orion commented upset.

"She will cause trouble, I have a feeling. There is also something else I have to tell you..."

"Now what?" Orion resigned to more bad news.

"I'm having a child..." Koren announced. Orion came to a halt turning to her and staring lovingly into her eyes. Kneeling before her, he kissed her womb.

"A girl... certainly as beautiful as you. She will be our redemption..." Orion said the prophetic words standing to kiss her passionately, restraining himself from taking her right there in the hall.

The inhabitants of the castle had gathered at the main courtyard waiting in silence to know why they had all been urgently summoned. Chancellor Usor came through the crowd from the back and climbed into a makeshift stage that had been erected for the occasion. Making full use of the place's acoustics he addressed the crowd in a solemn voice with sadness in his eyes.

"The monarchs of Bandah and Astra have perished by an act of violence. Prince Eligius is the sole heir and ruler as demanded by law and tradition, since the heiress of the Astrian monarchy is also dead. Due to the prince's young age he is not fit to lead our kingdom at the moment, fact that did not deter him from entering into a marriage contract, which has indeed occurred today. A marriage rite has been officiated with Lady Koren... it has come as a surprise, but it is in effect legal. Our kingdom has been under siege for too long, and for the sake of peace and prosperity we have accepted this union to avoid further bloodshed. It is our hope that when the prince comes of age he can rectify the situation and restore a just monarchy... not one forged on violence, deceit and cunning. From now on, the kingdom will be ruled by the Princess Regent Lady Koren, who has decreed that those not willing to serve the new government may leave the castle at once." The crowd exploded protests and jeers.

The majority of the castle inhabitants declared their intention of leaving, and when they tried to do so hours later instead of free passage they found death. Orion thought that this would send a message out to those who wanted, or thought to attack the newly established kingdom. Without mercy or regret Koren sent Kalani to the little house in the forest to murder her parents. One of her motives was to silent her father forever, lest he announce she was part dragon and she found herself targeted by rogue ones. Mistress Flora was almost happy to welcome death, for anything that remained of her saddened heart was completely broken, faced with the horrible monster her beloved daughter had become. Master Lorean tore out his heart and gave it to his wife before they both embraced to receive Kalani's fire.

Orion gathered all the generals and high ranking officers only to have Kalani slaughter them, that way he could put men he trusted in charge. Death, decrees and promises of loyalty forged new alliances and loyalties, until the kingdoms of Astra and Bandah were legally united and under Koren's rule. As expected, Orion sent a large army to Cyrus, to arrest the Viceroy for usurpation of the throne of a legal heir. Cyrus was suffering the ravages of violent conflict in its territories, and even though the soldiers fought courageously for their Viceroy, the castle fell to the new Bandian military. Viceroy Atle was dragged from the castle, nearly dead after an intense fight, for he had not easily surrendered. The following day after being taken to Bandah and sentenced to death for treason, his brutally tortured body was hung in display at the main courtyard for all to see. The new government wanted to send a clear signal of what could happen to the Vice kingdoms that dared to fight the establishment. With his men in control, Orion was not afraid that his new and thriving army could be defeated easily. He was also aware that soldiers were embracing the possibility of a long truce, or no battle at all.

After one month of intense diplomacy, struggles and acts of assertion, Koren was certain that she had conquered. The King's tower was now her home and she declared that for her personal protection General Orion would reside there too with the member of their respective cabinets. It was known secret that Orion barely set foot in his accommodations, for their union would never be able to be concealed, no mater how hard they tried. Their bodies beckoned each other from afar, their eyes found each other's too easily and their smiles declared a not so secret devotion.

There were no large revolts, or violent struggles, for the land thirsted peace coming from whomever it came. The Vice kingdoms had accepted the situation reluctantly to avoid any further conflict in their territories, giving up a fight which they had never embarked upon. Relative calm return to daily life, as the reconstruction of homes, villages and cities got under way. Although it did not mean that the people had forgotten, or forgiven, that General Orion had fed their children to the ogres… They knew deep inside that someday they would gather their strength to defeat the demon and avenge their loved ones.

On the second month of rule, Koren and Orion made a campaign to Albah, hoping to capture the Golden Sword. Upon their arrival to the Demi-goddesses' temple they were told that the sword was no longer there. In a fit of fury Orion ordered his men to destroy the forest, weakening the Demi-goddess enough to make her feel pain. Koren demanded from Arkana the whereabouts of the magical sword as she brutally tortured her. Arkana remained resolute in her silence; which upset Koren tremendously, to the point that she severed her head from her body. Arkana didn't die thanks to her godly nature, so her head was taken away to Bandah for punishment. The Demi-goddesses head was displayed as morbid decoration for a while until more suitable arrangements were made. Arkana's constant lament for her forest, her nymphs and her body became intolerable and Koren banished her head for good to the queen's tower. Once there, Prince Eligius found her on one future occasion and they established a close friendship... A friendship that in the future would uncover the location of the Golden Sword, for Arkana would carry the hope inside her of returning to her beloved forest.

Prince Eligius cried himself to sleep nightly after being turned a prisoner in his own castle. The place that had once been his playground had become a terrifying dungeon plentiful of silence and solitude. His sole companion was a detestable ogre named Grinda, whom he barely understood. Kalani was also a source of comfort, visiting daily to offer her friendship. It was the dragoness who presented him his most valuable possession, the statue of his mother. Unfortunately, both of them were unaware that the queen was alive. Althea had turned her into a stone statue to protect her from Koren's attack with the intent of returning her to a normal state after danger had past. That opportunity never arose. Queen Violet became this way another prisoner of the tower, condemned to a state where she could only hear her son's cries and despair without being able to comfort him. Wishing to hold him every second, Violet was suspended in time with suffering so sterile as her existence. Tortured by solitude, Bickett would sit next to his mother's statue every night before going to bed to relate his days, his dreams and all the things he secretly wished would come to pass. He would tenderly kiss the cold cheek of what was once his mother, without suspecting that she could feel it and it was her greatest joy.

The ogre Grinda came to love Eligius as her own son with the passage of time and tried to raise him as best as she could. They spent endless hours in the afternoon sword fighting and sharing the knowledge that no one ever suspected an ogre could possess. He learned the magic, military arts and all the secrets of the land of the ogre tribes. Grinda instructed him about the magic of the trees, the fungi, the birds, the mountains and the ogre languages. More than ever Eligius wanted to be called Bickett, and soon his real name was forgotten. He was more ogre than human. Kalani supplemented his knowledge whenever she could, reminding him that it was better that he never give an indication of his knowledge or power, lest they throw him in a dungeon until his death. Bickett had figured out that Koren and Orion's plan included his demise at his coming of age. Koren obviously wanted to be a widow and a queen, it was an outcome that everyone expected and accepted. Bickett was furious thinking about how little he mattered to anyone. The kingdom had moved on without him, the nobles barely paying attention to his presence in the monthly audiences he was forced to attend. He felt already discarded from Bandah's future. Bickett was only a vestige of a royal line that would soon disappear for good, merely a nuisance.

The months and years to come were the happiest for Koren for she was living with her true love and their children. It didn't matter that it all had to remain hidden from the world. A strange peace descended upon her soul, as life was finally a blessing. They did indeed have a firstborn daughter, a tiny replica of her beautiful mother, which they called Ona. A year later a son arrived, Ander. Orion was a proud father, and he loved his children immensely. The couple didn't want to test their luck and live together openly, much less show off their offspring, knowing that as time passed it was possible that some enemies were getting confident. If it were proven that Koren was unfaithful to Prince Eligius, their unconsummated marriage would be annulled and Koren would be killed for treason. The kingdom would fall in the hands of chancellors until the prince came of age... if he did. The poor boy had a long list of death sentences upon him.

By this means, the children Ona and Ander also became prisoners exiled to the queen's tower. The tower had been sealed off to cast Bickett away, and the children were placed in Koren's old quarters to avoid suspicion. Only trusted people of the court had access to the children, especially since the girl's resemblance to her mother was remarkable. Koren took to wear a dark cloth on her face while in public outings, so that people would forget what she looked like, hoping to conceal any possible connection to Ona. Even though she wished deeply to have them by her side they could not be in her tower, the risk of discovery was too great. Eventually, Ona and Ander came across the other prisoner in the tower, but that is another story...

Every so often the castle would bustle with excitement at the arrival of some daring knight coming to challenge Koren for a duel to win Kalani's heart. The result was always the same; she would toy with them to kill them at leisure, and then hung their dead bodies from the castle's gates. It was a severe warning, so that anyone thinking of challenging to a duel would see the possible consequences. The duels were a grotesque spectacle, where her sword was the stellar performer, always sharp and shiny. If she wanted to show off she would put out her lethal claws and eviscerate the challengers to the crowd's delight. The soldiers and guards applauded and cheered wildly, when the entrails of some unfortunate soul spread over the courtyard. Bickett watched the scene from his tower cowering in fear, knowing that his fate was no better. He tried to escape the tower however possible, which upset Koren. She would administer Grinda a sound thrashing for not keeping a proper eye on him, and to Bickett for trying to escape. Koren had to resort to a magical spell to keep him in the tower, conjuring that every step Bickett took away from the castle grounds would impart unbearable pain. The next time he tried to run away, he couldn't get far subdued by agonizing pain. Grinda would always find him after noticing his escape, but this time he lay almost unconscious from suffering, wailing in pain on the ground. The ogre would take him into her arms and cradle him as she returned him to his prison.

In other parts of the land, life went on as usual, people moving on from their sorrows and plowing ahead because only by doing so one can live in peace. However, far away from everything in the magical forest of Astra, there was someone who was intent on remembering the past... An old witch, that lived in the trunk of a generous tree with her disfigured sister. Another witch who had been severely burned by an evil woman and required her care. The caretaker was Lula.

She had seen the signs in the stars and had escaped the castle of Bandah just in time to save her life, knowing that she would also have to come to her sister's help. What she hadn't imagined was that she would also have to care for a little girl. Girl, who might turn out to be the hope of many, and who would wipe away evil and the blood tainted curse that reigned on the land. Lula had been inside that little home in the tree when she heard with deaf ears the magical sound of time, of the universe, of the sun and the stars... A chimerical chant making its way through the forest and she knew that it was the signal. The old witch walked fast with her clumsy legs to the place were the song originated, only to see with her blind eyes how a beautiful white creature left a baby girl in a bed of moss. The animals moved out of her way so that she could take the one of her kind in her arms. Lula observed the child intently in spite of her blindness, seeing her clearly as a big smile formed in her ancient mouth. It was whom she thought...

End of book 1